UNQUENCHABLE PASSION

"You don't seem like an Indian," she blurted. . . .

He paused before asking gently, "Are you afraid of me?"

Straightening her back, she looked directly at him. "Why should I be?"

"Because I want you and I have the strong impression that you feel the same."

She gasped, her large gray eyes widening with shock. Men never came right out and said this. . . . She raised her slender hand to slap him only to be grabbed tightly by the wrist.

With a quick movement he pulled her to him, his rib cage crushing into hers. He put his mouth to her ear, whispering, "You're a beautiful woman. One doesn't see your kind of beauty very often."

"Please let me go," she murmured, her voice barely audible. "Please." She fought her shivers of pleasure, but they continued to dance up and down her spine; she closed her eyes feeling faint. She knew that if he took her at this very moment, she would not resist . . .

Wings of Desire

Paula Dion

BALLANTINE BOOKS • NEW YORK

Library of Congress Catalog Card Number: 78-66650

ISBN 0-345-27322-2

Manufactured in the United States of America

First Edition: December 1978

With loving gratitude to my husband, Charles, without whom this work would not have been possible.

Also, fond acknowledgment to my friend Nancy Ashbaugh, my astrologer, Sonia Page, and all those who so kindly took an interest in this endeavor.

All that is, and all that
will endure, are God's
monuments.
They are, and will be,
eternal.
Those passing through
may lose their way,
but ultimately,
the route will be found.

P.D.

New Mexico

1800

THE INDIAN stood naked, watching the gray downpour of rain fall on the surrounding Chihuahuan Desert. Safely protected inside the entrance of a cave, he was grateful for shelter. His long black hair hung down his backbone, damp from humidity; his firm muscles glistened with perspiration. The rain brought him no relief from the sudden high temperature, natural to summer in the desert. His skin burned feverishly.

Nightfall was coming soon. Bats that lived in the cave would sleep, forfeiting their nocturnal search for flying insects because of the heavy downpour. The smell of their manure was strong in the hot air. He breathed its odor, wondering about these "little brothers."

Medicine men had told him that the souls of these bats belonged to lost men of an ancient hunting party, who, through a mysterious form of witchcraft, had been turned into bats. Properly respectful of the creatures, he wondered why the Great Spirit, Nayiizone, had permitted their fate to be such.

The Indian also pondered the tale of the medicine man who had once, long ago, gone into this cave to make "big medicine." When last seen, he had been wandering away from the cave entrance, beating steadily on a tom-tom. No man had ever looked upon his face again. For many moons since, on the anniversary of this deed, a brave from the Indian's tribe would come to this place to leave an offering of food for the medicine man's spirit. This year the Indian had gladly volunteered to observe the rite.

A crunching sound caused the Indian's attention to divert to his woman, who slept soundly on the ground before him; the dwindling fire cast an amber light on her smooth skin. His heart swelled with love for her. He studied the seeds of their nightly passion, shining —glistening—along her thighs. He hunched down to run his long fingers over her high, firm breasts. She stirred slightly.

Quickly he pulled his hand away and stood up. His mind was on other things, feeling himself mysteriously drawn to the deep pit that stretched out before him, not far from the darkening cave entrance. He moved toward it, and getting down on his stomach, leaned his body as far over the edge as it would go without falling. There was still enough light for him to see the steep slope downward, and the sheer drop to the floor of the pit made him both nervous and excited.

What strange mysteries were at the bottom of this deep bat cave? What lay beyond? Would the spectral manifestation of the medicine man be lying in wait for all who would venture within? The Indian slowly considered this. Perhaps he could go down there with the medicine man's food offering instead of leaving it up here. He *could* drop his longest rope and tie it securely above the edge, he reasoned. Then he could go down to see what was there. What a tale he would have for the tribe, and his and his woman's son, when they rejoined them. His insides churned with excitement. Tomorrow he would try.

He lay down next to the woman and entwined his legs around hers, falling asleep to the sound of the rain rhythmically pelting the desert around them.

The rain was gone by morning. The Indian stretched himself awake and breathed the cool, damp aroma of the surrounding ocotillo cactuses. Leaping to his feet, he released the heaviness in his groin. Then he took a stone knife and went to gather mescal.

The woman awakened, stretching her slender, frail form lethargically from side to side. A warm glow spread deliciously over her body, bringing back the memory of the last evening's lovemaking. Smiling, she got to her feet and languidly put on a fringed buckskin dress and moccasins, wondering what event would come into her life on this shining new day.

Suddenly she froze, remembering why they were here. The memory of something else was slowly edging its way into her consciousness. Frightened, she pushed it aside. She wished they had never come, trying desperately to fathom the reason for her fear. She was unable to, knowing only that for mysterious reasons she had resisted coming to this place and that now that they were here, she wanted to beg the Indian to come away with her at once.

She didn't, however, and instead busied herself by making a fresh fire, then gathering rocks from the surrounding area. Using two sticks tied together as tongs, she lifted the rocks and scattered them on the fire. When their favorite cactus was dropped before her, she cut out the heads and laid them on the heated rocks. Piling on fresh grass and dirt, she left them to bake.

Her task completed, she squatted down to watch the Indian who stood near her, lost in his own thoughts. She stared at his face, the most cherished of all faces, with its strong features and long, sweeping eyelashes, smiling softly at him with profound pleasure.

From the time she'd been a small child the sight of him had filled her with an unexpected yearning; he alone held the promise of complete fulfillment. She'd always known he would be her destiny. When they were grown and together, their love had brought her to a special oneness with the Great Spirit. With him she had soared to unknown places. Yet now she was filled with a great sadness. Something was wrong.

What was happening? Was something beginning or ending? She didn't know, finding herself mesmerized by his face, which bore a peculiar kind of intensity. She sensed he was about to do something.

The Indian put on hard-soled moccasins and pulled

a buckskin shirt over his bare chest. After tying a skin around his waist, he proceeded to secure his long rope on a large rock. Satisfied it would hold his weight, he threw the other end over the mouth of the pit.

He stopped, turning to look at the woman. Her frail body appeared strained; veins stood out prominently on her neck. She was perched on the ground, emanating the aura of a hungry animal waiting for the right moment to lunge forward and attack prey. He moved close to her. Sinking down on the ground, he reached out to touch her exquisite oval face with its high, well-defined cheekbones and delicate features, pausing to look deep into her large, black, almond-shaped eyes. Overcome with love for her, his breath caught in his throat.

She returned his intense gaze, fear causing the back of her neck to tingle; the world seemed to hang in silent, suspended motion. Helplessly she watched as he turned away and got up.

Again he checked the knot of his long rope. He threw a leather sack containing the food offering for the medicine man over his back, tying it to himself. Then, gathering grass and bark, he adeptly tied them together. Squatting down by the kindling fire, he lit the crude torch and then went to the edge of the pit, easing his body over the side. Holding the rope with one hand, he made his way down, careful to hold the torch away from his body, careful not to look at the woman again.

She moved quickly to the precipitous drop and watched his descent until she could see his flickering light no more. She wished this day had never dawned.

Dusk came and still she waited. The blazing orange sky was slowly giving way to evening, and she could hear the swish, swish of a snake writhing from its daytime concealment. Bats spiraled out of the cave, filling the sky with their blackness and throwing their own peculiar odor into the air.

She breathed it in, thinking, little brothers, send him back to me.

The next day passed slowly. Paralyzed with terror, she was incapable of performing the simplest task. She tried to eat the sweet, baked mescal, but the food caught in her throat. Sensing he was gone forever, she mourned; her body swayed back and forth in perpetual motion. She thought of their young son, who awaited their return to the tribe. Her whole being ached for her child's touch, wondering if he was now destined to reach his manhood without benefit of his father's wise guidance.

The second night she woke from an uneasy sleep and lay shuddering in the stillness. In a daze, she jumped up, compelled to take the stone knife that lay on the ground next to the fire. She sat down cross-legged, clutching the knife to her. In the agony of her mourning, as generations of Indian women had done before her, she sheared off nearly all of her hair with the knife.

Afterward she sat surrounded by the long, black strands, depleted, sapped of energy. Her skin was feverishly hot, her body shaking. Her hands were wet from tension.

She threw the knife down and crawled to the edge of the pit. Resting on her stomach, she leaned over, searching the deep drop of the cave, squinting into the darkness. She screamed his name over and over until her throat was dry and scratchy. Exhausted, she turned over on her back and let out an anguished cry.

Then, unexplainably, she sobered and sat up. Her face uplifted to the heavens, she spread her arms out wide, like an eagle. She closed her eyes and slowly chanted a wail of sorrow for several hours. When she opened her eyes, a strange scene appeared before her, rising like a flame from the dust. It did not frighten her; instead, she felt strangely detached from it.

She saw herself when she had been yet a woman-child and had seen a vision of her death as through an impenetrable blackness—a strange force sucking her into it. In her terror she had breathlessly run to the tribal shaman and fallen to her knees, begging for understanding of what she had just seen.

The shaman had put a heavy hand on her young shoulder and looked searchingly into her great black eyes, murmuring softly, "Let us go to the water and dwell on this, child. There, the Great Spirit will speak to us."

Hand in hand, they had walked in the darkness of the night to a nearby brook, their pathway bathed in moonlight. At a certain point he had released her and squatted down, motioning for her to do the same. He had closed his eyes and rocked his body back and forth, swaying to either side, all the while spewing the same guttural sound over and over. She had sat and watched him, hypnotized by the motion and the sound. After a time, he had opened his eyes and looked at her, saying, "Now we will listen and be spoken to."

She had listened with great attention, hearing the wind gently rustling the leaves in the trees; the gentle splash of water as it fluctuated lovingly over stones in the brook; feeling the wind blowing against her face. She had looked over at the shaman and seen him nodding his head, knowing he was being spoken to by a great force whose voice remained silent to her ears. She had waited for the shaman to speak to her, a deep sense of peace fusing her mind with her body. When the shaman had finally spoken, she had quietly given her attention, afraid of making the slightest move to distract him.

"Yes, child, you saw your death in that dream. But you must not fear death. It is the will of the Great Spirit that it will come to you in that way. Remember always, all things die and are reborn again."

"But why that way, shaman? Why will I die in that way?"

"In another time, in another place, you used your magic unwisely. You will die prematurely again and again until you truly learn to walk in the light of the Great Spirit."

"How," she had begged, "how did I use my magic unwisely?"

"It took place by the great caverns to the west. Your tribe warred against another tribe and your parents were massacred in a bloody battle. For revenge, you lay in wait for a hunting party from the other tribe and cast a spell over the men responsible for the death of your parents."

"A spell?"

"You transformed them into bats for all eternity."

"Shaman, can I change this?"

He had closed his eyes and remained quiet for a time. When he had looked at her again, his eyes had been glazed by sadness. "I do not know."

The scene dissolved before her now as suddenly as it had appeared. She shivered. Was the shaman right? she wondered. Could it be true? And why did this episode come to haunt her this night? Confused, she started to chant again, then abruptly stopped.

For an instant she thought she heard something. She strained to catch the sound. Yes, she was sure of it. The Indian was calling to her. Her name was echoing from somewhere in the cave.

Quickly she moved back the edge of the pit and called weakly, "I'm coming. I'm coming." She slid her shaking body over the side and found a footing. She grabbed the rope, but her moist hands slipped away from it.

Quickly she took hold of a sharp, protruding rock. With one free hand she groped for the rope, but the total blackness concealed it from her touch. She moaned as the jagged edges cut into her fingers and caused them to bleed. Her head was spinning confusedly. The pain in her fingers gave way to numbness.

She jerked back. Back into the endless blackness. Back into the weightless depth. Down, down, falling into space. Her muffled scream echoed and vibrated throughout the caverns.

Silence fell.

BOOK I

───◦⦅∞⦆◦───

Greenwich Village,
New York

1899

One

HONOR WENTWORTH lay deep in sleep, her long legs stretched over the scarlet coverlet, her arms hugging a pillow to her small breasts. Daylight was seeping into the room; bits of dust danced on a stream of light coming in through a crack in the drapes. Inch by inch, morning light crept over her still body.

With its short, straight nose and full, pouting lips, her face looked younger in sleep than its twenty-one years. Her long, honey-colored hair lay in a mass of tangled profusion on the bedsheet.

An emotion flickered across her face; she began to toss restlessly. At once her peaceful face clouded as the storms of a dream began to thunder in her head. She clutched at her stomach and grimaced; small drops of perspiration formed above her upper lip. From the deep recesses of her sleep she called out, "Mummy, Mummy. I'm hungry. Mummy." Honor kept crying these words until they began to penetrate her consciousness. She slowly opened her large, almond-shaped gray eyes to see the small, frightened face of her son peering at her from the side of the bed.

"Mother, are you all right? You were dreaming again. Are you all right?"

She sat up and pulled him to her, gently stroking his cheek, soothed by its velvety softness. She shook her head to clear it, but it was a few moments before she could pull herself back to the reality of her bedroom. She glanced around, taking in its familiarity, and began to relax.

She cleared her throat. "It's all right, Elijah. Really

. . . I'm fine. It was just a dream. Go get dressed, my
darling. Miss Gilly will be getting up. You can help
me get breakfast. Would you like that?" Her words
came out in a rush.

"Yes, Mama." He nuzzled closer to her warm body,
wiping away the tears that had fallen down her cheeks.
She kissed his forehead, then sent him out so that she
could proceed with her morning ablutions.

After splashing cool water on her face from the
white iron washstand adjacent to her brass bedstead,
she pulled off her nightdress and put on an ivory-
colored linen chemise. Struggling into a corset, she
pulled it in so tight it cut off her breath, forcing her to
sit on the edge of the bed until she was able to breathe
easier. Yawning and stretching, she rose and moved to
the window, her mind still clouded from sleep. Pulling
open the brown muslin drapes, she stared down at the
sun-drenched street.

Her mind wandered through the labyrinth of narrow
streets that lay beyond her sight. She decided the West
Village harbored the most interesting nineteenth-
century houses in the whole of New York. The
Georgian and Federal types of architecture, the back-
alleyed, converted stables, held an unlimited fascination for her. There was a special vibration about her
particular area on Christopher Street that never failed
to capture her imagination.

She often thought of the early settlers and how it
had been when they came here. Greenwich Village
had always been a village, the first one an Indian community called Sapakanikan. The first Dutch settlers
had quickly cast out the natives, taking over their
fertile, rolling farmland for their own profit and pleasure. Her employer, Miss Gilly, always had a colorful
story to tell about the Dutch grandparents who had
raised her; she delighted in recounting the details over
and over. But her memories had nothing to do with
her ancestors' indiscretion with the Indians. They
centered around her happy childhood in this house.

At the first break of day, Gilly always said, she

would be roused from sleep by three loud blasts from a cowherd's horn resounding far and wide over the fields. In answer, from every street and doorway was heard the jingle-jangle of scores of loud-tongued brass and iron bells that hung from the necks of hungry Dutch cows. Gilly would lie in her small bed listening as the cows noisily followed the herder to green pastures for their morning sustenance.

Gilly and her family would then breakfast on fish, rye bread, grated cheese, and sausages. All this would be washed down by tankards of beer, which, according to Gilly, were always in abundance. Her grandfather would then go off fishing and her grandmother would settle down with her knitting. Gilly often said that a Dutch family of that era could scarcely be clothed in comfort without the steady presence of those clicking needles.

Honor smiled, thinking of it all. How interesting and uncomplicated it always sounded. Now she intensely studied the angles of the wisteria vine creeping under her window, then focused her attention back on the street below. Except for an occasional horse and carriage passing by, the street was still. The clickety-clack of hooves falling on cobblestones echoed in the early-morning quiet. Resting her forehead against the windowpane, she sighed deeply, wishing she could preserve this moment of tranquility.

She knew well, though, that soon, too soon, the street would fill with a multitude of people going about their daily business. Squealing children would cluster about. The bustle and squeaks of carriages, and the whinnies of countless horses in a seeming protest to their enslavement, would thicken and become deafening. Noise . . . noise . . . noise.

She grew irritated with the rising heat; beads of perspiration formed on her forehead. She considered opening the window to relieve the stuffiness of the room but knew she couldn't. The sour stench of manure, lying in various-sized heaps from one end of the street to the other, would fill the room.

For a moment she found herself caught again in the nightmare of her dream. For as long as she could remember, she'd always had the same one, over and over. She closed her eyes, seeing herself in her dream falling into a great black pit—screaming—reaching out. Then everything would change suddenly to her mother and her. Honor was so hungry, begging her mother for food. But no matter how hard she pleaded, her mother refused her, until Honor's whole being permeated with terror. Now Honor shuddered, forcing herself to push that feeling aside.

Deciding she'd better hurry, she put on a full-skirted pair of embroidered, handkerchief-linen underdrawers, a corset cover, and finally a flannel petticoat. Already too hot, she slipped on a white shirtwaist that boasted a high, choking satin collar. At once she felt an itch at the base of her throat.

How confining clothing is, she thought, pulling on a brown, flaring, gored skirt. Impatiently she noticed that the heavy brush binding on the skirt had to be replaced. Its constant contact with the pavement on the city streets always reduced it to a dirty fringe.

She moved to a tall chiffonier with its oval mirror swinging at the top, squinting at her reflection. Picking up a hairbrush, she attacked her hair with it until the honey-gold highlights shone and static crackled in the air.

She paused in her brushing to study a pencil sketch she had once drawn from a *Vogue Magazine* photograph of the Chihuahuan Desert in New Mexico, now yellow with age, tucked into one corner of the mirror. The sketch always had a calming effect on her. She wondered what it would be like to live in all that peace and quiet, away from the noise and crowds of New York.

Examining her hair, she was satisfied it had been brushed enough. Carefully maneuvering a roll of false hair on top of her head, she pulled her own long hair over it into a high pompadour, fastening it in place with a tortoise-shell comb and a multitude of pins.

Reaching under the bed for her shoes, she sat down to slip them on and button them.

Honor paused then, glancing about the oversized bedroom. To her left in the far corner stood her sewing machine, various shades of fabric carefully piled on the floor next to it. To her right stood an easel with a table next to it cluttered with brushes, oil, and various painting paraphernalia. Interspersed throughout the room was an array of tufted willow chairs, and a nice-sized armoire that housed her clothing.

In this well-used room she could lose herself in painting or sewing, and the outside world would then cease to exist. She loved it here, finding it difficult to imagine living anywhere else after all this time. She finally jumped up to straighten the bed.

Engulfed by the heat of summer, weighted down by layers of clothing, she hurried down to the kitchen to make breakfast.

It was Sunday, and Julian was coming.

Julian Borg awakened, stretched, and thrust aside the quilt tangled around him. Mignon lay on her stomach next to him, her face pressed fiercely into the pillow, causing him some alarm. How can she breathe that way! he wondered. He pulled the quilt off her, studying the soft lines of her naked body, pink and flushed, her well-rounded buttocks slightly tensed. He turned his head to look at the clock on the table next to the bed, thinking of Honor, who at this moment would be waiting for him.

I should get up and get dressed, he thought, fighting the urge to stay in bed and make love again. He looked back at Mignon and softly groaned. "Damn," he murmured softly. He moved closer to her, brushing her long, black hair away from her neck, kissing the soft folds of her body. She turned her face to his, her dark blue eyes opening, inviting him.

Without giving much consideration for her pleasure, Julian entered Mignon, quickly, the clock next to him ticking off the time relentlessly. He rode her warm, pulsating body harshly, his head pounding as he suddenly climaxed and fell heavily on her, grunting. He lay still for a moment, then rolled off her, demanding softly, "Get dressed."

Mignon stretched lethargically before getting up and moving to a water closet in the hallway just outside the bedroom. Returning, she carefully piled on the layers of her clothing, now slightly creased, hardly taking her worshipful eyes from Julian. Once dressed, she sat down on a large, plush chair, studying Julian's lean, muscular body with great care as he prepared to shave.

She watched as he vigorously worked up a lather in a china shaving mug, noticing a satisfied look on his face when he studied the texture of the lather. She got up to move closer to him as he set the vessel down and honed a straight-edged razor on a leather strop, softly humming to himself.

She smiled at his reflection in the mirror as he generously lathered his face, then shaved, careful not to get too close to his full, bushy mustache. She was fascinated by the studied concentration he devoted to his grooming, thinking the perfect, classical lines of his features both sensual and vulnerable.

"Am I to be dismissed early today, Julian?" she asked, feeling a need to break in on his thoughts.

Julian stopped and turned to her, not sure if he had caught a resentful tone to her voice. She was smiling sweetly. He couldn't quite tell. He returned to his shave. "I have an engagement, love. Do you mind?"

"Would it matter if I did?"

He looked at her again, then turned away, saying nothing, deciding that reticence was the best course of action.

"Are you seeing Honor Wentworth today, Julian?"

He started. When had he told her that he was seeing Honor? He thought for a moment, but couldn't recall. He must have been drunk, he decided. "Yes," he answered, working to keep a note of indifference in his voice.

"Someone told me that she has a bastard."

Julian turned sharply to look at her. "You've been asking questions about Honor?"

"Does she?"

"Yes."

"I see."

Julian stopped shaving, giving Mignon his full attention. "What do you see?"

"Not many women would flaunt a bastard in—"

"She doesn't flaunt anything! What's this sudden interest in Honor about?"

"Did she tell you the circumstances?"

"I've never asked. It's her business, after all."

"You're not curious?"

In answer, Julian merely turned back to the mirror.

"Do you sleep with Honor, too, Julian?"

He sucked in his breath, exasperated. "Do you really think that's any of your business?"

She didn't answer.

"Well, if you must know," he continued, "we don't."

"It's rather hard for me to believe that you, of all people, would actually devote time to a woman you don't sleep with."

"That's a nasty thing to say. One doesn't have to sleep with everyone, you know," he added defiantly. Mignon laughed softly, and he realized she was enjoying his apparent irritation.

"Are you serious about this—Honor?"

He cut himself; blood spurted from his face. He wet a cloth and dabbed at the cut, angry at her persistent questions. He paused for a moment, wondering if he *was* serious about Honor. Involuntarily, the creases in his brow deepened when he thought of her. He had to admit that in the time he'd known Honor, she'd hardly been out of his thoughts. But he knew that, to be perfectly honest, it was the challenge that Honor represented that intrigued him the most. Women had always come easily for him. Too easily, perhaps. But not

Honor. She held on to her virtue tenaciously. It was a game he couldn't resist playing.

He turned suddenly and looked sharply at Mignon. His green eyes flashed with annoyance at her bold intrusion into his private affairs. He wished she'd leave and let him be. "What's the problem, Mignon?" he asked gruffly. "Are *you* suddenly getting serious about *me?*"

Her eyes narrowed. "Would it bother you if I were?"

Damn it, anyway, he thought, why did she have to pick today for all this? He struggled for a light tone. "Forget it, love. I'm not the marrying type. The last thing I see in my life is being saddled down to one woman and a bunch of kids. Good Lord!"

She burst out laughing. "Julian, you are funny!" After a moment's pause she asked, "But don't you sometimes wish you could have a meaningful relationship with one woman?"

"No!" He forcibly resisted an urge to reach out and shake her.

"Other men eventually do, Julian. What makes you so different?"

Julian wiped his face with a wet towel, grabbed a blue bottle of after-shave lotion, and generously splashed his face with it. His cut stung. He walked to the armoire, pulled out a white shirt and a pair of pants, and put them on, saying, "What makes me so different? Let me think about that for a moment." He spoke carefully and concisely, wanting to make his point clear. His voice came out harsh. "What makes me so different is that I love flesh. All kinds of flesh. All shades too, if you must know. I could never content myself with making love to just one woman for the rest of my life. If I were stupid enough to get married, I would be obnoxiously unfaithful. There would be no point." He clumsily fastened a collar and cuffs to his shirt, then sat down on the bed to put on shoes and socks. She's rattling me, he thought. Why am I letting her? His expression froze in anger. "Aren't you ready to leave?"

At once Mignon moved to him, wrapping her arms around his waist, the feel of his body comforting her. "Don't be angry, Julian. Please don't be angry."

"I'm not angry," he lied. He took her arms from his waist, then moved to the mirror to brush his pale blond hair. He reached for pomade but changed his mind. Honor liked his hair free, not slicked down.

Mignon got her purse and walked to the door. She turned to him, her voice hesitant. "When will I see you?"

"Soon, love. Soon."

He watched her stand mutely at the door, seeing her eyes fill with tears. He remained silent. To his relief, she finally turned and left.

He moved to the window and stared out, agitated. He wouldn't see Mignon again, he decided. She had all the signs of a woman out to tie him down. The questions she'd raised about him had unsettled him; his life suddenly loomed before him as empty and meaningless. He wondered if something was wrong with him. There had never been one woman to whom he'd ever considered devoting himself exclusively. He knew Mignon was right. Other men did settle down eventually. Why did the thought of marriage panic him so?

Could he be different with Honor? He considered this for a moment. He did like her. Really liked her. Would she be so terrible to settle down with? He quickly checked himself. None of that, he thought.

He ran his thumb across his square jaw, thinking deeply. Why wouldn't Honor sleep with him? She already had a child. How could she just stop doing it? Perplexed, Julian abruptly turned from the window and stalked out of the room, grabbing his straw hat from the dresser on the way. The devil be damned, he thought with determination as he rushed out into the morning sunlight, he *would* have his day with Honor.

He would no longer consider any other possibility.

Gilly Van der Donck slowly settled her aging body at the breakfast table, savoring the aroma of eggs and steaming coffee set before her. Taking small, birdlike bites of egg, she focused her gaze on Honor, who was fluttering about the kitchen in what Gilly interpreted as an attitude of nervous compulsion. She watched Honor open and shut cabinet doors rapidly in an apparent search for something, thinking that the sunlight, streaming in from the kitchen window, made Honor's hair look like a golden halo around her head.

"Well, what are you up to today, Honor Wentworth? What mischief?" She smiled at Honor with affection and good nature.

"Julian will be here as usual, Miss Gilly," Honor answered, her cheeks flushing. "We're going to church and plan to spend the whole day together."

Gilly noticed Honor nervously glance at the kitchen clock. So Julian was late again! He always kept Honor waiting, and his lack of punctuality consistently irritated Gilly.

Honor glanced worriedly at her son. "Will you and Elijah be all right without me?" she asked diffidently.

"Will we be all right?" Gilly smiled. "I should say." She turned to Elijah, who was greedily gulping down large bites of toast spread with a huge mound of strawberry jam. "What say you, Elijah Wentworth? Will you enjoy spending another day alone with Miss Gilly?" She waited while he swallowed his mouthful of toast.

"Yes, ma'am."

As Gilly ran her hand over his dark hair, she noticed his large, black eyes starting to fill. She turned back to Honor. "He's missing you already, but yes, I can certainly keep a five-year-old busy. Our Sundays alone are always well occupied. Now tell me," she probed, "what are your plans after church?"

Honor's face changed, the fine lines of her features suddenly both mobile and animated as her hands moved excitedly. The timbre of her husky voice grew rich and lilting as she spoke. "Well, Julian and I are invited to your cousin Drew's for lunch. Apparently Drew is expecting quite a large gathering today. His guests are always so exciting and different." Honor smiled. Half to herself, she said, "Did you know that Julian holds the center stage at these parties? People are drawn to him somehow. He's so interesting." She looked at Gilly. "Did I tell you he's writing a book?"

Gilly scrutinized Honor for a moment, inexplicably depressed. She had a presentiment about Julian that she couldn't quite put her finger on. It disturbed her. "Yes, you told me." Gilly paused before continuing. "Tell me, Honor, what is coming to pass between you and this . . . Julian? Has he stated his intentions yet?"

Honor sat down at the table and poured herself a cup of coffee, lapsing into silence.

Gilly waited a moment, then went on. "You are not to give me and this old house a thought, you know. You've taken good care of both of us these past five years and you would be missed. But nothing—nothing would give me greater pleasure than to see you with a home of your own, and for Elijah to grow up with a father."

Honor looked up and smiled at her employer with affection. How she loved her. Her thoughts traveled back to a biting winter day five years earlier in Washington Square. It was there that Gilly had come into her life. She could see it clearly. The day had been so gray . . .

Homeless and unmarried, Honor's belly had been swollen with child. Despite her condition, she had persistently stood in the cold, shifting her weight from one foot to the other, beseeching the passersby with her pleas for a few pennies. She hadn't allowed the humiliation of her circumstances to outweigh her need to get some nourishment for herself and the kicking child who thrashed about inside her. It had been days since she'd had a decent meal, and she was starving. Besides, begging had not been new to her.

She'd turned, noticing an old woman with stooped shoulders coming her way through the park, huddled in her long, heavy coat against the cold. The old woman had stopped walking suddenly, seeming to be out of breath. Honor had watched her sit down on a bench, sharply sucking in her breath.

Gilly, too, remembered the day well. She had glanced about the park, her attention falling on the sight of a young girl standing near her. The girl was tall, at least five feet seven, with honey-colored hair and gray, lustrous eyes. She had been especially struck by the girl's face, the most beautiful she had ever seen.

The features were straight and even, with high, well-defined cheekbones, her complexion softly pink. There was an arresting glow about her face that, to Gilly, had radiated a nimbus of inner light. Gilly couldn't specifically put her finger on it, but she'd sensed something different about this girl. Something apart from her obvious beauty, separating her from the others who roamed the streets in abject poverty. A sign of the times, her late grandfather had always said.

She'd noticed an aristocratic air in the girl's demeanor that had seemed paradoxical to her present, unfortunate circumstances. Gilly had looked at her large belly with a twinge of pity. To her surprise, she'd felt a great surge of maternal instinct for this beautiful child. It had awed her to experience this new emotion. Gilly was childless. On impulse she'd walked up to her. "Come home with me and have some supper, girl."

Honor had carefully studied Gilly's soft, wrinkled face and affluent clothing for a moment. Then, without a word, she'd trustingly gone with her to an old brownstone in the Village.

And stayed.

"Well, has Julian proposed?" Gilly asked, bringing them both back to the sun-flooded breakfast table, years removed from that cold, gray day in the distant past.

Before Honor could answer, the doorbell rang and she ran to answer it, grateful for its auspicious interruption. She pulled the door open to see Julian, dashing in a crisp white shirt, white pants, and straw hat.

He greeted her with a jubilant "Good morning, love," smiling that expansive smile that always caused a wave of shock to flow through her. His catlike green eyes were full of mirth and gaiety, taking her in from head to toe. The hot sun played on the highlights of his pale blond hair that stuck out from under his hat.

Honor resisted an impulse to reach up and tenderly fondle the flaxen strands, thinking that his presence seemed to fill the entire house with vitality. She felt limp from the emotional impact of Julian's being. Her loving him frightened her because she knew full well he was not a man to commit himself to any woman. She'd heard the rumors of his escapades. In one way she wished she'd never met him. In another way . . . She sighed. What would become of them? she wondered. What would become of her?

Two

HONOR AND Julian strolled down the street laughing, their entwined hands swinging back and forth in gay abandonment. Drew's party long behind them, they were both light-headed and giddy from a full day of food and wine.

Honor suddenly realized she hadn't the slightest idea of where they were going. "Julian," she laughed, "where *are* you taking us?"

Julian let go of her hand and put his arm around her small, cinched waist. "To my place for a glass of sherry." Feeling her tense, he stopped walking and turned to her, his green eyes serious. "All right, love?" He sweetly smiled at her, feeling her relax as she nodded in agreement.

Their mood shifting, they both became quiet and thoughtful as they turned a corner and came to Fifth Avenue and Julian's house. Honor had been to his home many times as a guest at the gala parties he enjoyed giving. She loved his house, one of a group on Fifth Avenue that had been constructed by the first builders in what had then been New Amsterdam. Those men had followed their Dutch style of building high-stooped houses far from the canal to protect basements from periodic flooding, even though no threat from local waters existed here. Nevertheless, these houses boasted a sturdy, secure look.

Honor stood quietly as Julian unlocked the front door. She paused at the entrance that was enveloped in darkness. The grandfather clock in the entryway was chiming five times. She wondered if Elijah was having his supper. While Julian made his way through the house to turn on the gas lamps, she recalled the first time she'd seen Julian here.

Gilly's cousin Drew had brought her, promising an interesting party. He'd introduced her to Julian, who had reached out to kiss her hand, his touch electrifying her. She remembered a pretty, dark-haired girl holding on to his arm possessively. She wondered what had become of that girl. She'd never seen her again. That first night Julian had extricated himself from her and devoted himself exclusively to Honor, who'd been very taken with him.

After that first evening she had regularly seen him on Sundays. She thought of the operas they'd been to, the plays, the rounds of parties. He'd opened up a whole new world to her. It wasn't long before she was painfully aware that she was deeply in love with him. Painful, because she'd never really known if her feelings were reciprocated.

She hadn't had time for men before; Gilly and

Elijah had filled all her time over the years. Her only friend had been Drew, and their relationship had always remained just one of friendship. So all her hopes lay in Julian.

She knew from Drew that Julian had a reputation for being wild and frivolous, but she'd sensed a goodness in him that she'd decided only needed to be tapped by the right person. She'd made up her mind early that *she* would be that person. Now she wasn't sure.

If only he wouldn't continually try to get her into bed with him, she fretted. She wouldn't get caught in that trap again. At least she didn't think so. It was getting harder and harder to resist him. But she had to hold out for marriage and respectability. She had to. She owed that much to Elijah. More than that, she realized that she desperately needed to belong to someone, and wanted so much for Julian to be the one.

Deep down, Honor knew that she was deluding herself. Perhaps she should face it before it was too late. She was wasting her time on Julian. She had considered that more than once but couldn't bear the thought of never seeing him again. Their Sundays together were the bright spot of her life. He could change. He must!

Julian suddenly reappeared out of the shadows, asking, "What are you thinking?"

Startled out of her reverie, she smiled, pushing her thoughts back to the high Dutch stoops. "That we're perfectly safe from a flood."

"A flood?" Puzzled for just a moment, he burst out laughing. "Your mind seems to go in all directions, Honor Wentworth. I can never guess what you're thinking. I like that about you, do you know that?"

Julian led her into the dining area, where he poured sherry into small crystal glasses, handing one to Honor. She watched him lean his muscular body back against the square oak dining table, one foot crossed over the other, aware of his intense scrutiny.

Finally becoming uncomfortable, she averted her

gaze down to the sherry. "Well, what are you thinking now?" she asked, trying to keep her voice light. He didn't answer, but she knew. She sensed it from the shiver that ran through her in response to his penetrating eyes. She lost her struggle for composure.

"Perhaps I should be leaving now, Julian. Elijah and Miss Gilly will be wondering about me." She flinched as his stare turned hard. Suddenly he was foreign to her. Then he changed, his eyes softening. He was again the charming Julian she loved.

"You won't go till we've finished our sherry, will you, Honor?"

She stared at him thoughtfully for a moment. "No. No. Of course . . . I'll stay. Of course."

"Go into the library, love, while I get a bit more comfortable."

Julian strode from the room, his thoughts racing. He was determined that tonight he would have her. The waiting was over, he decided.

Honor stood hesitantly for a moment as she watched Julian ascend the staircase. Turning away, she walked slowly in the direction of the library, her thoughts muddled. She knew she should have left, and for a moment she wavered over whether to simply flee at this moment and offer some excuse to him later. She quickly checked herself. That was foolish! They would share a glass of sherry and she would leave immediately after. What was the problem? She'd always been capable of handling his advances in the past. Tonight was no different from any other night, and Julian was, after all, a gentleman.

Her confidence restored, she strode into the library. She'd always loved this room, in which Julian's stamp was everywhere. Slowly absorbing all the familiar details, she settled her gaze on the walls, which were covered with a vibrant red material that she found pleasing. The portieres were made of a cotton tapestry in an Oriental design. Turkish stripes hung on the windows, and a stationary corner seat was covered with plush red material that matched the walls.

A low, wide Turkish couch, trimmed with heavy loops and tassels, filled the center of the room. Honor moved to it and sat down, two Oriental pillows cushioning her back. She put her sherry down on a small table next to her and leaned back, pulling out the pins that secured her large hat with its white egret plume and satin-faced brim. After she had removed it, she placed it next to her on the couch.

She glanced at the Morris chair situated directly across from her, the cushions perfectly matching the tapestry of the couch. Off to her left there was a large Turkish chair that was covered with the same tapestry as the portieres. She looked up, noticing a simple stencil decoration on the ceiling in perfect harmony with the Oriental details of the room. A dark green denim covered the floor.

A low bookcase across a corner stood in close proximity to the kidney-shaped writing table at the window. Was that where he worked? She suddenly found herself passionately curious about how Julian spent the hours of his life here.

Julian bounded into the room, startling her. As he fell into the Morris chair, thrusting his legs out in front of him, she noticed he had removed his shoes and socks. She watched him take a large gulp of the sherry he'd brought in with him, thinking the gaslight illumination in the room cast ominous shadows across his face.

A few top buttons of his shirt were open, his shirt collar and cuffs removed. Honor noticed the absence of hair on his chest. She thought his skin looked amazingly smooth for a man. Nervously she broke the silence. "How is your book coming, Julian? Have you been busy with it?"

He sighed, putting down his sherry and reaching into a small gold box for a cigarette. He moved to the writing table in search of matches and lit up. Julian came back to his chair and, as an afterthought, offered Honor a cigarette. She hungrily accepted. He lit it for her, a smile spreading over his face. "You're the only woman I know who smokes, do you know that?" She smiled back at him and shrugged.

He sat down and leaned back, taking a long drag, and finally answered her question. "I haven't worked on my book for a while. But as long as Aunt Wynne keeps on supporting me, I can bide my time. My problem is that I'm itching to travel again. A lazy existence by most people's standards, I suppose."

Her heart pounded. Was Julian planning to leave New York? She put her cigarette out and reached for her sherry, afraid to look directly at him and have him see the anxiety in her eyes.

He took a long, thoughtful breath. "Tell me something, Honor. What do you want out of life? Really want, beyond the everyday trivia?"

Honor's face registered surprise at the intensity in his voice. "No one has ever asked me that before. I didn't think men were interested in what a woman really needs or thinks."

"I'm interested."

She sipped her sherry, thinking deeply. "I suppose what I want is to be a whole person. A secure, content person who can live without fear."

"Fear? Fear of what?"

"Why, I don't really know. Of the unknown, I suppose. Of knowing myself. I want to explore all the hidden, mysterious parts of me. To explore without reservation." She looked at him hesitantly, then went on. "I've never said any of this aloud to anyone before, but I dream of this. It may sound like an odd dream, but it's mine."

Julian was quiet for a moment, studying her thoughtfully. "Your mind is not like other women's. I've never enjoyed anyone's company quite as much as I do yours." To his surprise, he knew this was the absolute truth.

Honor's face flushed. Did he love her? If he did, then why didn't he tell her?

They both sat silently for a time, Julian finally breaking the quiet. "We can't survive without dreams.

They're the very substance and essence of survival. Who really knows what life has in store for us?" He restlessly shifted in his chair, staring hungrily at her. "Come here to me, Honor."

She started visibly. "Julian . . . no."

"Why, Honor?"

"Julian—" Her voice broke.

He put out his cigarette. "We can't go on this way. You know that."

"Why can't we?" Foreboding gripped her.

"You know why we can't." He looked at her. "Don't you care for me?"

"Yes, Julian, I do." Her head was beginning to pound.

"Well, then—"

"Julian, please understand. I got caught once . . ." Her voice trailed off, and she sucked in her breath. When she spoke again, her words came out jumbled, hesitant. "I dearly love my son . . . I've never once wished he hadn't happened. But I won't . . . won't let that happen again. I can't."

"You've never told me the circumstances surrounding Elijah's birth, do you know that?"

"You've never asked me."

"I'm asking you now." He sat back and waited.

She hesitated for a moment. When she began to speak, her voice was barely above a whisper. "I was very young and unhappy. I've never told you, never told anyone outside of Miss Gilly, but the circumstances of my home life were not favorable." Her voice caught. Was she telling him too much?

"Are your parents still alive?"

"Yes."

"Did they help you?"

"No," she said slowly.

"I see. Well, go on."

She bit her lower lip for a moment. "There was this boy. His name was Thomas. He was from Ireland. A nice boy. Shy . . . and unhappy, too. We found ourselves alone one night. I don't know, I suppose we were both searching, trying to fill an empty gap. We reached out for each other and . . . it happened. It was the only time. He never knew about Elijah. Shortly afterward he came down with diphtheria and died." She grew quiet.

"Did you enjoy it?"

"Did I what?"

"Did you enjoy making love with him?"

Her face turned beet-red. "Why—I—really—" she sputtered in mild astonishment. She couldn't continue.

He let it pass. "What did you mean a moment ago when you said the circumstances of your home life were not favorable? What was wrong with your home life?"

"I . . . I was raised in a tenement on the East Side, Julian," she offered hesitantly. "You must be familiar with the neighborhoods in that section."

"You don't say," he murmured, a surprised note in his voice. "You know, I find that hard to believe."

"Why is that?" She tilted her chin defiantly.

"Because you're nothing like the people from that part of New York. You have such a dignified air about you. I really would have thought that in the deep, hidden recesses of your past lay an aristocratic vein."

"My mother came from an upper-class background in England."

"Yes. That's it. You must be like her. Are you?"

"I suppose. Yes. I really am."

"And your father?"

Honor didn't want to talk about her father. She didn't want to talk about any of this, fervently wishing Julian had never brought it up. She shrugged her shoulders dejectedly, knowing that she had to go on with it. What reason could she give not to?

"My father's background in England was quite the opposite from my mother's," she finally answered. "I'm sure you know how class-conscious the English are. It took great courage for my mother to marry him. But their biggest problem was that my father had never learned a trade. When he and my mother came to this country, they nearly starved. Actually, we lived our whole lives in a constant state of deprivation. I haven't seen them for a very long time, but I'm sure nothing's changed."

"Why didn't your parents help you when you discovered your pregnancy, Honor? What happened?"

"My father never knew. I'd gone to my mother at the time and she panicked. We're a large family, and there wasn't enough food to go around in the first place. With all my mother had to contend with, the thought of having another mouth to feed was too much for her."

"So?"

"So . . . She asked me to leave."

"But you were so young. What did she expect you'd do? Honor, that's horrifying."

"Well, after all, it worked out. I eventually met Gilly and I've been with her ever since. I've managed nicely."

"How do you think your mother explained your sudden disappearance to your father?"

"She said she would tell him that I'd gone to work for a family out of town."

"Have you been back to see your family since Elijah's birth?"

"No. Not once."

"Haven't you missed them?"

She looked away from him. "Sometimes . . . Sometimes I think of them. I wish I'd been capable of blocking them out completely. It would have made it less complicated for me. There are times when their images haunt me. But I know if I went back tomorrow we'd be strangers, my family and I. Yet, I expect I will return one day. I suppose I'll know when the time is right." She looked up to see Julian staring at her thoughtfully.

"How did you feel when you discovered your pregnancy?"

She thought back for a moment, then said, "I felt . . . happy."

"How could you feel happy over such a dreadful situation?"

"I think it was because I knew that finally I would have something that was mine. After all the years of having to share what little I had with my brothers and sisters, at last something was all mine. That, and the knowledge that life was growing inside me, filled me with such love." She paused for a moment before saying, "I'm sure that's hard for a man to understand."

"You know, Honor, it's always astounded me that you've never made any attempt to cover up the truth about Elijah. Do you really think it's wise to let people know he's illegitimate? Couldn't you fabricate a story? Why do you give people a reason to gossip about you?"

"If people talk, let them," she said with sudden fierceness. "To hell with people. I won't lie."

"I see." He smiled. "You're a spitfire, Honor Wentworth. You've always seemed so ladylike. This surprises me about you."

"I expect that after all you've heard tonight, there's quite a bit that astonishes you about me."

"Yes. I suppose so."

She tried to read his mood but couldn't. She hesitated, then asked, "Does all this make you feel differently about me, Julian? You know, I never meant for you to know any of this."

"But I wanted to know all about you. How could we ever hope to have any kind of relationship if there are secrets between us? But you're right. It does make me feel differently. I feel closer to you. Much closer now that you've shared your story with me. If you thought I'd think badly of you because of your background, you're wrong. After all, are you responsible for the life your parents gave you? I think not." He paused for a moment, then said, "I wish I'd been around at the time. I'd have helped you. I really would have." Their eyes met for a moment as they both lapsed into silence.

Honor watched him get up from his chair and pace restlessly, his movements catlike and sensual. The room suffused her with sexual promise. How she wanted him. She had trouble breathing. One part of her wanted to leave, but she couldn't. All her resolutions were rapidly dissolving. Tonight Julian had a power over her that was beyond the grasp of her understanding. She felt strangely sapped of all her physical strength. She wanted to run, but she was caught . . .

He interrupted his pacing and stood before her, leaning one hand over the couch behind her head, his free hand stroking her cheek; his knees pressed into her thighs through the layers of her clothing. "Your face is truly magnificent, Honor. I don't think you know how beautiful you really are." He sat down next to her, moving his hand under her long skirt.

Honor jerked away to the far end of the couch. "Julian," she whispered imploringly. "You mustn't."

"You have nothing to be afraid of with me, Honor. You know that, don't you?" He moved closer to her, again sliding his hand under her skirt, along the curve of her calf. "Don't you?"

She tried to pull away, but this time he held her down with one hand as the other traveled from beneath her skirt to her face, turning her mouth close to his. He kissed her for a long time, holding her so tight she couldn't resist. When he finally drew his face from hers, she gasped for breath, again trying to pull away from him. "I've trusted you," she cried. "Trusted you!"

He held her down firmly. "You can't say no to me this time, Honor. I need you. I really do." He began to remove the layers of her clothing with such speed and adeptness that she grew dizzy.

To her humiliation, she knew she was powerless to stop what was happening, but she wouldn't give in without a struggle. She wouldn't! She struck him over and over, her hands stinging from the impact, but soon she realized that the more she struggled, the more excited he became. "Julian," she pleaded, her anger toward him subsiding. "Please. Please. It's not right."

He didn't answer. Finally, to her embarrassment, all she was wearing was her chemise. She looked down to see her clothing strewn on the carpet. Feeling his stare, she looked into his eyes for a moment, helplessly submitting to his hands as they held her, gently roaming over her body. Her skin burned from his touch. She knew she was defeated.

Sensing this, he released her. He stood up and took her hand, looking at her, pulling her up to her feet with a shade too much force. "Come on," he murmured. "Come."

Never releasing her hand, he led her into the bedroom and pulled her thin chemise over her head. She didn't resist as he drew her lips to his moist kiss. He laid her down on the bed, releasing her only to undress.

In a moment he was all over her, fiercely kissing the soft folds of her body until little moaning sounds emitted from her. When she started to cry, he kissed away the tears, his fingers roaming and holding her. He roughly stroked her mons, then the taut nipples of her breasts, bruising her with his relentless searching and stroking until she cried out, opening herself to him, suddenly aching with desire. He savored this moment, knowing now she couldn't wait.

All at once he entered her with great force. He rode her hard, unmercifully, groaning as her hips rose to meet him. Together they rose higher and higher, climbing upward. Honor wondered if they would ever reach the summit. They floated, soared. Would they be able to return? Her cries of pleasure sounded like those of a wounded animal to her ears.

Suddenly something inside her . . . stopped. Something pulled her back in that fraction of a moment before she arrived there. At that moment Julian cried out, his body weighted and fell on hers.

She lay puzzled for a moment, wondering what had happened to her in that one mysterious second. Yet she felt good . . . good to be sharing this physical closeness with him despite it. "Julian," she whispered, "I love you, Julian."

He nuzzled her neck for a moment. "Marry me. Marry me, Honor, and save me from myself."

"I'll marry you, Julian. I'll marry you." Now she could never leave him. Now they belonged to each other. She cradled his head against her breasts and clung to him, the sticky dampness of their bodies fusing them together.

Three

HONOR SPENT the next afternoon painting in her bedroom by the north window. Her palette angled comfortably in her left hand, she stooped over a half-finished canvas depicting brown-ocher mountains against an indigo sky, painting flowers of cadmium yellow at the foot of a hill. The air was thick with the smell of turpentine and oils, and she breathed in the familiar odors while concentrating intently on her task.

Outside, a cacophony of city sounds blended together, filling her room with its din. The house was quiet, since Elijah and Gilly were spending the afternoon in the park. Honor enjoyed her aloneness, happy and at peace.

Mrs. Julian Borg. What a nice ring it had. She had everything to look forward to now. Everything. She stopped painting, letting her brush rest on a rag spread across her lap, as she began to wonder how Elijah and Miss Gilly would take the news of her forthcoming marriage.

Miss Gilly had often voiced her desire to see Honor married with a home of her own. But Honor had long suspected that Gilly did not entirely approve of Julian, his constant tardiness being a major bone of contention. Still, Honor reminded herself, Gilly had asked her more than once if Julian had stated his intentions, and she had worried about the propriety of his taking up Honor's time if he wasn't serious. In all likelihood, despite Gilly's predicted misgivings, she'd be relieved. Honor sighed. What Gilly thought was important to her.

Elijah. Elijah was not used to men, she thought, having grown up in a household comprised only of two women. What close contact he'd had with a man in his five years of life had been with Gilly's cousin Drew. A kind, gentle bachelor, for years Drew had been a frequent visitor in this house, and Honor treasured their friendship. Elijah loved him. Would her son be able to accept Julian . . . Julian as his father?

All the disquieting questions she'd purposely kept buried surfaced now. She wondered if Julian would feel comfortable in the role of a father. He was an only child himself and had no contact with children in his adult years. How would he and Elijah get on?

These thoughts were starting to spoil her otherwise tranquil afternoon, and she vowed not to let them. She was worrying unnecessarily, she decided. It would work out. Nothing would be allowed to tarnish the happiness and glow she was experiencing. She simply wouldn't permit it.

After spending a few moments meticulously cleaning her brushes with turpentine, Honor carefully wiped them with a rag and set everything down on the simple pine table next to her. She removed her paint-splotched blue smock, folded it, and laid it over the chair.

Moving to the multipaned window, the floor noisily squeaking beneath her, she glanced down at the street and focused her gaze on a gaggle of leap-frogging children playing Follow the Leader. The street had a happy hum to it today, or so it seemed to her. Smiling, she turned from the window and went downstairs to prepare for the evening meal.

Fried chicken for dinner. Elijah's favorite. Honor hummed as she attended to the small details of the meal and carefully set the table. When she heard Gilly and Elijah enter the house, she suddenly felt brave, deciding she would tell them her news at dinner.

After hands were washed and napkins placed across laps, the meal began noisily with Elijah's incessant chatter about every detail of his excursion to the park. Famished as well, he ate as much as he talked. Honor didn't interrupt, relishing a few more minutes' respite to organize her thoughts. Watching her young son gulp down his milk, she remonstrated, "Sip slowly, Elijah."

He paused, shrugged his shoulders, then good-naturedly obeyed.

Honor looked over at Gilly a bit timidly. She sucked in her breath. Now was as good a time as any. Steeling herself against the wave of panic about to envelop her, she blurted, "I've got an announcement to make."

Both Elijah and Gilly looked up at her questioningly. Gilly arched an eyebrow. "An announcement?"

"Yes." She studied both their faces, then said brightly, "Julian has asked me to marry him."

Gilly, about to raise a blue-rimmed teacup to her lips, paused in midair. She lowered it slowly to the saucer. "Marry him? Good gracious. Did you accept?"

"Yes. I have. We've set a date for the middle of November."

"November!" Gilly's eyes darkened worriedly. "Is four months long enough, Honor? In my day couples took their time and waited close to a year after announcing their engagement. I don't think that gives you enough time to get a trousseau ready. Four months!"

"I can do it, Miss Gilly," Honor said, anxiously looking over at Elijah, who was staring at her rather intensely. "You're going to have a father, Elijah. Isn't that wonderful?" She hoped the forced bravado in her voice belied her sudden insecurity about the situation at hand.

"Julian will be my father?"

"Yes. Won't that make you happy?"

"Will we still live here with Miss Gilly, Mother?"

"No, Elijah. We'll live in Julian's house. It's a lovely house, really. It's big, with a good deal of space for a little boy to grow up in." To her dismay he didn't respond, only continued to stare numbly at her.

She realized this was a shock for Elijah. His life was about to change and he hadn't been prepared for it. She tried to smile reassuringly at him as she reached across the table for his hand. Squeezing it, she announced proudly, "You'll even get to go to a private school next year."

He jerked his hand away from hers. "I don't want to go to private school." He stood up, pushing his chair away from the dinner table. "I don't want to go to private school." With that he rushed out of the room.

Honor jumped up, her first instinct being to run after him. But she paused, deciding against it for the present. He would need some time alone to adjust to both the idea of having a man around and a new home. It would be difficult for him, but he was quickly coming to an age when he would need a father's guidance. She had to think of what was best for Elijah. Everything would work out just fine.

She looked at Gilly, hoping for reassurance, and sat down, pushing her dinner plate away from her. Her appetite had disappeared.

"You are sure that Julian is the one for you, Honor?" Gilly asked, a strained note in her voice.

"Why, yes. I love Julian, Miss Gilly."

"You know this is all I've ever wanted for you, Honor. I knew the day would come when you would go. I wanted to see you married and for Elijah to have a father. So long as Julian's the right one. So long as you are really certain."

"I'm sure."

"Well, then. Four months. Let me see. I can help with your trousseau. I surely can." She clasped her hands together. "Why, we'll have such fun doing it. Won't we, Honor?"

"Yes, Gilly. We'll have a wonderful time getting ready." Honor relaxed, smiling broadly.

"Now," Gilly asked, "what about a honeymoon?

Have you and Julian decided yet? Give me all the details." She was beginning to enjoy herself.

Honor's words rushed out excitedly. "Well, of course we need time to smooth out all the details, but Julian suggested spending a few weeks abroad. In London, perhaps. He's lived there a bit in the past and liked it there very much. He thought I would enjoy England since that's where my parents are from. Julian has so much to say about London, Gilly. You know, he's been everywhere, really. He's spent a good deal of his life traveling from one place to another."

"Yes," Gilly said enthusiastically. "London would be a lovely honeymoon for you."

"I must work out an arrangement for Elijah, though. I can't just leave him here with you. We might be gone for as long as two months. That would cause too much of a strain on you."

"Nonsense. Elijah stays with no one but Miss Gilly. When you go, I'll hire someone to help out with the chores. I'll work it out. You're not to worry about this. The child stays with me."

"Gilly, I don't know what to say."

"Don't say anything but yes, Honor Wentworth." Her eyes suddenly misted over. "You must know how I love both you and Elijah. You've made these last five years very happy for me."

Honor looked pensively at her friend. "It's hard to think about leaving you, Gilly."

"Now, now. None of that. Go along to your son and have a nice chat. This was an awful lot for him to take in without any warning. He'll come around. You'll see."

Honor stood up, pausing for a moment to study Gilly's dear face before leaving the kitchen. She finally turned and made her way up the staircase to Elijah's room, wondering how to assuage his anxiety. She realized she had overwhelmed him at the dinner table. She'd have to proceed slowly with Elijah. Very slowly.

She entered his room cautiously, finding him on the floor playing with wooden soldiers. She sat down next to him and picked one up. "These are nice soldiers, aren't they?"

He kept his gaze downward, scowling.

"Can I play with you, Elijah? I'd really like to."

He was silent for several moments, then blurted, "Why do you have to get married, Mama? We're happy just the way we are. Aren't we?"

"Of course we're happy now. But we'll be happier. With Julian we'll be a real family, Elijah."

"But we're a real family now," he protested. "Isn't Miss Gilly like our family?"

"Of course she is, dear. But you know, this doesn't mean that we'll never see Miss Gilly again. We'll still see her. Often. I'll bring you to visit her any time you like, and she'll visit us, too." Her voice finally broke. "Everything will be all right, Elijah. I love you."

He looked at her fully now, his scowl melting. He reached over to wrap his small arms around her neck and hugged her. "Don't be sad, Mama. I didn't mean to make you cry."

"I'm not sad, darling. I just don't want *you* to be." She gently disengaged his arms and looked into his eyes. "Give Julian a chance, Elijah. Won't you?"

He solemnly stared back at her. "Yes, Mama. Maybe he can show me some new games. I'll be good."

She pulled him back to her and rocked him, her confidence slowly returning. It's going to be all right, she thought. Everything is fine.

It was two o'clock on the following Sunday. Honor dressed carefully in a new blue taffeta shirtwaist with a white yoke and collar, and a black, tailor-made, figured Sicilian cloth skirt interlined with crinoline and velvet running all around the bottom. Having dug into the scant savings she'd managed to accumulate from her wages from Gilly, she had splurged on her first store-bought outfit. Well proud of it, she imagined that after her marriage she would be able to afford many store-bought dresses.

Her honey-gold hair skewered in a bun, she took a

quick, pleased glance at herself in the chiffonier mirror
before rushing downstairs to double-check the parlor,
which she'd already tidied up twice. Julian was going
to spend the afternoon getting to know Elijah and Gilly
better. How she prayed it would all go well.

Honor entered the parlor in a rush, startling both
Gilly and Elijah. Gilly smiled patiently. "Relax, dear.
Everything looks fine."

Honor sat down, seeing the parlor as she knew
Julian would—outdated. The New England Colonial-
style furniture—straight-backed chairs and tufted settees—was showing definite signs of wear. Julian's
home had been redecorated only last year. Julian's
home, she thought. Soon to be her home as well. Her
skin prickled with anticipation. The doorbell rang, visibly jolting her. She jumped from her seat to answer it.

In the entryway, they kissed for a long time. When
at last Julian pulled away, he whispered to her, "Do
we really have to spend the whole afternoon here,
love? Why don't we skip out after a while and go home
to bed?" He drew her close to him again.

Laughing, Honor extricated herself from his arms.
"Not here, Julian. You're wicked. Really. Someone
will see. And no . . . we can't leave. I promised Elijah
and Gilly you would spend the afternoon." She
reached up to remove his brown derby and laid it on
the entry table. Then she took his hand and led him
toward the parlor. "Come on. Behave."

Gilly rose when they entered, moving to Julian and
offering her hand in greeting. "How nice of you to
come. We've been looking forward to it."

Julian placed Gilly's hand between both of his, saying, "Why, I've been looking forward to it all week."

Honor looked sternly in the direction of Elijah, who
had not moved from his seat. "Elijah, come shake
hands with Julian."

Elijah reluctantly stood up and moved to his pro-
spective father. "Good to see you, sir."

"How do you do, little man."

There was a long, awkward silence as Elijah did not

answer. Honor finally said, "Everyone sit down. Please. I'll fetch tea from the kitchen." Giving Julian a faint smile, she added, "Be comfortable." She scurried out of the room, quivering inside. She hadn't expected the gathering to be so strained.

Julian took a seat, as did Gilly, Elijah squeezing into the chair beside her. Julian stared at them for a moment, then said, "You have a pleasant home here, Miss Gilly. Has it been in your family long?"

"Indeed. My grandfather built this house eighty-two years ago. It's a good old house. I was born here. I've never lived anywhere else."

"Yes," Julian said. "These old houses have wonderful character." He looked at Elijah. "What are you up to these days, Elijah?"

Elijah glanced up at Gilly, then back at Julian and shrugged. "Not much, sir."

"I see. I see." Julian shifted restlessly in his chair.

Honor returned bearing a tray with a porcelain teapot, cups, and tea cakes, resting it on a high table. "Will tea be all right, Julian?" she asked. "Or would you prefer sherry?"

"Sherry would be fine. If you wouldn't mind."

"Of course not." She went to a mahogany cabinet and removed a bottle of sherry and a crystal glass. Pouring the amber-colored wine, she set it down on the high table, saying, "I think I'll join you." She poured herself a glass, first handing Julian his. Letting her drink sit for the moment, she poured tea for Gilly while asking Elijah, "Would you like a tea cake?"

Elijah nodded mutely in acquiescence, and Honor handed him a cake encased in a white linen napkin. She took her sherry and sat down uneasily on a chair close to Julian's.

After a moment Gilly asked, "Do you have family still living? Or are you all alone?"

Julian cleared his throat before speaking. "My parents are dead. The only relative I have left is my father's sister, Aunt Wynne. She lives here in New

York." He lifted his glass of sherry to his lips and finished it off in one swallow.

"How nice," Gilly said. "I'd like to have the pleasure of meeting her."

"Perhaps we could arrange it sometime in the future." He looked at Honor pleadingly, obviously uncomfortable.

"Yes. Yes," Gilly agreed. "Well, Julian, I want you to know how happy I am for you and Honor. What wonderful news. I wish you both a great deal of happiness."

"Yes," Julian responded woodenly. "Thank you."

There was another long silence, which Honor broke by saying, "Julian is well traveled, Gilly. He's had the most interesting life."

"Indeed," Gilly remarked. "Tell us something of your adventures, Julian."

"Have you ever sailed on a boat?" Elijah perked up, suddenly interested.

"Why, yes," Julian answered, fingering the rim of his empty glass. "Many times. When my father was alive, we did quite a bit of traveling together by boat."

Elijah put his half-eaten tea cake on the table next to him and moved from Gilly's side, planting himself on the floor in front of Julian. "Did you ever see anything *very* interesting?"

"Of course. There's a great deal to see in this world. As I look back, I think our venture to the Bering Sea was the highlight of my childhood."

"The Bering Sea," Elijah repeated, enchanted. "Where is that?"

"It's somewhere between Alaska and Siberia."

Elijah looked at him questioningly. "I've never heard of those places."

"Well, I'm sure you would have enjoyed it, had you been there. The most startling sunsets against gigantic steel-gray cliffs. I recall northern seabirds there that were the oddest-looking creatures I'd ever seen. They're called puffins."

Elijah's black eyes widened with delight. "Puffins?"

"Yes." Julian began to warm up. "Their coloring was black above and white below, as I remember them. A penguin's coloring, but their bodies were duck-like, and they had webbed feet. Their beaks were the weirdest-looking things imaginable—enormous. Their shape was triangular and their colors bright yellow and gold. Puffins nest in small colonies throughout the Bering Sea each summer."

"Mama once bought me a book on birds that she reads to me sometimes. Would you like to see it?" Elijah jumped to his feet and started to rush from the room to get it.

Julian stopped him. "Perhaps another time, little man." He looked at Honor. "Could I have another glass of sherry?"

"Of course." She rose quickly and reached for his empty glass.

Elijah went back to Gilly and sat down dejectedly without speaking.

Gilly, aware of his hurt feelings, put her arm around Elijah and held him to her. "Elijah is curious about so many things," she offered. "He's got quite an agile mind for a child so young."

Honor glanced around the room and began anxiously to divert the conversation to the honeymoon plans in London, but she found it impossible to keep up the flow of words. The afternoon drifted by aimlessly. She was finally convinced that Julian was really ill at ease. How strange, she thought.

At all the parties that she and Julian had attended together he had truly enjoyed being the center of attention, keeping people engrossed with his stories by the hour. Today he was decidedly distant—holding part of himself back.

She decided this situation was a strain for him. Perhaps it *was* hard to stay interested in talking to a little boy and an old woman for a long period of time. Still . . . She'd hoped the afternoon would have turned out differently. Perhaps the next visit will work out better, she consoled herself. Julian would surely be more com-

fortable now that the first awkward introduction had
passed. But she wished he'd tried to involve himself a
little more with Elijah. That was the important thing
today, his winning over Elijah.

The Queen cathedral clock chimed out the half hour
and the hour again and again. At the four o'clock
chime, Julian got up to leave. Honor was both relieved
and disappointed. She meekly followed him to the front
door.

"Will you be over tomorrow?" Julian asked as he
adjusted his derby on his head. "Come and have lunch
with me."

"Shall I bring Elijah along?" she replied hopefully.

He reached out to caress her shoulder, whispering
into her ear, "If you bring Elijah, how will I be able
to make love to you?"

She quivered inwardly, melting. "All right, then."

"All right, then," he repeated, tilting his head to one
side and lightly kissing her cheek. "Tomorrow." He
opened the door and went out.

Honor stood at the open door and watched him
walk down the crowded street until he was well out of
sight. She sighed, thinking, Tomorrow.

Rain pelted the streets of New York. Honor parted
the heavy drapes in Julian's study and stared out at it,
soothed by its steady, rhythmic sound. Dressed in a
flimsy lavender robe, she suddenly felt chilled and
hugged her arms tightly together. The summer has
raced by too quickly, she thought, mentally preparing
herself for the coming winter coldness.

The rain-gray afternoon was slowly giving way to
the darkness of night. She turned to look at Julian,
also dressed in a robe, seated at his writing desk puffing on a meerschaum pipe and avidly reading a book.

They'd spent the better part of the day in bed, making love. She knew she should be happy. Yet . . .
something was missing. She was with Julian but did
not really feel that way. There was an abyss between
them, growing wider with each passing day. As their

wedding day crept closer, Julian was becoming more and more detached, withdrawing into a private world she couldn't seem to penetrate. A wedding groom's nerves, she thought. That's all it is. How weak men are in the end, she decided. How they needed women to bolster them and carry on.

He looked up at her unexpectedly. For a moment she thought he had perceived her thoughts with that strange, canny intuitiveness of his.

He put down his book. "Come, Honor. Come sit on my lap."

She smiled and went to him, curling up against his chest contentedly. His hand moved inside her robe, caressing her smooth, round breasts. He pulled the robe open suddenly and bent his head down to kiss each rosy nipple, then bit one.

"Julian, that hurt," she gasped.

"Come, let's move to the couch," he laughed.

They sat down close to each other on the couch, Julian spreading his legs in front of him. His expression serious, he remained deep in thought.

"What is it, Julian?"

"Nothing, love. Nothing."

"Julian," she murmured hesitantly, "are you sorry you asked me to marry you?"

He suddenly gave her his full attention. "Now, why do you ask that? Of course I'm not. But *you* might be."

This stung her and she shrank back. "Why should I be sorry?"

"I'm not sure I'm such a catch. I'm terribly set in my ways. I don't deserve you, really. You're much too good for me, Honor Wentworth."

"Julian, how can you say that? You have wonderful qualities!"

Julian regarded her seriously. "I do need you, Honor."

"Well, you have me."

"Yes," he said, reaching out for her hand. "I do."

Changing the subject, she quietly asked, "Do you

think you could find some time to spend with Elijah, Julian? I'm really having a rough go with him."

"Still?"

"He's frightened by the prospect of his life suddenly changing."

"Well, next September he'll be off in a private school. That will toughen him a bit."

"He's still just a baby. I'm not sure I want him toughened up."

"Coddling him won't help anything, Honor. You've got to learn to let go of Elijah. He'll survive. We all survive in the end, don't we?"

"Yes," she answered. "We go on. But the thought of his being away from me takes some adjusting on my part."

"I spent my whole childhood away at school, Honor, and I can't see where it hurt me. I came home for holidays and summer vacations. Being sent away to school is not exactly being abandoned."

"No," Honor agreed, "it's not. I suppose it can even be beneficial." She grew quiet.

"Well," Julian said, "let's get dressed and go out to dinner."

Honor looked toward the window. "In this downpour? I could make something for us here."

"No. Let's go out."

"Yes. All right." She got up.

Julian stood up also and wrapped his arms around her. "But first . . ." He pulled her close, nuzzling her earlobe. "First," he repeated, leading her to the bedroom without another word.

She smiled half heartedly, wondering if they would be destined to avoid serious talk between them, and if making love would always serve as the answer to their problems.

Four

THE WEDDING was a week off. Honor sat with the folds of a yellow blouse resting on her knees, the last garment to finish for her trousseau, She drew a needle and thread in and out of the fabric, giving it some final touches. Elijah napped peacefully on her bed. She glanced up occasionally to look at his innocent face, sweetly cast in the shadows of the late-afternoon gloom of winter.

Gilly sat with her knitting on a chair next to the window, watching Honor give the yellow fabric design and structure. Restlessly abandoning her knitting, she let it lie in a brown heap on her lap and fixed her attention on the street below. A sad, serious expression came over her lined face. Looking back at Honor, she asked, "Did I ever tell you about the garden my grandmother had?"

"Yes, dear, you did," Honor answered plaintively, aware that Gilly's mind was wandering again.

Gilly became voluble, not hearing Honor's response. "To the Dutch housewife the garden was her only recreation. It lit up a small space of time that would otherwise have been spent with household drudgery. Right here, in front of this very house, my grandmother had a trim, stiff little garden that graced the narrow front yard. Her flower beds were surrounded with aromatic herbs for medicinal and culinary uses." She closed her eyes, lost in the pictures forming in her head, clasping her hands together on her lap, childlike and serene.

"There were tulip bulbs and coronation-pink roots

that had been ordered from Holland. She had white and red roses, stock roses, carnelian roses, eglantines, jenoffelins, crown imperials, white lilies, anemones, bare-dame, violets, marigolds, summersots, clove trees, and gilliflowers." Her eyes opened with a start. "I was named for the gilliflower. I'd almost forgotten that."

She drew in her breath sharply. "As a small tot, I would wander through my grandmother's garden, absorbing the beauty of the brilliant colors and breathing the sweet aromas. Oh, Honor, you should have seen it . . . You should have seen it."

Gilly paused, finding herself once again in the present. She wiped her watering eyes with the back of her hand. "Look at the street now. There are no flower beds waiting out the winter, making ready to spring their colorful heads from the sleeping ground." Sadly she lamented, "I've lived too long. Seventy-five years is much too long. Why has the world changed, Honor?" She fell into a comtemplative silence.

Honor sighed, finding it painful to see Gilly in such mental anguish. She wondered how Gilly would get on alone after the wedding. To escape this worry, she let her thoughts drift to Julian. Her body still felt warm and mellow from their shared physical closeness of the night before. Her brow wrinkled suddenly. Why, when she loved him so much, did she still find it impossible to reach the heights she had heard other women whisper about! The fault did not rest with Julian. She was sure of that. It was something lacking in her.

Sighing, she pulled her needle through the material and tied a knot, biting the thread off at the end. After placing the fresh-stitched blouse over the sewing machine, she stood up and bent over from the waist, stretching. She decided to put the whole business out of her mind, certain that it would improve with time; it was just a matter of getting used to him. Wrapping herself in a brown shawl to ward off the November chill, she moved to the oval mirror over the chiffonier.

She searched the reflection of her face, looking for

something. What? How did Julian see her? she wondered. Really see her? Smiling at her image, she could hardly remember a time when there hadn't been a Julian. How changed her life was. She wondered what direction her life would be taking if she weren't looking forward to being his bride, if she had stayed where she was . . .

The form and shape of images from her past began to resurrect themselves in her mind. No, she thought, I won't let myself think of them. Would their ghostly presence never let her be?

She moved to the armoire and opened it, gently running her hands over the newly made clothes. Thinking of the rags she'd been forced to wear as a young child, she was proud of how far she'd advanced.

Now she envisioned what her life would be like as Julian's wife. Living in that fine house, married to a man of real breeding. She would be respectable. Elijah would be sent to the finest schools. And most important of all, she would finally be loved. Love would free her of the childhood demons that continually plagued her. She believed this with the very essence of her soul.

She thought about this for a moment, keenly aware that Julian had never actually said he loved her. But he *was* marrying her. Didn't that speak for itself?

Honor smiled gaily as she pulled out her peach wedding gown of primrose faille and held it against her, remembering the night, four months before, when Julian had proposed. I'll save you, Julian, she mused. I'll save us both.

Two days later Elijah lay huddled under the far corner of his bed, clutching a wooden soldier to his chest. He could hear his mother calling him, hear her footsteps as she searched for him, but he remained quiet, smiling with pleasure at his causing so much trouble. She'll never find me here, he thought mirthfully. Then I won't have to go.

Suddenly his mother's head appeared at the foot of

the bed. He laughed out loud, thinking it funny to see her squatting down like that.

"Elijah," she muttered crossly, pulling him out from under the bed and to his feet. "Now look what you've done. Your clothes are dusty." Brushing the seat of his pants, she straightened his brown-striped wool tunic and bloomers as she admonished, "Julian is waiting downstairs to take you to lunch. You knew he was coming. Why on earth were you hiding?"

He looked up at her pleadingly. "Must I, Mama? Must I?"

Her face softened as she sank onto his bed and pulled him toward her. "Julian would like to get to know you better, Elijah. Why, in just a few days he'll be your father. Doesn't that make you happy? Don't you want a father, Elijah?"

"No! At least not him."

"Oh, Elijah. You don't really still believe that he doesn't like you, do you? We've been over that time and again. It's just not true." Her expression suddenly took on a worried look.

He weakened, not wanting to be the cause of her concern. He put his arms around her neck and kissed her soft cheek. "I'm sorry. I won't be naughty again."

She gently kissed him back and stood up. Her face brightened. "It's going to be all right, Elijah. You'll see. We're going to be so happy. Our whole lives will change for the better. Come." She walked out of the room ahead of him.

"Can I take my soldier along?" he called out.

"Yes," she answered. "Now come along."

Elijah stood hesitantly in the doorway, eyeing Julian with more than a little remorse. So he had to go out with him. He supposed there was no getting around it. But he fervently wished he could. He knew Julian didn't like him. He felt this very strongly, no matter how hard his mother tried to convince him otherwise. As Julian moved closer to him, his towering presence caused Elijah to wince slightly.

"Are you going to take that toy along with you, little man? You might lose it."

Elijah's glance shifted anxiously to his mother. He relaxed as she came to his rescue.

"I told him it was all right, Julian," Honor said as she began buttoning him into a heavy wool coat. Wrapping a Christmas-red wool muffler twice around his neck until it reached up to his nose, she kissed the top of his head and settled a wool cap on his dark hair. She smiled sweetly at him. "Have fun, darling."

He nodded and turned desolately to Julian. Together they set out into the chill of the winter day. Walking beside Julian, Elijah once again silently bemoaned his bad luck at having to spend time alone with him. Julian had let four months go by since the engagement had been announced without once bothering him. What had happened to change his mind now? Elijah wondered bitterly.

Trying to keep up with Julian's brisk gait was not an easy matter. Elijah's eyes were beginning to water from the cold, making matters worse. As they passed children playing in the winter slush, Elijah eyed them longingly. They were having fun. They didn't have to put up with Julian. Why, he wondered miserably, did his life seem so strange and complicated?

At last Julian stopped walking. Elijah looked up to see a large sign that he couldn't read. He supposed this was it. They entered the restaurant through an enormous, ornately decorated door. A pleasant-looking redheaded woman assisted Elijah in removing his muffler, coat, and wool cap; all the while he tightly grasped his wooden soldier. He smiled at her when she carried his belongings away. Hers was a friendly face. After a moment a tall man with a strange-sounding accent led them to a table. Elijah obediently stayed two paces behind Julian.

Elijah sat uncomfortably in the large restaurant chair, remembering to put the starched white linen napkin across his lap as his mother had told him to do. Setting his soldier next to his plate, he wished he were home alone with his toy, playing games. He glanced over at Julian, who was preoccupied with the menu. Leaning back, he looked around the oversized room, studying the green plush seats and thick burgundy carpeting, thinking it all stiff and unnatural. So grim and serious. Not at all like the warm, sunny kitchen he ate in at home.

He heard Julian give the order to the waiter, though he had no idea what he would be getting. He guessed Julian knew what he was doing. The waiter brought Julian a round glass filled with a dark substance, and Elijah watched him lean back and sip it. They quietly eyed each other.

Julian finally broke the silence. "Do you know how the Brevoort came to be named, Elijah?"

Elijah stared at him dumbly. "The Brevoort?"

Julian laughed softly. "That's the name of this restaurant."

"Oh. No, sir. No, I don't."

"Well," Julian began enthusiastically, "there was a Henry Brevoort who had a farm right in this area when Washington Square was a potter's field. He—" His voice faltered and he grew quiet.

Elijah stared blankly at him, not responding. He wondered why that seemed so interesting to Julian.

After a moment Julian said slowly, "The French food here is really wonderful." He paused. "Have you ever had French food before, Elijah?"

"No, sir."

They lapsed into silence again. Elijah watched Julian shift his body uneasily and perceived that he was making him uncomfortable. He winked and then smiled at his soldier.

"Is something funny, Elijah?" Julian asked.

Elijah sobered immediately. "No, sir."

After a while the waiter set their plates of food in front of them. Elijah cautiously eyed the anemic-looking chicken covered with a strange-smelling sauce. He didn't want to eat it, but he'd promised his mother he would be good.

The rest of the meal passed quietly and uneventfully. Elijah wasn't sure if he had liked the chicken, but the chocolate pudding for dessert had made it all worthwhile. By the end of the meal he had finally begun to relax and was even enjoying himself. Then, duly wrapped in his winter clothing, he found himself once again out in the cold air.

Julian looked down at him. "Did you enjoy the meal?"

Elijah pulled his muffler down below his chin. "Yes, sir." He noticed steam coming from his mouth when he spoke. He puffed a few times, watching it.

"Perhaps we could do something else when your mother and I return from our honeymoon. What do you like to do?"

Elijah thought for a moment, then brightened. "Mama once took me to a play. I liked that more than anything."

"Well," Julian said. "Well. Perhaps we could arrange that sometime. But I think we'd best go home now. Your mother will be worried if you're gone too long."

They ambled along comfortably together, slush soaking Elijah's shoes. His toes were already beginning to feel numb. He wondered if Julian really meant it—would really take him to a play. He guessed that Julian must really like him after all to want to do that. Perhaps they could be friends. Today hadn't been so bad. Actually, it had been fine. He just might get used to the idea of sharing his mother with Julian. He just might.

"High time you settled down, Julian. High time. I'd almost lost hope."

Julian looked across the table at his aunt, thoroughly exasperated. "Must you continually harp on that, Auntie?"

"Well, you must admit it has taken you rather a long time." She rubbed her wrinkled hands together. "Deal the cards. Deal the cards." She pushed back the silver-rimmed spectacles that had slipped down her short, pushed-up nose.

"I will when you get out the cribbage board," Julian retorted sardonically.

"Ah." She pushed her chair away from the table and ambled to a cupboard to secure the board, her large, flabby bulk preventing her from moving too quickly. Out of breath, she returned to the table and placed the deck of cards on it.

Concentrating intently on the six cards dealt to her, two facedown, she sputtered excitedly, "Well, this looks good, doesn't it? I'll get you this time, Julian. I'll beat you yet." She paused for a moment and looked over at him. "What have you been up to these days?"

Studying the cards, Julian said offhandedly, "I took Honor's son out to lunch today."

"Have you been spending much time with the boy?"

"Well, actually, no. Today was the first time I ever took him out alone. He's really a nice boy."

"Do you mean that you've been engaged for four months and only now have spent some time alone with the boy who'll be your stepson in a few days? That's just like you. Just like you."

"Must you always criticize me, Aunt Wynne? Don't you ever have anything nice to say?"

"Well, I suppose I will when there is something in your life to reflect that."

"I'm getting married. You've nagged me for years about settling down. Isn't that enough?"

"Yes, I suppose. Twenty-seven points! Twenty-seven points! What do you have?"

"Fifteen," Julian said unenthusiastically.

"I told you I'd get you. I told you. Deal again."

"Must we play tonight, Auntie?"

"You're really afraid you'll lose, aren't you, Julian? Ha!"

Julian sighed. "For God's sake." He shuffled the cards and dealt out the appropriate number. He wished she'd just play and stop that eternal chattering.

"Honor is really lovely. Just lovely. But you've never told me much about her, really. Where are her parents?"

Julian gulped. Why did he always feel intimidated by his aunt? "Her parents are dead," he lied.

"And the boy's father?"

He looked at her carefully. Had she heard something? No. Her life was too secluded and shut off from the outside world. He doubted it. But still . . . It *was* possible. He squirmed uneasily in his chair. "Her— husband died also. Before her son was born."

"How has she taken care of herself and the boy?"

"I told you she was a working girl, Aunt Wynne."

"Ah, yes. I remember now. I suppose she's had a hard time of it."

"Yes, she has."

"Well, I've supported you in style for all these years. I suppose I can continue well enough when you have a wife and son, too. But don't you think it's high time you considered some sort of job now that you're getting married?"

Julian threw the deck of cards down. "So that's what all this is about!"

"You've never taken on much responsibility. You never learned how. First your parents spoiled you, and when they died—leaving you penniless, I might add —I just naturally took over. We've all made life too easy for you, Julian. Much too easy."

"My father meant to leave me well taken care of. He always said I'd be provided for. He just miscalculated, that's all. All those bad investments."

"Your father, my brother, squandered away every nickel our parents left him. Squandered it all away on drink and women."

Julian stiffened. "If you think I'll sit here and allow you to slander my father, you're sadly mistaken, Aunt Wynne."

"Well, perhaps your father couldn't help it. He was too handsome. More handsome than any man had a right to be. And charming. You're so like him, Julian. So like him."

He looked away from her, wishing he were anywhere tonight but here. "Could we please change the subject?"

"I haven't minded supporting you, Julian," his aunt continued relentlessly. "Not at all. I just don't know if I've really done you a favor, that's all."

"Well, just forget it, Auntie. Just forget it. If you think I'm going to grovel for your money, you're sadly mistaken." He pushed his chair violently away from the table.

Her blue eyes narrowed with distress. "Calm down. Calm down. I'm not going to cut you off for no reason. When I go it will all be yours, anyway. It's just—just that I wished you showed some incentive for doing something. You breezed through college easily enough. But what have you done since? I ask you, what have you done?"

"I've been writing a book."

"Yes, you've been writing a book. And where do you think that will lead you? Nowhere, that's where. Nowhere."

Julian stood up. "I think it's time I left, Aunt Wynne. There's no point in carrying this conversation any further."

Her lined face reddened. "Julian, it's just that I think you should take some of the responsibility for your new family. Every other man does."

"It seems to me I've heard that one before. What other men do. Well, dammit, I'm not like other men."

She stood up and reached out for his hand. He tried to withdraw it, but she pulled it back, patting it. "There, now. Let's not be cross with each other. You know how I care for you, darling boy."

Julian looked contrite. "Don't you think you're being a little hard on me, Auntie?"

She regarded him seriously, her eyes clouding over with moisture. "The problem with you, Julian, is that not one person in your life has been hard enough on you. We've all loved you too much." She released his hand.

He leaned over and reluctantly kissed her on the cheek. "I will be going now. We'll play our game of cribbage some other time." He turned to leave, but her voice stopped him.

"Are you sure I can't come to the wedding?"

"We've . . . I've decided on a private ceremony. We'll stop in to see you later in the day for brandy."

"You know I wish you luck and happiness, darling boy."

"Yes, Auntie. I know." He put on his overcoat and hat and set out into the night.

Julian walked for what seemed like hours. His thoughts were muddled; his mind raced from one disturbing idea to another. Why did his life have to change? he wondered. Why hadn't he left well enough alone? He'd been happy before. No one made demands on him. He came and went as he pleased. He seriously doubted that he knew what he was doing. *Marriage*. It had an ominous ring to it.

He thought about Honor for a moment. He couldn't deny that she was good for him. Probably the best thing that had ever happened to him. She'd always made him feel more special than he actually was. He knew himself very well. He really was not all that Honor thought him to be.

To him, their relationship was perfect just the way it was. Why did it have to be muddied up with marriage? Wasn't there a woman alive who could be happy without chaining a man down? But he knew, deep down, he wasn't being fair to Honor. He was the one who'd pursued her, not the other way around. He was the one who'd proposed in a sudden, insane desire for normalcy in his life. He knew his life-style before Honor had been wrong. It had led him nowhere. Still . . . it had been fun.

He frowned suddenly, thinking of Aunt Wynne's trying to pressure him into getting a job, of all things.

She'd never objected to supporting him before she'd known of his wedding plans. He wondered if she knew about Elijah's illegitimacy. For a moment there he'd really suspected that she did. He realized he was being ridiculous. If she knew, she would have said so, he thought wryly, understanding his Victorian aunt all too well.

Aunt Wynne might forgive his transgressions. He was a man. But a woman's? Never! At all costs she must never find out. That would probably give her the only reason to ever seriously consider cutting him off. Suddenly fearful, he wondered why he was taking this chance. Of all the women he had known, how had he gotten into this predicament over Honor?

Honor . . . Honor . . . Honor . . . Did he love her? He didn't know. What the hell was love, anyway? He certainly liked her more than any woman he'd ever known. That was one reason why he chose her. But was that enough? Should there be more? She was beautiful and bright . . . wonderful company . . . a marvelous bed partner. Yet he'd always sensed that she held back part of herself. This bothered him, for he wanted everything from her. Everything.

Still, she claimed to be deeply in love with him. He wondered what that must feel like, to be deeply in love. Perhaps he'd never know.

He abruptly stopped walking, finding himself in front of an all-too-familiar building. Now, how did I find myself here? he wondered. He hesitated, then climbed the steps and went inside, walking in the direction of one particular door. What the hell, he thought. He knocked and waited.

The door was flung open and Mignon stood before him, a startled expression on her face. "Why, Julian Borg. What brings you here at this hour?"

"Can I come in, Mignon?"

"I haven't seen or heard from you in four months, Julian. Four months! Give me one good reason why I should let you in."

He smiled, mocking her. "Because, my love, you

know damned well you've missed me too much not to."

She burst out laughing. "Well, you haven't changed, have you? Not a bit." Her shoulders slumped over in defeat as she moved to the side of the doorframe to give him entry.

Julian walked in and shut the door behind them, blocking everything else from his mind.

Exuberant, Honor was on her way to St. John's in the Village with Elijah at her side. Her steps were quick and light, reflecting her happy spirit. Her wedding day shone brightly on her long-awaited expectations.

Julian would meet her at the church. Afterward they would retire to Miss Gilly's for a glass of brandy and the white-frosted cake that lay on the kitchen counter. Then there would be a quick visit with Julian's Aunt Wynne before returning to Julian's home to spend the night. In the morning they would board a ship that would take them to England for their honeymoon. Honor smiled in anticipation.

She headed down Christopher Street, clutching Elijah with one of her gloved hands. With the other she carefully held the great folds of her gown high above the ground in an effort to keep it from being soaked by the slush on the street. Her three-quarter-length brown coat was buttoned to her neck, and she proudly wore a new, mammoth-sized burgundy velvet and silk hat. The salesclerk had assured her the hat was made for a blonde. Everything she wore felt right today.

Elijah skipped along beside her, hanging on to her hand, trying to keep up with her long strides. Honor glanced down at the child bundled in the warm coat, the sailor cap resting on the dark hair, the large, dark eyes glistening with excitement. A surge of love for her son rushed through her. She squeezed his hand. What a beautiful day, she thought, despite the obstacles that made their journey difficult.

When they crossed a street, they had to sidestep

various-sized piles of horse manure or cautiously make their way through the endless traffic tie-ups that occurred daily in New York. Impeded continually by the traffic snarls they helped create, the electric trolleys were forced to keep a step behind horsecars for long stretches. Seldom did they reach their designated speed of twenty–twenty-five miles an hour. The result was mayhem. Trolleys, carriages, cart men, pedestrians . . . They all seemed to melt together in one cohesive muddle.

Walking through this bedlam was nearly impossible, but Honor was too impatient to ride a trolley. She could have taken the elevated railroad, but riding in those trains frightened her, although by walking beneath them she risked the possibility of oil or cinders falling on her from the stubby little coal-burning locomotives that moved them. The foul air made her cough and the noise hurt her ears, but, considering her choices, Honor walked.

At last they turned into Waverly Place and approached the church. They stood before the huge Greek-revival building, looking up at its famed pillared portico. She wasn't sure whether she and Elijah should wait inside or greet Julian from the portico. She decided to wait outside. Her heart tripped at the thought of Julian coming up toward her, his handsome face close to hers . . . that expansive smile.

There was still no sign of him, but she was early. She knew well that it was hard for Julian to get out of the house promptly for anything. But of course this wasn't merely *anything*. Surely his wedding day would spur him on a bit. She smiled, feeling her nose pinch from the cold, and waited.

Honor wasn't sure how much time had gone by. Was it one hour, two? Elijah was running up and down the church steps, unleashing the great storehouse of energy in his young boy's body. She watched him, swallowing hard, gripped by fright. Julian wouldn't *not* come, would he? He wouldn't do that to her. Julian loved her. She knew that he loved her. But where was he? Could something have happened? No, nothing. Nothing had happened. Julian, her voice echoed and vibrated inside her, where are you, darling?

Elijah ran to his mother and searched her face, seeing her pain. He wished he could kiss away his mother's hurt, but he sensed that kissing her wouldn't help. Instead, he asked cautiously, "Julian is coming, isn't he, Mama?"

There was a silence. When she finally answered him, her voice didn't sound like his mother's. It was strained and hoarse. "I don't know. I don't know," she repeated.

"He knew where to meet us, didn't he?"

"Yes. He knew."

"Could Julian be lost, Mama?"

"No. He's not lost." With that she shakily sat down on the top step, hugging her knees tightly.

Elijah raced away from her down the steps, searching one end of the street to the other. He ran a few steps this way, then the other, his heart pounding. He told himself that Julian would surely appear at any moment. Then his mother would be happy again. He darted back and forth for a long time, slowly aware that the cold was growing more biting. His nose and cheeks hurt from the sting of it.

Snow began to fall softly, quietly, covering the city with its whiteness. The stillness of the street was palpable, as if all things were suddenly frozen in time. There was no one anywhere in sight. Elijah felt quite alone with his mother, who was sitting on the church steps in an anguish he couldn't quite understand. For a moment he considered the possibility of Julian's having been in an accident, then decided against it. He recalled Miss Gilly's and his mother's frequent remarks about Julian's constant tardiness. That's all it is, he told himself; Julian is late again.

He thought that over carefully. Julian was often late for appointments, but not this late. Not that he could remember. But why wouldn't he come? Elijah wondered. He could make no sense of it at all, and a feeling of anger began to rise inside him.

At this moment he hated Julian. Truly hated him, for he finally had to face the fact that Julian would not be coming down the street toward them. He just knew it. He's not coming, he thought angrily. It was lies. All lies.

Elijah turned toward the church and climbed the steps, bringing himself closer to his mother's unhappy face. He sat down beside her, put his arms around her waist, and laid his head on her arm. He looked up at her, his dark eyes serious and pleading. "Mama. We'd better go. Please, Mama. Get up and let's go home. We have to go now. It's getting late. Mama."

Gilly greeted them at the doorway with a letter clutched in her hand. The letter, delivered only moments after Honor had left for church, had thrown Gilly into an angry, frustrated state. She had not needed to be told its contents. In a strange way she had already known. From the time she'd awakened that morning she'd had a strong, inexplicable premonition of the day's coming events.

Now the sight of Honor's pale, pinched face reflected her own pain, and Gilly mutely handed the sealed envelope to Honor. She then bustled Elijah off to his bedroom to remove his wet clothing, wisely knowing the only way she could help Honor was to leave her alone.

Halfway up the staircase Elijah stopped, turning to Gilly. "Why did he do this to Mama, Miss Gilly? Why?" His eyes were brimming over with tears. "How could he be so awful?"

Gilly gently took his hand and continued their ascent. "It is shocking, Elijah. But you will come to discover there's a lot in this world that's startling and horrible."

"Does this mean that Mama and Julian won't get married?"

"I'm afraid so, Elijah."

"But she wanted to marry him. It was important to her. It's wrong of Julian. Wrong of him to hurt my mother so."

"Yes, dear. I know. Let's just put Julian Borg out of our minds for good, shall we? We'll just concentrate on giving your mother privacy for a while and being as considerate as we possibly can. Our love will help her get over this."

"Yes," Elijah said soberly, looking older than his years. "We'll be extra good and nice to her."

In the privacy of her room Honor sat down trembling, not bothering to remove her damp hat or coat. Her body felt drained, bereft of energy. She stared at the envelope for a clue. Her name was sprawled on it. Nothing else. The handwriting was all too familiar. Dear God, she thought, how will I live through this? What will I do?

Pulling herself together, she reluctantly took off her gloves and opened the white square, withdrawing a note. She read the words through a haze of tears that spilled heavily down her cheeks.

My dearest Honor,
    By the time you read this I will have boarded ship one day early and will be on my way to England in the morning—alone.
    Forgive me if you can, but I can't marry you. Call it a weakness in me, or call it whatever you like, but I can't go through with it. I need, I must have, my freedom.
    I should have let you know sooner. Forgive me.

Julian

Some small part of her had anticipated the worst; she felt both utterly crushed and curiously relieved.

Five

DREW COURTENAY jumped atop a high, round table in his sitting room, his small frame shaky from intoxication. With one hand he held his champagne glass high, and with the other he adjusted his gold pince-nez that had slipped down his long, pointed nose. He shouted, attempting to be heard over the throng of people milling about, "Happy New Year! Happy nineteen hundred!"

His guests turned to him, gaily acknowledging his toast and creating such a high intensity of sound that Honor laughingly cupped her ears with her hands. Drew jumped off the table and found himself face to face with her.

"Happy turn of the century, pretty Honor. It's good to have you here." He paused reflectively for a moment. "Are you feeling better these days?"

"Yes, Drew, much better . . . Thanks." She smiled at him.

"Good . . . good. Well, have fun, beauty. I'll be back in a bit."

Honor watched Drew disappear into the crowd. She helped herself to a glass of champagne from a tray and attempted to move about, heading nowhere in particular. It was not an easy matter, for Drew's large sitting room was overflowing with people. Honor noticed that many drinks were spilling onto the wisteria-blue carpet; one barely missed the skirt of her long, sweeping gown of amber chiffon. Smoke rose in a gray haze, causing her eyes to tear. She stopped wandering, finding it impossible to gain distance. Searching the faces carefully, she realized that not one person was familiar to her. These were all new people tonight. Sipping her champagne, Honor contented herself with watching them.

She was especially fascinated by the theatrical-looking women with their painted faces and large, vari-colored plumed hats. Reaching up to touch her face, she wondered how she'd look with makeup, while mentally comparing her Gainsborough-styled hat bearing two sweeping aigrettes with theirs. Her attention wandered to the men. She was sure nearly all of them were actors. It seemed to her that Drew had more than the usual number of theater people present at the party tonight despite the fact that, as owner of a legitimate establishment on Broadway, Drew's prime interest had always been actors.

The men amused her as she heard them thrill to the sound of their own booming, articulate voices. They did not appear to be talking *to* people so much as *at* them, apparently lost in a private world of their own importance. They might as well have been addressing a stage audience.

Tonight, for the first time since Julian had deserted her, Honor was responsive to the world around her. *Julian.* Something still tore at her insides at the thought of him. She wondered if she'd ever be free of the anguish he'd caused her.

She'd hesitated when the invitation for the party came, glad now that Gilly had talked her into it. She knew she'd led a very cloistered existence during the past six weeks. She couldn't have continued that way much longer. It certainly hadn't solved anything, and burying herself would not bring him back. Indeed, she knew she couldn't go back to him if he should return. Not after what he'd put her through. No. There was nothing left to do but return to the world of the living. It was good to be with people again. She relaxed, enjoying the hubbub around her. Life does go on, she thought. One does survive.

Raising the champagne glass to her lips, she became

aware of a man standing near her. A tall man, dressed in the manner of a Westerner, he wore a black cloth waistcoat over a long-sleeved white linen shirt, indigo-blue denim Levi's, high black leather boots, and a ten-gallon cowboy hat. He appeared awkward to her, and decidedly conspicuous in this sophisticated crowd of seasoned New Yorkers. Of all the strange people that Drew had ever invited to his parties, this man looked the most out of place to Honor. She wondered where Drew had found him.

As if reading her thoughts, Drew elbowed his way through the crowd toward Honor. "Have you met my cousin yet?"

"Your cousin? No."

"That tall cowboy standing over there. He's staying with me while he's visiting New York. Would you like to meet him?" She nodded, and Drew moved to his cousin, chatted with him for a moment, then drew him in her direction.

Honor gazed up at him, finding his looks pleasant. He stood over six feet tall, a towering, lanky figure. His brown hair, hanging from beneath his hat, was long and unruly; his full mustache covered most of his face. She was immediately struck by his dark eyes, which were his most outstanding feature, communicating a vast reservoir of kindness and strength. She couldn't help but feel drawn to him.

"Honor," Drew said, "this is my cousin."

The cowboy smiled warmly at her, removing his hat. "Good evening, ma'am."

Honor watched him nervously shuffle his cowboy hat from one hand to the other. She smiled back. "Hello."

"Are you an actress, too?" he drawled.

"God, no," Drew assured for her. "Honor is just an old friend. She's just Honor. Isn't she something, though? If I thought I had a chance, I'd marry her tomorrow." He winked at her humorously.

Honor flushed and Drew smilingly turned away, deserting them to greet yet another guest entering the room. Enveloped by the noise and chatter, she and the cowboy stood together quietly for a few minutes. As she sipped her champagne, she was aware of his intense stare.

He shyly broke the silence. "My cousin neglected to properly introduce us. My name is Lucus Kant." He cleared his throat. "You are Honor . . . ?"

"Wentworth." She smiled.

"Sounds English. Is it?"

"Yes, my parents come from England." Suddenly intensely curious about this man, she asked, "Where are you from, Mr. Kant?"

"Call me Lucus. Uh, Santa Fe, New Mexico. I'm a long way from home. You know, New York is all I ever dreamed it would be, and a lot of what I hoped it wouldn't be. I feel so damned closed in. I've never seen so many people thrown together at one time in my life." He smiled and gestured broadly, adding, "And I think most of them are in this room."

"New Mexico!" she gasped. "Tell me about it. It isn't a state yet, is it? And I thought the people were mainly Mexican. You're not Mexican, are you?"

"No," he replied, laughing at her rush of questions. "I'm an American. But I speak Spanish real good. My daddy migrated to Santa Fe when I was an infant. Lord, it's beautiful country. It will be a state someday; we're fighting for it." He paused thoughtfully, moving a step closer to her. "You know, I think you would like it there very much."

In her mind's eye she suddenly saw her pencil sketch of the New Mexican desert that was on her chiffonier mirror. She tingled, her eyes glistening at the prospect of learning about the Southwest from someone who actually lived there. All she had ever known of it was from books. "Lucus," she said excitedly, "tell me about your town of Santa Fe—"

"Honor Wentworth. Of all people," a voice interrupted her.

She turned to face a young, dark-haired woman. Puzzled, Honor stared at her. The girl's face was familiar, but she couldn't place her. Then she remembered . . . The night she had first met Julian. This girl had looked different then . . . faded and unkempt. Honor stiffened, saying, "Hello. How are you?"

The girl laughed shrilly, clearly intoxicated. Honor sensed something in her behavior that was beyond control. She unconsciously stepped closer to Lucas for protection. This woman frightened her. "I'm afraid I don't remember your name," she said.

The girl's blue eyes looked feverish. "My name is Mignon Gionet. Does that mean anything to you?"

"Why, no, it doesn't. But I do remember meeting you once."

"What do you hear from Julian, Honor Wentworth?"

Honor visibly started, losing her composure. She struggled to regain it. "Julian? Why, Julian has left the country."

Mignon reached out for Honor's arm and slipped, falling to the floor. Lucus grabbed her and helped her up. People were turning in their direction. Honor was acutely aware of curious eyes on them.

Mignon's voice grew loud. "Tell me something, woman to woman, did Julian ruin you for other men as he did me? Can you bear to have another man touch you after Julian?"

Honor's face reddened. Her eyes searched the room for Drew, wishing he'd take her away from this woman. She turned to Lucus and looked at him pleadingly.

"Answer me, Honor Wentworth. Answer me." Without warning, Mignon lunged at Honor, clawing her face, and toppling Honor's hat to the ground.

For a split second Honor was too stunned to move. Then, in a blaze of matching fury, she slapped Mignon's face, screaming, "You bitch! You bitch!"

They tore at each other with savage vehemence. Honor was vaguely aware that Lucus was frantically trying to pull them apart . . . and that Drew rushed over to intervene. Honor could feel their hands, hear their voices muted in the background, but they were a blur. She had Mignon on the floor, her face pressed into the carpet. Crazed, she was on top of her, tearing at her hair, banging her head repeatedly into the carpet. All she could think was, You had him. You had him. You bitch. Bitch.

Mignon stilled under her without warning. Honor could feel Drew pulling her up. When she was on her feet, her knees buckled and she started to sink down. Lucus grabbed her arm to steady her.

Trickles of blood streamed down her face. Lucus took a handkerchief from his pocket and gently dabbed at the cuts. His handkerchief was a red blur before her unfocused eyes. She was vaguely aware of the sound of Mignon's moaning.

Drew got down on the floor beside Mignon and looked up at Lucus. "Take Honor outside. I'll take care of Mignon."

Honor was now keenly aware of eyes staring at her. She covered her face with her hands, letting Lucus lead her out. Once in the open air she stopped, sucking in her breath. The cold wind revived her, clearing her head. Suddenly wondering what this stranger must think of her outrageous behavior, she looked at him guardedly and was shocked to see him smiling. "Are you amused, Mr. Kant?"

"Yes, ma'am, *very* amused. Are you all right now?"

"I think so."

"You wouldn't want to tell me about it, would you?"

"No. I wouldn't." He was still grinning. "Would you please stop smiling!"

He didn't. "You've got fire, girl. I wouldn't know it just to look at you."

Despite herself, she couldn't resist the rising laughter in herself.

"Say, look," Lucus said, "why don't we get away from here and go for somethin' to eat?"

Honor reflected for a moment on his suggestion, knowing she couldn't go back inside. Why not go with him? she reasoned. "All right." She shivered against the cold. "Do you think you could retrieve my hat first, and ask Drew's housekeeper for my cape? She'll know which one it is."

"Right. I'll get my coat also." He pulled open the door, then stopped to turn back to her. "You won't get into another brawl, will you?" he teased.

"I'll try not to, Mr. Kant." She burst out laughing. She liked him, this cowboy named Lucus Kant.

After a few moments Lucus returned with her plush seal cape, neatly embroidered with black soutache and beads, and helped her into it. "This is a real pretty piece. I've never seen one like it. At least not where I come from."

"Thank you. It was my Christmas gift from Gilly."

"Gilly?"

"The woman I work for."

He nodded, shyly taking her by the elbow. He drawled, "You lead the way."

She smiled at him brightly. "I'm famished. Are you?"

"A mite."

They walked briskly down Broadway, Lucus hanging on to his wide-brimmed cowboy hat as bitter gusts pushed against them. Trusting that Honor knew where she was going, he looked down at her, saying, "Will there be a place open at this hour?"

"I'm sure the Vienna Bakery will be. Many places will be. It's New Year's Eve."

He laughed. "New Year's Eve in New York. Back home that wouldn't make no never mind. Everythin' closes early, no matter what."

"There it is," she said, pointing to her right.

Lucus moved ahead of her, wedging his tall frame through the door and holding it open until she had passed by him. They sat down at a round oak table, and Lucus removed his gloves. Briskly rubbing his frozen hands together, he looked over at her, studying the gash on her cheek. "Does your cheek hurt?"

"It stings a bit, but it's not too bad."

Keeping his steady gaze on her, he suddenly realized how completely thunderstruck he was by this woman.

Her beauty took his breath away. Yet her looks seemed to change with her mood, he realized, recalling how different she had looked on the floor at Drew's, fighting in a savage rage. At that moment she had lost her fragile, Dresden-doll look, her face becoming vulnerable and open. Her wild abandon had excited him more than he'd ever dreamed could happen.

Now, sitting across from her, he thought she looked very ladylike and serene. There's many sides to this woman, he mused. That's for sure. He smiled shyly. "You won't get mad if I tell you that you're the most beautiful woman I've ever seen, will you?"

"No, I won't get mad. Thank you."

"What will you have?"

"A Viennese roll and coffee."

Lucus turned and ordered two cups of coffee and hot Viennese rolls from the elderly, baldheaded proprietor hovering close by.

Unbuttoning her seal cape, she leaned forward, asking, "What do you do at home? What is your job?"

"I work on a cattle ranch."

"Do you like it?"

"Well, I never thought about it before. I guess so. It's good to be outdoors most of the time. Good to be under the sun and feel the wind beatin' on your face. It's a good life."

"Is that all you've ever done? Cattle ranching?"

"Yes. It's not what my daddy wanted me to do, but it's all I've ever wanted."

"What did he want you to do?"

"He was a preacher. He was always at me to follow in his footsteps. Sometimes when I think on it, I feel bad that I let him down."

"Are you religious?"

"You could say that. But it's not the kind of religious that has anythin' to do with being closed up in a buildin' sayin' prayers."

Hot coffee and rolls were set down before them. Lucus waited for the proprietor to move away before saying lightly, "You're full of questions, aren't you?"

"Yes, I suppose I am." She sipped the steaming coffee, then asked, "Do you think you'll always work for someone else? Don't you want a place of your own?"

"I suppose. You never know. New Mexico is wide-open country. With a little money I can do anythin', I guess."

"Please, Lucus, please tell me about the Southwest."

"You're really interested, aren't you?"

"I've always had a keen interest in New Mexico. I can't explain why. It's always drawn me somehow. As a child I pored through any books I ever found on the subject. But you're the first person I've ever met who actually lives there."

He thought for a moment. "When you spend your whole life in a place, it becomes old hat. But I can tell you this, you've never seen anythin' so pretty as a New Mexican sunset or the Sangre de Cristo Mountains when they're covered with snow. God, it's beautiful country. Clean country. Pure. Untouched, you know?"

Her eyes shone, picturing it all. "Is Santa Fe near the Chihuahuan Desert?"

"No, but I've been there. I've got a friend that lives in Carlsbad."

"Carlsbad?"

"You would like it in Santa Fe. I told you that before. Maybe someday you'll get to see it all for yourself."

"I can't explain why, but I know I will. For some unexplainable reason . . . I must."

"What would you do if you were there?"

"Why, I'm not really sure." Her eyes suddenly widened with mischief. "Climb the Sangre de Cristo Mountains. I've never climbed a mountain."

Lucus laughed and sipped the scalding liquid.

She leaned forward. "Tell me about Santa Fe. Do they have modern conveniences?"

"You bet. For ten years now we've had street lights and telephone lines. Even some sidewalks here and there. Why, they've even paved San Francisco Street.

That's our main street. We're really advanced compared to most places."

"How interesting," Honor said. "I wouldn't have thought you'd have all that."

Lucus studied her face, mesmerized. Finally forcing his gaze away from her, he looked down at his hot seeded roll, watching the melting butter slide down over the plate. He lifted the roll, then put it down, wiping the slippery substance from his fingers with a white, starched napkin. He had suddenly lost his appetite. He looked up at Honor again. "You haven't told me anythin' about you. What is your life like?"

"I work for a maiden lady, taking care of the house and doing the cooking. My son and I—"

"Your son?"

"Yes. I have a son who recently turned six."

"You don't have a husband lurking around somewhere, do you?" he asked anxiously.

"No. I don't have a husband."

"Well, that's a relief."

"Oh, is it?"

"I'd like to see more of you before I go back home. Do you think we could?"

She eyed him carefully for a moment. "Do you have a wife there, Mr. Kant?"

"No. I've never been married. Never even came close to it. At least not until—" He stopped. Blushing, he lapsed into silence. A strange feeling washed over him. He knew suddenly, inexplicably, that this woman would be his destiny. "You're goin' to think I'm crazy, Honor," he blurted. "We've only known each other a few hours. But I think I've met the woman I'm goin' to marry."

"And who might that be?" she laughed.

"You can tease if you want. But I'm serious."

"You can't be serious."

"Can't I?"

"Don't you have one special woman back in Santa Fe?"

"Yes, you might say that. But that won't come to anythin' permanent."

"Why not?"

"Just won't." Realizing she must think he was out of his mind, he changed the subject by asking, "Well, can I see you again?"

"Come over tomorrow afternoon at three for tea. All right?"

A smile spread over his face. "Tomorrow at three. And the next day, and the next day, and the day after that, too."

Honor laughed. He was crazy. Impetuous. And yet . . . so really very nice. So easy to be with. She was already looking forward to tomorrow. How quickly life can change, she thought.

Six

DREW AND Lucus sat in the dimly lit kitchen looking out the window, watching the snow fall. Drew turned away from the window, bringing his attention to his cousin. He thought he was more quiet than usual, more pensive than he'd previously been during his visit.

He recalled the impression Lucus had made on him when they were children, when Drew and his parents had made their yearly pilgrimage to Santa Fe. Before Drew's father had put his foot down and stopped those visits.

To Drew, Lucus had been the kindest boy he'd ever known, devoid of all the nastiness inherent in young children. Yet, even then, Drew had sensed a great sadness in him, a heavy weight pressing down on his young shoulders. Lucus was so different from other children their age. So terribly serious. And always quoting the Bible.

Drew recalled listening to his mother and father whisper to each other late at night, when they thought he was asleep, about how dreadful it was that his mother's sister had died in childbirth, leaving Lucus to be raised alone by Abram, his father. Drew's mother never had anything good to say about Uncle Abram, always referring to him as "that religious fanatic."

Yet it seemed to Drew that Lucus had turned out well in spite of it all. He was a likable chap. Extremely so, despite that ever present aura of deep sadness. Drew sighed, leaned back in his chair, and finally broke the silence. "What did you and Honor do yesterday?"

Lucus's face lit up. "We rented a carriage and went sightseein'." He pulled on his mustache thoughtfully. "What a woman, Drew. What a woman. In all my thirty years I've never felt this way about anyone. Well, to be honest, there haven't been too many women in my life in the first place. Just one I've been halfway serious about. But she's married. Mostly I never seemed to find the time before. Cowherdin' is a lonely, solitary life."

Drew was incredulous. "You mean back home there's a woman you care deeply about? A married woman? That's hard to believe, knowing your religious background."

"Loneliness does strange things to people sometimes, Drew."

Drew tapped his forefinger on the kitchen table, thinking deeply. "Are you serious about Honor?"

"Believe it, Cousin, I am. You know, I knew from the first night I met her that she was the woman I'd been waitin' for. I even told her that evenin'."

"What was her reaction?"

"She didn't think I really meant it."

"And now? Does she believe you?"

"Well, I haven't actually brought it up since. Been waitin' for the right opportunity."

Drew regarded him quizzically. "It's odd, but I never thought of you as being impulsive before. I can't imagine you proposing to a girl on the very first night."

"I guess I'm as impetuous as any man who falls in love."

"Don't you think you're moving a bit too quickly?" Drew asked carefully. "You admit you haven't had much experience with women. And you haven't had time to get to know Honor well."

"Time has nothin' to do with it, Drew. I'm sure about my feelin's for her." Lucus paused. "I take it you don't approve."

"Of course I do. Honor would be a catch for anyone. Why, she's one of my oldest friends. No one thinks more of her than I. That's just it. I worry about her. I really want her to be happy."

"You don't think she could be with me?"

"I think what bothers me is that you and Honor come from such different backgrounds. I guess I worry that you don't really have enough in common with her."

"I know we live in different worlds, but she's really interested in mine. Did you know she's always dreamed about living in New Mexico? Since she was a child. Why, she'd love it there."

"She may love New Mexico, Lucus, but does she return your feelings?"

"I think she does," Lucus replied hesitantly. He thought for a moment. "She's got to!"

Drew sighed, suddenly despondent. "You're leaving the day after tomorrow. What will you do then?"

"I've got a plan. Honor can join me later in Santa Fe. I know she can't just pick up and leave right now. We'll be married there later. She'll come. You'll see. She'll come."

"What about Elijah?"

"Elijah? Well, I mean for her to bring the boy, too. It'll work out just fine." Lucus shifted his lanky body in the hard, straight-backed chair. "You know, Honor told me she wasn't married when Elijah was conceived. Not many women would be honest about somethin' like that."

"How do you really feel about that, Lucus? Can you accept it?"

"Listen . . . who am I to hold that against her? As a matter of fact, I respect her for her honesty." He paused for a moment, then recited, " 'There is not a just man upon earth, that doeth good, and sinneth not.' "

Drew laughed suddenly. "You're still quoting the Bible, I see."

"If a man would just take the time and look, that's where all the answers are, Drew. I should know. I've studied the Bible my whole life."

"Well, as I remember, you didn't have a choice. The one thing that's most clear in my mind from the days when my family and I used to visit you in Santa Fe is your father's Bible lessons after dinner every night. Didn't you ever tire of that?"

"Can't say I did. Well . . . that's not completely true. There were times when I wanted to go out to play and skip the lesson. Lord, he'd whip me good over that. I didn't try to get out of it too often, I'll tell you."

"I'm sorry."

"My daddy did the best he could by me," Lucus said defensively. "It wasn't easy for him to raise a boy without a mother. He did what he thought was right. I didn't always agree with his thinkin', but I never blamed him for anythin'. Don't forget, religion was his whole life." He leaned back, reminiscent for a moment. "Lord, his sermons in church were really somethin'. When I was a kid I just knew the devil was chasin' me, so I prayed real hard to save my soul."

"Do you think you did?" Drew asked teasingly.

Lucus laughed. "I doubt it." He glanced at the kitchen clock and stood up. "I'm meetin' Honor in half an hour. I'd best get goin'."

"Are you going to ask her to marry you today?"

"Yes . . . I am."

Drew smiled. "Good luck, Lucus."

Lucus nodded at him as he strode out of the kitchen. "Thanks, Cousin. I'll need it."

Drew sat at the kitchen table for a long time after Lucus had left, mulling over this surprising turn of affairs. He would never have dreamed that Honor could seriously care for someone like Lucus. Except as a friend.

To Drew, it seemed a mismatch. They didn't look right together. Honor was, after all, remarkably sophisticated for her age. And Lucus? Well, Drew was fond of him, but Lucus was simply Lucus. He couldn't possibly be more different from a man like Julian. Perhaps that was it, Drew decided. Right now Honor needed someone totally different.

He thought about what Julian had done to Honor, and wished that somehow he could have prevented it. He'd tried to approach her a number of times about what he considered to be Julian's true nature, but she'd only laughed his words away. He'd been afraid of going too far, knowing she was desperately in love with Julian. He supposed Honor had thought she would be the one to change him. So much for that.

Julian had always been a bastard where women were concerned, Drew thought, the way he jumped in and out of affairs with no apparent consideration for the consequences. Drew had to admit that he had been in awe of Julian for years. His complete success with women had always made Drew slightly envious. Still, despite his envy, Julian's liaisons had always had a humorous edge to them. At least until his involvement with Honor. For Drew, that was a different matter entirely.

Of all the women Julian could have had, Drew wondered why he had chosen Honor. She was too decent for him. Too innocent, despite the fact that she had a child. That altered nothing. Drew knew she'd been inexperienced. He'd never forgive himself for having introduced her to Julian. Never. She'd never have met him had it not been for himself.

And he'd brought Honor together with Lucus. How ironic! Drew knew that Honor wanted to be married with a home of her own. It was perfectly natural. Yet he couldn't imagine that she'd seriously consider Lucus's proposal. Impossible, he decided. Totally impossible. She wouldn't. He knew her too well for that, certain that if she did, it would result in disaster. He was also convinced that Honor was still in love with Julian, although she'd never said so. What kind of life would that be for Lucus, he fretted, married to a woman who was in love with another man?

Drew sighed, shrugging his shoulders, knowing he was worrying far too much. After all, he reasoned, they were both grown-up people and very capable of making their own decisions without his butting in. Putting it out of his mind, Drew was positive it would all turn out for the best.

Lucus rang the doorbell of Honor's house. He felt skittish, his heart thumping wildly in his chest. The door opened and there she was, looking as radiant as ever. He had to restrain himself from reaching out and embracing her.

"Come in," Honor said. "Please come in."

Elijah was behind her, running toward him. Lucus picked him up and tossed him high in the air, delighting in the sound of the boy's squeals.

"Are you going to stay for dinner, Lucus?" Elijah asked. "Are you?"

"You bet I am. You couldn't stop me."

"Come play with me, Lucus," Elijah pleaded. "Please."

Honor stepped in. "Not now, Elijah. You go on to your room for a while. I must speak to Lucus alone."

"Oh, Mama."

For the first time Lucus realized that Honor looked very upset. He turned to Elijah. "Go on, boy. I'll play later. I promise."

"You promise?"

"I promise."

"All right, then."

Lucus watched Elijah scamper up the staircase, then turned to Honor. "What's the matter, darlin'?" he asked gently.

"You'll never guess what's in the *Times* today, Lucus." She looked on the verge of tears.

He took her hand and felt it tremble. "Calm down, now. Calm down. What did you read? What's in the paper?"

She pulled him into the sitting room, whispering, "Gilly is having tea in the kitchen. I don't want her to hear." After they were seated on the pink satin couch, she asked, "Do you remember Mignon?"

"I don't know as I can ever forget her."

"She's dead, Lucus. Dead!" she shouted. Honor looked in the direction of the kitchen, realizing she had raised her voice. She lowered it to a whisper. "She killed herself. Poisoned herself. Yesterday. It's just awful. Terrible!"

"Good Lord."

"She was so young, Lucus. Not much older than I."

"Does the newspaper say why she did it?"

"They don't know. She didn't leave a note. Nobody knows." She grew quiet for a moment. "No, that's not true. I know why. I'm sure of it."

He reached over and squeezed her hand. "Are you ready to tell me about it?" He returned her steady gaze and finally saw her relax. He held on to her hand.

"Mignon and I were both involved with the same man. Julian . . . Julian Borg. He left the country . . . Deserting us both, I suppose. Although I had no way of knowing about it at the time." Her voice was husky with emotion. "I keep remembering how she behaved the night of Drew's party. How completely frantic she was. She couldn't get over him. I'm certain that's why she killed herself."

Lucus weighed her words in his mind for a moment, feeling a sharp thrust of jealousy despite himself.

Since that first night, and Honor's fight with Mignon, he'd wanted to prod her about what had really happened. Now that it was out in the open, he found himself almost violently fearful of this . . . this Julian. How did she feel about Julian now? He had to know. "And what about you, Honor?" he asked.

"Me?"

"Are you over it? Over this man? I have to know."

She lowered her head. "I don't want to hurt you, Lucus. I like you. I really do."

"Then answer me. Are you still in love with this Julian fellow?"

She hesitated for a moment, then looked straight at him. "I don't know."

"I see."

"I'm sorry, Lucus."

"There's nothin' to be sorry about." He released her slim hand.

"Let's talk about something else, shall we, Lucus? I can't discuss it any more."

Lucus leaned back and took a deep breath. "This is probably the wrong time, Honor, but there's somethin' I've got to talk to you about. I'm leavin' day after tomorrow. I don't have much time left."

"Yes?"

He plunged in. "You once said you'd always dreamed about livin' in New Mexico. I know that's easy to say. I know your roots are in New York and you're accustomed to a certain kind of life. But it could be better someplace else. It *is* better in New Mexico. That I do know. Most people consider New York a dying city. You've got to admit, it's gettin' overpopulated."

She studied him seriously for a moment. "What are you trying to say, Lucus?"

"I guess I'm trying to say that I care about you. I know we haven't known each other all that long, but I can't stand the thought of leavin' you . . . or of never seein' you again. I don't care about other men who've been in your life in the past. All I care about is us.

You may not love me now, but you could grow to love me, Honor. I'm willin' to take the chance."

Honor frowned. "Lucus—"

He cleared his throat and moved closer to her. His words came out in a rush. "Marry me and come to New Mexico. It's a good life there. You know it is. Lots of open space to breathe. . . . Beautiful country. It would be good for Elijah, too. I could teach him things. He could even learn to ride a horse. I have a house in Santa Fe, left to me by my father. I haven't used it for myself, but I could open it up. You could fix it real pretty." He looked into her eyes. "You joked about it the first night we met. But I was serious then, and I'm serious now. I love you, Honor."

Honor bit on her lower lip, "I don't know what to say, Lucus. We really haven't known each other long enough. I need time—to think."

"You can have all that you want. I won't rush you for an answer right this minute. If you decide to agree, you and Elijah can follow me to Santa Fe. We'll be married when you arrive and I'll legally adopt Elijah. I would be proud to have him for my son."

She stared at him helplessly. "Lucus, I—"

He cut her off, his voice intense, "I love you. Let me make you happy. I know it would be an adjustment for you to leave New York, but you wouldn't be sorry. I can promise you that. I'm willin' to take the chance that you'll learn to return my feelin's someday. I think you will. You'll forget this Julian. You'll see." He stopped talking, noticing her great dark eyes filling with tears. He felt anxious . . . confused. "Did I say something that upset you?"

Honor shook her head, her voice quivering. "No. You haven't. Thank you for asking. We'll write to each other. We'll see. We'll see." She stared into his kind face and took one of his great, large hands into her own. "Dear Lucus. Dear . . . dear . . Lucus."

Honor and Drew stood inside Grand Central Station with Lucus only minutes before the departure of his train. Drew shook his cousin's firm hand, saying, "It was truly good to have seen you again after so many years, Lucus. Truly good."

"Same here, Drew."

Drew moved away to give them privacy. "I'll wait for you in the carriage, Honor."

"Yes, Drew. Thank you."

Alone with her, Lucus took both of her soft hands in his. "You know you could get on the train with me right this minute. Drew would see to it that Elijah followed."

Honor laughed. "What makes you so impetuous? You know you're asking the impossible."

"Am I?"

"Lucus, you're a fine, decent man and I think a great deal of you. But you mustn't press me like this."

"I'll leave and you'll forget all about me," he said ominously.

"I won't forget you, Lucus. I promise you. We'll write to each other. We've agreed to that."

"Is it Julian? It is, isn't it?"

"At this moment I can honestly say it has nothing to do with him. He's gone, after all."

"It's killin' me havin' to leave you like this, Honor," Lucus murmured, still hanging on to her beautiful hands.

"Lucus, please don't make this so hard on us."

The train whistle blew, signaling its imminent departure. Lucus's face darkened anxiously. "I'll write. I love you." With that he pulled her to him, bending down to kiss her full lips.

Returning his ardent kiss, Honor felt close to tears. When he released her and walked away, she almost ran after him, almost begged him to stay. But what would that accomplish? she asked herself. Tomorrow or the next day she wouldn't be any more sure of what she wanted to do.

She finally turned dejectedly to join Drew in the carriage. Sidling up next to him, she whispered, almost under her breath, "He's gone."

Drew cracked the reins, prompting the horse forward. "You know, I'll really miss him. It makes you feel good just to be around Lucus."

"Yes. I know what you mean. There is something special about him. Being with him made me feel so safe and protected, somehow. Now I feel alone again."

Drew studied her profile for a moment. "Are you in love with him, Honor?"

She returned his glance. "No. I'm not. I wish I were. Why can't we fall in love with the right people?"

"Some people do. You should wait for that to happen to you."

"What makes you think I will?"

"I suppose I'm afraid that you've been through too much, and that, love or no love, Lucus represents a safe haven for you. But that's too easy, Honor. Anything worth having is worth waiting for. You're still so young. You have years ahead of you." He paused for a moment, then asked, "Have you ever considered what it really would be like to live with a man you didn't love?"

Honor's gaze sharpened as she replied tersely, "I haven't said that I intend to marry Lucus."

"No," Drew said. "You haven't said that. But do you?"

She looked away from him. "I don't know. How can I possibly tell what will happen?"

Drew stared straight ahead. "Well, whatever you do, Honor, you can count on me to back you. I want you to know that."

Her expression softened as she touched his arm and said, "Thank you, Drew."

"Well, then. What are we so sad about? We're both acting as if someone just died. Can I buy you lunch before I take you home?"

She smiled at him. "Of course." Then she retreated into her own private thoughts, wondering why this magic ingredient of love was so important, anyway. Love only hurt you. By not loving Lucus, she might be able to create the best of all possible marriages.

Something tugged at her. What *was* happiness after all? It wasn't simply love. It was also the joining together of two people who both liked and respected each other. She did feel these things for Lucus. She did!

Yet she knew she was lying to herself. It wasn't enough that Lucus loved her; she wanted to love him in return. Why hadn't it happened to her with him? He was the finest man she'd ever known. There was a kindness and decency about him that assured her he would make a good husband and father. She almost felt angry because falling in love with him had eluded her.

Of one thing she was certain. Ultimately, the right choice would be made despite Drew's seeming lack of confidence in her ability to make her own decisions. Still, her doubts nagged at her. What did she really want? She fervently wished she knew.

Honor stared into the darkness of her room, tossing restlessly on the bed. Her scattered thoughts made sleep impossible. It had been five months since Lucus had left New York. Five months of receiving pleading, lovesick letters from him. Five months of searching her soul for the right course of action.

Since Lucus's departure for Santa Fe, her days had drifted aimlessly into weeks and months. Existing in a kind of limbo, Honor had joylessly attended to her duties around the house. She'd painted, read, and played with Elijah. She'd joined Drew for an occasional game of cribbage and attended a few of his parties. But where Drew's friends had once fascinated her, she'd now come to recognize that she had nothing in common with them.

Something had been missing. She could see it in her art. A single ingredient—enthusiasm for just being alive—had decidedly been absent, and as more and more time had gone by, she'd become panic-stricken. Everyone around her seemed to have a full life. Everyone but her.

She'd finally come to believe that marriage might be

the answer. Perhaps somewhere within that institution
she could find herself again. Perhaps she would find
joy. So she had made her decision. She would go to
Santa Fe and marry Lucus. But now, at the thought of
it, she grew chilled.

What really awaited her there? She was so confused.
Surely she and Elijah would have a good life with
Lucus. He was a good man. She liked him. Really
liked him. That was the trouble! Liked . . . liked . . .
liked! She didn't love him. Why couldn't she *love* him?

If only she could feel for Lucus what she'd felt for
Julian. If only. Would she ever feel that way about
Lucus? she wondered. Could she learn to love him?
She wanted to, desperately. She didn't know . . . She'd
frustrated over this so many times since Lucus had left,
she couldn't think about it anymore.

She got out of bed and sat in a chair, wrapping a
thin shawl around her shoulders. A new life, she
thought. Exciting. Yes, but why was she so afraid?
After all, she couldn't stay in New York and spend
the rest of her life pining for what she couldn't have.
Yet she knew deep down she was running away and
that her outward boredom was just a cover-up for this.

Honor had to get away from New York. Above all
else, she had to make a life for herself and Elijah
away from all the ever-present reminders of her love
affair with Julian. After all, she reasoned, outside of
her bond with Miss Gilly, what really kept her here?
But deep down she knew. She was always plagued
with the nagging thought that Julian might return
someday. All the more reason to get out while she
could, she decided. All the more reason.

Julian, she thought. Julian. Damn you, anyway. If
only I could hate you. Was that the way Mignon had
felt? Mignon. She couldn't let herself think of her.

But was she being fair to Lucus, marrying him
while she knew full well she didn't love him? Knew she
was using him as an excuse to escape her life in New
York? She realized suddenly that she was being hard
on herself, that this wasn't the complete truth. There

was more to her decision to marry Lucus. He was by far the kindest man she'd ever known. There was something so very dear about him. Elijah adored him, and that in itself was a prime factor. She would be a good wife. And Lucus accepted her just the way she was. Their forthcoming marriage made more sense than anything she had ever considered before.

She would go. Just one thing remained . . . one thing she must do before she could leave. She had to go back to where she came from, ending her self-imposed exile. Just once. She felt she couldn't leave until she did that. She would face the past so that she could release it and have done with it. Then she would be able to go on with a clear conscience.

She whispered into the darkness, "That night, Julian, that first night . . . you said we really didn't know what life had in store for us. Did *you* know, Julian?"

Seven

HONOR HURRIED toward her destination on a sweltering summer day. The pavement scorched the soles of her high-button shoes, the intense heat causing her to experience a slight vertigo. In order not to look too conspicuous, she had dressed in her oldest white shirtwaist and a flowing brown skirt that was fraying hopelessly at the hem. But she knew that even her oldest clothes looked too good for this part of town.

Holding her head high, she pulled her brown, wide-brimmed hat firmly to one side and turned down Avenue A, to be greeted by the strong stench of un-collected garbage and unswept manure wafting through the unbearably hot air. For a moment she considered turning back but then bravely moved forward, weaving through a maze of people circulating aimlessly along the garbage-strewn street, their tattered clothes clinging damply to them.

Perspiration glistened over the blank, listless faces of the people surrounding her, and she forced herself to set her gaze downward to avoid their vacant stares. She passed idle men and women sitting dejectedly on stoops, fanning themselves impotently with newspapers against the sizzling sun. Honor well knew that they were seeking refuge outdoors from the summer infernos of their impoverished tenement rooms. The air outside was just as hot and heavy, she thought. The narrow, overcrowded streets brought little escape.

She lifted her gaze to the pushcarts, pulled by skeletal, undernourished horses, making their way down the dusty street at a tortoise's pace, carrying their daily wares of half-rotten fruit and vegetables. Every now and again she saw women rushing forth with a few pennies to purchase some apples or potatoes.

Various heavily loaded wagons, preceded by yapping dogs, passed creaking carts with difficulty. They were slowly being pulled by whinnying horses, their heads spiraling, trying to shake off the steady presence of flies that buzzed incessantly around them.

Filthy children with dirt-encrusted faces and lice-infested hair scrambled about, reminding Honor all too well of herself a few years ago. Young girls, most of them not looking much more than ten, rocked small, crying infants in their arms. Honor knew why. These girls, babies themselves, were rearing their infant brothers and sisters alone while their mothers worked.

Little boys with faded knickers blocked her path every so often, eyeing her with mocking interest. She thought of Elijah, more grateful than ever that her escape from the squalor of these streets had protected him from it as well. His clean, wholesome existence provided a stark contrast with this bleak, dissolute world.

Along the way Honor glanced into alleyways and saw sprawling and disfigured forms lying about in random heaps. The sight and stench of them sickened her. She passed long-aproned shopkeepers standing wearily under large signs advertising groceries or dry goods. Some sat snoring on wooden crates beneath worn, tattered awnings that fluttered sadly from gray, cracking tenements. One rotund store owner looked Honor's way and began to shout in a thick European accent, "Looking for some fun, dear? Come on! My storage room has a bed!"

Honor hastened her steps, but even at a safe distance away she could still hear his degrading, insulted shouts prompted by her rejection. Nothing has changed here, she thought. The slums are still vile, still lacking in pride. This was how she had always felt about the people and the environment. The old bitterness crept up her throat like the taste of bile, choking her. At once she felt violated.

Honor stopped walking when she came to the building that had once housed her school. Vivid memories flooded through her mind. She found herself moving back in time . . .

The red brick structure was perched over a live chicken market, and Honor remembered the rising sounds of scratching and squawks that had filled the classroom daily. The room had lacked chairs or even benches, so the children had done their studies on their knees, which had caused Honor's legs to ache. The odors emanating from the chicken market had made her nauseated, adding to her misery. But she had let nothing deter her from her unwavering objective.

Unlike most of her classmates, Honor had been determined to learn to read. Yes, she would learn. She had decided early that an education would release her from the bondage of her environment. That it had not quite turned out that way didn't matter now. What was important was that she did ultimately escape—which had been the driving force of her childhood.

The pressures of her life had been eased by the

startling discovery that she could draw. She'd spent the few free hours of her childhood with pencil and paper in hand, capturing the faces of people, cats, dogs— whatever roamed the streets. And she'd found joy in it.

Deliberately, she'd kept herself occupied, filled with conviction not to weaken and succumb to what the rest were led to. One by one, others turned to prostitution and crime to secure money for food. She did share hunger with them, scavenging for food in huge ash barrels, and begging. She had not felt demeaned by the begging. When her stomach was empty, survival had been the only consideration. She had always been hungry. That was what she remembered most.

Yet she'd never felt as if she'd truly belonged with these people; she'd felt misplaced, as if it had somehow been a terrible mistake. She'd felt different. Holding her head high, she'd kept herself apart from the rest. As if then she couldn't be touched by it all. But she recalled too well what the turning point had been for her. The precise moment in time when she'd decided she had to rise above her surroundings. It had happened two months before her twelfth birthday.

Flora, six months younger, had been Honor's only friend. The only person in the world in whom she could confide. At eleven, Flora had already been a prostitute for a year. No matter how hard Honor had begged her to stop, she would have her way.

Flora's parents were both dead. An aunt, who already had nine children to care for, had reluctantly taken her in. But only to sleep. She'd been left to feed and clothe herself, to roam the streets at will. She'd never gone to school. She hadn't the time, accommodating as many customers a day as she could squeeze in, vowing to save enough money to get herself out of Avenue A for good.

Still, Honor had liked her. Loved her, really, for in spite of her hard life Flora had been cheerful, forever seeing the humor in all situations. Honor could see her now, cocking her head sideways, her chestnut curls bouncing, as she cleverly related the endless idiosyncrasies of the men who'd bought ten minutes of her time in a back alley. Flora could make Honor laugh at it all, despite her friend's fervent disapproval.

Many a night she and Flora, perched on the front steps of Honor's tenement, would share a cigarette and dream of a happy, fun-filled future away from this environment.

Flora would promise, over and over, that when she'd saved enough money to get out, she would take Honor with her. They would live high, she'd vowed. Move to Fifth Avenue. Do all the things they'd ever dreamed of doing.

Honor would listen to her, enraptured, pulled in by her fantasies, wanting so terribly to believe them all. Until finally she'd come home from school one day to be matter-of-factly told by her mother that Flora was dead.

"Dead!" Honor had screamed. "She couldn't be dead. How?"

"A drunken bloke," her mother had answered, "just took it in his head to cut her up with a carving knife. Serves her right, I must say. That trashy baggage."

Honor had screamed until her voice became a raw, hoarse whisper, frightening her mother out of her wits. She had finally gone to bed and remained there, trance-like, for three days. At last, her grief spent, Honor knew what she had to do. She drew herself in even tighter than she had before, escaping into a private world in which Avenue A did not exist.

For a long time afterward, Honor retreated to the public library, where travelogues offered an escape from the harsh environment surrounding her. She'd been particularly drawn to literature about and photographs of a Territory called New Mexico, wondering what it would be like to live in all that open space. No sounds of carriages creating endless clatter on cobblestone. No crowds. A magical place where one could breathe freely. A place of separateness.

Now she realized with a jolt that that was exactly where she was going. New Mexico! How strange, she thought. But the dream coming true did nothing to deaden the memory of a childhood spent in pain. She closed her eyes for a moment, seeing it all before her. The past was not buried, she thought. It still lived to torment her. Raising her head high in defiance, she walked on.

Finally she came to the building that was most familiar to her. Commonly known as the double-decker, or dumbbell tenement, it was an architectural structure that New York had the unenviable distinction of having invented. A type of housing unknown to any other city in America or Europe, it stood tall, extending seven stories into the air. Honor knew that at least one hundred and fifty persons lived within the confines of its walls.

The first floor housed two stories, one on each side of the entrance. Hesitantly, Honor walked inside and stood in the center of the hallway. It was a sixty-foot-long corridor, less than three feet wide, almost totally dark. It received no light except that from the street door and another, fainter beam emanating from a small window in the roof. She blinked, her eyes adjusting to the dimness.

She started to move toward the narrow stairs hugging one side of the hall. Honor's progress was halted at the sight of a young boy urinating against the wall. Turning her head away from him in disgust, she waited until the beating sound of his urine ceased. He dashed past her out to the street, and she moved to the dilapidated stairwell, looking up to see foul-smelling slime oozing down the steps. Gagging, she quickly took a handkerchief from her pocket to cover her nose and mouth, and avoiding the wetness, prepared herself for the long climb ahead.

Each floor was divided into four sets of apartments, with seven railroad rooms on each side of the hall. Of the fourteen rooms, only the two facing the street and the two looking onto the small yard at the back of the building received direct light and air.

Air shafts ran the height of the dwelling on both

sides to provide light and air to the inner rooms. But the shafts were too narrow and high, with no intake of air at the bottom. So, instead of freshness and sunshine, the rooms were foul from stale air and semi-darkness.

The shafts also acted as conveyors of noise and disease. And if a fire were to break out, they would serve as flammable flues, rendering it impossible to save the building from destruction.

As Honor reached the landing of each floor, she stopped to catch her breath. She glanced at the familiar surroundings, almost obscured from her sight by the darkness. Opposite the stairs on each landing there were two water closets used in common by the people living there. These were lighted and ventilated by the same air shafts that opened onto the other rooms. The stench of urine and excrement was so strong that she had to steady herself on the banister to keep from keeling over.

Finally, her lungs seeming to collapse, and half-sick, she reached the fifth landing. Moving to one of the doors in the rear, she lifted her hand to knock, then stopped, leaning back against the wall and closing her eyes. She rubbed her temples, feeling the outline of protruding veins. Fervently wishing she could loosen her corset, she sucked in her breath and turned to pound again.

A woman appeared, clutching a dirty, frayed apron in one of her hands. She held the door open, looking at the young woman in front of her as though seeing a ghost. The two stared at each other for what seemed to Honor an eternity. At last the older woman let out a cry, spreading open her arms. Honor moved into them, to be held tightly. The two stood crying, rocking each other. Almost inaudibly, Honor murmured over and over, "Mother . . . Mother . . . Mother."

Olive Wentworth pulled Honor in, closing the door behind them. "Sit down, luv. Sit down. I'll make you a cup of tea." Nervously she cleared off some dirty underwear from a cracked chair.

The chair squeaked as Honor sat on it. She watched her mother move to the grimy sink, put water in a stained saucepan, and place it on the coal-burning stove.

Honor's gaze traveled from her mother to a broken faucet from which water was dripping endlessly into the sink. She looked down at the floor, which was littered with discarded shoes and articles of clothing. A rope was tied from one end of the small room to the other, bearing the weight of wet wash hung to dry.

She looked back at her mother, almost crying all over again at her appearance. Her red hair was lifeless, unkempt, pulled into a tight ball at the back of her head. Her black blouse was coming open at the seams, the sleeves rolled up to her dirt-encrusted elbows. Her long black skirt was wrinkled, dusty, and frayed at the bottom, and hung loosely over her tall, thin frame.

It was her face that shocked Honor the most. The skin that had once looked like alabaster, framing large blue eyes, was now a sickly gray. Puffs of flesh swelled beneath her eyes, and her even, white teeth that had once shone were now yellow and rotted. Honor worked hard to conceal her shock as her mother poured tea into a cracked cup and sat down in a chair opposite her.

"Where is everybody?" Honor asked lightly.

"The children are about on the streets somewhere, luv. I don't see them much any more. God knows what they're up to. Your dad is dead, you know."

A shiver went through Honor. "When?"

"A couple of years ago. In one of his drunken stupors, you know. Rowdy that night, he was. More than usual. He was throwing furniture, punching anyone who came close to him. The children had all run out, thank God. Then he started coughing, funny-like, blood coming out of his mouth. He fell down, luv, and that was it. He was gone." Olive sucked in her breath. "It was a blessing, you know." Abruptly she got up to pull the wet clothing from the line, keeping her back to Honor.

It was with both dismay and relief that Honor absorbed this news. Why should she care that her father was dead? Too many times in her childhood she had been the target of his violence. She recalled his drunken rages and senseless beatings that had left her swollen and aching for days. She'd been terrified of him, remembering how she and the other children would cower in their beds when they heard him storming into the apartment in the early morning hours, drunk and hostile. When he finished quarreling and beating her mother, he'd pull Honor from her bed, singling her out for further physical abuse.

He'd hated her for reasons that were still a mystery. She shivered, remembering how he'd yank at her blonde curls, warning her of the pitfalls of vanity. Through all the years she'd been at home he'd carried this same theme until she thought she'd scream if she had to hear it again. Everything about her was somehow a threat to him. He'd always called her "your Highness," mocking what he'd considered her "high-falutin ways."

Yes, she'd been terrified of him. She felt it even now. His vibrations were still everywhere in the room. What a relief he was dead. What a relief never to have to fear him again, she thought. He was the reason she'd waited so long to return home.

Deliberately forcing all this from her mind, she looked at her mother, asking, "How do you get on now for money?"

Tossing the last piece of wash into a basket, Olive turned back to Honor. "Well, I'm laid off now. But I been working in a sweatshop since he died. When I work, I put in an eighty-four-hour week. At a pittance, I can tell you that. But I'm careful not to do anything to get fined. The sweater I worked for is a bastard." Her brows drew together anxiously. "He fines the girls for talking, or breaking a needle on the sewing machine. Even for smiling. Can you imagine that? The bloody bastard. But at least when I work I can put a little food on the table and make the rent."

Honor's face looked pained as she listened quietly.

Olive paused and studied her oldest child. "What about you, Honor? You look like a fine lady now. You know, I've lain awake nights thinking of you. I hope when you look back you understand." She sat down across from Honor once again. "I couldn't let you stay here with a child on the way. There were five mouths to feed and your father to contend with. I couldn't let you stay, luv."

"I know, Mother. I know."

"I never meant for you to stay away permanently, though. I really thought you'd be back after a time, to visit at least. Why didn't you come home before now, Honor?"

"I . . . I just couldn't come home and face Father again. It seemed best to sever my attachments completely."

"Where have you been all this time, luv?"

Honor directed her gaze to her lap, fingering the rim of the teacup. "A maiden lady took me in when I was seven months gone. I've been with her ever since. I take care of the house for her and do the cooking. But it's not like a job. She's family for me and Elijah."

"Elijah? You had a boy? What's he like?"

"A fine boy, Mother. Sweet and beautiful." She paused for a moment. "I'm leaving New York next week to get married. Elijah and I are moving to New Mexico. I wanted to see you before I left . . . to see how you were getting on."

"Yes, I see."

Honor squirmed in her chair, feeling uncomfortable. Out of place. She got to her feet, placing the untouched cup of tea on the table next to her. "I must go now."

Olive's eyes misted over. "Do you have to go so soon, luv?"

"Yes, Mother, I do. My son is waiting for me at home."

"I did the best by you that I could. You know that, don't you? Don't you, Honor?"

"Yes, I know."

"You were the most beautiful child I'd ever seen. When you were in a carriage, strangers would stop just to get a better look at you. You were the best looking of all my children."

Honor suddenly felt as if she were suffocating. She had to leave immediately. Nodding mutely at her mother's comments, she felt a terrible sadness wash over her. She should never have come. She was wrong to have thought that if she came back and faced all this, she'd be free of it. She knew now that could never happen, she could only go on as best she could and try to give *her* child a happy life. Maybe that would make up for it somehow. This was the only thing that made any sense.

Olive got up from her seat. "There were some good days then. Way back to when you were a baby. It wasn't always bad. Believe me, Honor."

"I do, Mother," Honor said while moving to the door, Olive following her. She turned suddenly and hugged her mother to her. She stepped back and pulled some bills from her pocket and put them in Olive's hand, watching her gnarled fingers close over them. "Goodbye, Mother."

"Goodbye, luv. Good luck."

Honor looked into her mother's large blue, vacant eyes, then quickly turned and descended the staircase, her thoughts racing.

In that one stark moment of having to face her inadequacy at attempting to deal with her past, Honor knew herself. She could never face it, and this was *her* problem. Only hers. No one else was to blame. That sad, wasted woman up there had brought her into the world and had done the best she could. There was nothing else. Somehow, Honor would have to learn to live with it all and do the best *she* could. Yet, strangely, because she'd recognized her own weakness, the old bitterness had disappeared. In its place Honor experienced a new emotion—compassion.

Exhausted, she faced the street and squinted from the glaring sun. She had to get away quickly. She ran, not feeling the heat, no longer seeing the pushcarts or the people. It was all a blur.

She ran faster. Faster. Wishing to be home. To hold Gilly's hand. To hide. She'd never fully comprehended to what degree Gilly's brownstone in the Village had insulated her from the ugliness of the world. She'd been too successful in pushing it farther and farther into the recesses of her mind.

Gilly. Gilly. Gilly. Her name and image blazed through Honor's mind. Was there any way to repay her for all her kindness and generosity? Out of breath, she pushed open the door of the house, to find Elijah sitting on the floor, sobbing.

He ran to his mother, crying, "She won't talk to me! She won't talk to me!"

A cold chill went through Honor. She bent down and kissed his damp cheek. "Where is she, Elijah?"

He pointed to the sitting room.

Honor found her slumped in a large easy chair, her knitting on her lap. She got down on her knees in front of her dearest friend. Gilly was sleeping, she told herself. Wasn't she? Honor put her hands over Gilly's still ones, gently murmuring, "Gilly. Gilly. Wake up. Wake up." Her body remained lifeless. Panic washed over Honor. "Gilly! Please!"

Honor lowered her head to Gilly's breast, listening for the sound of a heartbeat. She jerked back, staring at her with numb horror. "My God," she muttered, strangling a scream that was fighting its way out of her throat. She turned to see Elijah standing in the doorway.

"She's dead, isn't she?" he asked. "She's gone to heaven."

Honor quickly got to her feet, struggling for the calm she would need to keep going. She had to think clearly and force herself to function. Moving to Elijah, she took him by the hand and led him outside to the stoop. "You stay right here," she instructed. "Don't move until I come back. Do you hear?"

Tears continued to slide down his cheeks. "Where are you going?"

"I'm going to hail a cab and get Drew. I'll be back as soon as I can. Do you understand?"

He nodded. "I understand."

Her head pounding, Honor rushed off. She couldn't believe this dreadful thing had happened. It was a terrible mistake. She had to hang on. She had to! Drew would help, she tried to assure herself.

She secured a cab and settled back into the seat in frozen silence. Her body rigid, she steeled herself against the profound wave of grief sweeping over her. When the cabdriver let her off at Drew's and she finally saw his face, she allowed the barrage of tears their release. Falling helplessly into his arms, she cried over and over, "Gilly is dead. My God. Gilly is dead."

Eight

IT TOOK two full weeks for Honor to come back to her old self after the shock of Gilly's death. Her departure for New Mexico, already delayed a week because of the tragedy, could no longer be postponed. She and Elijah would leave on the afternoon train. There was no reason to keep Lucus waiting any longer.

Smartly dressed in a seal-colored Eton suit trimmed with rows of silk, Honor walked through the silent rooms on the upper level of the brownstone, absorbing all the familiar details. Two generations of Gilly's family had lived in this house, she thought, and now the house would be sold. She wondered if strangers would value its heritage as she did.

She also wondered what Drew would do with the furniture and bric-a-brac after Honor and Elijah left. He'd wanted to ship some of it to Honor in Santa Fe, but she'd asked him not to. She had no way of knowing how large or what style of house she'd be living in. There might not be enough space to accommodate all these pieces. The only object she'd packed away in one of the trunks had been the Queen cathedral clock she'd always enjoyed so much. Honor didn't need any other physical reminders of Gilly. She'd always be alive for her.

Wandering into her bedroom, Honor looked at it stripped of her personal belongings. It was hard to comprehend that she wouldn't be sleeping in her own bed tonight—that she'd never use it again. Elijah had been born in this room. Memories lingered everywhere about her. Gilly and this house had represented the first calm in her otherwise stormy existence. She half resented the thought of strangers intruding and living here. It didn't seem right.

Suddenly tired, she stopped wandering. Drew wouldn't be returning to take them to the railroad station for awhile. She went downstairs to put on the kettle for tea. Elijah was with Drew, Drew having insisted on buying him a new outfit for the trip. Dear Drew, she thought. What would she have done without him the past two weeks?

Waiting for the water to boil, she sat down at the kitchen table, her mind going over the news that Drew had brought her yesterday after he returned from an appointment with Gilly's attorneys.

Gilly had named Honor her sole heir. How much inheritance this involved would be determined by the attorneys after the house was sold and Gilly's bank accounts gone into. Honor did not imagine it would amount to much. Gilly had lived a frugal life. Still, the idea of being sole recipient had overwhelmed Honor.

What a kind person Gilly had been, and how dearly Honor had loved her. Still hurting, Honor recalled that on returning to the house that last, fatal day, she had been concerned with finding a way to repay Gilly for all her generosity. Now she'd never have the chance. And Gilly was *still* giving to Honor. Always giving.

She heard the front door open and the sounds of Drew and Elijah entering. She invited Drew to join her for a cup of tea before loading the packed trunks into the carriage and leaving for the train station, wanting to linger over her last moments in this kitchen as long as possible.

Standing between Drew and Elijah, Honor began to experience a wave of excitement as she observed the throng of people and the flurry of activity surrounding them in Grand Central Station. Reaching up to adjust her English hat with its black Russian coq plume, she dwelled pleasantly on the prospect of her first departure from New York. A strange, foreign world waited out there, she thought, enticing and full of the promise of adventure.

Elijah hung on to her expectantly, reluctant to leave her side even for a minute. He was dressed in his new, navy blue, serge blouse-suit with large lapels and a wide sailor collar, trimmed in one corner with a silk-embroidered red and white star. A whistle and cord dangled from his neck. His knickers met with silver buckles at each knee, and Honor noticed that his dark blue stockings were beginning to sag. She put her arm around him protectively, hugging him to her.

Drew interrupted her reverie, his words coming out too fast, causing them to slur together. "I'll attend to the sale of Gilly's home, Honor. You're not to worry about a thing."

"I know you will, Drew. I'm not worried."

"As soon as the attorneys settle everything, you'll

receive your full share. The only thing that will come out of it will be the attorneys' fees. I'll take care of everything."

"You'll never know what a help you've been, Drew. I've always counted on your friendship."

"We'll always be friends, Honor. If you should ever need anything . . . anything at all . . . I'll be here."

She smiled, "I know that, Drew."

"Perhaps when Elijah is a little older, you can send him to visit with me for a summer. I would show him a grand time."

"That would be wonderful for Elijah. I'll remember that."

"Do you have everything?" he asked anxiously. "Are you sure you haven't forgotten anything?"

"I'm sure," she answered, smiling.

"In case you have, I can mail it to you. That won't be any trouble." His face slowly saddened.

Honor sobered. "You will write, Drew, won't you? We mustn't lose touch with one another." She suddenly felt the impact of leaving everything behind that was familiar.

"I'll send all the news regularly."

Honor shuffled her feet impatiently. She looked around, unexpectedly at a loss for words, then glanced at Drew. "I really think we should get on board, don't you?"

"Yes. Yes. I suppose so." He bent down to Elijah's level. "I'll miss you."

Elijah released his mother's hand to wrap his arms around Drew, hugging him. "I'll miss you, too."

"You be a good boy for your mother."

"I will. I will."

Drew stood up and turned to Honor, taking hold of her hand and kissing it. "I wish you all the happiness imaginable."

She leaned forward to kiss him on the cheek. "Take good care of yourself, Drew." Then she took Elijah's hand and climbed the steps of the train. She looked back for a moment to wave.

Honor watched the skyline of New York disappear from sight, the train racing and vibrating beneath her. Standing next to her, Elijah had his nose pressed fiercely against the window, fogging up the area surrounding his face. They were on their way! The palms of her hands perspired with nervous anticipation. The very air she breathed felt charged with both excitement and expectation. How she savored it all.

She thought back to her earlier apprehension at leaving the city. How silly she had been, she decided. A wealth of new experiences awaited her out there. Hers for the taking. Leaning back in her seat, she studied her son's face with pleasure. "Are you happy, Elijah?" she asked.

He turned to her, his face breaking into a wide grin. "Oh, yes, Mama," he said, sitting down. "Isn't this fun? I've always wanted to ride a train."

She smiled back at him. "I didn't know that."

They settled back, and Honor recalled the sadness in Drew's face when he saw them off at the train station. What a dear friend Drew was, she thought, knowing they would miss him.

Now Honor became aware of the sounds of laughter and music floating toward them from somewhere in the train.

Elijah jumped to the edge of his seat, his eyes growing wide. "Let's go see where that's coming from, Mama. Shall we?"

"Yes, let's. I'm too excited to sit still," she said, jumping up and reaching for his small hand.

They moved closer and closer to the sounds, soon finding themselves in the midst of a group of young women and assorted children who were laughing heartily and clapping their hands in time to the music played by a young, raven-haired girl on a mandolin. Elijah squealed with pleasure. Honor turned to see a little girl with long bottle curls and white bows bouncing on her toes, improvising a dance to the music with unrestrained abandon.

To Honor's surprise, Elijah leaped from her side

to join the other child. She watched as he jubilantly clapped his hands and stamped his feet. He swung himself around in the small area of the corridor, spurred on by the exuberant crowd around them.

Honor laughed, amazed at Elijah's ease in performing so spontaneously in the midst of strangers. The dance over, he fell into her arms giggling and breathless. She cuddled him in her arms, kissing the top of his head. She couldn't remember when they'd had more fun.

The mandolin player turned to Honor, saying, "Your son is very charming. Don't you agree?"

Honor smiled. "Yes, he is." She hugged Elijah closer to her, planting kisses on his damp, round cheeks. He slipped away to join the children.

"Where are you headed?" the girl asked.

"Santa Fe. In New Mexico."

"Oh, then you'll be changing trains at Dearborn Station in Michigan."

"Yes, we will."

"How exciting! You'll be taking the rest of your trip on the Limited. I once took it to see my grandmother in California. It really is the most beautiful train in the country."

"Is it?"

"Oh, yes. They started the Limited about ten years ago, you know. It had to do with a big advertising campaign. They were promoting tours to the Indian villages of New Mexico, emphasizing the Spanish culture of the Southwest. They thought a luxury train would attract more tourists."

"Well," Honor said, "we've really got something to look forward to, then."

The girl smiled agreeably, picking up her instrument to strum another tune. Honor found a vacant seat and sat down to enjoy the music and the people, feeling as if she'd entered a new, almost foreign world of gaiety and good will.

Much later, back in their sleeper, Elijah laid his

head on Honor's lap and went to sleep. She gently stroked his forehead, smiling at the picture in her mind of his dance, wondering about all the hidden parts of his personality that hadn't surfaced yet, and if he would always reveal each facet to her. She hoped he would always be as happy as he was now. And now Elijah would have a real father! She rejoiced in thinking about it.

Sighing contentedly, she listened to the sounds of the mandolin still being played in the distance. Its soft tune filled the air with the strains of a romantic ballad of a far-off land. Something about the melodious notes evoked memories of Julian. Her heart stopped. *Julian.* No! She wouldn't allow herself to think of him. It was her marriage to Lucus she should be thinking of.

It was precisely five o'clock, three evenings later, when they reached Dearborn Station, an hour before the Limited's departure. Striking up an acquaintance with a young, freckle-nosed, carrot-topped brakeman by the name of Shinny, they were offered a tour of the train. Honor had never seen anything like these cars. There was something new to look at everywhere they turned.

Shinny informed them, in a high-pitched, nasal drawl, that the vapor-steam from the locomotive served a dual purpose: it ran the train, and it also conducted heated water through the pipes for warmth during the winter months. He also explained that the train was lit by Pintsch gas. And not every train had *that,* he boasted.

Amazing, Honor thought as he led them into one of two first-class coaches. Finding it impressive, she looked with pleasure over the interior of carved mahogany and maroon plush. This was where they would stay. Lucus had insisted on first-class accommodations when he'd forwarded her the money for the trip.

Honor ran her hand over the thick velvet, delighting in the feel of it, thinking it all lovely. But as they progressed with their tour she decided the parlor-smoker was the most beautiful of all with its antique oak paneling, golden-brown sofas, and wicker settees cushioned in yellow silk.

Elijah was far more impressed with the two sleepers, decorated in Louis XV style with bronze hardware, French oak trim, and peacock-blue upholstery. In his exuberance he ran to touch everything, Honor finally grabbing hold of his hand and laughingly moving him along.

To their surprise, they discovered that the lounge car featured an extensive library and had comfortable brown leather chairs. In sharp contrast with the Victorian furnishings in the rest of the train, the decor here was Southwestern and Indian, artfully blending together a color scheme of muted browns, blues, and orange. Shinny proudly boasted that the circulating ice-water and soda fountain in the lounge signified the coming of "modern" equipment.

Elijah ran gleefully to the soda fountain. "Can I have something here? Can I?"

"Later, Elijah." Honor turned to Shinny. "Where do we eat on this train? I'm starved."

Shinny pointed them in the direction of the Fred Harvey Diner, with a promise to show Elijah the rear platform and engine later, and then they were on their way.

Honor and Elijah stood expectantly at the entrance of the diner. Before long they were led by the person in charge into one of the many small rooms offered for private dining. Honor stared curiously at the waitress, who smilingly deposited a frosted pitcher of ice water and a bouquet of orange marigolds on their table.

The waitress, like all the others they had seen, was clothed differently from what Honor had expected. She was wearing black shoes and stockings, a plain black dress with an Elsie collar and a black bow, and a heavily starched white apron. She reminded

Honor of a character in an Ibsen play, the outfit having a somber and dramatic quality so characteristic of his work. The woman's hair was pulled severely off her face and tied back with a white ribbon. Honor had the distinct impression that she wasn't wearing a corset, and envied how comfortable she must be feeling.

Honor brought her attention to the menu and was amazed at the selections. It was difficult to decide on just one entree. There were bluepoints on the shell, whitefish with Madeira sauce, young capon with hollandaise sauce, roast beef, English-style baked veal pie, and prairie chicken; seven different vegetables and four salads, including lobster salad au mayonnaise; and a wide variety of pies, cakes, and custards, followed by cheese and coffee. Seventy-five cents did seem high to her, though.

She looked over at Elijah, who was busy fingering his setting of English silver. "They have veal pie, Elijah. How does that sound to you?"

"Like you make it, Mama?"

"Well, no, I think not. But I'm sure it's fine."

"All right."

Much later, the meal finished, Honor slowly sipped her coffee, watching Elijah greedily digging into his peach pie. He'd been quiet over dinner, which wasn't like him. "Everything all right?" she asked.

"Yes, Mama," he said between mouthfuls of pie, "it was all quite good."

"Tell me, Elijah, how do you really feel about going to live in New Mexico? You won't miss New York, will you?"

He was thoughtful for a moment. "I don't know, Mama. But I wish Miss Gilly was here," he said, his eyes filling with tears.

She reached across the table and grasped his hand. "There, now. Don't feel bad. Miss Gilly was very old, and very tired. I know she's happy in Heaven. We mustn't think of her now."

Elijah looked shocked. "Not think of her! Didn't you love her, too, Mama?"

"Oh, Elijah, I loved her more than you'll ever know. But we must accept death as the natural course of things. Everything that lives must die." She stroked the back of his hand with her thumb. Perhaps he was too young, but it was a difficult thing to understand at any age.

"You're not going to die, are you, Mama?"

"Not for a very, very long time."

"Do you promise?"

"Yes, honey."

Her face brightened. "Can I go look for Shinny now? He said he'd show me the engine. Can I?"

"Yes, go on. But don't be too long."

Honor dawdled over her coffee for several minutes after Elijah had left, staring out of the small window next to her. What lives must die, she thought over and over. But do we live again? She had always wondered about this, drawn to the idea that it could be possible. Unexplainably, she suddenly felt very lonely.

The train screeched and forged ahead, carrying her closer and closer to the threshold of a new life. She settled back to watch the summer countryside slip by, the muted colors and shadings changing with the time of day, finally obliterated by nightfall.

BOOK II

───◦─◦◇◦─◦───

Santa Fe, New Mexico

1900

Nine

ELIJAH'S FACE was firmly pressed to the window in their compartment as the slackening train sputtered into the depot, the tumultuous sound of brakes screeching an ear-deafening wail. With a sudden jolt it halted, jerking the passengers forward.

"I see Lucus," Elijah shouted gleefully. "I see him, Mama. Look!"

Honor slid over to the window. Yes. There he was. Taller than she remembered. Thinner. Doubts rushed into her mind, and she used all her efforts to push them out. Turning to Elijah, she said, "Let's get organized. Hurry, now."

Lucus was waiting at the bottom of the steps leading down from the train. Honor smiled and held out her hand to him. "Lucus! How are you?"

He looked happy. "Just fine. Just fine. How was your journey?"

"Full of surprises. Very enjoyable, really."

Following behind her, Elijah jumped into the conversation, gushing over with exuberance. "It was exciting to make a trip by train, Lucus. I was never on one before."

Lucus looked down at him and put a gentle hand on his shoulder. "I'm glad you had fun." He paused for a moment before saying, "Lord, it's good to see the both of you. Well, now, you two come on to the buggy and I'll see about gettin' your trunks. There's a stagecoach that would have brought you to Santa Fe, but I wanted to take you in myself. I couldn't wait."

The train coughed out steam profusely, causing

110

Honor to feel slightly ill from the odor. When they finally reached the buggy, some distance away, she breathed a sigh of relief as she sidled into the seat.

"Can I go with you to get the trunks, Lucus?" Elijah asked.

"Why, sure." Lucus looked at Honor. "You'll be all right?"

"Of course. Go on." Retying the bow of her hat, Honor watched Lucus and Elijah stride away. Feeling travelworn, she hoped they didn't have a great distance to go before arriving in Santa Fe.

A short time later, the trunks secured tightly with a long rope onto the rear of the buggy, they were off. Elijah was sandwiched between them, still full of energy and expectation. Honor opened her parasol, angling it comfortably over her head against the sun, and settled back.

For a long time they rode in silence, passing first through a canyon and then along the vast terrain of high desert surrounding them. Honor eyed the ubiquitous cacti curiously. After a while they found themselves journeying beside a long river stretching north, the sun dancing on its surface. Yet, in all this time she hadn't seen a house or any signs of life. "Do people live in these parts, Lucas?" she finally asked.

"There are a few ranches scattered here and there. Not like Santa Fe. Santa Fe is a real town."

"How far is it to Santa Fe, Lucus?"

"Sixteen miles."

"That far?"

"We'll be there before you know it. Are you comfortable?"

"Yes," she lied, beginning to feel weak from the impact of the exceptionally dry, penetrating heat. She wondered if Lucus had been wise not to have let them take the stagecoach, realizing it would have protected them from the steady, relentless rays of the hot, burning sun beating down on them.

By now Elijah was tired also, and wearily resting his head on her shoulder, fell fast asleep. They con-

tinued in silence, Honor occasionally casting furtive
glances at Lucus. She felt slightly ill at ease with him,
not knowing how to keep the conversation going. They
continued their trek in silence through this odd-looking
land with its bumpy, archaic roads.

Overheated, sticky, and profoundly exhausted,
Honor at last got her first glimpse of Santa Fe. Dusk
was approaching, and everything about her was cast
in a warm, rosy glow. She gratefully savored the slight
breeze wavering through the air, cooling her.

Lucus pulled up before a trough and alighted to
give the horse a long, much-needed drink. "This is the
town square. The plaza. Nice, isn't it?"

Honor looked around carefully. Nestled in a valley,
the Santa Fe town was built around this charming
square with its tall, arching trees and abundance of
wooden benches resting beneath outstretched limbs.
A row of portals extended around the square, pro-
tecting the mud sidewalks from the sun. The four
corners led to the main streets at right angles to each
other. At the east end of town a massive cathedral
rose high in the air, setting it apart from the rest of
the structures. She looked around and saw enormous
mountains to the east, south, and west lying back
against the sky.

She loved the look of Santa Fe, thinking how imaginative it was, that its design was much more prefer-
able to the sight of ungainly houses simply placed on
either side of a road. She wanted Elijah to see it and
gently nudged him awake. "We're here, Elijah. We're
here!"

Elijah sleepily opened his eyes. "This is Santa Fe?"

"Yes," Lucus answered. "This is it. What do you
think so far?"

Elijah looked around and thought for a moment,
then said, "Why, I don't know. It smells so pretty."

Lucus laughed. "That's right. It sure does. That's
because of all the flowers growin', I guess." He got
back into the buggy, cracking the horse's reins and

prompting him forward, then expertly maneuvered the vehicle through the winding streets.

"Are we close to the house, Lucus?" Honor asked.

"Won't be long now, darlin'. We're not too far. You know, I was raised in that house. I've always had a soft spot for it. I even painted it for you, inside and out. And Doña María is waitin' with a nice hot meal for you and Elijah."

"Doña María?"

"I hired her as our housekeeper and cook. She's a good woman. You'll like her." He looked over at her. "What's your first impression?"

Honor scrutinized the houses in their path. She'd never seen anything like the architecture that pervaded Santa Fe; it was not at all what she'd expected. The Mexican adobe houses that she recognized from photographs in books were regularly interspersed with structures made of brick and stone; these had bay windows, turrets, and stained glass: a startling discovery. She finally answered Lucus with a surprised note in her voice. "Why, a lot of the houses here are identical to the houses back home. I never expected to find that."

"Strange as it might seem, darlin', sometime back there were a might too many people who wanted to do away with Mexican culture. They thought if they built themselves these types of homes, the Mexican influence would just go away."

"But why would they stay here if they felt that way? Why not just leave? It doesn't make any sense."

"A lot of things in this life don't make any sense. But there are still whole sections of town that are built in the old tradition."

"Is your house one of them?"

"You bet." He looked at her, adding slowly, *"Our* house."

She smiled and nodded, falling into silence. New York was fast becoming more and more remote to her. Santa Fe was as she'd imagined it would be, Anglo architecture notwithstanding.

In sharp contrast with sooty and stained tenements, here the houses were spotless, framed against a myriad of trees, shrubs, summer flowers, and green grass. Honor saw pots and pots of red geraniums blooming on low, blue-painted windowsills. What a welcome sight it all was. And above all, there was no nerve-jangling roar of elevated trains. This was truly a peaceful place.

A sparse scattering of dark, Spanish-looking people walked by them at a leisurely pace. Honor studied the women carefully. Their mode of dress was identical to what women wore in the East, except for their long, veil-like head coverings, which she thought beautiful. "What is that the women are wearing on their heads, Lucus?"

"Mantillas. I guess you would call it the Spanish version of a bonnet."

"They're exquisite." Honor leaned back and closed her eyes. The streets were suffused with stillness, except for the occasional yapping of dogs and the sporadic sounds of children laughing. She could actually hear the soft breeze rustling through the trees. What a beautiful sound, she thought.

She opened her eyes to see a small group of children playing. Elijah would enjoy life here, she felt certain. It seemed to her to be a place where children could grow unencumbered by the pitfalls of city living. Children had the entire outdoors in which they could play freely in the sunshine. There was no need for them to scuttle out of the way of scores of carriages and people on crowded streets.

Darkness was slowly settling over them when Lucus abruptly pulled the horse to a stop before an old adobe house. Elijah sprang from the buggy in a sudden surge of renewed energy. "Is this where we'll live, Lucus? Is this it?" he squealed.

"It sure is," Lucus said, running around the buggy to help Honor down. "It's all ours."

Honor and Elijah followed Lucus from the street through a large, exquisitely carved brown door that brought them into the dim courtyard. There was still enough light to see the multicolored zinnias, orange marigolds, and blue, white, and pink hollyhocks that climbed the courtyard walls. Honor was very overwhelmed. "What a lovely garden!" she cried, smiling.

Looking around, she could see that the house was built in the form of a square, the courtyard standing in the center. The doors of various rooms in the house opened onto the enclosed garden. "How convenient," she said, studying the portal that ran around the courtyard, serving, she was sure, as a sheltered communication between different parts of the house. She noticed a hive-shaped structure on the ground. "What is that, Lucus?"

"That's a *horno*—an oven. An old Mexican method for baking. The bread is delicious. You'll love it."

Elijah ran through one of the doors, calling, "Come here, Mama. Look here."

Honor followed him and found herself in a large barren room with an unplastered ceiling. The roof, supported by beams, was cheerfully painted in various shades of yellow and orange. A fireplace stood in the corner of the room, its mouth in the shape of a horseshoe.

"This is called a *sala*," Lucus said as he strode in behind them. "The family sitting room. It's the largest room in the house. I left it unfurnished so you could do what you liked with it. The bedrooms are in good shape, though. I had furniture shipped special from the East."

"I'm going to look around some more," Elijah called as he scampered out of the room, leaving them completely alone for the first time.

Lucus studied her, his dark eyes brimming with emotion. "This house has been empty too long. You and Elijah are just what this place needs." He paused. "Just what I need." He walked over to her and enfolded her in his arms. "You'll never know how happy I am that you're here."

"I'm happy, too, Lucus. Really."

"The preacher will be here on Sunday to marry us. I'll be stayin' at the Exchange Hotel till then. I thought we could have the ceremony in the courtyard. I've been plantin' out there for months with just that in mind. I wanted it pretty for you." He paused for a moment, a concerned look spreading over his face. "Is four days enough time for you to get ready?"

"Of course it is," she assured him. "Sunday will be fine. I have a beautiful dress for the ceremony."

"You'd look beautiful in anythin'." He tenderly cupped her chin and brought her lips up to meet his. Releasing her, he said, "Let's christen this house with a name. What do you say?"

Honor laughed. "That's an idea. But what?"

"How about Casa de Contento?"

"Casa de Contento," Honor repeated. "But what does that mean?"

He looked at her meaningfully. "House of Contentment. And that's just what it's goin' to be. Say, you know, I'm goin' to have to teach you to speak Spanish."

"Well, that'll be fine. I'd love to learn."

They were quiet for a moment, both suddenly awkward with each other. Elijah burst into the room, breathless from running. Lucus turned to him and squatted down in front of him. He reached out for both of his small hands. "Did you see Doña María in the kitchen?"

"Oh, yes. She seems nice."

"Well, you go on back in there and ask her for a hot chocolate drink. We'll join you for dinner in a minute, Son."

Elijah smiled broadly. "Am I your son now, Lucus?"

"Well, you will be very soon."

Elijah planted a kiss on Lucus's cheek, then ran in the direction of the kitchen.

Honor had watched this exchange quietly. A great surge of happiness flowed through her. She smiled and walked over to Lucus, wrapping her arms around his waist and resting her head on his broad chest. At that moment she was exactly where she wanted to be, and with the man she wanted to be with. What a good, secure feeling it gave her.

Today was Honor's wedding day. She should have been happy. But from the moment she'd awakened at the crack of dawn, she'd had second thoughts about what she was doing. It had taken every ounce of courage she could muster not to pack and run. What had stopped her, she supposed, was the realization that there was no place to run to. Now she put on her gown of pink satin cloth with its embroidered braid, nervously fussing over herself.

She and Lucus really should have waited, she thought. She could have come to Santa Fe without setting the wedding date so quickly. They'd had no real courtship, just that small space of time shared together in New York. Although she'd been doing fine up until this morning; had even been excited about the wedding, and happy with her choice of Lucus. Earnestly she tried to fathom what had precipitated this sudden change of heart, but she couldn't. She looked up to see Elijah standing in the doorway.

"Is Lucus here yet, Elijah?"

"No." His large black eyes looked solemn.

Honor studied him curiously for a moment. She sat down on the edge of the bed and patted the place beside her invitingly. "Come. Sit next to me for a minute."

He did, staring down at his hands.

She put her arm around him. "Now. What is it?"

"Nothing."

"I know something is wrong, Elijah. You can tell me."

He looked up at her, his eyes fearful. "What if he doesn't come?"

She knew instantly what was bothering him. "He'll

come, Elijah. In just a few minutes, I imagine. There's nothing to worry about."

"Julian didn't."

Honor swallowed hard, knowing how deeply he'd been affected by that. Her rejection had been his, too. "Lucus is nothing like Julian," she said gently. "He's dependable. I trust him. That's why I chose Lucus. He won't let us down, Elijah. I promise you that."

"Are you sure, Mama?" He was brightening.

"Yes. I'm sure. Now, go see if you can help Doña María in the kitchen. I'll be out shortly."

Elijah kissed her and then scampered off, leaving her shaken. No matter how she felt about this marriage, she knew she couldn't let Elijah down again. He'd had enough to cope with in his young life. She had to go through with it. She *would* go through with it. At that moment she heard Lucus enter the house and call to Doña María. She breathed in deeply and walked out to him.

When Lucus saw her, his eyes misted over. "You look beautiful, Honor. Really beautiful."

"Thank you, Lucus." He looked nice, she thought, dressed in a dark blue frock coat and pants, cowboy boots reaching up to his knees. His mustache looked trimmed, and Honor realized he'd had his otherwise long, unruly hair cut a few inches.

"Where is everyone?" Lucus asked.

"Elijah is in the kitchen helping Doña María."

"Good. Good. I'll go see what I can do." He started to move away and then stopped, turning back to her. "I'm an awful proud man today, Honor," he told her before turning and going into the kitchen.

Honor went back into the bedroom and shut the door behind her, slowly sinking into a chair to wait out these last few minutes of her life when she belonged to no one but herself.

Under a cloudy, overcast sky Honor and Lucus solemnly exchanged their marriage vows before a rotund, pink-faced minister who recited the long ceremony with dramatic flourish. When it was finally over, Honor let out a small sigh of relief. She had gotten through it. It was done.

She felt excitement generate around her as the small handful of guests smilingly rushed forward to offer their hearty congratulations. Honor awkwardly smiled back at the unfamiliar faces, all the while nervously smoothing away imaginary wrinkles from her gown, and tucking in some honey-blonde curls that had strayed from beneath her pink-flowered silk hat.

Standing in the midst of these people, Honor suddenly felt lost and frightened. She studied their faces, feeling strange with them and with herself. Lucus held her possessively by the elbow for a few moments before moving away to mix. She watched him gaily stride about the courtyard, once again shocked to realize he seemed as unknown to her as the people who encircled them.

Clutching her small white fan to her side, she worried if being a wife would somehow change her identity. She was no longer Honor Wentworth, but Honor Kant. Her new name sounded strange and foreign. She dearly wanted to go back in time and be Honor Wentworth again. She knew who Honor Wentworth was. Who would Honor Kant turn out to be? What lay before her? She anxiously searched for the face of her son and went toward him, comforted by his familiarity.

He encircled her waist with his small arms. "I'm so happy for you, Mama," he said, looking up at her. "We're all going to be happy, aren't we?" His black eyes searched hers for reassurance as he clung to her tightly.

She hugged him to her, kissing the top of his dark head. "Of course we'll be happy. Didn't I promise you that we would?"

"I love Santa Fe, Mama. The people are all so friendly here."

"Yes, darling, it's quite wonderful."

"Can I have some wedding cake now?"

"Of course. Go on." She watched him run to the table where Doña María was distributing white rum cake on blue porcelain plates. She sighed, feeling lost again. Suddenly Lucus was at her side.

"Come and have some wine, darlin'. We haven't toasted each other yet." He led her to the table and poured half a glassful for her. Handing it to her, he held his glass up high, saying, "To our long life together."

"Yes," Honor said faintly, "to our long life together." She swallowed the wine, feeling it flame through her chest, comforted by its warmth. At that moment she resolutely decided she would make the best of this marriage. She *would* make a go of it.

A slender Spanish boy walked up to them, carrying a guitar. Reaching for her hand to kiss it, he bowed dramatically and said, "I will sing a folk song. Just for you, Mrs. Kant. Please. Sit."

She and Lucus found a seat as all the guests encircled them. The boy sang beautifully, his sweet voice magnetizing everyone. The song had a curious rhythm, Honor thought, with stressed notes and runs, the words tumbling together.

> *Ojos trigueños, color de café,*
> *Dáme un beso de buena fé.*
> *Ojos azules, color de ciel*
> *Dáme un beso, un beso de miel.*

> Deep brown eyes of coffee hue,
> Give me a kiss, loving and true,
> Fair blue eyes, clear as the sky,
> One honey kiss, for that I sigh.

Everyone applauded loudly. Honor was beginning to enjoy herself. Smiling, she turned to face a small woman sitting next to her when a cloudburst suddenly pelted them, forcing the wedding party into the *sala* amid squeals from the women and disgruntled moans from the men.

The long day over at last, Honor lay in bed fingering her wedding ring of shaded gold hearts, flowers and grapes. The bed creaked as Lucus joined her and gently pulled the blanket away from her naked body. She cringed at lying there exposed before him, and folded her arms over her breasts.

Barely noticing her reaction, he reached for her, cradling her in his arms. "Are you happy, Mrs. Kant?"

"Yes, I'm happy," she lied. "It was a lovely wedding. Too bad about the rain at the end, though."

He traced the outline of her face with his fingertips. "I can't believe you're really my wife."

She smiled weakly as he uncrossed her arms and awkwardly fondled her breasts.

"I love you, Honor."

"I know," she said. "I'll do my best to make you happy, Lucus. I really will."

"I know. Hush, now." Breathing heavily, he lingered over her full breasts, gently stroking them until her nipples stiffened. He moved his hand down over the curve of her stomach, continuing along the inside of her thighs and lingering there. *"Lado del lado de mi corazón."*

"What does that mean?" she whispered, beginning to tremble beneath his touch.

"Side of the side of my heart." He continued to caress her lightly, bending his head to plant kisses over her stomach.

Surprising herself, she gasped, tingling with excitement, her hips lifting upward. Abruptly he pulled his hand away and turned over, entering her.

Clasping her arms around his neck, she moaned, feeling an intense heat flow through her. Suddenly Lucus groaned, his penis slackening inside her. She was incredulous. If he had slapped her, she couldn't have been more stunned. He couldn't be finished! No, it was impossible!

He rolled off her and squeezed her hand. "I love you, Honor."

Her eyes stung with tears. She couldn't speak . . .

could only lie there in an agonized silence. In a moment he was snoring, fast asleep. Her body aching with frustration, she turned onto her stomach and pushed her face into the pillow. Suddenly all the disquieting thoughts she'd forced into the inner recesses of her mind tumbled forward, their impact chilling her.

Julian, she thought. Julian had been so different. So alive and caring about her responses. She'd never achieved a full orgasm with him, but sex had been pleasurable and fun. Oh, Lord, she agonized, why had Julian left her? Why?

Honor couldn't fight the truth any longer. She still wanted Julian . . . still needed him. The memory of their lovemaking flooded over her with startling recall. She hadn't let herself think of it before, but now she knew with a chilling certainty that every moment she had spent with Julian, every touch and exchange, would forever haunt her. She was helpless before this truth.

What do I do now? she wondered. Is this my destiny? To live with one man while wanting another? In New York she had thought it would turn out differently. She'd really believed that marriage to Lucus would be the answer to all her troubles.

Perhaps she'd expected too much, too soon. Time was on her side. After all, they had all the time in the world. It could still change for the best. She must be patient. Yet, despite her efforts to reassure herself, Honor buried her face deeper into the pillow to muffle the sounds of her weeping.

Ten

HONOR SAT at a round wood table in the courtyard and finished sipping her hot, thick chocolate drink. Leisurely she leaned back in her chair and studied this structure that was her new home, the first that really belonged to her. It felt good to be mistress of her own house, she thought; her day-to-day existence here during the past four months did not diminish her thrill over this fact.

She put her empty cup aside and got up slowly, wondering how to occupy herself. Doña María didn't leave much for her to do in the way of household duties. She decided to dust the *sala* whether it needed it or not, and moved in that direction.

Away from the sun-filled courtyard, she relished the coolness of the *sala,* for no sun reached here. This room had emerged as her favorite in the entire house. She'd derived great pleasure in furnishing it, thinking it a perfect study of a New Mexican interior.

She looked around, enjoying all the details of the large sitting room. The striped blankets that she'd purchased at the marketplace were neatly rolled against the walls. She'd adorned the room with a number of engravings of saints, the Virgin of Guadalupe being the most predominant. With Lucus's help she'd lined the walls with colorful calico to a height of four feet. A rug woven in designs of Navajo origin covered the floor. Hand-carved, dark wooden chairs and tables were placed at appropriate, comfortable locations; replicas of saints fashioned from knots of pine rested on the tabletops. How cheerful it all looked.

Picking up a feather duster, she swished away invisible dust from shining brass candlesticks that stood on a long trestled table. A silver-mounted saddle hung from a peg, but it was too high to reach without the aid of a stool.

Doña María appeared at the door. "Shall I prepare the *horno* for the bread, *señora*?"

"Yes," Honor answered, turning to her. "That would be fine." She set the duster down and moved to the open doorway to watch Doña María working outside.

Panting heavily, Doña María heaved dry red cedar into the hive-shaped oven. Honor knew the cedar would burn until the thick mud walls would be too hot to touch. Then the oven would be carefully swept out and the mud floor covered with round bread. After the door was closed tightly, the vent would be stopped up with a rag kept for that purpose. In three or four hours the crisp loaves would be an even brown. The bread was as delicious as Lucus had promised it would be.

Now Honor turned her attention to the *sala* fireplace, from which she carefully swept ashes into a dustpan. She thought this fireplace truly astonishing. Built in one corner of the room, it occupied an exceedingly small amount of space.

The mouth of the fireplace was designed in the shape of a horseshoe, not more than eighteen inches high and the same width at the bottom. The back was slightly concave, and the little circular hearth in the front was raised a few inches above the level of the floor. Andirons were not widely used in the Territory by Mexicans, so piñon pine was placed on end against the back wall, giving out far more heat than the larger variety in American homes.

It didn't smoke, either, Honor thought, recalling a winter day when thick gray clouds had unexpectedly spewed from the fireplace in Julian's house. They had both run from room to room, opening windows and gasping for air. Yes, she decided, this was far more efficient.

She looked around once more, finding nothing else to do. Striding into her bedroom, she took a new, long-fringed black rebozo from a drawer and walked back to the courtyard. "I'm going for a walk before the noon meal, Doña María," she announced.

"*Sí . . . Sí . . . Sí,*" the housekeeper muttered, casting a gloomy glance Honor's way.

Honor knew her strolls often made her late for a meal and that this upset Doña María. She turned away with a silent vow to be more considerate and let herself out through one of the courtyard doors, closing it behind her. She stood there hesitantly at first, wondering where to go, then decided to walk in the direction of Elijah's school. She had no intention of disturbing him, she just wanted to have a destination in mind. Smiling, she turned eastward.

Soon she would take a sketch pad and pencil with her on these outings and capture the faces of the people and their surroundings on paper. But for now, she preferred to absorb it all as a spectator.

Luxuriating in the aroma of the hot, pitchy blaze of piñon pine that burned steadily in fireplaces and filled the winding streets with its essence, Honor walked along at an easy gait. By now she was a familiar figure to those who noticed her daily strolls. Strangers were a common sight to the natives, who were long accustomed to outsiders drawn to their beautiful city, but Honor stood out with her rare beauty and shining honey-blonde hair in a land of *cabello negro*.

Her rebozo thrown over her shoulders, the ends dangling below her small, cinched waist, she pulled it around her to ward off the autumn chill. Walking through the crooked streets in this part of town, she was flanked on both sides by the old-style adobe houses made of bricks of sun-dried earth sprouting forth in complete harmony with their environment. Modern structure had not yet invaded this section.

The mud roofs of the houses were flat and had a parapet running around them. The water that collected there was carried off by wooden spouts that extended into the street, reminding Honor of the guns of a small fortress jutting out through embrasures. From every rooftop she could see strings of bright scarlet chili peppers hanging down to dry in the sunshine.

Santa Fe seemed a magical place to Honor. Perhaps her life with Lucus was not as idyllic as she wished it could be, but living in such positive contentment in this environment made it all worthwhile. It *was* worth it, she thought. And away from their bed, Lucus was an ideal husband. He was a dear, considerate man. If she didn't allow herself to dwell on the poor sexual aspect of their marriage, she was happy. One couldn't have everything, she convinced herself. The marriage was working despite that.

Passing the houses in her path, she saw each *madre de familia* stooped over, conscientiously sweeping her front doorway with a short wheat-straw broom, sweeping so thoroughly it seemed the ground would be brushed away. Honor lost herself in the melodic sounds of an aging vendor moving by her in a covered wagon, singing his song of wares. *"Du-RAZ-nos, me-LON-es, ce-BO-llas, chi-les."*

Totally absorbed in the sweetness of her solitude, Honor was startled back to reality when a young Mexican woman appeared before her, reaching out for her arm in greeting.

"You are Señora Kant, are you not? I am Doña Consuelo Medina de Martínez." She hugged Honor and kissed her on both cheeks. "Welcome to Santa Fe," she said, smiling.

Honor thought this woman was the most beautiful she had ever seen. Small and slim, with tiny hands and feet, she had dancing dark eyes that dominated her delicate, oval face. Her black hair was pulled back tightly beneath her mantilla of chantilly lace, and her olive skin looked the texture of satin.

"Thank you, *señora*," Honor said. "How nice to meet you."

"Forgive me for not coming to your home for the introduction. I am an old friend of your husband's. I did mean to introduce myself when you arrived in Santa Fe. I have been rude. But how nice to find you this way. Please . . . you and Lucus join my husband, Estéban, and myself for a fandango at a hall not far from our home this coming Friday evening. We would be honored if you would join us."

Honor wondered if she should accept before asking Lucus first. Deciding to take a chance that he would be agreeable to the invitation, she said, "Thank you. We'd love to."

"*Bueno.*" Consuelo smiled. "Two Cerillos Street at seven." She went on her way, turning back briefly to call, "*Hasta luego, señora.*"

"*Hasta luego,*" Honor called back. She continued her walk, thinking about Consuelo. She had liked her instantly, and wondered why Lucus had never spoken of her if they were old friends.

She turned a corner and saw the school where Elijah spent his days. The building was not a hundred yards away from a flat piece of ground overlooking a river, and where a small wheat farm was situated. As she drew near, the children bounded out for recess, Elijah among them.

With shining eyes the youngsters grouped together to watch a Mexican farmer drive his goats round and round on yellow wheat that was spread over a threshing floor, urging them to trod out the grain from stalks. Elijah looked up unexpectedly, noticing Honor, and waved.

She waved back and quickly turned to head for home as copper church bells rang out the noon hour.

Honor spread a toast-colored tablecloth on a level patch of ground, setting a picnic basket in the center. She could hear the rhythmic thud of an ax falling on wood and the muted conversation between Lucus and Elijah, somewhere in the brush behind her.

She settled herself on the large cloth, looking off into the distance. Against the clear blue of the sky she saw mountainsides flaming with aspen leaves that trembled in the soft breeze. Their brilliant gold color was generously interspersed between green pine and spruce. Below the aspen, strong-scented clumps of the butter-yellow blooms of chamiso spread widely over the rich earth.

Her eyes roamed farther, over thumb-sized willow trees and cottonwoods arched low over muddy riverbanks. Massive cliffs were covered with leaves in autumn colors of red, purple, yellow, and orange. This was a place, Honor thought, where everything seemed different and yet the same. As if nature were standing still to give one time to pause and contemplate its mystery.

Elijah suddenly appeared out of the brush carrying a small load of chopped cedar in his arms. He dropped it by the burro that had been drawn painstakingly up the mountainside with them. "We're almost finished, Mama," he announced breathlessly.

"Good. Are you hungry?"

"Yes. Starved."

"Well, tell Lucus to hurry up, then, so we can eat."

She watched him dash away, the sight of him startling her for a moment. He was getting taller and his shoulders seemed to be expanding every day. Her son was growing up. It saddened her somehow. If life were an hourglass, she thought, we could measure time running out by the steady growth of our children right before our eyes.

Lucus appeared, bearing a high stack of wood in his arms; Elijah was behind him with a smaller one. "Well, I think we've got enough cedar for a while," Lucus said, dumping the wood down. He looked at Elijah. "We'll get this stacked on the burro later. All right?"

"Right," Elijah answered, diving for the tablecloth and a cold chicken breast.

Lucus squatted down and soon was greedily eating chicken and crisp bread. He looked over at Honor. "It's pretty up here, isn't it?"

"Yes, it is. You know, we can't stay too long, Lucus. We're going to a fandango tonight. Remember?"

He glanced away, then said, almost in a whisper, "I'm surprised at this invitation from Consuelo."

"Why?"

"Just am."

Honor's face broke out in a teasing smile. "Is she an old flame of yours? Should I know about it?"

He grinned. "Nothin' serious, darlin'. Nothin' was ever serious before you."

She studied him thoughtfully for a moment, wondering if she was jealous. She wasn't. "Are we going to leave after we finish eating?" Honor asked.

"No, ma'am. I'm goin' to take Elijah bird watchin'. You goin' to join us?"

"No, I think not."

"Why, Mama?" Elijah pleaded. "Please come. It'll be such fun."

"No. The two of you go on when you're ready. Since we're staying a while longer, I want to read a letter from Drew that I haven't had time to get to, and maybe make a few sketches."

Lucus studied her, then said perceptively, "You really enjoy bein' alone, don't you, darlin'?"

"Yes, I suppose I do. Do you mind?"

"No. That's fine." He reached out to tousle Elijah's hair. "My son and I have lots to do together. Don't we?" Elijah nodded enthusiastically while gulping down his food.

Later, the meal over, Honor watched the two set off together. Elijah suddenly stopped in his tracks and ran back to her, throwing his arms around her and smiling broadly.

"I love you, Mama."

Something caught in her throat. "And I love you. Now go on."

Watching them until they disappeared from her view, Honor experienced a feeling of exhilaration. Her son was very happy. That made everything worthwhile. She was happy, too, in a way. Everything was going to be fine, she reasoned.

She leaned back against a tree and removed the unopened letter from her skirt pocket. Tearing open the envelope, she settled back to read this long-awaited letter from Drew.

My dear Honor,

The sale of Gilly's house has been completed, for an excellent sum, I might add.

Aside from that, much to my surprise, since she was so thrifty, there remained quite a large sum of money in the bank left to Gilly by her grandfather. It's amazing how little she used of her money throughout her lifetime.

In short, the attorneys will see to it that a full accounting will be mailed to you in the near future. Right now I would estimate the figure to be around $25,000.

You, my dear, are now indeed a woman of means. How very pleased I am for you.

Regards to all.

Your devoted friend,
Drew

Honor reread the letter twice, letting the full impact sink in. She was so taken aback by this news, she didn't really know what to make of it. She had expected something from the sale of the house, but she had no idea Gilly had a great deal of money tucked away. Gilly had never discussed finances with her, only informing her a couple of years ago that whatever she had would one day be Honor's.

Dear Gilly, Honor thought, dear Gilly. She had known what this would mean to Honor. No matter what happened in Honor's life now, she would never again experience poverty.

Honor clutched the letter to her for a moment, then jumped up and ran in the direction of where Lucus and Elijah had disappeared. How happy they would both be upon hearing this news. She couldn't wait to see their faces.

The night was still, save for the sounds of the buggy jerking and creaking beneath them. Lucus reached over and pulled her close to him, smiling as she rested her cheek on his shoulder.

"You'll enjoy the dance tonight, Honor. They're always lively and fun. Dances are important to the people here. It's their main social outlet." He stared at the straight, even line of her profile, illuminated by the moonlight. Looking away, almost whispering, he asked, "You are happy, aren't you, Honor?"

"Why do you ask that now?"

"I don't know. Sometimes I get the feelin' you're not really with me."

"Lucus. Lucus. Of course I'm with you. And I am happy. I don't regret coming to Santa Fe. It's home to me now."

"I never knew what I was missin', not havin' a family. You and Elijah make me real happy."

He pulled up before a Spanish-style structure and helped her out of the buggy. Encircling her small face with his hands, he bent his head to kiss her. She sank against him, passionately returning his kiss, and he wondered why she didn't respond this warmly when they made love. There was something wrong, and he didn't know how to make it right.

Releasing her, he took hold of her hand and steered her to the gate entrance. Consuelo appeared out of the shadows, startling them as she pushed open the gate with a sudden thrust.

Honor jumped. "Consuelo, you startled us."

"I am so sorry. I did not mean to. I have been

waiting and watching for the both of you." She looked at Lucus. "How good to see you here, Lucus."

"It's good to be here, Consuelo. You're lookin' well."

"*Gracias*." She turned to Honor. "How lovely you look, Honor. What a beautiful gown. It is from the East, is it not?"

Honor drew her shawl close to her against the evening chill. "Yes. Organdy ruffles were the rage when I left New York."

"*Sí*. It is lovely. Well, now, both of you, come. The fandango will soon begin."

Taking Lucus's arm, Honor followed, her eyes widening with pleasure as they approached the entrance to the hall. She could see wide, white-walled rafters artfully decorated with pink-flowered paper, the dozen or so posts tightly wound with cheesecloth. Brown tile, with an embossed, yellow-flowered pattern running across it, covered the full length of the floor. The orchestra, consisting of a fiddler and guitarist, sat on a high platform at one end of the room.

The strains of a lively Spanish rhythm were already permeating the crowded hall. The fandango had begun. Led by Consuelo, Honor and Lucus moved inside.

Looking around the gaslight-illuminated room, Honor noticed a sprinkling of black-shawled women who seemed content to stay seated and watch the activity around them. Those who chose to dance rose to their feet.

Lucus leaned over and whispered to Honor, "Watch what everybody else does and do the same."

Nodding, she turned to look for Consuelo and realized she had disappeared. The room stilled for a moment, the musicians pausing. Then the guitarist struck a chord and the dancers clapped their hands in unison. The ladies advanced, one by one, and stood facing the partners of their choice.

Honor laid her shawl over a chair before moving in front of Lucus; she could feel excitement ignite the air around her. The music abruptly changed to a waltz. Each man then took his partner in his arms, dancing in perfect step to the music. Honor moved into Lucus's arms also, letting herself be led around the dance floor through the throng of people around them.

Bodies whirled around her and the women's long skirts moved up and down, creating a flurry of muted color and synchronized movement. Through the din she could hear both the sounds made by high-button shoes clacking on the tile and the steady laughter emitting from people thoroughly enjoying themselves.

Honor smiled as she whirled faster and faster under Lucus's strong grip. Honey-gold ringlets formed on her damp forehead. Her cheeks grew pink, her neck flushed. She kept up with Lucus in joyous abandon, wishing the dance would never end.

When it finally did, she and Lucus stood back and faced each other, laughing and winded. Holding on to his arm with one hand, Honor used her white fan vigorously with the other as she was guided to a table where wine and a mild brandy were being served.

That was when she noticed a small man with a thin mustache standing nearby, engaged in a heated conversation with a group of men. Something about this man commanded attention, and she liked him immediately.

He was wearing a gentleman's Mexican horseman-cloth habit with which she'd become very familiar. His black jacket was adorned with silver ornaments and toggles; his dark-colored trousers covered his boots that were without spurs. Rows of silver buttons ran up the side seams of the trousers and around his waist. His shirt was white, and he wore a matching white cravat tied in the front. His large gray sombrero was gold-embroidered at the rim and bore a silver lace band. Honor wondered about the weight of it on his head. The man turned suddenly, spotted Lucus, and walked up to him, embracing him affectionately.

"Lucus Kant! It's been a long time since we've met. How are you?"

"Fine, Governor. Fine. Let me introduce you to my wife, Honor." Lucus turned to Honor and held her by the elbow. "Honor, this is Señor Miguel Otero, our territorial governor."

"How nice to meet you, Governor Otero," Honor said.

"A pleasure, *señora*," he murmured, reaching for her hand to kiss it. He turned to Lucus. "Do you still work on Manuel Rodriguez's ranch, Lucus?"

"Yes, Governor. I still do."

"Good. Good. And you, *señora*, I'd hoped I would meet you. You have aroused much interest in Santa Fe. I have heard much about you. You are from New York, are you not?"

She nodded, smiling.

"I received some of my education in your city," the governor went on. "I am well familiar with it. Tell me, what do you think of Santa Fe?"

Honor brightened. "I'm spellbound, Governor. I've never seen so much beauty anywhere."

"*Sí*, foreigners often feel that way. We are three races, yet each miraculously retains its own individual identity. The Indian continues to follow his old ways of working with nature. The Spaniard remains strangely arrested in the traditions and customs of his Andalusian heritage." He gestured broadly to no one in particular. "And the descendants of our sturdy Anglo pioneers of the Santa Fe Trail days carry on their spirit of adventure of life. It is a city like no other," he finished enthusiastically. Smiling warmly at Honor, he added, "You will be happy here."

"I know I will."

"It was a pleasure meeting you, Señora Kant. You and Lucus will have to attend our parties at the Palace." He reached out to kiss her hand, then once again embraced Lucus. Murmuring "*Adios*," he moved to a group of people standing nearby.

"What an interesting man, Lucus."

"That he is. We call him our 'little governor.' Miguel is the first native governor New Mexico has had since becoming a Territory. He sure makes life fun for the people." He laughed. "Miguel is outrageous, you know. He uses every holiday as an excuse for the pardon of some murderer or robber, or for overthrowing acts of the courts. He's also made the Palace of the Governors the social and political center of New Mexican affairs. Just like it used to be. The people love him."

Consuelo approached them timidly. "Are you enjoying yourself, Honor?"

"Yes, thank you. I am."

"I would like you to meet my husband, Estéban."

A small, dark man, he smiled warmly at Honor and bowed slightly. *"Señora."*

Lucus cleared his throat. "Nice to see you again, Estéban."

Honor noticed Consuelo's face become motionless as she fingered the gold filigree brooch that held her white blouse closed at the throat. It seemed to Honor that she detected a hint of sadness in Consuelo's expression.

Lucus touched Honor's sleeve, saying, "Say, excuse me a minute. I see an old friend over there. I'll bring him over to meet you."

Honor nodded to Lucus, then brought her attention back to Consuelo. "Do you have children, *señora?"*

"Si, four. Three boys and one girl."

"I have one son. Perhaps one day he could meet your children."

"That would be nice. You will come for tea soon, will you not?"

"I'd be delighted. Tell me—"

Lucus was back, breaking in on the conversation, a delighted tinge to his voice. "Honor, this here is my old friend Will Jeevers." He turned to Will. "Will, this is my wife, Honor."

A soft-spoken, flaxen-haired man about Lucus's

age, Will Jeevers reached out to squeeze Honor's hand gently. "A pleasure, ma'am."

"What are you up to, cowboy?" Lucus asked, slapping Will good-naturedly on the back.

"Still have my ranch in Carlsbad, Lucus. I meant to see you this trip. There's somethin' I want to talk to you about. Private-like."

"Sure, Will. Let's step outside." He started to move away, then paused to look at Honor. "Do you mind, darlin'?"

"Of course not. Go ahead."

Lucus elbowed his way through the crowd, Will following behind him. Outside, they sat down on a bench and Lucus rolled a cigarette, offering it to Will. He accepted it, and Lucus made himself another, taking a deep drag before he asked, "What do you think of my wife? She's somethin', ain't she?"

"She's sure a good-lookin' woman. Where'd you meet her?"

"In New York. I was there for a while visitin' a cousin. 'Bout time this cowboy settled down, don't you think?"

"Yeah, I suppose so."

"Your wife with you this trip?"

"Nope. When I left Carlsbad, our boy was sick with a high fever. She stayed to tend him."

Lucus leaned back in his seat. "What'd you want to talk to me about?" he asked.

"How'd you like to be my partner on my ranch in Carlsbad, Lucus? I been thinkin' on this for some time now. Nothin' I would like better than to have an old friend in with me whom I can trust."

"Partner?"

"I figure if you've got fifteen hundred dollars, that would do it. I could use the money to buy some more cattle I been wantin', and I would sure enjoy havin' you with me."

Lucus dragged on his cigarette, thinking deeply. When he finally looked at Will, his expression was one of regret. "Can't do that, Will. But I'd sure like to. I really wish I could."

"Is it the money, Lucus? 'Cause we could always work somethin' out."

"It's not the money. I got me some money saved. It's my wife. She's a New York gal, used to a different kind of life than we have here. Why, she's just adjustin' to Santa Fe. I can't just move her to Carlsbad so soon after she got here. I don't think that'd be right. You know?"

"Well, I expect you're right. But the offer stays. There's no rush. I need a partner, but I can wait on it. You ever change your mind, you just let me know."

"I sure will. Maybe next year. Who knows?" With that Lucus stood up. "We'd best be gettin' back."

He entered the crowded room and waved to Will, who returned to the group of people with whom he'd arrived. Lucus walked up to Honor and asked, "Did I miss anythin'?"

Honor smiled. "No." She eyed him curiously. "What did your friend want?"

"He wanted to know if I'd be interested in joinin' him on his ranch in Carlsbad, as his partner."

"Carlsbad? Isn't that a long way from here?"

"It's a distance."

"What did you tell him?" she asked anxiously.

"I told him no. But it really sounded good. I'd like nothin' better than to be partners on a ranch with Will Jeevers. We're old friends. He and I were always together till he and his daddy moved to Carlsbad."

"Are you sorry you turned him down, Lucus?"

He smiled. "No. Put it out of your mind."

The music suddenly swelled around them, causing Consuelo to turn to Lucus shyly. "Will you dance with me, Lucus?"

Lucus looked uncertainly in Honor's direction.

She smiled at him. "Go on, Lucus. I'll be fine." She watched them dance off, studying them intently. They looked so comfortable together, so completely carefree. For a moment a fierce possessiveness for Lucus washed over her. She decided she was being silly and determinedly turned away to accept a glass of wine from Estéban.

Honor was long back at her easel well into December, painting scenes and people taken from her accumulation of pencil drawings. She painted small streams shimmering in the morning sun, snowcapped mountains against turquoise skies, Mexican women with black mantillas or black shawls covering their heads, and the open, sensuous faces of young Mexican children.

All the faces of Santa Fe held a certain fascination for Honor. The young men with their curving nostrils and fierce, black mustaches, suggesting flaming Latin passions. The graying heads and thin white noses. Bronze Indian faces, open and childlike beneath red fillets binding straight black hair. If it were possible, she would have drawn them all.

She enjoyed painting the old women's faces best, seeing in them a sensitive and proud Castilian dignity that blended with a trace of Indian stoicism. Old and withered as dry brown leaves, their faces revealed the sum total of a history that was slipping by too quickly in the name of progress.

Honor worked hard at her paintings, losing herself in them, but finally she put her brushes down and temporarily abandoned her easel. Christmas was fast approaching. Her first Christmas in Santa Fe. The air was crisp and cold, the blue sky cloudless and the noonday sun warm, but it didn't feel like Christmas to Honor without snow. Nevertheless, the whole city pulsated with plans for the coming holiday, and she, too, threw herself into the spirit of it and made her own plans.

A blue cedar now stood in the *sala*, its graceful, lacy branches decked with purple berries that she and Elijah had carefully strung together. Candles were fastened among the branches and would be lighted tonight—Christmas Eve. The fireplace burned continuously now, and crackling piñon permeated the air with its piney fragrance. Elijah's long white stocking hung expectantly over the fireplace and the dancing fire.

Lucus and Elijah sat cozily at the foot of the tree, making satin ribbon bows to be fastened to the tree as well, while Gilly's Queen cathedral clock chimed the hour.

Honor stood in the center of the room, not moving, watching them with more than a glimmer of contentment. The whole scene before her, Lucus and Elijah sitting together, the tree, the crackling fire, all blended together for her in a happy holiday spirit.

A knock at the courtyard door sent Honor to answer it. She opened the gate to find Consuelo standing there with Lita, her youngest daughter, who was clutching a doll. Honor smiled. "Consuelo, what a nice surprise! Come in. Come in." She closed the gate behind them and led them into the *sala*. "Sit down. Please."

Lucus turned their way. "Nice to see you, Consuelo. Lita."

Elijah looked up. "Good afternoon, ma'am."

Honor smiled at Lita, standing shyly at her mother's side. "Join Lucus and Elijah, Lita. You can help make the bows."

The child looked questioningly at her mother through large black, luminous eyes, then slowly moved forward to join them on the floor.

"What a lovely girl, Consuelo. Just lovely."

"Gracias."

"Well," Honor said gaily, "why don't I get some sherry and spice cakes from the kitchen? Doña María just baked the cakes this morning."

"Sí. That would be nice. I will help you, Honor." Consuelo got up to follow her into the kitchen.

"Are you ready for Christmas, Consuelo?" Honor asked as she retrieved a decanter of sherry from a cupboard.

"Sí, we are." She placed the cakes on the large

platter Honor handed her. "Will you be going to Mass tomorrow?"

"No. But we do plan on going to vespers tonight. I've never been in a Catholic church. I'm looking forward to it."

"*Bueno. Bueno.* We will be there as well. Perhaps we will see you."

Honor put the decanter, three glasses, and four small dishes with silverware on a tray and carried it out to the *sala,* Consuelo behind her with the platter of cakes.

"Lucus," Honor said as she entered the room, "let the children make decorations alone for awhile. Come and talk with us." She lowered the tray onto a long table flanked by chairs.

Lucus looked up and nodded. He patted both the children on the head and stood up, stretching. "Lord, I was gettin' a mite stiff sittin' down like that."

The three sat down, Honor and Lucus side by side, Consuelo across from them. Honor poured the sherry and then handed them each a porcelain dish with a spice cake on it. She put two cakes on another dish and brought it to the children. Back in her seat, she was suddenly aware that Lucus's eyes had not left the children. "Now, Lucus," she said, smiling, "they can manage the tying without help."

Lucus reluctantly turned from the children and picked up his glass of sherry. "Yes. I know." He glanced at their guest. "You're lookin' mighty well, Consuelo."

"*Gracias.* And you too, Lucus." She took a sip of sherry, her gaze never leaving his face. "I understand you will be going to vespers tonight."

"Yes. Honor wants to go. She's never been to a Catholic service."

"There will be much activity afterward. Christmas is a wonderful time, is it not?" She continued to stare straight at him.

"Yes," Lucus answered. "Tell me, how is Estéban? His ranch doin' well?"

"*Sí*, it is."

"And your other children?"

"Also well, Lucus."

"Good. Good. And your mother? I haven't seen her for a spell."

"*Mi madre* grows very old. She will not leave the house now."

"Well," Lucus said. "That's too bad."

Honor squirmed in her chair, feeling left out—an intruder in her own home. It occurred to her that Lucus and Consuelo seemed to lose themselves in each other when they were engrossed in conversation. She'd noticed this before. She observed the way Consuelo stared at Lucus, her face flushing and eyes shimmering. She thought deeply for a moment, recalling having teased Lucus before about Consuelo's being an old flame. Now she suspected it was true. With glaring clarity she knew that Consuelo was in love with her husband! She decided to keep her own counsel on this matter, not wanting Lucus to view her as a suspicious, jealous wife.

Suddenly Consuelo looked at Honor, bringing her back into the conversation. "Many people have told me that you have drawn them on paper, Honor. How wonderful it must be to be an artist. *Sí?*"

Before Honor could answer, Lucus said enthusiastically, "You should see her paintin's, Consuelo. I've never seen anythin' like them." He brushed sherry off his thick mustache with the back of his hand. "They're really fine."

"And what do you plan to do with your paintings, Honor? Will you sell them at the marketplace as all the other local artists do?"

"I really hadn't considered that," she answered. "I've never thought about selling my paintings. They're just something I do for myself."

"You should think about it. One day you could make a lot of money selling them."

"Yes," Honor said. "One day. Perhaps."

Consuelo finished her sherry and spice cake. She

looked over at Lita, still on the floor with Elijah. "Lita is getting big. Is she not, Lucus?"

"Yes, Consuelo," he said. "She sure is."

"Well, I must go now." She rose and drew her shawl around her shoulders. "Lita, come now." The child obediently got up and moved to her mother. "Perhaps we will see you tonight, *sí?*"

Honor stood up to walk her to the gate. "Yes. That would be nice."

"*Sí.*" Consuelo looked over at Elijah. "Merry Christmas, Elijah."

"*Hasta luego,* Lucus."

"Take care now, Consuelo. Give my best to Estéban."

After the gate closed behind Consuelo and her daughter, Honor rushed back into the *sala* to find Lucus still seated at the table, staring off into space. "Come, Lucus. I'll help with the bows now." Getting down on the floor beside Elijah, she looked back at Lucus questioningly. "Won't you join us?"

He smiled. "Sure. Sure."

The afternoon swept gaily past them. Finally, the bows fastened to the tree and the candles lit, the three set out at twilight in the buggy.

When they arrived at the cathedral, they found the service had already begun. The men were sitting on one side, the women and children on the other, their voices sounding the low, surging chant of the Ave Maria, rosaries slipping softly through their fingers. The priest rendered forth the Latin service with great flourish; sweet-faced young altar boys assisted him. Honor and Elijah took their seats in the rear with the other women and children, Lucus sitting with the men. Honor looked around, not seeing Consuelo anywhere, and secretly felt glad.

Fascinated, she studied every detail of the cathedral, seeing the beauty of Christmas reflected in all the reverent faces around her. Candles gleamed on the altar, and those in tin sconces along the walls lit up the Stations of the Cross, casting a soft, warm glow over the people and emitting a waxy smell throughout the church.

Honor shifted in the hardwood pew, beginning to feel stiff. She carefully studied the priest, thinking that he seemed to be involved in a secret, solitary rite that all but excluded the parishioners. She wondered about these people who never doubted, never questioned their faith. It was as if they looked upon the priest as God himself. To observe these rituals as a bystander was interesting, but Honor knew she could never believe in them. Something was missing for her in this church, though she could not define it.

After vespers, the men, women, and children filed out quietly. Honor, Lucus, and Elijah came out into the cold evening air and were greeted by the sight of large, leaping bonfires in front of the cathedral.

"Look, Mama," Elijah squealed excitedly. "Look at that!"

"How beautiful!" Honor exclaimed, looking farther away and seeing that bonfires had also been lighted around the plaza. "Do they always do this, Lucus?"

"Yes, they do. It sure is a pretty sight. Wait. There's more."

They got into their buggy and rode in the direction of their house, passing more bonfires in front of many homes. An entire city of dancing fire fusing against a black, star-filled sky lay before them. Suddenly there was music as well. Guitarists and violinists strolled by them down the starlit road, exuberantly playing as they went.

"Oh, Mama," Elijah gasped. "Isn't it all lovely?"

Lucus abruptly pulled the buggy to a stop. "Look over there," he directed, pointing to a young boy seated beneath a window, playing a guitar while softly singing a Spanish refrain.

"What is he doing, Lucus?" Honor asked.

"Playin' the bear."

"Playing the bear?" Elijah repeated. "What is that?"

"An old Spanish custom. He's serenading a girl in

that house. A girl he's in love with. See her? At the window?"

"Yes," Elijah answered. "I see her."

Smiling, Lucus cracked the reins and started forward.

Honor wrapped her arms around Elijah, and he did the same to her, humming as they happily hugged each other, enraptured with the night, the stars, the blazing fires, and the music filling the air around them. Their life had never been as sweet, thought Honor, never.

It was June 1901, and the idyll was over. The first year in Santa Fe had passed swiftly in a flurry of teas, dances, and new friendships. In one way Honor felt she'd just arrived. And now Lucus was telling her it was time to leave. It wasn't possible. He couldn't be thinking clearly.

Facing him, she felt angry, somehow betrayed. She turned from him, pacing up and down the *sala*, spitting out her anger. "You've already made up your mind, haven't you? Without consulting me first?"

"Will asked me to come in with him on his ranch in Carlsbad nearly a year ago. I told you about it at the time."

"But you refused him then. What changed your mind now?"

"Listen, I've been thinkin' of leavin' Manuel's ranch for several months." He grabbed hold of her and pulled her around to face him. "I have enough money to buy in. It'd be good not to have to work for wages any more. I look at it as a way to insure our future security. I may never get another chance like this again."

"But, Lucus, we're settled here. I dearly love this house. And Elijah's made friends. He loves his school. We've only been here a year, Lucus. Don't you think it's too soon to uproot him again?" She silently wondered if it wasn't too soon for her to be uprooted as well.

With pain etched on his face, Lucus said, "I know you and Elijah are happy here, darlin'. But he'll make new friends. And I'll build you a new house. I know you'll be happy in Carlsbad, too."

"Lucus, I don't want to stand in the way of your getting ahead. I understand how you feel about wanting your own ranch. But why can't you do the same thing right here? There must be opportunities for you here in Santa Fe if you're tired of working for wages. I have all that money from Gilly just sitting in the bank doing nothing. Use some of it to buy yourself a spread and cattle."

Lucus couldn't restrain his anger. "I don't give a damn about your money, Honor. You'd better get that straight right away, if you haven't already. I'll make it on my own or not at all. You keep your money."

"But, Lucus, we're married. My money is yours, too."

"I'm not goin' to discuss it, Honor." He was quiet for a moment, then asked, "Don't you trust me to make the right decisions for us?"

His voice had a tinge of hurt to it, and Honor began to feel guilty. Lowering her voice, she said, "Of course I trust you."

"Well, then. Know that I'm makin' the correct choice for us now. Why, it'll affect all of us."

"Yes, I know, Lucus. That's precisely the point."

"Honor. Please."

Her resentment spent, she felt fear well up in its place. She moved to him, reaching out for his hand, her voice pleading. "Lucus, let's not go. Something tells me that we shouldn't. Please, Lucus. Please."

"Honor." He pulled her over to a chair facing the fireplace and lifted her onto his lap, cradling her in his arms and stroking her golden hair. "You'll like Carlsbad. So will Elijah. I promise you. It'll be good. You'll see. It'll be good."

Honor vacillated between wanting to believe him and knowing in her heart that this move meant trouble for them. What form the problems would take was not discernible to her, but she sensed it nonetheless.

She thought of the sweetness of her life in Santa Fe, the beauty of the environment, the warmth and friendliness of the people. She'd really known more peace here than she'd ever known at any other point in her life. How painful to have to put it all behind her.

The last suitcase was locked. Estéban waited outside in a buggy to deliver them to the stagecoach that would carry them to the railroad station. Honor tarried in the *sala* with great reluctance, feeling compelled to stay there.

How strange the room looked to her now with the furniture covered with blankets, the rugs and brass and pictures all packed away. She wondered if she could have some items shipped to Carlsbad later on.

Oh, well, she thought, sighing outwardly, perhaps another adventure awaits me in Carlsbad. An adventure full of new surprises. She'd been reluctant about moving to Santa Fe. And look how good it had all turned out. She'd make a go of this, too. She'd always made the best of whatever life had offered her. And she would do the same now. She was determined to.

Elijah ran into the room and pulled on her hand. "We're ready, Mama. Let's go."

From the moving buggy she watched Casa de Contento diminish in size behind them. She turned to Lucus. "Do you think we'll ever come back, Lucus?"

"Sure, darlin'. We'll be back for visits."

I wonder, Honor thought. I wonder.

BOOK III

Carlsbad, New Mexico

1901

Eleven

HONOR ENTERED Carlsbad proper by buggy, wind ripping violently around her. Thick whirls of dust blew in her face, completely obscuring the wind-swept road from her vision. The day, which had been still and clear when she left the cabin on a shopping expedition, amazed Honor with the suddenness of this storm. The frightened horse snorted and whinnied loudly, jerking against the reins, and trying to control him was very difficult.

Had she not been so close to town, she would definitely have turned back for home, but now she kept moving until she came to the dry goods store, barely able to make out the sign. She quickly jumped down and tied the horse's reins to a post, then ran for the front door. She had difficulty opening it against the wind, and when she finally did, she had to use all her weight to close it again.

Completely breathless from the effort, she leaned back, exhausted, against the shut door. Rubbing sand from her eyes, she looked up to see a stone-faced woman coming her way. "It's bad out there," Honor offered.

The woman nodded at Honor but did not respond, and adjusting her bundle under her arm, moved to the exit. Honor stepped out of her way, staring after her, puzzled. Then she heard a voice calling out to her.

"Quite a day out there, isn't it?" A woman with an open face and brown hair piled high on her head smiled at Honor from behind the counter.

Relieved to find the first pleasant person in this community of sour, unfriendly people, Honor smiled back broadly. "Yes, it certainly is. I never would have come out today if I'd known how the weather would turn out."

She watched as the stranger came waddling out from behind the counter. Portly, with short, stubby legs and a long torso, she wore her gown cut low, causing her ample bosom to bounce up and down when she giggled, which she did frequently. Honor judged her to be in her thirties.

"I'm sure the storm won't last too long," the woman offered. "These winds come up quickly and seem to disappear just as fast."

"I hope so," Honor said. "I wouldn't like to have to go home in that. It's frightening."

The woman held out her hand. "My name is Sophie Long. I run the store."

Honor smiled and shook her hand. "Hello. My name is Honor Kant."

"You're new in town, aren't you?"

"Yes. My family and I moved here from Santa Fe just three months ago."

"Santa Fe!" Sophie exclaimed. "My parents once visited there. My mother always told me how charming it was."

"Yes," Honor said. "It really is a colorful place—full of history."

"Do you speak Spanish? I understand you couldn't live there unless you did."

"Yes. A bit. But a great many of the residents are bilingual. You can get along without speaking Spanish."

Sophie smiled. "You look tired. Would you like to join me for tea? I have a wood-burning stove in the back room, where I keep a kettle going."

"Are you sure I won't be taking you away from your duties?"

"Great heavens, no." Sophie giggled, gesturing

around the empty shop. "I believe I can tear myself away from all this thriving business."

Honor laughed. "I'd love a cup of tea."

"Well," Sophie said in her high-pitched voice, "follow me."

Settled in the back room, Honor removed her bonnet, shaking it free from the clinging dust and laying it across her lap. In a moment Sophie handed her some tea, and Honor relaxed in the hardwood chair, relishing it and the good company. She couldn't remember when she'd last had a woman friend to talk to. "Are you a native of Carlsbad, Sophie?"

"Oh, yes. I've never lived anywhere else."

"Never?"

"No. When I was young I used to dream about leaving Carlsbad and visiting all sorts of exotic places. But I never did."

"Do you have a family?"

"Do you mean, am I married?"

Honor nodded.

"No. I've never married. I had a chance once when I was very young, but it didn't work out."

"Oh? Why not?" Honor caught herself quickly and apologized. "I'm sorry. I really didn't mean to pry into your private life. You don't have to tell me."

Sophie grinned. "It's all right. I don't mind talking about it. It was a very long time ago, after all. You see, my parents didn't approve of the boy who'd proposed to me. He was a wanderer, Gerald was. Didn't stay too long in one place. I'd met him at a picnic and fell in love. It wasn't too long after that when he asked me to marry him. But my parents didn't think I'd have too secure a life with Gerald." She paused thoughtfully. "I've always regretted listening to my parents. I think I would have been happy with him. He was so gay and full of fun." She smiled. "How that boy could make me laugh."

Honor's expression saddened. "I'm so sorry, Sophie."

"Well, let's not get glum. For all I know, he's still

wandering and my parents may very well have been right all along."

"You live alone, then?"

"Yes. For the past five years I have. I lived with my mother and father up until that time. They died within months of each other."

"It must be lonely for you."

"Sometimes. But I keep busy. I work here at the store six days a week. That just about takes up all my time. And then there's church on Sunday." She rested her teacup and saucer down on the table next to her. "Tell me about yourself," she said enthusiastically.

Honor sipped her steaming tea cautiously and then answered, "I'm afraid you would find it boring."

"Boring? Heavens, no. Really, I'm interested."

"Well, my husband, Lucus, has joined Will Jeevers as a partner on his ranch. That's why we moved to Carlsbad."

"Will Jeevers," Sophie repeated. "I know his wife. She shops here frequently."

"Lucus is very happy here. In Santa Fe he worked for wages, and he enjoys being half owner of a ranch."

"Do you have children?"

"I have a son. Elijah. He's close to seven years old."

"You're not from Santa Fe, are you? I mean, you weren't born there, were you? There's something different about your accent."

"You're right. I was born and raised in New York City."

"My, my," she giggled, "you certainly are a long way from home."

Honor smiled, warming up to her completely. "Yes, I am."

"Well," Sophie said, "you've traveled a bit. Tell me about New York. It's a big, modern city, isn't it?"

"Yes, it is. But it's getting quite overcrowded . . . And the air is terrible there. Not like New Mexico on a clear day. But there is so much there. You could never run out of things to do. That's what I miss. It has such fine restaurants. And the theater. I always enjoyed the theater." She paused briefly before continuing. "Santa Fe was also full of activity. Carlsbad is so bleak by comparison. I have to admit I was a bit disappointed when we first arrived. The town has nothing much to offer and the people are so closed. In Santa Fe everyone was so friendly and hospitable."

"Yes. The townspeople are closed to outsiders. I dare say they're even closed among themselves as well. And I must agree with you about the lack of things to do. There is nothing here save a local saloon that the men frequent after a long day on the spreads. There's church on Sundays, of course. And there are plenty of fishing holes. But I'm afraid that's the extent of it."

"Haven't you found it dull?"

"Perhaps. But I'm used to it. I don't really have a source of comparison. This is my home. I've never lived any other way. But for someone like you, Honor, who has known another kind of life, Carlsbad would take some getting used to." Her voice brightened. "But when the weather warms up, we do have a town picnic occasionally."

Honor nodded. "Well, thank heavens I have a hobby that keeps me busy."

"A hobby?"

"Yes. I draw and do oil paintings."

"Do you really?" Sophie's hazel eyes danced with interest. "How fascinating. Did you know there's an artists' colony not too far from Carlsbad? Now, that's an interesting pastime for an idle day. I'd almost forgotten that. Perhaps I can take you there sometime."

Honor smiled. "I would enjoy that, Sophie. How nice you are."

"I would love to see your paintings, Honor. I've

simply adored art work since I was a very young child. How exciting to have a gift for it!"

"Why don't you come out to our cabin on Sunday and I'll show them to you? Can you?"

"Can I? Why, I'd be delighted to!" she exclaimed. "What time do you want me?"

"Any time in the afternoon. Lucus and Elijah will be off fishing, and we can have a nice visit all by ourselves." She looked around. "Do you have a pencil and tablet handy? I'll draw you a map. The cabin is a bit out of town and hard to find."

"You just wait a moment. I'll get them."

In a moment Sophie rushed back, crying, "Well, it's just as I predicted. The storm is over. It's clear again."

"That's a relief," Honor said as she reached for the tablet and pencil and drew Sophie a map. She handed it to her and stood up. "I'll see you on Sunday, then?"

"Yes. On Sunday." She walked Honor to the door.

Honor suddenly turned to her and laughed. "I need material to make my son some clothes. I'd almost forgotten why I came into town today."

Sophie joined in her laughter. "Well, come on back, then. I'll show you what we have."

Honor stood in the sparse cabin that was now her home, lining up her paintings along a wall so that Sophie could get a good view of them. "These are all of them." She sat down in a large maple rocking chair and waited, watching her new friend waddle up and down the room, carefully studying each painting and talking rapidly all the while. How Honor enjoyed this cheerful, exuberant woman; Sophie was the one bright spot in an aloof, unfamiliar community of which Honor did not yet feel a part.

"My goodness, my goodness," Sophie kept saying. "How realistic they are. I've never seen anything like them. Never. Why, there's no one in Carlsbad who's capable of this work. Not a one. What talent!" She turned to Honor. "Why, with all your paintings alone, we could open a gallery. I know quite a few ladies from church who would love to buy some of these."

"Then you really like them?"

"Like them? I should say." She pursed her lips, thinking for a moment, then said, "When you came into the dry goods store the other day and we chatted, I sensed a great sensitivity about you. And that quality would have to take an artistic direction. It just would." She regarded Honor questioningly. "I expect you'll be doing many more, won't you?"

"Yes, I plan to." Honor looked at her quizzically for a moment. "Would you like to sit on the porch for a while?"

"That would be nice." She was halfway to the front door when Honor's voice stopped her.

"Sophie?"

"Yes."

"I'm going to have a cigarette. Do you ever smoke?"

"Yes, on occasion." Her eyes danced mischievously. "Do you think it's all right?"

"No one will see us around here."

Sophie laughed. "Then let's."

"Wait for me on the porch," Honor called as she walked into another room. "I'll bring out two."

Moments later they were comfortably seated on rockers on the porch, languidly puffing in silence. Honor finally broke the quiet, saying, "I'm so glad I've met you, Sophie. The people in Carlsbad are so strange."

"I know. I've lived here all my life, and there's only a small handful of people I can call friends. The women don't mean to be rude, Honor. They're good people at heart. But their whole lives, from sunrise to dusk, are made up of nothing but hard work. I expect it doesn't leave them time to think about the amenities. And, as we discussed the other day, they tend to be closed to outsiders. Believe me, that will change somewhat."

"Yes," Honor said, "I expect so."

Sophie looked around. "You're really so isolated out here. It must be lonely for you."

"You're right, but I don't really mind it. I love the openness of the land. It's peaceful."

"I can see that," Sophie agreed.

"Sophie?"

"Yes?"

"A few minutes ago you said you knew some ladies at church who would be interested in buying my paintings. Are you sure?"

"Oh, yes. There are quite a few who frequent that artists' colony nearby. They're always coming home with something."

"I see." Honor grew quiet.

Sophie cocked her head to one side. "What are you thinking, Honor? Do you want me to ask around and see if anyone would like to come out to look over your work?"

"Not exactly."

"Not exactly?"

"You had a good idea a moment ago. Why don't we open an art gallery?"

Sophie burst into giggles. "Honor, I was joking about that! You're not serious?"

"But I am. It's an excellent idea. I've got a bit of inheritance money tucked away. For a long time I've tried to think of a way to do something with it. If we opened an art gallery, we could sell my paintings. Perhaps we could get others from the artists' colony interested in doing the same. I'll put a deposit on a place in downtown Carlsbad and we'll finance the rest with the bank."

Sophie rocked back and forth without a word.

"Well?" Honor asked.

"I've got my position in the dry goods store, Honor. Why, they depend on me."

"But you just work there, Sophie. I'll make you a full partner. This would be your chance to be a proprietress. You can run the gallery. That will give me time to continue painting."

"Do you really think there's a living in selling only art?"

Honor thought about that for a minute. "Perhaps we could stock oil paint and artists' supplies as well. The artists in the area must surely be sending away for what they need. It would be a great convenience for them."

"Yes. That's an excellent idea."

"Then you're interested?"

"I've only just met you, but I can't think of anyone else I'd rather be in business with. We get on so well. It's just . . . women don't own their own business. The bank would never give us any money. Now, if Lucus would put the loan in his name—"

"No. I won't have it. We'll do it ourselves."

Sophie shrugged, then stated, "There is a place for sale in town. Next door to the dry goods store."

"Would it be suitable?"

Excitement began to surge in Sophie's voice. "Oh, yes. It would be perfect. It's Mr. Klemmer's sundries store. He was in just the other day telling me about it. He wants to retire. But I've no idea how much he wants for it."

"Leave it all up to me. I'll stop and see him in the morning before dropping in on the bank president." Honor jumped from the rocker, threw her cigarette down, and stamped on it. "Won't it be an adventure, Sophie? What do you think?"

"If we can do it. Then yes, it surely would be."

"Well, then," Honor said, "we'll do it. We'll just do it."

The next morning Honor dressed in her best white shirtwaist and flowing burgundy walking skirt. With her plumed hat angled comfortably on her head and a parasol at her side, she knew she looked citified. Exactly the impression she wanted to create.

As she approached the bank she straightened her shoulders with determination, tilting her chin upward. She walked in and approached a thin, bespectacled man behind a cage who was penning figures into an oversized ledger. "I wish to see Mr. Lowell, please," she declared.

He looked at her over his spectacles. "The president?"

"Yes," she answered impatiently. "The president, Frank Lowell."

The clerk shrugged. "Just a minute."

Honor watched him rise begrudgingly from his seat and move to a door at the rear of the bank. Knocking, he disappeared inside and closed the door behind him. Honor impatiently paced while she waited. After a few moments he came out and opened the cage door, letting her pass through.

Honor faced Frank Lowell with more than a little amusement. Having met him once before, she considered him a pompous ass. He was a large, bulky man with a cherub's face and a red, bulbous nose that he had the habit of often honking into a worn handkerchief. He stood up and grandly held out his hand. For a moment she had the impression he was actually going to bow.

"Ma'am."

Honor shook his hand. "My name is Honor Kant, Mr. Lowell. I'm sure you remember me. I wish to talk to you about a business matter."

"I see." He smiled. "Please, sit down." He motioned to a chair positioned next to his desk. "Now, what can I do for you?"

"My friend, Sophie Long, and I wish to secure a loan from your bank."

"Sophie Long. From the dry goods store?"

"Yes. That's correct."

"And what would you and Sophie be needing a loan for, Mrs. Kant?" He honked into a handkerchief.

"Miss Long and I wish to buy Mr. Klemmer's store and open an art gallery. I've just left Mr. Klemmer, and we've worked out the arrangements very nicely."

"An art gallery?" His eyes registered surprise.

"Yes. An art gallery and artists' supply store."

He smiled broadly and leaned back in his chair, which creaked under the burden of his weight. "Do you really think there's a need for a gallery in Carlsbad, Mrs. Kant? We're plain, simple people here."

"Women enjoy the arts, Mr. Lowell. I'm sure we can turn it into a thriving business."

He clasped his pudgy hands over his vast stomach. "And how much of a loan did you want for this venture?"

"Mr. Klemmer is asking five thousand dollars for the store. I will put up five hundred dollars as the down payment."

"I see. Well." His smile seemed frozen on his face. "Tell me, won't your husband be in this business with you?"

Honor had the distinct feeling he was about to patronize her. She wouldn't tolerate that. "No," she answered firmly. "My husband is involved in his own business matters. This is exclusively my affair."

"I see. Well, now, Mrs. Kant, why don't you think about this a bit longer? You wouldn't want to rush into anything, would you? Perhaps your husband could come in and talk to me about this. We might be able to work something out."

Honor stiffened. "I said no, Mr. Lowell. I want to do this by myself."

"But, ma'am," he said, expansively gesturing his palms outward. "Collateral. What collateral do you have for a loan that size?"

"I think, Mr. Lowell, you conveniently forget about the money I had transferred here from the bank in Santa Fe. That money is in my name and for me to do with as I wish."

"Yes. As I recollect, it's a sizable amount. You could buy Mr. Klemmer's store outright and still have plenty to spare."

"Now, that wouldn't really be good business, would it, Mr. Lowell?"

He paused, leaning forward on the desk. His smile had suddenly vanished. "No, I expect not."

"Well, then?"

"I'm not sure, Mrs. Kant." He was avoiding her eyes. "Let me think about it."

The back of Honor's neck was beginning to prickle with annoyance. She pulled herself up straighter. "Let me assure you, Mr. Lowell, that if you won't finance this business operation, I will promptly remove all my money from your bank." His stunned expression almost made her laugh.

He looked directly at her and responded with a hesitant note in his voice. "You don't want to do anything hasty, do you? I expect we can arrange this, Mrs. Kant. I'm sure we can."

"How long do you need to get the papers drawn up?"

"Let me see now," he replied in a contained voice. "Today is Monday. Would Friday morning be convenient?"

"Yes, Mr. Lowell, that will be fine. Miss Long and I will be here at ten." She stood up and reached over to shake his hand, then turned to leave, his honking trailing behind her.

Honor's whole being pulsated with a sense of victory as she rushed out into the sunlight. She could hardly wait to tell Sophie. And Lucus! She couldn't wait to tell him as well. Honor Wentworth Kant was about to be a businesswoman.

Lucus wound barbed wire around the shaky fence post, the jagged tip catching deep into his forefinger. "Damn," he muttered as he pulled the wire out, watching blood trickle down his tan hand. Taking a handkerchief from his shirt pocket, he tied it around his wound and knotted it by pulling one end with his teeth. He sat down and rested his back against a post. Keeping his forefinger high, he awkwardly rolled a cigarette.

The gray smoke rose and circled over him. He watched it with a kind of detachment, more conscious of the throbbing in his finger. Letting his mind drift, he thought of Honor, whom he was frankly worried about.

Sophie Long had been the only friend she'd made in the few months they'd been in Carlsbad. Lucus was acutely aware that people here lacked the open hospitality that had existed in Santa Fe. Also, he realized that their temporary, makeshift cabin was a poor substitute for Casa de Contento, and he wondered if he'd ever find the time to build Honor a real home as he'd planned to before moving here.

But she never complained, he reminded himself. She didn't seem unhappy on the surface. He just wanted everything perfect for her. He'd promised her that their life would be just as good here as it had been in Santa Fe. She had to be experiencing disappointment even though she never expressed it.

He closed his eyes and thought about the long day stretching out before him. His shirt was starting to cling to him with perspiration. Irritated with both the heat and his boredom, he decided to quit early and take Honor riding through the Guadalupe Mountains. Tingling with anticipation, he took a long drag on the cigarette, satisfied that this idea was the best damn one he'd had all day.

Honor had just arrived home when she heard the sound of horse's hooves approaching the cabin. She moved to the kitchen window, parting the gingham curtains to see Lucus approaching. He's early today, she thought, and wondered why. She ran to the door and greeted him eagerly.

"Hi, darlin'." Lucus bent down to lightly kiss her pink cheek. "You're all dressed up. Are you goin' somewhere?"

"No. I've just come from somewhere. I have so much to tell you, Lucus."

"Well, good. Why don't you change into somethin' more comfortable? I quit early so we could take a ride through the mountains. You can tell me all about it on the way."

She noticed his finger. "What happened, Lucus?"

"It's nothin'."

"Don't you want me to attend to it?"

"No. You just go get ready."

"All right." She headed for the bedroom, calling back to him, "I won't be long."

Ten minutes later their horses were swaying and bouncing beneath them. Lucus looked over at her with pride, admiring the ease with which she handled her horse. "Well," he said, "you goin' to tell me about it?"

She faced him directly and said, beaming, "Sophie and I are going into business together."

"Business? What kind of business?"

"A gallery and artists' supply store. We're buying the sundries store. Mr. Klemmer is retiring."

"Well, now. You don't say."

"I'm putting up the deposit and we're taking out a loan for the remainder. I've already cleared it with the bank." She paused, laughing. "Mr. Lowell did give me some rough moments, though."

"He did? Why?"

"Banks are hard put to give loans to women for business ventures, Lucus."

"He didn't stand a chance with you, that I'm sure of."

She looked at him slyly. "Is that a compliment?"

"It sure is. You're a fiery woman, Honor, and I love that about you. The man who crosses you is a damn fool."

She smiled radiantly.

"What kind of arrangement have you worked out with Sophie?"

"She will run the store so I can continue painting. I'm making her a full partner, Lucus. What do you think?"

"I think it's a mighty good idea. I really do. Will you be sellin' your paintin's in the gallery?"

"Yes. And, I hope, canvases from other artists in the area as well."

"I sure hate to see your paintin's go. I'm really attached to them. Can we hold on to a couple?"

She smiled. "Of course, Lucus. Why don't you pick out a couple of your favorites and I'll put them aside."

"Good."

"Then you're happy for me?"

"Sure am. How about yourself?"

"Yes. Very."

"That's all I need."

"Lucus, you are a good man."

"I know, and don't you forget it."

She laughed. What a dear he really was. At moments like this she felt very lucky to have him.

They continued their trek through the rocky, uncharted paths in reflective silence. After some time had passed, Lucus glanced at her and asked, "Are you gettin' tired, darlin'?"

"Yes," she answered, "a little."

He dismounted first, then helped her down. "Let's stretch out on the ground a bit, sweetheart." He pulled a blanket from behind the saddle, where it had been rolled and tied to his horse, and spread it out on the ground.

They lay down, smelling the sweetness of the mountain air. At day's end, the sky was a brilliant sea of orange, bursting and erupting like a volcano above the mountains. The gentle slope of rocky terrain spread out before them as far as the eye could see. They were blissfully quiet for a long time.

Honor finally broke the silence. "You know, I can't see New York in my mind very clearly any more. I try to see the streets and the people, but it's all foggy. I think I push away the memory of all that congestion . . . that crowded feeling of too many houses . . . too many people thrown together. Now . . . now . . . I look at all this space. All this wonderful, unending space." She paused for a moment. "I used to look at pictures of these very mountains when I was a child. Now here I am." She smiled. "I would like to run and fly through all this space. I'm free here, Lucus."

He looked at her. "You're really not sorry we left Santa Fe?"

She turned over on her side, raising herself on one elbow to face him. "I can't say I'm not sorry at all. But I like it here very much." She reached over to push back a lock of dark hair that had fallen on his forehead.

Lucas looked so young today despite the creases in his brow and the lines dancing out from beneath his dark, gentle eyes. Unexpectedly she found herself in a quickening state of strong sexual arousal. It had been a long time since she'd experienced desire. She'd blocked it out, stoically submitting to Lucus's brief, sporadic lovemaking. But today she wanted him with every fiber in her being. She wanted to be close to him—physically close. If only . . . Perhaps, she thought, if she took the initiative and made him take his time. She slid her slender hand down over his firm stomach and opened his belt buckle.

Taken by surprise, he jerked away from her. "Honor."

She sidled up next to his lean body, pulling his mouth to hers, thrusting her hand down under his Levi's to his quickly hardening sex. "Let's get undressed," she whispered, removing her hand and beginning to take off the layers of her clothing. He followed suit, then drew her to him and mounted her.

"No, Lucus, wait. Wait!"

But he couldn't. In a moment it was over. After, he lay on his back, his right arm flung over his eyes. "I'm sorry, Honor. Really."

"It's all right," she said wearily.

She dressed and so did he, turning on his side afterward and falling asleep. For a moment Honor thought she'd be sick, but it passed. She deliberately kept her mind blank, stubbornly refusing to let unpleasant thoughts enter in. Sitting motionless, she stared off into the distance.

Blinking, she tried to focus her gaze on something unusual in the sky. She squinted for a moment but couldn't make it out. Turning to Lucus, she jostled him awake. "Wake up, Lucus. I want you to look at something."

He stretched, then sat up. "What?"

Pointing to the sky, she asked, "Lucus, what is that blackness up there?"

His eyes followed the direction she was pointing in. "I don't know," he answered. "It looks like a dark cloud of smoke. It could be a prairie whirlwind." He paused. "No, I don't think so. This thing doesn't seem to move. Look at it. It stays in one spot near the ground, and the top keeps spinning upward." Half to himself, he muttered, "What is it?"

They didn't talk for a while, watching, waiting for something familiar to reveal itself, something recognizable. They suddenly turned and looked at each other, knowing they were thinking the same thing.

"Are you game, darlin'?" Lucus asked.

Her curiosity aroused, she jumped up, tugging on his hand. "Let's go see, Lucus!"

They tied their horses' reins securely to a rock and went on foot, but it was a difficult journey. Holding hands, they were forced to climb awkwardly over jagged rocks, since there was no accessible path. Honor's long brown skirt repeatedly caught on razor-sharp spindly cactuses. Silently, she cursed her cumbersome clothing, but, mesmerized by that black apparition in the sky, they kept on going.

Finally they were close enough to see what it was. They stopped—disbelieving. Bats! Millions of them spiraling upward. There seemed no end to their number as they erupted from the mouth of a large cave.

"Lord, Honor," Lucus said, "there must be a hell of a big cave in there to hold that many bats. Look at the size of the opening!" He moved close to the entrance and lay down on his stomach, peering into the inky darkness. "I wonder how far back it goes?" he said, quickly rising to his feet.

He began searching for something in the area, and she turned away from him to look at the cave opening.

A strange sensation gutted the pit of her stomach. Was it fear? She didn't know. Why did this cave seem so familiar? She couldn't begin to explain it, but she knew she had been here before. When? Chills danced up and down her spine.

Turning back to Lucus, she watched his movements in a daze. "What are you doing?"

"You'll see." He piled some dead cactus in a heap, then drew some matches from his shirt pocket and lit the pile. When the blaze caught, Honor jumped, frightened by it.

"What are you going to do with that?" she asked in a constricted voice.

Not answering, Lucus squatted down and pulled out a cactus stalk flaming at the tip with hot fire. He moved to the edge of the cave and threw it in, watching the bright blaze fall into the ebony abyss, trying to judge the distance from where he had tossed it to where it finally went out, spraying its sparks on the rocks inside. He suddenly realized that the flaming stalk had fallen downward and had temporarily halted the bats' ascent. "I'll be damned," he murmured softly.

Night was enveloping them. Honor shivered. "We'd better get back, Lucus. We won't be able to find the horses."

He got to his feet. "You're right, darlin'. Let's go." Reaching for her hand and feeling its icy cold, he said, "Lord, you're freezin', girl. Why are you like ice?" He put his arm around her, hugging her to him. "Hey. There's nothin' to be scared of."

"I'm sorry, Lucus. I'm being foolish."

"What is it, darlin'?

"I'm not sure. But there's something strangely familiar to me about this place. It frightens me. I can't explain it." She turned away from the cave to bury her face in his chest. "Take me away from here, Lucus. Please."

Puzzled, he gently patted her head for a moment. "It's all right." He drew her away from him and clasped her hand. "Come on, now. Let's go home."

He led her away, turning his head slightly, his gaze riveted on the sight of the gigantic cave. To Lucus this place seemed cloaked in an aura that was strange and mysterious. He wished he knew what it was. It had already left its mark, magnetizing him. One thing Lucus was sure of. He would be back.

As Lucus sat at the square pine table sipping his evening coffee, he thought about the bat cave, unable to erase the memory of it from his mind. For two weeks since their trek there, he'd been unable to think of anything else. The cave seemed to be drawing him—pulling him—compelling him to return. Over and over the same question filtered through his mind: What could be down there? He decided the time had come for him to go back there and find out. In the morning, he thought, I'll go back.

He glanced at Honor, sitting quietly by the evening fire and sewing, lost in her own thoughts. Elijah sat at her feet, engrossed in a schoolbook. He walked out and went to the shed behind the cabin, gathering together a kerosene lamp, a hand ax, a rope, and some wire, and putting them in a place where they'd be undisturbed.

He started back to the cabin to tell Honor of his plan, then stopped in his tracks for a moment, recalling Honor's puzzling fear on the night of their discovery. He decided not to tell her about it—yet. Afterward, he thought; then he would share it with her.

Twelve

LUCUS SAT down to rest on a high hill. He looked off into the distance, thinking that the mountainside seemed like a vast blue-green sea spread out before him. For a moment he doubted the saneness of his decision to explore the deep cave alone. Was he mad? What if he got down there and couldn't find his way out?

He pondered this for a moment, then quickly decided that his imagination was too fired up for him to turn back now. He got to his feet and moved on.

The rugged slopes and rock-strewn ridges disappeared behind him, bringing him closer and closer to his objective. Seemingly from nowhere, a mule deer sprang majestically before him and froze with fear. Lucus slowly turned away from it and tossed a rock off to the side, the sound scaring the deer off. He continued his climb, thinking about the animal's flight. We're all afraid of the unknown, he thought.

Once he arrived at the cave, Lucus dropped his gear to the ground and stood quietly before it. In the morning sunlight the orange-cast cave entrance appeared even more huge than it had at dusk. Larger—deeper—more menacing.

He watched cave swallows sweep down and up the entryway, and turkey vultures gliding gracefully above the surrounding canyons. There were no signs of bats anywhere. A chill ran through him. Was there danger below? Fear and anticipation gave him a lightheaded feeling. "All right, *amigo*," he said aloud, picking up his ax, "let's get goin'."

His eyes roamed over the growth in the vicinity, searching for a netleaf hackberry shrub to provide wood to build a ladder. The area brimmed over with prickly pear cactuses bursting with their purple fruit of summer. Spindly ocotillos were growing upward in dense patches. The smooth-leafed sotol was in full bloom, bearing a large cluster of whitish flowers growing at the tip of a tall stalk high above the center of the plant. The light green foliage of mesquite sprang up from the brown earth. Juniper and soapberry trees rustled in the summer breeze. At last he saw the shrub he was searching for.

He swung the ax high in the air, bringing it down with a thud on the bush. Adeptly, he chopped off a great pile of suitable branches. When satisfied that he had enough, he got down on his knees and constructed a long ladder, using the branches for steps and tying them together with rope and wire. He checked and rechecked the knots and the tightly twisted wire, then relaxed. It was primitive, but safe.

Dragging it into the cave and to the edge of the pit, he threw it over and secured the top tightly to a large boulder. After filling a lamp with kerosene, he carefully stored the reserve in his knapsack, and pulling this over his back, tied the straps across his chest, moving forcefully back to the edge of the drop. First adjusting his wide-brimmed cowboy hat securely on his head, he swung his tall, thin frame over the side.

He made his way down, the ladder undulating beneath him. When he finally felt his feet touching something solid, he stopped to light the lamp, then looked around. He found he was not on the floor of the cave, but perched precariously on a narrow ledge some distance above it. Damn, he thought, I miscalculated.

He glanced upward, knowing he should return to the top, lengthen the ladder, and start down again. After pondering that for a moment, Lucus decided to hell with it. He'd just jump to the bottom. The distance seemed to make this feasible, he decided. He'd worry about reaching the ladder when he returned. He took a deep breath and leaped, reaching the bottom with a thud. He was fine.

Quickly moving to the entrance of a tunnel off to the right, Lucus lifted his lamp high and went in. He walked for a while before finding himself in a vast underground chamber. As far as he could tell, it extended ahead several hundred yards before turning off to the right. To what? he wondered.

To the left, he made out another tunnel that seemed to go in the opposite direction. Its floor appeared to be more level, so he took that route, finding himself in the bat cave. He had a sudden vision of bats descending on him, swarming over his head. Nervously he turned back to explore the other tunnel.

There was total silence. It was unnerving. The only sound was the echoing of his own footsteps as he penetrated farther and farther into the virgin depth, making his way through winding caverns. He carefully surveyed the twisting passageways with his kerosene lamp, fervently wishing it threw out more light than it did. He soon realized that nothing in particular stood out or seemed unusual. After a time he began to wonder if this expedition had been worth the trouble after all.

Suddenly, without warning, a strangely magnificent, beautiful sight loomed before him. What in the world was this? he wondered as his startled gaze roamed over a colony of massive stone pilings. Their enormous size and eerie beauty staggered his senses.

Some structures hung suspended from the ceiling, falling in long, graceful points, descending in thick groups. Others erupted from the earth, resembling giant sand castles. It was as if God had reached in and, driblet upon driblet, created a subterranean city of stone. Exquisitely sculptured by some divine order of arrangement, each frozen droplet had a place and a purpose.

Lucus moved close to the structures to touch them, one by one, feeling their icy coldness. Their perfection was so intense, it struck something deep inside of him, overwhelming him. A feeling of reverence closed his throat with emotion as he fought back tears. He'd never dreamed anything like this existed. Nothing he'd ever seen could compare with these structures.

Some of the more delicate points broke under his fingers. He decided to use them for a recognizable trail and laid them prominently on large rocks. A worrisome thought flashed through his mind. What if he couldn't find the trail on his way back? He considered this possibility for a moment before electing not to worry any further. He was sure to find it.

He walked on, moving trancelike through networks of winding, twisting corridors and vaulted chambers. To Lucus each one was more ornate than the last with its multishaped forms and complex composition. The shapes varied from swirling stone portieres to great gleaming pillars, their rich luster wet to his touch.

A frozen waterfall, shining white, cascaded down a wall, so real in his imagination that he could almost hear the sounds of its splashing currents. One room had an indefinable air of regal majesty, a royal splendor of delicate forms and a wide spectrum of hues. Translucent points hung from the ceiling, sparkling almost with pride in the intense solitude. For how long? Lucus wondered. Centuries?

He stood still for a moment, overcome by a startling idea flashing through his mind like a white light. I was sent here to act as the cavern's messenger. To tell the world of this. To bring people to it. I know it . . .

Kneeling in reverence, he seemed to hear his father's voice, seemed to see his father appear before him, chilling him to the bone. "Go out into the world and do God's work, Lucus. Do you hear me, Son?" Lucus nodded vigorously. "Hear well, and give heed to the Scriptures. Many are called, Lucus, but few are chosen. Do you hear me?"

"Yes, Father. Yes, I hear you. I hear you." Lucus shuddered as the apparition vanished as suddenly as it had appeared. He stood up, carefully willing himself back to the present. Recalling that incident from his childhood, he wondered why he relived it now with such startling clarity. Could his father have really known he would be brought to this spot on this very day with a mission before him?

Lucus became infused with a profound vigor. Now he had to see it all and saturate himself with its unearthly beauty. He didn't feel tired. He didn't feel anything except a pulsating, rhythmic pounding in his head that urged him to go on.

He moved through a keyhole-sized entrance into another room that also gleamed with its own peculiar splendor. A pond twisted through the base of some of the structures, the lamplight reflecting a vibrant emerald-green water. He got down on his knees to take a cautious sip from his cupped hands. Satisfied that the water was pure, he drank until his thirst was quenched. Refreshed, he continued with his explorations.

Where he couldn't walk he crawled on all fours, struggling across narrow ledges, laboriously moving down unknown passageways, passing great black pits along the way. He inched past mammoth-sized openings that seemed bottomless, wishing with his whole soul that he had more light. He was quickly growing tired. Very tired. He stopped to rest near a pit to get his bearings.

Putting the lamp down, he moved tentatively to the edge of the pit and stared into its blackness, wondering if he could determine its depth. He loosened a large boulder and pushed it over in order to see how long it would take to reach bottom.

He slipped—going headlong over the side with the boulder.

Desperately he grabbed hold of a jutting rock and held on, his feet dangling in the air. In a blind panic he searched for a firm footing. The sound of the boulder rolling in the black depths beneath him echoed and reechoed in the stillness until it became too faint to hear. He never heard the boulder hit bottom.

Finally he found a footing, and with a strength he didn't know he possessed, he pulled himself slowly up to the top. His heart pounding loudly, he felt incredibly cold as he sat in the lonely quiet, his sudden spurt of energy now depleted. Lord-a-mercy, he thought. With wildly trembling hands he picked up the lamp and slowly, cautiously, went on.

Had an eternity gone by? He was losing track of time, having no idea how long he had been crawling and climbing in the deep, feeling a million light-years away from the surface of the earth. He sighed with profound relief when he at last reached a large room and could stand up and walk again.

Here the expansive size of the structures was even more overwhelming than those he had left behind. Giant domes of great magnitude rose up to the ceiling. Or did the law of gravity pull them down in the hard, solid mass of stone? Clusters of small shapes erupted from the ground, resembling large growths of algae and coral on an ocean floor. Lucus felt suspended in a timeless place. The outside world was remote. Reality was here. Nothing else mattered. God keep me strong, he prayed, to bring the world to this.

Suddenly, without warning, Lucus was thrust into complete inky darkness—alone . . . lost. The lamp, exhausted of its kerosene supply, had gone out. He dared not move. Terror gripped him and confusion muddled his mind, making him helpless. Slowly and steadily, he sucked his breath in and out, forcing himself to calm down and not to panic.

His head clearing gradually, he loosened his knapsack and let it slip to the floor. Continuing to breathe deeply, he knelt down and groped in his sack for the reserve of kerosene, pulling it out with shaking hands. Struggling to maintain self-control, Lucus refilled and lit the single source of light. Coughing from the smoke that emanated from it, he pulled his knapsack on again and stood up on trembling legs. Jittery and completely unnerved, he decided it best to return.

The thought of retracing the trail was overwhelming. At the start of this expedition he'd had the feeling he might not be able to find his markings. What if he couldn't? His whole body shook with fear. Honor didn't know where he was. No one knew. He'd never be found!

In a blind terror, Lucus started to run headlong into the blackness, his lamp casting a dim light before him. He suddenly tripped and fell, his head smashing against the base of a large structure. Feebly he tried to raise himself. "My God, what if I can't get out? What if I can't find the way? Help me, Father. Help me."

Everything looked fuzzy as Lucus fell heavily to the ground, unconscious.

The yellow and red striped bowl slipped from Honor's hands, shattering into a thousand pieces. "Don't get near it, Elijah," she called. "Stay where you are until I sweep it up." What has gotten into me? she wondered. She was so terribly nervous today.

Sophie, who'd been seated at the sturdy kitchen table, jumped forward. "Good gracious!" She reached for the broom resting against the barren wall.

"Thank you, Sophie. Please finish your tea. It won't take a moment," Honor said, taking the broom from her. She was sweeping the broken pottery into a pile when she heard the sounds of a horse approaching the cabin. She looked at Sophie. "Lucus is home early today." Calling out to Elijah, she instructed, "Open the door, dear. Father's home."

Elijah pulled the door open, and she looked up, expecting to see Lucus's tall frame. Instead, it was a cowboy from the ranch. "*Buenos días,* Juan." She looked over his shoulder. "Is my husband with you?"

"No, *señora.* I thought he was here. He is needed at the ranch. Do you have any idea where I could find him?"

"No, I don't."

Juan shuffled his feet. "Well, I will be getting back. Would you tell Lucus we could use his help when he gets home?"

"Yes, of course."

"*Adíos, señora.*"

"*Adios,* Juan."

Elijah tugged at his mother's skirt. "Where do you think Father is, Mama?"

"He'll be along, Elijah." She ran her hand across the top of his shiny dark hair. "Go on and play now."

The shards of the bowl picked up, Honor poured herself a steaming cup of tea and sat down at the table to join her friend. "This is peculiar, Sophie. It isn't like Lucus to go off without telling anyone. How strange."

"I'm certain it's nothing to worry about, Honor. After all, Lucus can't very well tell everyone where he is every minute of his life, can he?"

"No," she agreed. "I suppose not. But it's still not like him. When he left this morning, he said he'd be branding cattle all day. He just wouldn't go off when he was needed. He's much too responsible." The palms of her hands were beginning to perspire. "Do you think there could have been an accident? Lucus could be lying injured on an isolated road somewhere."

"Honor," Sophie said soothingly, "you're making too much of this. You mustn't let yourself get upset. I'm sure Lucus is fine. Why, he'll probably be here any minute, and you'll feel foolish for worrying so."

"Yes, I expect you're right." She got up, walking to the window to watch for him. She was starting to feel silly. "You're probably right, Sophie. He'll be here any minute now."

Lucus moaned and rolled over onto his spine. His head felt heavy, throbbing; everything around him was blurred. He rubbed his eyes for a moment, then squinted them open, shivering from the cold. He'd never felt so lonely in his life. Aloud he said, "Relax, cowboy. It's goin' to be all right. You're goin' to make it."

Carefully, he tried to stand up, almost falling again, his wobbly legs lifeless and limp. He had to do it, he told himself. He had to get back. He reached down for his lamp and put one foot before the other, slowly, laboriously, the pounding in his head and his weakened legs resisting him. It took every ounce of strength he had left to keep going. Painstakingly, he made his way back across narrow ledges, moving at a snail's pace.

Cautiously, Lucus climbed over boulders in his path, slipping shakily on loose rocks. Breathing heavily, he stopped often, confused, his thinking disoriented. Yet he found the trail, and at each recognizable point he breathed easier, hanging on to the thin thread of hope that he would make it. He had to, convinced there was important work waiting for him out there . . . God's work.

Exhausted, his head aching unmercifully, he fell once again. I've got to get up, he told himself. I can't give up now. I just can't. Pulling himself up on all fours, he lifted his lamp and looked ahead of him, relief flooding his face. Was he imagining it, or did he see a flicker of sunshine ahead? Slowly he raised himself and moved forward, bringing his body nearer and nearer to that light. I've found it! I've found it! He rejoiced, thanking God for his deliverance as he ran for the ladder with a surge of renewed strength.

He looked up, a sinking feeling coursing through him. He'd forgotten the separation of the ladder from the bottom. The distance had seemed fairly proximate when he'd jumped down. Now, in his weakened condition, it looked much too far. He laid his lamp down on the ground and removed his sack, relieved to have the weight lifted from him. With firm resolve he found a footing and inched his way up. When he reached the ladder at last, he felt faint. Hang on, he told himself. You're all right now. You're going to make it.

Once safely out of the cave, he lay down on the earth, pressing his face into the dirt. The hot sun warmed his chilled body, reviving him. After several minutes he sat up and turned to face the cave entrance, staring at it thoughtfully for some time.

Then he yelled hoarsely into its depth, "You scared me away, but I'm not frightened that easily. I'll be back. Do you hear me? I'll be back."

Thirteen

"Look at it! Look at it! God sent me. I know He sent me. Honor . . . Honor . . . Honor. My God, it's beautiful. So fantastic. So magnificent." Lucus tossed restlessly in delirium for more than twenty-four hours, his body wet with perspiration, his words garbled.

Honor sat in a hardwood chair next to the bed, pressing wet cloths to his forehead. The furrows in her brow deepened with worry as she thought back to when she'd found Lucus, wondering how he'd made it home in his condition. She'd heard a voice calling her name from somewhere outside the cabin. Opening the door, she'd seen Lucus sprawled on the ground before her, babbling. Now she shivered at the memory.

Lucus's body ceased its thrashing about. He became very quiet. Honor cried in alarm, "Lucus! Lucus! It's Honor, Lucus!" He opened his eyes, and she relaxed.

He turned to gaze at her. "What happened?" he asked, his voice sounding steady and clear.

She changed places to sit on the edge of the bed, putting her arms around him. "I don't know what happened, dear. I found you lying outside, half out of your mind. Where were you, Lucus?"

"The cave, Honor. Remember that cave we found?" She nodded. "I went back. I had to see what was down there. My God, Honor, I've never seen anythin' like it in my life. It's the most fantastic thing in the world. Exquisite stone sculptures of all shapes and designs. A city of rock formations. It's beyond description." He thought for a moment. "I fell and hit my head a few times while I was down there. I guess I got hurt bad. Lord, my head aches."

"Calm yourself," Honor ordered. "I have hot broth on the stove for you. I'll get it."

She thought about what Lucus had said as she slowly poured broth into an earthen bowl. A city of rock formations? What could he have seen? Perhaps his head injury had made him believe he saw something unusual. It sounded absolutely unreal. She picked up the soup and a spoon and hurried back to the bedroom.

The weeks of Lucus's convalescence passed swiftly. With his strength renewed, the pattern of his days fell into the same sequence as before the accident. But beneath the surface of his every move and thought, everything was totally, irrevocably different. There was the cave to contend with, looming larger than life in the deep inner recesses of his mind.

He couldn't concentrate on his chores at the ranch, could no longer focus on Honor and Elijah. Lucus thought and dreamed incessantly about the cave. He was convinced he'd been chosen to bring a graceless world to the caverns; that God wished him to do this. People coming face to face with the perfection of His work would have a heightened awareness of His existence. Though how he would go about this was not readily clear to him. The responsibility weighed heavily upon him.

Now Lucus's thoughts drifted to his father. He hadn't lived up to his father's expectations of him, and this still sorely rankled his spirits. Yet, despite their tumultuous, unbending relationship, Lucus had been awed by Abram Kant until the very end. Abram had left Lucus with a legacy of sorts, the wisdom of survival in an uncompromising world. His father would always be with him. Always. He thought of this as he and Honor huddled in bed under a warm quilt, a kerosene lamp casting a warm glow over them.

"What are you thinking, Lucus?" Honor asked, looking at him with a new tenderness.

"I'm thinkin' about my father. Did I ever tell you that he was a preacher?"

"Yes, you once mentioned it."

"But he wasn't simply any preacher. I mean he was *the* preacher of the faith. I wish you could have seen him in a pulpit. He had this loud, boomin' voice that echoed and bounced off the walls. He'd raise a fist into the air and drop it on the lectern to pound the Gospel out. He was electrifying. People would come from miles away just to hear him preach. They truly loved him."

"Did you, Lucus?"

"Did I love him?" He pondered for a moment before answering. "No. But I can tell you I sure respected him. Was scared of him, too. I didn't disobey him often. I wouldn't dare."

She turned on her side to see him better. "Did you miss not having a mother?"

"Well . . . I guess I did. When I was real young, I used to envy other children who had mothers. I once confided that to father. He got awful mad at me. He said envy was a sin."

"I'm sorry, Lucus."

He smiled at her. "That was a long time ago, Honor."

"Lucus, what makes you think about all this now?"

"The caverns. There's somethin' there I want—to claim. Not for myself, but to share with the world. I don't know how I can do that exactly. But there's got to be a way. My father used to say, 'Go out and get your heart's desire, Lucus. No matter what it is. God means us to fight for what we want. The man who stands afraid throughout his life is the man who fails the test. Fightin' to reach goals is every man's destiny. Fear,' he would always say, 'will make you a mental cripple.' I think my test now lies in the caverns. I know we didn't find the cave by accident. And my purpose there would help me make up for a lot, I think."

"Make up for what, Lucus?"

"He wanted me to be a preacher like he was. He

always said it was the biggest disappointment of his life that I wouldn't carry on his work for God after he died."

"Didn't it matter to him what you wanted to do with your life?"

"He never considered that. Do you know, at the end, before he died, he wouldn't even speak to me."

"Lucus, how terrible."

"He was a stubborn man, that one."

"But tell me," Honor asked, "how does this test you speak of lie in the caverns?"

"I know God sent me there for the purpose of acquaintin' the world with the perfection of His work. And that won't be easy."

"How do you know that?"

"Just do, is all. Someday I'll tell you about it. Trust me."

Honor nodded, trying to digest his words, but felt disappointed that he was holding something back. Keeping that to herself, she asked instead, "Where do you go from here, Lucus?"

"That's somethin' I have to figure out. It'll take some doin', I'll tell you. But I really believe every man has the test of endurance and faith, don't you?"

"I'm not sure. But if that's the test, I daresay some fail badly." She paused for a moment. "Like my father."

He turned to her. "You know, you've never spoken of him before to me. You've never described any of your family. Tell me about them."

She closed her eyes and rubbed her forehead with her fingertips. "It's not very pretty. I'd rather not."

"Darlin', anythin' that's part of you can't be that bad. I want to know everythin' there is to know about you. Share it with me, Honor."

Honor was quiet for a time. "I come from a nightmare." She looked into his dark eyes, full of such gentleness, and felt easier. "My parents both migrated to New York from London. I suppose they were full of hope then. Young, recently married, starting life in a new country that seemed full of promise. My mother's people were of an upper class in England. My father's weren't. Her family's objection to the marriage caused their decision to leave. I suppose her people made life very rough for her."

"That's why they left London?"

"Yes. I don't know what opportunities they thought would be waiting for them. My father didn't have the language barrier that other immigrants had, but he was unskilled. He couldn't find decent work. They went deeper and deeper into debt. The children came and my mother couldn't help. She was always big with child and held down by caring for us. We lived in squalor, in a dirty, filthy, rat-infested tenement. We were always hungry. But that wasn't the worst of it. In his desolation, my father started to drink. As the years went by it grew worse and worse. When he was drunk, he had a temper he couldn't control. He would break furniture. He would punch my mother—" She stopped talking, her throat choking from emotion.

Lucus sat up, his expression one of disbelief. "Go on, Honor. Tell me the rest."

She swallowed hard. "Do you really want to hear it?"

"Yes."

She ran her tongue across her upper lip, trying to quell the increasing anger. When she spoke again, her voice was hesitant. "Of all the children, I was the one my father would single out for beatings. Once . . . I remember my mother screaming with terror and his fists coming down on me until I finally blacked out. My ribs were broken." She looked over at Lucus and saw tears streaming down his face.

He reached for her, stroking her, rocking her.

After a few minutes she said, "It's all right, Lucus. Strangely enough, it made me strong inside. Stronger than I might have been otherwise. Perhaps that was *my* test of endurance."

"An awful lot has happened to both of us, in a way," Lucus mused. "All that matters now is what we do with the remainder of our lives. How fully we live, and how much we put into the rest of it, will go a long way toward making up for the past. The important thing is to salvage whatever time we have left on this earth and do the most with it that we can."

Moved by his words, Honor came closer at that moment to loving Lucus than she'd ever been before. "Lucus?"

"Yes, darlin'."

"Haven't you wondered why there's been no sign of a child coming along?"

"I suppose I've been so content, darlin', I hadn't given it much thought."

"I so much want a baby, Lucus. I want to bring new life into the world. Why do you suppose I'm not with child yet?"

"We'll have a baby. We will. Don't worry about it."

"Lucus?"

"Yes?"

"Take me with you to the cave. I want to go down and share it with you."

"It frightened you, Honor."

"I won't be afraid. I promise."

"Sure, darlin'. I'll take you." He kissed her eyelids . . . her cheeks . . . her mouth. "I'll take you."

Honor had one bad moment on the ladder when she looked down and had to halt her descent to fight a wave of dizziness. Was she mad, forcing herself to return to this place? She was suddenly overwhelmed by a powerful thrust of déja vu penetrating her consciousness. She'd never been as terrified in her life as she was at this moment.

"Honor, are you all right?" Lucus called up.

She struggled against the dizziness, swallowing hard. Determined to overcome her fear, she concentrated on Lucus, knowing he would catch her should she fall. In a moment she felt better. "Yes, I'm fine," she murmured.

She continued the descent, glad for one thing—the

man's Levi's she was wearing that she'd had Lucus purchase for her. Her body felt free and comfortable, the pants giving her much flexibility of movement. When she finally reached the bottom of the ladder, she turned to look down at Lucus, who was waiting for her on the cave floor.

"The ladder doesn't reach all the way," she called.

"It's not far, Honor. Jump. I'll catch you."

Unsure, she hung on to the ladder and sucked in her breath. Then, closing her eyes, she plunged, nearly knocking Lucus over when her body hit his. She burst out laughing, relieved that her inner tension had subsided. Tucking a stray strand of blonde hair into her white bonnet, then buttoning her warm jacket, she was suddenly anxious for the exploration to unfold.

They both carried a kerosene lamp, the combined light affording greater visibility. She let Lucus guide her through the twisting corridors until they reached the first spectacular structures. She was thunderstruck by the sight before her.

"Did I exaggerate?" he asked.

"No," she whispered, "you didn't." She looked at his face reflected in the lamplight, suddenly aware that his eyes had taken on a frenzied glaze. She'd never seen him appear that way before. It disturbed her. Nevertheless, she put it out of her mind as she followed him through a keyhole-sized opening into a chamber that boasted enormous, swirling, stonelike draperies. She watched Lucus put his lamp close to them. The curtains seemed to burst into flame. When he moved away, they absorbed the light and continued to glow a few seconds longer. "Lucus," Honor whispered, "look at it! Look at it! It's lovely!"

He smiled at her. "I'm going to name this room after you. I'll call it the Queen's Chamber. It fits you. I make this room a gift to you."

She laughed. "I don't suppose I make a very regal queen in men's pants."

"You look like one, believe me."

She curtsied dramatically and Lucus bowed to her.

They burst out giggling like small children, then stopped as their voices rebounded repeatedly in the stillness.

"How eerie," she said, suddenly aware that Lucus was staring at her intently.

He moved toward her and clasped her to him, hungrily kissing her, his sex taut and hard.

She drew her head back with a surprised look in her eyes. "Here, Lucus?"

"Why not?"

They removed their packs and Lucus spread his jacket on the ground. He grabbed her and pulled her down. Panting heavily, he undid her Levi's, whispering, "It seems right to make love here where no one else ever has. It's fitting." He took his pants off as well and lay down beside her, running his strong hand down her taut stomach, then between her firm thighs, spreading them apart and stroking her gently.

Something caught in her throat. She was burning, aching beneath his touch. In a frenzy of desire she closed her eyes when he entered her, suddenly, unbelievably, seeing *Julian!* It was Julian looming over her, Julian's hands pushing her buttocks up to meet him. Julian's flesh was the flesh fusing with hers. She couldn't bear it. It had to be blocked out. It had to! "No," she shouted. "No!" She moaned as Lucus's body fell heavily on hers.

Afterward he regarded her baffledly. "What happened?"

She didn't know how to answer him. "It was nothing," she muttered inanely. "Nothing."

His face looked so hurt and confused, Honor wanted to cry. He started to say something but stopped, turning away instead to put on his clothes. At a complete loss, Honor was grateful he hadn't pursued this issue with her. What could she say?

They continued their exploration in tense silence. Unable to erase what had just happened from her mind, she wondered if the invisible presence of Julian would always come between them. An unbearable yearning pitted her stomach. She felt skittish and resisted further conversation.

It seemed to her that many hours had elapsed. She was exhausted when they finally started back, but nonetheless impressed by all she'd seen. She could well understand why Lucus had been affected so strongly. For the first time in her life she believed she'd really seen perfection.

They decided to rest not far from the cave entrance and eat the food that Honor had brought along.

Seated on the cold ground, hungrily eating a large chunk of yellow cheese, she stared into the darkness. "You know I feel close to God here, Lucus. I've never been what you could call religious. I've always felt that formal rituals rob people of their own special, individual relationship with God. You lose your personal identity praying in a group. It becomes cluttered with other people's versions of how things should be done. But here! It's hard to explain. This is the real temple. The temple of God's work. You can't deny Him here. You can feel Him—alone and special. How right you were about it all."

"Yes," he agreed. "There's a mysticism about this place. The first day I was here I fell down on my knees to pray." He paused reflectively, unable to reveal to her that momentary vision he'd experienced then. Instead, he asked, "Do you think other people will feel the same as we do?"

"Perhaps. Yes, I'm sure many will sense the same thing." She leaned toward Lucus, asking tentatively, "Do you believe in reincarnation?"

He looked surprised. "I've never thought about it. No. No, I don't think there is such a thing. Why?"

"Would you think I was mad if I told you I'm sure I've been here before? Not down below, but up here at the cave entrance."

Lucus laughed loudly. "Honor, you're imagining things."

"It's not funny, Lucus. I'm serious."

He reached for her hand. "There's a logical explanation for your feelin's. I'm sure of it."

She tore away from his hold. "I—" She stopped, irritated at his unwillingness to take her seriously. Picking up her lamp, she got up and started to walk away.

"Don't go too far without me," Lucus cautioned.

"I won't," she called back testily.

Left alone, Lucus sat in the pervading silence and pondered over Honor's strange, unpredictable moods. She'd been on edge with him lately. Nervous and moody. He'd always been fascinated by the many sides of her personality, but this facet bothered him. She did need to have a baby, he decided. His thoughts traveled to her puzzling behavior earlier, when they'd made love. What a strange woman she is sometimes, he thought.

He looked around him, wondering where all this was going to lead. Before, his life had always been reasonably uncomplicated. Now he had this driving force to show the world these caverns. Instinctively, he knew his life was going to change radically, for this obsession wouldn't let him rest. He had to realize this dream. The thought jolted him. Was it only a dream? Or was it within the realm of realistic possibility? At this moment he didn't know.

Honor's voice startled him out of his reverie. "Lucus! Lucus! Come here!"

He picked up his lamp and ran toward the direction of her voice.

"Look at that," she half whispered when he'd reached her. "Look!"

Two skeletons were lying on the ground before her, one on top of the other in their final resting place . . . entwined forever in this stone temple of God.

Fourteen

It was a hot, dusty Saturday evening when Lucus wearily entered the Running Water Saloon in Carlsbad. He looked around at the men, all sporting bowlers and large-brimmed cowboy hats, who were noisily huddled over an assortment of round tables, drinking whiskey and playing cards. The heavy presence of cigar and cigarette smoke made his eyes smart.

He walked to the long mahogany bar, freshly polished and shining. In sharp contrast, the hardwood floor was badly in need of repair and varnish and creaked beneath him. The ceiling was covered with gold wallpaper that had a red flower design running across it. The walls were overlaid with a deep red paper intermingled with a busy gold pattern. Mammoth-sized oil paintings of nude women hung on every wall, the one over the bar of a buxom blonde especially capturing Lucus's attention.

A few electric bulbs hung from the ceiling providing sparse, barely adequate light. A potbellied stove stood next to the bar. In the winter months it would provide heat, though not enough for the large room. Two doors in the rear boasted a sign indicating the dining room. Lucus looked up at a clock on the wall. It was eight o'clock.

He rested his foot on the low brass rail at the base of the bar, his toe scraping a spittoon. Looking up, he saw two deer heads with massive antlers hanging over the huge mirror opposite him.

Nonnie, a young Indian with jet-black hair cas-

cading down his back, was tending bar. "Whiskey, Mr. Kant?"

Lucus thought for a moment. He'd been up since daybreak branding cattle on the ranch and was bone-tired. "Yes, Nonnie, make it a double." The Indian poured whiskey into a water-spotted glass. Lucus took a coin from his pocket and laid it down. He picked up his glass and sauntered over to a table adjacent to the bar where Will Jeevers and some of their ranch hands were gambling. "How're you doin', fellas?" Lucus asked, pulling a chair from a nearby table to where they were seated.

"Pretty good, pretty good," they chorused.

Will peered over his cards at him, pushing his cowboy hat back on his blond head. "Want to join in, Lucus?"

"No. Not right yet."

"Did you finish brandin' all the cattle?"

"There's still a mite more to do tomorrow."

Will nodded, his concentration back on the game.

Lucus sipped his whiskey, feeling it flame down into his chest. He sat back and studied their faces, wondering if this was the right time for serious talk. Deciding it was, he plunged in. "Any of you men interested in seeing some caverns I found?"

They glanced up at him for a moment, shrugged their shoulders, and continued with their bidding.

"I discovered the most spectacular caverns I've ever seen over in the Guadalupe Mountains. There's miles and miles of beautiful stone formations down there. I tell you, it's like nothin' you've ever seen."

He stopped talking for a moment to check their reaction. They glanced up at him occasionally, but their faces remained expressionless. He continued. "Part of it houses millions of Mexican fantail bats. But they don't bother you none. They sleep all day and leave the cave at dusk to hunt for insects." He paused for a moment before hopefully asking, "Anyone game?"

Putting down his cards, an aging cowboy with a

long, thin, wrinkled face looked sharply at him. Chomping on plug tobacco, he first turned and took aim at a spittoon, making his mark, then settled back and spoke to Lucus. "I've seen plenty of caverns in my day, Lucus, like Mammoth in Kentucky. You've seen one, you've seen them all. Can't be anythin' so special 'bout this one."

"But there is," Lucus said excitedly, "there is. There's nothin' like these anywhere. If you saw, you would know what I mean." He paused for a moment, then declared, "There's somethin' holy about these caverns."

A suspicious look crossed their faces. They glanced at each other and shrugged.

Nonnie, who'd been listening from behind the bar, approached them. "I know what caverns you're talking about."

Lucus turned to him with interest. "Do you?"

"For hundreds of years my people have told the tale of a huge cave in the Guadalupe where bats live. We've always known about it."

"Has anyone ever gone down and explored?" Lucus asked expectantly.

"No," Nonnie stated emphatically. "No one would ever go down there. Indians have great superstition about entering dark places. No Indian ever has. Of that you can be sure," he added. "But there was a half-breed hanging around those caverns sometime back. He was in here a couple of times talking to me about it."

"A half-breed?" Lucus said. "Is he still around?"

"I haven't seen him for a while now. I think he went to California."

"What was his name, Nonnie? Do you remember?"

Nonnie thought for a moment. "Clay. Clay Birdsong. You never know, Mr. Kant. He just might drift back this way one day."

Disappointed, Lucus shrugged and nodded, then asked hopefully, "Would you be interested in goin' down with me and seein' it, Nonnie? It's a sight like nothin' else."

"No, Mr. Kant, not me. You won't see me going into no cave."

"But you admit that the Indian fear about goin' into dark places is based on superstition." Nonnie didn't answer. Frustrated, Lucus turned to the others, cajoling them. "Believe me, there's nothin' to be afraid of. Nothin'. I've even taken my wife down there."

Juan, the young Mexican from the ranch, who'd kept out of the discussion so far, looked at Lucus incredulously. "You took a woman exploring in a cave? Man, you must be loco. If it's as big as you say it is, you could get lost and never get out."

"I've made my own trail. You can't get lost. Believe me." He turned to his partner, hoping for some sign of support. "What about you, Will?"

Will stared at him, his blue eyes full of questions. "I'll think on it, Lucus."

Lucus looked helplessly at all of them. He reached for his whiskey and finished it. "Well, if any of you change your mind, let me know. But I'll get someone to go down with me," he stated confidently, pushing his chair back to get up and talk to other men, relentlessly continuing his search for someone to share this great, profound experience.

The men watched his tall figure join another group on the other side of the room.

Juan spoke first. "Man, he must be loco. A holy cave? What's he talking about?"

"He's crazy, all right," the elderly hand said. "From the first day I met him I thought there was something strange about that Lucus fellow."

They sent Nonnie for more whiskey and returned to their card game. Will Jeevers stared at Lucus across the room for some time.

Lucus and Elijah were heading into a shed when they heard Will's voice call out, "Hey, Lucus, you got a minute?"

Lucus stopped and turned toward his lifelong friend. "Sure," he answered. "What're you up to, Will?"

"I want to talk to you about somethin'. Why don't we go into the house and have some of Sanchez's rotten coffee?"

Lucus nodded and walked back to Elijah. "Go help Juan feed the horses, boy," he instructed, giving Elijah a reassuring pat on the back.

"Yes, Father."

Lucus loped into the house with Will and helped himself to a steaming cup. He placed his drink on the table next to him and stretched out his long legs. "It sure feels good to sit. It's been quite a day."

"How's your pretty wife doin', Lucus?"

"Not too good, Will. I don't know. She's been nervous and irritated lately. It could be her disappointment that we can't seem to have a baby."

"I'm sorry to hear that."

"Sometimes," Lucus said, "I wonder—"

"Wonder what?" Will asked.

"I get the feelin' sometimes she'd like to pick up and run."

Will laughed. "Come on, Lucus. When a woman gets married, she don't run nowhere. When she's married, she's married. There's no choice in it."

Lucus shrugged, then changed the subject. "You didn't bring me in here to talk about Honor. Was there somethin' special you wanted, Will?" He waited patiently, watching Will take off his hat and rub his tired eyes.

Will looked over at him. "We've been friends for a long time, haven't we, Lucus?" Lucus nodded and smiled as Will continued. "I guess I know you as well as anybody can know someone. But I'm havin' trouble understandin' you lately."

Lucus remained silent.

"Everybody's been sayin' you're a little crazy, Lucus. The ranch hands. Some of the people in town. Everybody's been gossipin' about you and that cave.

For two months now you've been talkin' about it constantly to everyone you run into. It's not just your talkin', people are backin' off because you seem obsessed with it. They don't understand you. To tell you the truth, you scare them a mite." He picked up his coffee and sipped it slowly.

Off in the distance Lucus could hear the barking of a coyote. He listened quietly to the familiar sound, not responding, watching Will.

"Where is all this leadin' you, Lucus? Why are you doin' this?"

"Well, I'll tell you this, Will. I'm not crazy."

"But why?"

"Isn't it enough reason just to want to bring beauty into people's lives?"

Will shifted his lean body uncomfortably. "Come on, now, Lucus. When you jabber about beauty to cowboys in these parts, they don't know what you're talkin' about. If you pushed the point, they'd probably tell you that their idea of beauty is a good romp in the hay. I'm tellin' you, Lucus, you've got to stop it."

Lucus stared desolately into space. "I just want to share it . . . I want everyone to see it. Somethin' is drivin' me about this thing. I can't fully explain it. But I'm convinced that I didn't find that cave by accident. I'm positive there's a purpose to it all. I'll never stop talkin' about it. Not until people come and see for themselves. That's got to happen." He paused before adding, "It will."

Will sighed. "You've been different from the time we were kids . . . forever quoting the Bible and such. I always took your side, Lucus, when others poked fun at you. I don't know how many black eyes I wound up with to prove it. But you're a grown man now and I can't fight your battles for you any more." He hesitated for a moment. "You've always been like a brother to me, Lucus. Do you think I enjoy hearin' people call you crazy? Leave it alone, Lucus. Leave it alone."

Lucus was quiet for a moment before declaring, "I can't."

Will shrugged. "Well, I don't claim to understand it, but I guess there's no stoppin' you." He hesitated for a moment, then said, "I did run into a guy in town who's interested, though."

Lucus's face lit up. "Who?"

"A fella named Cyrus Zabez. He's heard the talk about the cave."

"Will—"

"Wait a minute. It's not the cave itself he's interested in, it's the bats."

"The bats?"

"Somethin' about bat manure. Guano, he called it. He said it's a good fertilizer and the fruit growers in California have a need for it. He told me when I see you to ask you to come to town and look him up."

"Fertilizer?"

"That's what the man said."

"I'll look him up. Thanks for tellin' me, Will."

"I just can't get through to you about this, can I, Lucus?"

"Not a chance, Will. Not a chance. As a matter of fact, I want to take time off from the ranch and go down into the cave for two or three weeks."

"Two or three weeks!"

"There's miles and miles of cave down there, Will. I've got to explore it. I plan to bring along enough supplies to keep me goin'. And every few days Honor will lower down anythin' I need."

"Lucus, that's crazy!" Will shouted.

Lucus closed his eyes for a brief moment. When he spoke again, his voice was shaky. "It's not crazy. You'll see. There's somethin' there . . . somethin'. Someday I might—" He broke off, not knowing what it was he might do someday.

Fifteen

AN UNSEASONABLE cold spell settled over Carlsbad far too late in the year. The sun remained frozen behind large gray clouds—everything was bleak. Yet the weather appealed to Honor's somber mood. Clambering up the decaying wood steps of the art gallery, she felt more in tune with the world just the way it was, having no desire for the cheerful glare of sunlight.

She burst into the small room with a sudden release of kinetic energy, taking Sophie by surprise. She found her in the midst of giving a customer a sales pitch about a painting. Honor motioned her to continue and sat down on a chair to wait.

"You're going to just love owning this picture, Mrs. Costa," Sophie said to her customer.

Mrs. Costa picked up her painting and walked to the door. "I know I will. Thank you, Sophie." She looked Honor's way. "Nice to see you, Mrs. Kant. How are your husband and son? Well, I hope."

"Yes, they are, thank you."

Sophie followed her customer to the exit. "You come again soon now," she said. "Bye-bye." She turned back to Honor with a broad smile. "Why, I haven't seen you in almost two weeks. I've been missing you. I was going to take the buggy out to the cabin today after closing to see if you were well."

"It's been nothing like that, Sophie. My health is fine."

"Well, will you have a cup of tea with me?"

"Yes. That would be nice."

"Good. Good." Sophie moved to a room adjoining the gallery where she kept a small wood-burning stove and some dishes. "I'll just be a minute," she called through the muslin curtains separating the two rooms.

"Has business been good, Sophie?"

Sophie's happy voice from behind the curtains said, "Business has been surprisingly good." She brought out two cups of tea and set them on a small birch table next to Honor, then sat down opposite her friend.

"The gallery is certainly not in the black yet," Sophie continued. "But we're getting there. I can't get over the response from the ladies in town. And quite a few of the local artists have dropped in for supplies. Do you want to see the bookkeeping ledger?"

"No, not today. Next time."

Sophie leaned back in her chair, studying Honor quietly for a moment. "You're down today," she remarked. "What's the matter?"

Honor picked up her porcelain cup, then nervously set it back down. Her face clouded, and she burst unexpectedly into tears.

Sophie leaned forward. "What is it, Honor? What's wrong? Please tell me."

Honor removed a handkerchief from her skirt pocket and wiped her eyes, containing herself. "Do you have any cigarettes around, Sophie?"

Sophie's eyes danced mischievously. "Yes . . . let's indulge." She scrambled over to the front door, locked it, and pulled down the shade. Moving to a desk, she took two cigarettes and matches from a drawer. First offering Honor a light, she lit her own, then sat down again and puffed. Billows of smoke circled above them. After a while, she asked, "Why are you so melancholy today, Honor? Is it Lucus? Has something happened?"

"Yes, it's Lucus." Honor took a long drag on the cigarette. "He hasn't been the same at all since he spent those two and a half weeks alone down in the cave. Something's happened. Lucus is completely different from the man he used to be."

"How so?"

"He won't touch me, Sophie," she said hesitantly. "He's even taken to sleeping on the ranch most nights. When he's home, all he speaks of is an experience he claims to have had while down in the cave. He said the apparition of his father appeared to him there— several times."

"Apparition?"

"Yes. I knew all along that he was holding something back. I'd felt so left out. Then he finally confided in me. Now I can only wonder if all this hasn't affected his mind."

"Couldn't you perhaps divert his interests elsewhere, Honor? I really think Lucus needs a change."

"Lucus says he must devote his life to the cave. That he's been chosen. I couldn't keep him away now. It's too late. You know, when he spoke in this vein at the beginning, about his being chosen, it sounded so romantic . . . so noble somehow. How could I know it would turn into an all-consuming obsession? That's really it, Sophie. He can't think or talk about much else." She started to cry again. "He's rational in all other things. But something's terribly wrong, Sophie."

"Oh, dear, oh, dear."

"I simply don't know what to do. I have nowhere to turn."

"Will you leave him?"

"Leave him? But how can I? Sophie, my place is with my husband—no matter what! I have no other choice. You know that."

Sophie thought for a moment, then said, "There's someone I want you to go see, Honor, someone I believe can help you. A gypsy woman. Bruja, she's called. Everyone has told me about her. I'll wager she can give you a potion for Lucus that would help. I know where she lives. I'll draw you a map."

"I don't believe in gypsies, Sophie. There must be something else I can do."

"You go see her, Honor. I've heard the most marvelous stories about her and all the people she's helped. It's worth a try, isn't it?"

Honor's voice was strained. "Yes, I suppose . . ."

The gypsy's house, more of a decaying shack than anything else, was nestled on a hill behind giant hackberry trees. Hidden behind thick branches and green leaves, the dwelling had been difficult to find even with Sophie's directions to guide her. Honor had combed the area for close to an hour in search of it; now the shadows and glow of dusk settled around her.

Honor hesitantly approached the front door, which was slightly ajar. She knocked gently and waited. When there was no answer, she timidly pushed open the door and entered, to see an old woman stirring a strange-smelling concoction brewing over hot coals. She watched the woman crumble dry leaves between wrinkled, crooked fingers and drop them into a kettle. The gypsy was seated next to a fireplace with her back to the door, so Honor couldn't see her face. She made no sign that she was aware of Honor's presence.

Honor looked about the room, absorbing its details. The floor was covered with drying leaves and roots clumped together in various-sized piles. Herbs hung in bunches from cracked beams in the ceiling. The house reeked of a pungent odor that made Honor feel nauseous.

The furniture was sparse, and what there was looked to Honor to be on the verge of falling apart. Her gaze settled on a stained calendar with 1902 printed across the top.

The old woman quickly turned her head in Honor's direction. Coal-black eyes stared out from an ancient, shriveled face. The sight of her face made Honor quake as she stood motionless, staring at her. All her features were sunken in; the gypsy had no teeth. A black satin dress covered her reed-thin frame, and a long black mantilla was draped over her small, birdlike head. She looked frail, but her voice, strong and harsh, belied her outward appearance.

"How long have you been married, *señora?*" the gypsy asked, almost accusingly.

"Why . . . it'll be two years very soon," Honor answered, moving closer to her, yet cringing beneath the old gypsy's piercing stare.

After a moment's silence the gypsy announced cryptically, "A potion might not solve your problem, *señora.*"

Honor searched the old woman's face. "You know why I'm here!" she blurted. "But how?"

The gypsy didn't answer, but turned away to reach for a worn sack from which she withdrew an assortment of small brown bags. She opened them and inspected their contents, all the while clucking her tongue and shrugging her shoulders. Then she handed Honor two small bags. "A man who has completely lost his taste for women could be beyond help. I perceive he is out of his element. One day your husband will enter a monastery. It will come to pass, *señora.*"

Honor was dumbstruck, full of disbelief. Wishing now she'd never come, she wanted to run from this place and this woman. Following some doubtful seconds her words came out in a rush. "How do I use these herbs?"

"Brew one teaspoon from each of these bags in boiling water and have him drink it. See that it's used up, *señora.* But do not expect miracles. I am called witch, not God." She turned back to the fireplace to inspect the mixture in the kettle.

Honor took some coins from her pocket and held out her palm. "Will this be enough, Bruja, for the herbs?"

The gypsy kept her gaze on the kettle. "*Sí, sí.* Put it on the table, *señora.*"

After depositing the money, Honor turned quickly to leave, but the woman's harsh voice stopped her.

"You will not escape, *señora.* A past life is fighting for recognition from you. *She* will reach out to embrace you once again. We are forever locked in a divine repetition of experience. *Her* end will be *your* end."

Honor was stunned. "What do you mean?"

"I am busy, *señora*. Good day." She continued to stir the foul-smelling brew with a long wooden spoon.

"Please t—" Honor choked back her words as she headed for the doorway. When she paused there to look back, the wizened figure in black was still crouched by the fireplace.

Honor was both puzzled and confused. The old woman and the house were shrouded in a mystery beyond her comprehension. What was she being warned of? Did it have anything to do with her feelings about the cave?

She walked outside, grateful to be out of the shack at last. A wild gust of wind swept around her, forcing Honor to pull her shawl tightly around her shoulders.

It was far into the night when Honor finally reached home, the kitchen window bright from the warm glow of kerosene. Looking in before entering, she saw Lucus seated at the kitchen table opposite a bulky, redheaded man with a long red beard. She recalled meeting this man once in town. He and Lucus were deeply engrossed in conversation.

Seated on Lucus's left was a man of about thirty whom she had never seen before. In his quiet attention to the animated discussion, he displayed a keen intelligence and intensity that caused Honor to study him. From his bronzed skin, his strong, even features, and his lustrous ebony hair, she assumed he was an Indian. Honor was struck by his cleanshaven face and the shortness of his hair, cut in the Anglo style, so unlike the long, flowing Indian fashion she had become so familiar with. His clothes were much like those of the other men. But his blue and green plaid shirt was open slightly at the throat, revealing a strong neck, and the soft fabric did little to disguise the broadness of his chest or his muscular arms. She felt slightly foolish at analyzing him so closely, then justified it to herself by saying that it was only her artistic instinct at work.

She drew her eyes away from him and sought out Elijah, who was studying his schoolbooks at the far end of the table, his young face in serious repose.

She moved quickly into the cabin, depositing the two brown bags next to the water pump at the sink.

"I was worried about you. Where have you been?" Lucus asked.

She wondered why he never worried about her whereabouts when he was away from home for days at a time. Avoiding his question, she asked, "Have you eaten? I'm sorry to be so late."

"Yes, we have. Honor, you remember Cyrus Zabez, don't you? The man interested in the guano at the caverns?"

"Yes." She held out her hand to him. "How have you been, Mr. Zabez?"

"Just fine, ma'am," he said, shaking her hand.

"And this is Clay Birdsong, Cyrus's business partner."

Clay nodded his head. "Ma'am."

As their eyes met, Honor was riveted by the penetrating, almost hypnotic stare of his coal-black eyes, challenging her. With his unflinching gaze he seemed to rip away her mask of self-composure and to assess her deepest secrets in an instant. It was as if this stranger were commanding Honor to admit a passion more compelling than she had ever experienced before. A scintillating tremor swept through her body, making her feel both excited and guilty. Honor's legs trembled almost uncontrollably, and a whirring noise vibrated in her head. As though she were speaking from some far-distant place, she heard herself responding, "Nice to meet you, Mr. Birdsong." She could not remove her large gray eyes from his. Overcome with embarrassment, she forced her attention toward Lucus.

"Come and sit with us, honey," Lucus said. "Cyrus and Mr. Birdsong here have some news for us."

Her husband's voice broke the spell, and she glided to Elijah, putting a protective arm around his thin shoulder.

"How is your schoolwork coming, dear?"

He looked up at her warmly and said, "Pretty good, Mama."

She gently kissed his small forehead, then seated herself as far as possible from the handsome Indian. "Well, what is your news?" she asked.

"Well, ma'am," Cyrus said, "like I was just telling Lucus here, my partner, Clay, and myself are finally able to begin mining the guano in the cave. It's taken some time, but our placer-mining claim to the guano and other mineral rights for twenty acres around the entrance of the cave has been approved."

"I see." Her eyes kept darting from Clay to Cyrus. She held herself rigidly, trying to remain expressionless.

"Yes . . . well," he continued, "this is our proposition to Lucus here. We'd like him to be our foreman. He's interested in the cave, and we know we can trust him to take over. Mr. Birdsong and myself will be around for quite awhile, but eventually our other business interests will take us elsewhere. We can't pay Lucus a fortune, but we can give him enough to get by on. If it goes well, we'll up his wages."

Honor grew serious. "You're sure there's a need for guano fertilizer, Mr. Zabez?"

Clay answered for him in a clear, resonant voice. "Yes, I can assure you there is. I've just recently come from California, and the fruit growers there are clamoring for it. They're willing to pay ninety dollars a ton. There is a need, Mrs. Kant."

Honor swallowed hard. There was something overpowering about this man, something that made her reluctant to really speak her mind about this matter in front of him, and she couldn't ignore it. At once she felt both ridiculous and annoyed at herself for being intimidated. She finally asked, "You'll have to blast to do that, won't you?"

"That's correct," Clay answered, his voice deep and his gaze direct.

She willed herself to look away from him to Cyrus. "Wouldn't the blasting cause damage in the caverns, Mr. Zabez?"

Cyrus looked uneasily at Clay, then replied, "Why, no, ma'am. I don't see how. The bat cave is some distance away from the cavern structures."

"I see," Honor commented again, worriedly casting a glance at Lucus. They were all suddenly quiet, as if knowing what was on her mind. She was sure this new job would rob her of Lucus's presence completely. She had to stop him.

Abruptly Cyrus pushed back his chair. "Well, we'll leave you two to talk it over. Come and see me in the morning, Lucus, and let me know what you decide. It was a pleasure seeing you again, Mrs. Kant."

She nodded. "A pleasure to have seen you, Mr. Zabez."

He walked toward the door with her husband, leaving Clay still seated at the table. Clay's jet-colored eyes hadn't left Honor's face. "I hope to have the pleasure of seeing you again, Mrs. Kant." His eyes suddenly filled with amusement as he stood up.

Honor stared back at him uneasily. "Yes. I hope so." She was greatly relieved when he turned his back. But as he was leaving, Honor could not help noticing his narrow hips and long, strong legs encased in soft brown leather pants. She wondered what in the world had gotten into her, about his magnetic attraction.

"I'll see you in the morning," Lucus called. "Good night." He closed the rough-hewn door and turned back to Honor, a puzzled expression on his face.

She averted her gaze to Elijah. "Get ready for bed, darling. Morning will be here before you know it."

Elijah closed his schoolbook and got up, walking over to his mother and kissing her sweetly on the cheek. "Good night, Mama."

"Good night, Elijah." To disguise her anxiety, she hastily removed the soiled dishes and busily began washing them at the sink, aware that Lucus had not been distracted by her movements.

"What's the matter, Honor? Don't you want me to do this?"

"I don't understand why you *want* to do it."

"You don't understand? Darlin', you of all people should. It'll keep me where I want to be . . . at the cave. And once people get to workin' there, I know I can interest them in going farther in and seein' it all. You never know where this can lead." After a pause, he said with new resolve, "I want to do it, Honor."

Honor abandoned the dishes and dried her hands with a towel, her tongue nervously tracing her upper lip. She thought carefully for a moment, then, folding her arms across her breasts, turned to face him.

"How can you allow yourself to play a part in turning the caverns into a money-making operation?" she demanded, her voice shrill.

"Cyrus will do it with or without me," he said defensively. "At least if I'm there I can watch over things."

"I thought the reason we came to Carlsbad was so you wouldn't have to work for wages any more. That's the reason you bought into Will's ranch, isn't it?" Lucus didn't respond, so she kept on, the pitch of her voice rising further. "What about the ranch, Lucus? What happens there if you become foreman of this mining operation?"

He cleared his throat. "I knew this opportunity might be coming. I've already talked to Will. He has someone who will buy out my share." He waited for her to digest this new information. "I really want to do this, Honor."

She couldn't contain herself any longer, lashing out at him in anger. "We'll never see you. All you live for now is that cave. If you work there, you'll never tear yourself away at all!"

"Honor," Lucus pleaded, "I thought you understood."

"No," she shouted, "I don't understand! I don't understand anything about you any more!"

They were both suddenly quiet, the air throbbing and heavy between them. Honor sat down at the table, her shoulders slumping in defeat. She felt him come close to her, put his arms around her, and rest his bristly chin on her head.

"This is important to me, Honor. I want to do it."

She turned into his searching embrace, wrapping her arms around his waist and burying her face in his flat stomach. After a few moments she lifted her face to his. "Lucus," she whispered. "Lucus, I—"

He interrupted her words by pulling away, quickly walking to the other side of the table as though to place a defensive barrier between them.

A tightness creased her chest, strangling her breathing. "We can't go on this way. We just can't." Her voice was strained, sounding alien to her ears.

"Honor, please don't."

"Don't what? Talk to me about it, Lucus. Please talk to me."

She watched him stare helplessly at her, then turn to stride across the room. She jumped up, yelling, "Don't walk out! Please, Lucus. Pl—" He was gone, slamming the door behind him.

Sixteen

HONOR SPENT a restless night, finally falling into a fitful sleep in the early hours of dawn, and did not awaken until after the noon hour. When she opened her eyes, she was sluggish and irritated, shiver-

ing with the memory of that one recurring nightmare of plummeting into endless darkness.

It was the first time in a very long while that this
dream had returned to haunt her. She wondered if
she'd ever be completely free of it.

Elijah was nowhere to be found, which increased
her terror until she remembered he was off fishing with
a friend. Suddenly faced with the reality that Elijah
was growing away from her with his own interests,
she felt lost and despondent.

She'd been right about the mining operation's robbing her of Lucus completely. In the three months
that the guano mining had been working, he'd only
slept home twice. She sighed deeply, not being able
to bear thinking about it any more.

She ate breakfast listlessly, pushing eggs from one
side of the blue-edged plate to the other. Realizing
she would never finish the meal, Honor left the food
where it was, to pick up a shirt that needed mending,
only to drop it back in the sewing basket. The lonely
day stretched out before her. Frankly angry at the
prospect of this today, she paced the kitchen, unable
to sit. She still hadn't dressed, and her nightgown
clung damply to her body.

She wandered into the bedroom, moving to the pine
closet that housed her clothing. Opening the doors, she
ran her hands over the garments she'd brought with
her from New York, fondling the green chiffon prin-
cess gown; the blue broadcloth Eton suit trimmed with
folds of matching velvet; the peach satin evening
gown decorated with lace and velvet ribbon; the in-
door dress made of London smoke cloth, embroidered
with silk braid; the gown of primrose faille with its
white satin collar and cuffs; and more. She had a sudden desire to put something pretty on, but just as
quickly lost the impulse. There was no longer any
place to go, nor any reason to dress fashionably. She
was wasting away, she thought.

How incongruous it seemed to her that all that
money Gilly had so kindly left her was sitting in a

bank gathering dust while she lived such a bleak life. She could travel with that money. Could do anything, really. She thought about that for a moment, knowing it wouldn't be any fun to travel alone. True, Elijah would enjoy it with her. But that wouldn't be the same as sharing it with her husband, and that was impossible now.

She sighed heavily, knowing she should get out of the cabin. But where would she go? And to do what? Unlike Santa Fe, Carlsbad was indeed limited by what it had to offer in the way of diversion. She supposed she could drop in on Sophie at the art gallery but decided against it. She'd just be in Sophie's way; she wasn't really needed there. Her gaze fell on a drawing pad lying on a small corner table. Why not go out and find someone interesting to sketch? she asked herself. She hadn't drawn in weeks. She considered that idea for a moment but decided against it, too. The faces of Carlsbad weren't as interesting to Honor as they had been in Santa Fe. They all seemed to blend together in a nondescript way. Everyone looked alike to her.

The caverns flashed through her mind. They would be lovely to draw, she thought. She froze for a moment, that familiar chill going through her. Could she face the cave again and that bewildering fright? No . . . yes! She wouldn't give in to fear. Besides, anything was better than facing another solitary day in the cabin.

Moving to her dresser, she pulled a pair of men's dark blue pants from a drawer together with a white, starched shirtwaist top. Anxious to leave before she changed her mind, she dressed quickly. Making a brief survey of her attire in the mirror, she caught her thick blonde locks at the nape of the neck, holding them in place with a red print bandana. Then, loading up a knapsack, she secured a large pad under her arm. Juggling a kerosene lamp and a jacket with her free hand, she rushed out into the blinding sunlight, filled with a fixed determination.

She hitched a horse to the buggy and placed the sack and sketch pad on the seat next to her. Sharply snapping the reins, she called out, "Come on, boy. Let's go."

She jostled along, her thoughts running wildly together. She questioned if she was going to the cave not just to sketch, but to see Lucus. Well, after all, what would be wrong in that? Lucus *was* her husband. Of course she wanted to see him.

She thought back to how much Lucus had been in love with her, and how afraid she'd been of marrying him and not returning his love. Was that what had happened? Had she been right, that liking him and respecting him were not enough? She convinced herself that she'd failed him. Why else would he be deserting her now?

Yet she had seen marriages of convenience flourishing all around her, apparently unaware that something was missing. *Something* . . . that magic, illusive ingredient called love. It was the one element she couldn't feel for Lucus. Perhaps if I'd given him a child, she told herself, it would have made a difference . . .

Approaching the vicinity of the cave, she urged the horse to stop. She put the knapsack on and grabbed her pad, then got down and tied the horse's reins to a tree. Climbing to the top of a hill near the cave entrance, Honor stood there motionless, studying the men at work. This place had robbed her of her husband. She fervently wished the caverns had never come into their lives. Reflecting on that, Honor realized she could never sustain her feeling of resentfulness, for she clearly believed the hand of God had truly touched the cave.

She grimaced to see a shaft sunk not far from the front, yet moved closer in to watch the flurry of activity taking place. Fury at the workmen and the whole operation overcame her. The shaft was offensive, the caverns now desecrated. Couldn't Lucus see this?

She stepped even nearer to see miniature cars,

running on rails constructed of two two-by-fours, being drawn to the bottom of the bat cave by the utilization of an old wagon axle. Below, the guano was being shoveled into bulky gunnysacks, sewed up, and then loaded into the cars. Later the sacks were transferred into a large iron bucket and cranked to the surface by a revolving gasoline winch.

Mules shuffled their hooves impatiently, standing in readiness to haul loaded wagons to the Carlsbad freight yard. The choking stench of bat guano hung heavily in the hot summer air.

In search of Lucus, she approached the workmen but didn't see him anywhere. Everyone was too absorbed in the work at hand to take notice of her arrival. Except one man. Before her stood Clay Birdsong, bare to the waist, his taut muscles gleaming with perspiration.

She could feel her face flush as his eyes roamed from her face and honey-blonde hair to the pants covering her long limbs. She froze, self-conscious under his gaze, completely embarrassed at his open appraisal of her. Looking around awkwardly, she cleared her throat before asking him, "Where would I find Mr. Kant?"

He walked up to her, so close she could smell the sweat emanating from his body.

"He's at the bottom of the shaft." His voice sounded amused. "It's the first time I've seen you here."

Summoning courage, she said, "It's the first time I've ventured here since the mining operation began."

"How have you been?" he asked gently, while his eyes glinted with another, unspoken question.

Honor was choking with sexual excitement. She wanted to run her hands over his straining muscles, to feel his body pressed to hers, his full lips touching her own . . . She attempted to check herself as a warm throbbing moved up along her inner thighs. Was she going crazy? She hardly knew this man. She glanced at her feet impatiently. "I've been fine," she answered awkwardly, denying the truth.

"I don't remember your first name. I'm sorry."

"It's Honor."

"Mine is——"

"I know. Clay."

His eyes filled with laughter, mocking her. "You have a good memory."

She was having trouble breathing. "Yes, I expect I do." She paused. "I must find my husband," she said aimlessly, wanting to move away from him and yet finding herself frozen to the spot where she stood.

Cyrus Zabez spoke without warning behind her. "Mrs. Kant, nice to see you. It's been a long time."

She spun around to face him, grateful for the intrusion. "It *has* been a long time. I hardly recognize this place." Smiling wanly, she added, "You've been busy."

"Yes, ma'am, we've been busy, all right."

"Excuse me," Honor said, "both of you." She walked to the edge of the shaft, stark confusion muddling her mind. She looked down, relieved to see Lucus at last.

He glanced up, surprise flooding his face. "Are you coming down?" he called.

"Yes."

"I'll send up the iron bucket. You can come down in that."

Regarding the makeshift ladder still hanging from Lucus's first descent, she asked, "Couldn't I use this?"

"The bucket is safer. Wait a minute."

When the iron bucket reached the top, she stood back—uncertain. Unexpectedly, Clay Birdsong was there in an instant and in one easy swoop had lifted her into it. He moved aside, openly staring at her, his black eyes glistening. Startled and speechless, Honor was grateful when the crank went into motion, causing her descent. At the bottom she hastily climbed out, relieved to be away from the Indian's powerful attraction, though realizing that because of him she'd completely forgotten her fear of going down.

To Lucus she said, "I'm going into the chambers

for a while." She put her gear on the damp earth for a moment in order to don her jacket and light her lamp.

"Fine. I'll look for you when I finish here."

Once organized, she walked away from him and moved down the passageway, the noise from the shaft filling the stillness with its endless din. She could hear the flat cars running back and forth as well as Lucus' voice echoing down the tunnel, directing orders to the workmen.

She moved further inside, clutching the sketch pad and holding the lamp in front of her. The noise gradually faded, until she was wrapped in a hushed tranquility. She found a comfortable place and sat down, adjusting the kerosene light in a position to throw off the best illuminating rays.

Taking off her sack for better comfort, she took out a pencil and looked around. An onyx sculpture closely resembling draperies swept across a wall, catching her attention. She studied them thoughtfully before beginning.

For a moment the stone curtains blurred. All she could see was Clay Birdsong's staring face. She was keenly aware that he'd aroused feelings in her that she found astonishing; she hadn't thought she could feel such an intense sexual attraction for a man ever again. It had been so long . . . He seemed different from most of the Indians and other people in Carlsbad with whom she'd come in contact. There was something very well educated in his manner of speech.

Irritated with her thoughts, she pushed his image aside and began to draw. Page after page of the sketch pad became filled with swirling designs. Eruptions bursting from the ground found their likeness on paper. She experienced an elation so keen, she lost track of time. When she ran out of blank spaces in the pad, she stopped, picking the drawings up to examine them.

Had she really done these? she marveled. She felt disconnected from them somehow, as though the sketches had nothing to do with her. How strange, she thought. She studied each drawing, then altered shadings and added detail, losing herself in her own private world. The only reality was the sharp strokes of her pencil.

She stopped working suddenly and looked around. The base of her spine was cold and she shivered instinctively. A strange sensation flooded over her as she became aware of feeling closed in—buried, almost. She decided she'd been down here alone for too long. A deep voice startled her out of her solitude.

"Mrs. Kant."

Looking around, she saw Clay Birdsong standing in the aperture near her. She watched him move toward her, noticing the ripple of muscles in his arms and chest. His thighs emanated strength, almost bursting out from his mud-encrusted pants.

He squatted down next to her and picked up her sketches. "These are really good."

She studied him, the faint light casting a thin shadow under his high cheekbones, giving his bronze skin a tawny look. For the third time since they'd met she found herself overwhelmed by his startling good looks.

"What are you going to do with them?" he asked.

"Do with what?"

He laughed. "Your sketches."

She was having trouble concentrating. She forced herself to look away from him and back at the open pad. "I'll probably redo them in oils and sell them at my art gallery."

"Your art gallery?"

"Yes. My friend and I own the Carlsbad Art Gallery in town."

He nodded, staring down at the rapidly executed pictures.

Honor's hands moved over the pages, touching them gingerly. She felt a great sense of awe from the creation of these images. To her amazement the stone sculptures of the cave came alive on the paper. Her attention drifted back to Clay, with whom she was embarrassed at being alone. Guardedly, Honor looked into his face. "What are you doing here?"

"I was curious to see what you were doing down here by yourself. Do you mind?" He smiled.

"No, I don't mind." She averted her gaze to the ground, unable to continue looking directly at him. "You don't seem like an Indian," she blurted. Her face reddened. What had made her say such an outrageous thing?

He burst into a roaring laugh. "I guess that's because I'm just half Indian. My mother was white." He paused. "Do you always say the first thing that comes into your head?"

"Not always." She glanced around, groping for an excuse to leave without offending him. She had to get away from him, unable to bear for another moment the electricity sparking the air between them. She got to her feet, jumping when he reached out to touch her hair.

"I've never seen blonde hair like yours," he said. He paused before asking gently, "Are you afraid of me?"

Straightening her back, she looked directly at him. "Why should I be?"

"Because I want you, and I have the strong impression that you feel the same."

She gasped, her large gray eyes widening with shock. Men never came right out and said this. He was awful. Falling prey to her first instinct, she raised her slender hand to slap him, only to be grabbed tightly by the wrist.

With a quick movement he pulled her to him, his rib cage crushing into hers. He put his mouth to her ear, whispering, "You're a beautiful woman. One doesn't see your kind of beauty very often."

"Please let me go," she murmured, her voice barely audible. "Please." She fought her shivers of pleasure, but they continued to dance up and down her spine;

she closed her eyes, feeling faint. She knew that if he took her at this very moment, she would not resist.

He laughed, gently releasing her. "Someday, Mrs. Honor Kant. Someday."

Ineffectually covering up her feelings, she raised her chin defiantly. "You're very sure of yourself, aren't you?"

"Yes, I am," he replied with calm authority.

"Y——" She was cut off by Lucus's voice.

"Are you ready to leave now, Honor?"

"Lucus," she cried in sheer relief, wondering how much he had seen. "Yes, I'm ready." She quickly bent to gather up her drawings.

Clay sauntered over to her husband. "Howdy, Lucus. I was just on my way." Pausing, he turned back to Honor. "Nice to have seen you again, ma'am."

She watched him leave, surprised to realize she was truly sorry to see him go, and again was consumed with a longing to have his body close to hers. She felt feverish.

"Was he bothering you, Honor?"

"No, Lucus, he wasn't," she lied. "Let's go now. Let's just please go."

"Why don't we go home tonight? It seems such a long time since we've shared a hot meal together." He paused, his forehead creasing in a worried frown. "I've been so wrapped up here . . ." His voice trailed off.

Honor's eyes widened. Perceptively, she sensed his suggestion had something to do with Clay Birdsong's presence. She shrugged. "Of course. Elijah went fishing today. I'm sure there's a fresh catch waiting. Let's go home."

"What do you think of these paintings, Sophie?" Honor squirmed anxiously in her chair.

"I've never seen you so excited about your work, Honor," Sophie laughed. "Give me a chance to look at them." Her plump hands moved over the canvases, her hazel eyes scrutinizing them carefully. She finally set them down and leaned back in her chair.

"Well?" Honor demanded. "Tell me *something* about them."

"These are terribly good, Honor. I'm sure they'll sell. People are beginning to get very curious about what the caverns look like."

"They're different from anything I've ever done before. I want to do more of the caverns sometime."

Sophie looked at the oils again. "I've never gone there, but I expect you've captured them authentically. There's such an eerie, almost depressed quality about your paintings. Is that the way you see the caverns, Honor?"

"Not entirely. There is something mystical and spiritually uplifting about the place, Sophie. You can actually feel the hand of God down there. Except . . . except when you've spent a lot of time there alone—you feel as if you won't ever get out alive." Her voice grew intense. "The outside world diminishes. It's almost like a stone coffin. I expect that's what I communicate in my paintings. It's an indefinable feeling, but it's there."

"How depressing," Sophie exclaimed.

Honor laughed, breaking the tension. "Let's talk about something else."

"Yes, for goodness' sake, let's."

A considerable silence ensued until Honor suddenly asked, "What do you know about Clay Birdsong?"

Sophie looked at her in surprise. "You mean the half-breed who's Cyrus Zabez's partner in the guano operation?"

"Yes," Honor said, "that's the one. I know you hear all sorts of gossip when people pass through the gallery. You must have heard something about him."

"Why, yes, as a matter of fact, I have. Mrs. Costa was in just the other day telling me all about him. Mr. Costa apparently struck up an acquaintance with him, and he's been to their home several times. I've never seen him myself, but she tells me he's really quite a fascinating man. And extremely handsome."

"Well?" Honor prodded her impatiently. "Is that all?"

Sophie thought deeply for several moments. "Let me see. She told me that his father was a Mescalero Apache . . . a chief of his tribe. His mother was white. It seems his mother was kidnapped as a young girl and forcibly dragged to a Mescalero campground up north. She was forced into marriage with the chief and became pregnant with Clay. But she made a grand escape when Clay was a young boy, taking him to California and seeing to it he had a white man's education. I'm also told he became quite an astute businessman when he grew up, having his finger in more than one enterprise. I believe he has, among other things, an interest in a cattle ranch in Santa Fe." She paused for a moment. "Yes, that's it. Santa Fe."

Honor stared dreamily out of the window. "I knew there was something different about him. I sensed it." She glanced back at Sophie, flushing as her friend scrutinized her sharply.

"What's this sudden interest in Clay Birdsong, Honor?"

"Nothing special," she lied. "I just met him a couple of times and wondered about him."

"You're not going to look for any trouble, are you, Honor?" Sophie shook her head half reproachfully. "It seems to me you've got enough problems to cope with right now."

Honor looked at her guardedly. "I know you're a good friend, Sophie. Please don't worry about me. I'm able to handle my life."

"Are you?"

Honor remained silent.

"Honor?"

"Yes?"

"You've never told me whether or not you gave Lucus Bruja's potion. Did you?"

"Lucus hasn't been home long enough for me to find an opportunity to give it to him. It's hopeless."

"I'm sorry, Honor. I really am."

"I must leave now. Elijah will be out of school in half an hour, and I thought I would meet him so we could ride home together on my horse. His is at the blacksmith's for new shoes." She paused at the door, turning back to Sophie. "The gypsy warned me of something. It was all so strange."

Sophie's eyes widened with interest. "What was that?"

"She said I would not escape . . . that a past life experience would reach out to embrace me once again. She said *her* end will be *my* end. It's been haunting me. Do you believe it could be true, Sophie?"

"Horsefeathers," Sophie chortled. "You shouldn't let anything like that upset you. Bruja is an old woman, filled with superstitious nonsense," she added.

"You didn't think her potions were nonsense." Honor started out again, but Sophie's voice stopped her.

"Are you going to the town picnic on Sunday?"

"Yes, I was planning on it."

"Good. I'll see you there, then."

Honor climbed down the creaking gallery steps, forcing the gypsy's image from her mind and wondering, despite herself, if Clay Birdsong would be at the picnic, too.

Honor sat sideways on the saddle with Elijah behind her, his short arms stretched around her waist. The horse bounced beneath them as Honor juggled the reins. "Did you enjoy school today, Elijah?" she asked.

"Yes, Mama. But school seems such a waste of time. I would rather work with Father at the cave."

She turned her head to look at her son with surprise. "You need an education, Elijah. You're not even nine years old yet. There's time enough when you're grown to work for a living."

"Father used to let me help him with chores at the ranch. But when I visit him at the cave, he refuses to let me do anything. Why can't I help him sometimes now also?"

"There could be danger for a young boy working at the cave. It's a man's job, Elijah."

"Why is Father away so much?"

"The mining operation demands a lot of his time. He's needed there."

"We need him, too, don't we?"

"Yes, Elijah, we do."

"Mama?"

"Yes, darling?"

"What happened to my real father?"

Honor abruptly pulled on the reins, forcing the horse to a halt. Elijah had never asked about his true parentage before. She didn't know quite how to answer him. She looked around at him, finally saying, "Your real father is dead, darling." She was stung to see disappointment in his eyes.

"What was he like?"

"He was nice. A kind, gentle person. You would have liked him." She started visibly when she noticed his large dark eyes filling with tears. "Elijah, don't." She put her arm around him and stroked his thick, gleaming hair.

"I just wish I could have known him, Mama."

"I know, darling. I know. I wish you could have, too."

Elijah wiped his eyes with the back of his hands, his young face grave. "Well, Lucus is like my real father, isn't he?"

"Yes, he is." Suddenly Honor was furious with Lucus. Furious at everything that had brought them to Carlsbad and at this unhappy turn of affairs that left Elijah fatherless and herself without the comfort of a real husband. She had to swallow hard before she could speak again. "Are you all right now, Elijah?"

"Yes."

They continued their ride home in brooding silence. When they reached the cabin and dismounted, Honor turned to her son. "Next week, when school lets out for the summer, would you like to go to New York and visit Cousin Drew for a while?"

Elijah's eyes grew wide. "The one who writes you letters and owns a theater there?"

"Yes, that's him. He told me a long time ago that he'd be happy to have you visit him when you were old enough to make the trip alone."

"Am I old enough now?"

"I think so. It would be a wonderful adventure for you, darling. I could cable Drew tomorrow."

Elijah's dark eyes were thoughtful as he exclaimed, "I would miss you, Mama!"

"I would miss you, too."

Elijah suddenly clapped his hands together excitedly. "I would love to go. What fun!" He ran for the cabin door, pausing to turn back to her. "Are you making chicken for the town picnic, Mama?"

She laughed, deeply relieved to have diverted his thoughts away from Lucus. "Yes, I'll make chicken. Tomorrow you can help me." She moved toward him and reached for his hand, and they entered the empty cabin together.

Clay Birdsong stood in front of the Carlsbad Art Gallery, analyzing its appearance and location, trying to determine its success before going in. Unable to reach a conclusion, he leaped over the steps in a single, easy bound with his long legs. As Clay opened the door a bell jangled over his head, summoning a friendly-faced woman from the rear of the gallery.

Sophie parted the curtains and looked out. "I'll just be a minute. Make yourself comfortable."

"Thank you," Clay answered. His gaze slowly traveled over the paintings hanging on the walls, finally settling on a display of oils depicting the caverns. He walked closer to study them more intently.

He remembered how Honor had looked when he'd found her making the preliminary sketches. How alive her face had been with the excitement of creation; her luminous gray eyes concentrating on the subject, yet sparkling with delight. She'd seemed burning with an inner light, existing on some high, foreign plane. She'd overwhelmed him.

Sophie waddled up behind him, interrupting his thoughts. "They're good, don't you think?"

"They're excellent." He turned around to face her. "I know the artist."

"Do you?"

"Yes. Her husband works for me at the caverns."

Sophie's eyes widened. "So, you're Clay Birdsong."

"Yes, I am."

"Well, well. How nice to meet you. My name is Sophie Long."

He smiled warmly, revealing even white teeth. "A pleasure."

"I've heard so much about you, Mr. Birdsong."

He looked at her with interest. "From Mrs. Kant?"

Sophie hesitated shrewdly. "Well . . . actually from Mrs. Costa."

"Mrs. Costa? Yes, I'm acquainted with her husband. I've been to their home."

She cocked her head sideways. "Were you interested in purchasing a painting, Mr. Birdsong?"

"Yes." He pointed to one showing stalagmites reaching high into the air, alive with orange and yellow highlights. "How much is that?"

"Why, that one sells for seven dollars."

"I'll buy it," he said firmly, without hesitation.

"Fine. Fine." She stared at him curiously for a moment. "I'll get it down for you."

Clay watched Sophie gingerly remove the painting from the wall and carry it to a desk. As she began wrapping it in brown paper he said, "I understand that Mrs. Kant owns this gallery with you."

"Yes," she answered. "That's right."

"She's a talented artist. These paintings of the caverns are the finest oils I've ever seen."

"Honor is very good and getting better all the time," Sophie agreed. "That's how we got started with the idea of opening a gallery in the first place."

"You're close friends, I take it."

"We surely are. Honor is a marvelous person."

"Yes, I think so, too." He self-consciously averted his gaze to another painting on the wall. "She seems so," he added.

After a moment Sophie asked, "Is there anything else you'd like to see, Mr. Birdsong?"

"No. Not today." He reached into his pocket and withdrew a wad of bills, peeling off seven dollars.

Sophie took the money and handed him the wrapped painting. "Honor will be so pleased you bought this painting. It's the first one to go of the caverns."

"Are there other paintings of hers here?"

"No, not any more. They were sold long ago. But we have some lovely paintings from other local artists for sale."

He nodded, carefully placing the picture under his left arm. Reluctant to leave just yet, he stood hesitantly before her.

Seeing that something was on his mind, Sophie asked, "Would you like to have a cup of tea with me, Mr. Birdsong?"

Relieved, he smiled broadly. "Yes, I would. Thank you."

"Fine. Sit down and I'll bring it out." She moved to the curtained-off room in the rear of the gallery.

Clay leaned the newly acquired painting against the chair next to him and tried to make himself comfortable in the small chair. He needed to learn something from this woman and hoped she'd talk freely with him.

In a few moments Sophie returned, carrying a teapot and cups on a tray. She placed the tray on the table to one side of him. Smoothing the back of her indigo skirt, prior to seating herself, Sophie leaned slightly forward to pour tea, then asked attentively, "How do you find Carlsbad, Mr. Birdsong?"

"It's a nice enough town, I suppose. I probably won't be here long, though."

"Oh, are you planning on leaving?"

"I have several business interests in California. Before long I'll have to go there and see to them."

"What about the caverns? You are part owner of them, aren't you?"

"Yes. But we have the operation running smoothly. And Lucus is a good foreman. I don't imagine there's any reason for me to oversee the project much longer."

Sophie sipped the steaming tea cautiously. "It must be nice to be able to travel around. I was born and raised here. I've never been too far away from Carlsbad."

Clay downed the tea rapidly and looked directly at her. "Would you think me rude if I asked a personal question?"

"Why, no. Go right ahead."

"Lucus Kant and Honor don't have a very good marriage, do they?"

Sophie leaned back in her chair, studying him with renewed interest. "What makes you say that, Mr. Birdsong?"

"For one thing, Lucus spends all his time at the caverns. Even sleeps down there at night. It hardly seems like a close marriage."

Sophie carefully rested her teacup and saucer on the table, her thoughts speeding forward. "Do you have a personal interest in this, Mr. Birdsong?"

"Perhaps. Would you think it terrible of me if I did?"

"No, I wouldn't. It's just that . . . well . . . Honor has enough problems. I would hate to see her life any more complicated than it already is."

"Then the marriage is in trouble?"

"Well, Mr. Birdsong," Sophie replied slowly, "I suppose Honor is the only one who can honestly answer that. Perhaps you should ask her yourself."

"I believe I will." He stood up. "Thank you for your hospitality, Sophie. I'm sure I'll be seeing you again." He reached down for the picture.

"I'll see you to the door."

At the door, Clay turned to look at her. "Goodbye for now, Sophie Long."

"Bye-bye now, Mr. Birdsong," she said, grinning, then felt a swift pang of guilt for encouraging something that could only bring trouble.

Clay strode down the street toward his hotel, thinking about Sophie's reticence in answering questions concerning Honor's marriage. Just as it should be, he realized. After all, they were friends. Yes, he mused, Honor is surely the only one who can answer any questions about how things were between her and Lucus. He wondered for a moment why he was jumping headlong into this thing with Honor. It was as if he were compelled; there was no getting away from it.

He tried to reason himself out of it. After all, he told himself, Honor *was* married. Lucus could spend the rest of his life sleeping in that cave, and that still would not alter the fact that Honor was his wife and not free. Why was he looking for problems? There were plenty of single women around. All available. But he wanted Honor. Badly. The first time he'd laid eyes on her, he'd known he had to have her. There was something different about that woman, he decided. Very different indeed.

He sighed as he entered his hotel, wondering where his actions would lead him, for he was determined to do something about his feelings for Honor. He wished he could brush them aside, but he knew he was powerless in their grip.

Honor smoothed away the creases from the red-checked blanket as she spread it on the grass. Placing a full picnic basket behind her, she watched Elijah playing baseball off in the distance with his class-mates and some of their fathers. Returning to the task of putting out the food, she noticed Sophie waddling toward her.

"Honor, how good to see you. I've got news for you," Sophie gasped breathlessly. She squatted down next to Honor on the wool blanket.

Honor smiled. "Well, tell me. What is it?"

"You'll never guess," Sophie squealed. "I sold one of your paintings of the caverns yesterday to none other than Clay Birdsong. Aren't you pleased?"

"Clay?"

"Yes. He said your oils were the finest he'd ever seen." Sophie paused briefly before continuing. "I must say his good looks have not been exaggerated. He is really the most handsome thing." She giggled, her face flushing. "He—" She broke off and leaned forward, whispering, "Why, here he comes now. Right in our direction."

As Honor watched Clay stride toward them, she felt a tightness constrict her chest. He was wearing a white, long-sleeved shirt with light blue and navy stripes, a black vest, and a black silk cravat tied around his collar. His trousers were also black, and he was carrying a matching jacket over his arm. High black boots reached up to his knees. But Honor could not take her eyes away from the blue highlights in his ebony hair that were brought out by the bright sun and which danced as a soft breeze swept about his head.

He looked exceedingly attractive, she thought—so clean and shining. When he was next to them, she looked up, hoping her face didn't betray the impact he had on her. He smiled down at her with that ever-present amusement in his eyes she remembered so well from their first meeting.

"Howdy, Mrs. Kant. Sophie. Can I join the two of you on your blanket?"

Honor looked at Sophie, then back at Clay. "Why, of course." She moved to make room for him, freezing when he squatted in Indian style beside her, his body a fraction of an inch away from hers.

"It's a nice day for a picnic, isn't it, ladies?"

"It certainly is. Summer has come quickly this year," Sophie responded, darting her eyes from him to her friend.

Honor averted her gaze to her cotton skirt, smoothing out the pleats in the gingham. "I understand you purchased one of my paintings yesterday, Mr. Birdsong. Thank you."

"Thank *you*," Clay said. "I'm proud to own it. You've really captured the loneliness of the caverns in your work. I could see that the day you made your first sketches."

"You saw Honor's first sketches?" Sophie intertupted him.

"Yes, I did. And I was mighty impressed." He smiled, looking away in the direction of the baseball field. "Is your son here today, Mrs. Kant?"

"Yes." She pointed to Elijah, who at that moment was jumping up and down with excitement. "That's Elijah . . . There."

"You know, he wanders over to the cave every now and again. I've spoken to him a bit. He's very interested in learning about Indian culture. He's bright, that boy. And very mature for his age. I like him." He turned to Honor. "He looks like you, despite the fact you're so fair."

Honor could feel heat creeping into her neck. Her voice was hesitant when she spoke again, deliberately changing the subject. "Have you spent time down in the caverns, Mr. Birdsong? Away from the mining operation?"

"Some. Lucus took a group of us on a tour one day." He glanced around the crowded picnic grounds. "Where is Lucus?"

"He didn't come," Honor said. "He thought today would be a good opportunity to do some exploring."

Clay leaned closer to her. "If you were my wife, I wouldn't leave you alone so much."

Her gray eyes flashed at him with anger. "Well, I'm not your wife. And it's really none of your business, is it?"

He laughed, exasperating her. "You've got a temper, haven't you? Why do I always make you angry?"

Honor resisted the urge to slap him across one of his deeply tanned cheeks. His arrogance in speaking freely to her about private matters irked her terribly, especially when she knew it would be so easy to tell him everything.

Sophie got to her feet, saying diplomatically, "I must attend to some errands. You'll both excuse me, won't you?"

Honor looked at her pleadingly. "Do you have to leave right now?"

"Yes . . . yes. I'll see you all later. Very nice to have seen you again, Mr. Birdsong. Please come and visit our gallery again soon."

Honor fervently wished Sophie hadn't left. She was afraid to be alone with Clay, to say or do something she shouldn't.

"Let's take a walk down by the creek, shall we?" Clay suggested.

Honor looked around, searching for an excuse not to go, feeling confused, wondering what people would say if they saw her spending too much time with Clay. Unable to find an alternative, she decided she would have to risk possible gossip and not worry about it. She jumped up and straightened her white bonnet. In any case, a stroll was better than having to sit so close to him. "Yes, let's."

They walked in silence, the din of the crowd gradually fading in the distance. When they reached the shallow creek, Honor looked down at the muddy water gently splashing against large rocks. She felt shy with Clay, at a loss for words, so she concentrated on the babbling water instead.

After a time Clay spoke. "Let's sit down for a while." He spread his dark jacket on the ground, throwing himself down on it. Grabbing hold of her

slim hand, he pulled her down next to him. "I'm
sorry I upset you, Honor. I really don't mean to."

She glanced at him quickly. Was he mocking her?
"You don't upset me."

"Yes, I do. I behaved badly the other day. It's not
really the way I want it between us."

Honor stiffened, anger suffusing her. "What makes
you think there can be anything between us, Mr. Birdsong?"

"I wish you'd call me Clay. And there *is* something
between us. You know there is." He turned away to
stare into the brown water. For just a moment he
looked dejected. "I haven't been able to get you out
of my mind since that first night. You've been in my
thoughts constantly."

Her anger subsiding, Honor studied the lines of his
strong profile. The sun, reflecting off his bronze skin
and high cheekbones, filled her with aesthetic respon-
siveness. She felt tempted to reach out and trace
his full, beautifully shaped lips with her fingertips.
Looking away, she said, "I'm a married woman."
Her manner was suddenly diffident, her reserve
diminished. Lowering her eyes, she added, "You
really must stop pursuing me."

He turned to her, his jet-colored eyes flashing. "How
married are you? I know your husband is never home.
Many a morning I go to work and find that he's spent
the night down in the cave. What kind of a man would
devote himself to a cave . . . when he has a woman
like you at home waiting for him?"

Honor found herself furiously defending her husband. "Lucus can't help himself. Something about the
cave drives him. He really believes God has chosen
him to bring people down there. Lucus is convinced
there's a great significance about the cave. Something more than meets the eye."

"What about you?" Clay asked. "Do you believe
that, too?"

"I don't know." She shrugged her shoulders dejectedly. "Whatever man touches, he seems to ruin.

To me the cave symbolizes something perfect in an imperfect world. Perhaps Lucus *has* been chosen."

"Where does this leave you, Honor? How do you fit into all this? Do you find it fulfilling to sit home all by yourself? Is that really the way you want to spend the rest of your life? You're a beautiful, talented woman, and there's a whole world out there waiting for you. It seems such a waste."

She jumped up, on the defensive again. "You have no right to question me this way. No right at all. Please . . . let me be. Why, we hardly know each other. You can't barge into my life this way. This is all really none of your business."

Reaching up, he easily dragged her back with his heavily muscled arm. "It is my business. At least I'm going to make it my business." He looked into her gray eyes framed with lush lashes, his expression softening. "All right. Let's not fight. Let's just talk."

Still shaken, she sucked in her breath, blinking back tears. "What do you want to talk about?"

"You. Tell me about yourself."

"I'm not sure what you want to hear."

"Well, for starters, how did you come to live in New Mexico? You're not a native, are you? Your accent is different from most of the people in these parts."

Glancing at his intent face, she felt his interest and slowly began to relax. "You're right. I'm not from around here. I'm a New Yorker. I met Lucus there when he was on a visit. He asked me to follow him to Santa Fe to be married, and I did. Then . . . Carlsbad. We've been married for two years."

"Then your son is not Lucus's?"

"No, he's not."

"What was your first marriage like?"

She was quiet for a moment, then raised her chin defiantly. "I wasn't married before. Does that shock you?"

He laughed. "No. There's not much that could surprise me in this world."

In an effort to take him off guard as he had done

to her, Honor bluntly asked, "Is it true that your mother was kidnapped and forced into marriage with your father?"

He looked at her in amazement. "It's true that she was kidnapped, but I don't believe there ever was a legal marriage." After a long pause, he said, "In a way, we have more in common than you think." He smiled at her, pleased. "You've been asking questions about me. What else did you find out?"

She flushed, knowing she'd betrayed herself. She continued reluctantly. "That your mother escaped and took you to California . . . that you're educated and a good businessman."

He nodded. "It's all true. You know, people always looked down on me for being a half-breed. I decided early that the one way I could get back at them was to become rich and powerful. Then I would look down my nose at *them*."

"And are you rich and powerful?"

"I'm getting there."

"Do you know your father at all?"

"Strange you should ask that. A couple of years after my mother died, I spent some time on the Mescalero reservation in the mountains up north. I was curious about the ways of my father's people. More than that, I'd hoped at the time that I'd be able to meet my father . . . get to know him. Oddly enough, I've always felt more Indian, despite my mother's efforts to keep me in a white world."

"And did you meet him?"

"No. I was too late. He'd died a few years before. I stayed, anyway . . . for close to six months. I was looking for something. My identity, I suppose."

"Did you find what you were looking for?"

"No," Clay replied. "I don't believe anyone ever finds what he's looking for."

"Perhaps not." Honor's delicate face was suddenly grave.

"Don't be sad," Clay said. "You know, a beautiful

woman like you should laugh more. Don't you ever laugh?"

Changing the subject, she asked, "What drew you to the cave? Did you see it as just another opportunity to make money?"

"No, not entirely. During the time I spent with the tribe, my grandfather related a legend to me about some ancestors of mine who went into a cave in the Guadalupe Mountains and never came out again."

"Your forefathers?"

"Yes. The story intrigued me. Afterward, I set out to look for that cave, although I had no idea what I'd do when I found it. But I was sure I would discover it if I searched hard enough."

"There are other caves in these mountains, Clay. How do you know you've found the right one?"

"I was somehow drawn to that particular cave. It was like a magnet. I've never doubted for one minute that I didn't find the right one."

"Did you go down and explore, as Lucus did?"

"Actually . . . no."

"Why not?"

"I don't know. I can't explain it. At the time I was content just to be there—at the entrance. Anyway, I stayed for a while, then went on to California on business. I have an investment in some peach crops there. It never occurred to me that there would be any reason to return to Carlsbad."

"But you did."

"Yes, when it came to my attention that many California fruit growers were anxious to get their hands on bat guano for fertilizer. I immediately thought of the cave. I knew there were tons of guano just waiting to be mined. So I came back and got together with Cyrus and made a deal. But you know, I think I wanted an excuse to be around. I'm still intensely curious about the caverns."

Honor had been hanging on to his every word. She found herself wanting to tell him about the skeletons she'd come across, but she refrained. Was there a connection between what she had discovered and Clay's old relatives? She fleetingly wondered if her attraction to Clay had something to do with this new revelation and if there was some significance for her in it. Why did it seem to her that this was so? Don't be foolish, she chided herself. She was unduly imaginative.

Clay suddenly reached over to loosen the bow of her bonnet, gently taking it from her head and laying it down beside them. His arms enveloped her waist and he moved his face close to hers, finding her lips.

Her first impulse was to pull away, but she couldn't. Sinking against him, her mouth hungry for the taste of his lips, she clung to him with fervor.

He lifted his face for a moment, then fiercely lowered his mouth to hers again while easing his body over hers and drawing her down flat. Nuzzling her white neck, he uttered her name over and over in a soft, agonized whisper. "Honor. Honor. Honor. My God."

Suddenly she was frightened at the intensity of her own feelings. She began to fight him. "No. Clay, please. Clay!" The weight of his body held her down.

"Honor, I want you. I can't remember ever wanting anyone the way I want you. You're different for me. I can't keep myself away from you, even though I should. Don't fight me, Honor. Please don't." His body rocked rhythmically atop hers as he began to open the buttons of her blouse.

The surging heat in her loins at the sensation of his stiff manhood between her legs urged her to go on, to run her fingers through his sleek hair, to stroke her hands across his strong back . . . She wanted Clay more than any man before, but she couldn't prevent herself from thinking about her checkered past. "Clay, I can't! There's Lucus to consider!"

Clay froze, pulling himself off her. He sat up and closed his eyes for a few moments. When he opened them again, he murmured softly, "Lucus Kant is not man enough for a woman like you. And you know it.

Why don't you give us a chance? I'm falling in love with you, Honor. I've tried to stop it, but I can't help myself. I know you feel the same. I can see it. I can feel it."

Shaken, Honor started to reach for him longingly, then suddenly began to cry, rolling away instead. Her mixed emotions toward Clay tormented her. Part of her wanted to stay and make love with him—desperately needed to. Yet if she stayed, she'd never be able to smooth things out with Lucus. For once in her life she had to make a relationship with a man work. She forced herself to flee from Clay and his demands.

"Honor," Clay called, "don't run away. It won't solve anything. Honor!"

She couldn't stop running. She didn't care where she was going, only wondered in her flight why life had played this trick on her. Why *now!* She couldn't fall in love. She simply couldn't!

Seventeen

HONOR STOOD at the depot with Elijah, waiting for the departure of his train. She was anxiously trying to contain herself, afraid that he might see how dreadful she really felt about his leaving. She looked down at him, tenderly brushing back a lock of dark hair falling on his forehead. They'd never been separated before. What would she do without his presence? "Are you excited, Elijah?" she asked him.

He looked up at her. "Yes. I think it'll be a lot of fun with Drew in New York. Do you think he'll take me to the theater? I would so like to see a stage play."

"I should think so. He owns a theater, after all."

"Doesn't Drew have any children, Mama?"

"No, dear. Drew has never married."

"Do you think he'll like me?"

Honor laughed in spite of herself. "Elijah, he'll more than like you. I suppose you don't remember how attached he was to you when we lived there."

"I remember. Sort of."

"Well, you just be a good boy for him. Promise?"

"Yes, Mama. I promise."

She bent down, hugging him to her, caressing his baby-smooth cheek. "I know you will."

Elijah looked into her eyes. "I'll miss you, Mama. And all my friends here."

"I know you will. I'll miss you, too. So will Lucus. He felt so bad because he couldn't be here today to see you off, but he just couldn't get away from the job. You understand, don't you?"

"Yes, I understand."

"Oh, Elijah, what an exciting summer you're going to have! And you'll be back before you know it."

Impatiently Elijah looked around at all the people boarding the train. "I think I should get on the train now, Mama."

She bent down and handed him his satchel. "Now, I've already spoken to the conductor, Elijah. He'll watch over you and see that you change trains at the right place."

"Yes, I know."

"Have a wonderful time, darling."

"I will, Mama. Kiss Lucus goodbye for me, will you?"

"Yes, I'll do that, darling." She leaned over to kiss his face once again. "Take good care of yourself. Don't forget to write to me."

He began climbing the steps, calling out, "I will, Mama. I will."

She stepped back and waited until she saw him at a window waving at her. He was maturing so quickly, her little man. Frozen to the spot, she stood there watching his dear face at the window, not moving until the train finally coughed and sputtered, inching forward. She felt so lost—cut off from an integral part of her. When the cars pulled away, she let the tears fall. My darling, she thought, what will I do without you?

The depot emptied around her, suddenly bathed in silence. After a long while she, too, left, feeling desolate and abandoned. There was really nothing for her to return to at home.

Straightening her Alice-blue, paint-splattered smock, Honor removed her large straw hat and went to answer a knock on the door. When she opened it, she was shocked to see Clay Birdsong standing before her.

"Good morning." He smiled reassuringly.

Honor stared at him uncertainly for a moment, finally stepping aside to let him enter. "Come in. I was about to take a break." Her heart was pounding as he moved past her into the kitchen. What was he doing here?

He held up a white bonnet. "This is yours. You left it behind."

Her face flushed as she reached out to take it from him and laid it on the worn table. "Thank you."

"Have you been out painting so early? It's only ten o'clock." He made himself comfortable next to the table, watching her every gesture.

"Yes." She moved to the sink to fill a bright copper kettle with water. Her voice took on a note of forced bravado. "Isn't it marvelous? I've been out since dawn painting the countryside. Everything looks so different then . . . so fresh and new. Don't you agree?"

Clay stretched his long legs and nodded.

Her words continued to rush out as she put the kettle on to boil. "Elijah left for New York yesterday to spend the sum—" Her voice faltered. She stopped talking, nervously running her hand over her thick hair. She couldn't stand this false conversation another minute. "What do you want, Clay?" she confronted him boldly.

"To return your hat. To see how you are. Have you been well? You've got shadows under your eyes." His black eyes expressed his concern.

"No," she answered in a controlled voice, "I have not been well." She wrung her hands together, unable to contain her inner tension. "You shouldn't be here! Nothing can come of this!"

He stared at her intently. "You don't know how hard I've tried to keep away. I've made an effort to put my mind on other things. I've even bedded down with other women, trying to forget you. But nothing works. I think this has been the longest month of my life. I know it's crazy. Do you think I make a habit of falling in love with married women?"

"Clay, I—"

"No. Let me finish. I can't get you out of my mind, and it's tearing me apart. We have to talk." He got up and went to her, grabbing her roughly by the shoulders. "Please talk to me about this."

"Clay, why do you make it so hard for me?"

A tight muscle worked across his jaw. "Is there still something left between you and Lucus? I have to know."

The kettle shrilled, interrupting their confrontation, and Honor was able to break away from Clay's iron grip. She turned to extinguish the fire, keeping her back to him. In a constricted voice, she admitted, "No, there's nothing left between us. But I'm still his wife. You've got to understand that."

He spun her around to face him. "I only understand that I want you. And I know you want me."

"Clay, he needs me. If I weren't here for Lucus, I don't know what would become of him. I'm learning to live with my problems. You mustn't complicate my life this way."

"Sometimes," he said evenly, "there's no choice."

"What do you want of me?" she whispered, on the verge of hysteria. "What?"

"I want to marry you."

"Marry me?" Honor looked at him incredulously. "You must be mad!"

"Yes, I suppose I am. But we could make it work, Honor. I've never been so sure of anything in my life. People search for a lifetime and never feel for one minute what I feel for you. Look around at all the vacant, indifferent faces. Look at yourself. Do you really think that's what life's supposed to be? A passage of time lived in limbo? Take the chance with me, Honor. Are you really going to allow a time for us to slip through our fingers?"

Honor did not respond. She knew, irrevocably, that he was right. She couldn't fight him any longer. Clay's indomitable spirit devoured her, robbing her of all willpower. Something snapped inside her. My God, she thought. My God. Pleadingly, she stretched out her arms to him, her voice quivering. "Love me, Clay. Love me."

He hungrily embraced her, kissing her soft lips and neck. Her head swam as she clung to him, never wanting him to cease. His strong arms felt good—safe. When he released her, she led him into the bedroom and let him tenderly undress her, savoring each touch of skin on skin. His bronze body was a study in male perfection, emanating a fierce strength, his manhood already erect in anticipation. She stood naked, waiting, watching as he removed his clothing also.

He moved closer, holding her gently for just a moment before lifting her in his powerful arms like a child and laying her down on the bed. "I love you, Honor," he whispered. "I love you."

"Clay . . . Clay . . . Clay," she murmured, pulling his head down to her voluptuous breasts while his tanned hands stroked the length of her back and rounded buttocks. He teased her pink nipples with his lips and small bites until they stiffened. Then his head moved downward, planting the soft curves of her body with moist kisses until he reached her thighs.

Pulling them apart, he gently caressed her mons, then the folds of velvet skin.

She cried out to him, her body trembling, arching to meet his. He lifted himself onto his knees between her spread legs, pushing them farther apart with his strong hands. As he entered her, her hips responded to his rhythm. "Clay," she gasped. "Clay!"

Something was happening to her, shocking her senses. An incredible, joyous warmth rose up in her until she was well past the point of halting it, fusing their hearts together as well as their bodies. She joined with him in a way she had never coupled with any other man, screaming as she reached the peak with him. When he cried out, the weight of his body falling on hers, tears flowed profusely down her cheeks.

Honor at last understood what she'd never comprehended before. What she'd just experienced was different because love had given the act keener definition and meaning. The interaction of passion and caring flowing between them filled her with peace. She knew instantly that without shared love, sex was nothing but a sham. She couldn't stop crying, sobs racking her body. Wanting desperately to share her newfound knowledge with him, she caressed him, saying, "Clay, I—"

"Honor!" Lucus's voice cut through her like a knife.

They turned in unison toward the sound from the open doorway. "Oh, Jesus," Clay muttered as he rolled off her. He jumped up, hastily pulling on his pants and reaching out to throw a quilt over Honor's body. Pain emanated from the dark liquid pools of his eyes as he saw Honor's radiant face cloud instantly with acute shame. How deeply he wished he could have spared her. If only he could have held his emotions in check. Somehow he would have to explain this to her husband, but it would be impossible to remain in this room, the scene of adulterous loving, with him.

Lying in a state of shock, Honor heard the bedroom door close. Covering her eyes with her hands, she listened to the pitch of their muted voices rising in the next room, her acute embarrassment transforming her into a helpless, inanimate object. The sound of furniture crashing to the floor and against walls finally bolted her out of her trancelike state. She rushed to put on a dressing gown and raced out of the bedroom, to find Lucus and Clay tearing at each other. The sight of their fists lashing into the other's flesh filled her with a numbing terror. She couldn't move, could only mutter, "Please stop. Please . . . please . . . please."

Suddenly Lucus was on the hard wooden floor, blood trickling from the side of his mouth; he was unconscious. Running to him, Honor pleaded, "No more, Clay. Stop it. Please stop it."

Clay stood dazed for a moment, rubbing his swollen knuckles. Blood spurted unheeded out of his nose as he felt rendered helpless by her intervention. After a while he reached into his pants pocket for a handkerchief and dabbed at it, never taking his eyes away from Honor. "I'll get my things," he said softly.

Seated on the floor next to Lucus, she watched Clay go into the bedroom, then move to the cabin door. He turned and looked at her briefly, powerless to comfort her. Honor watched him walk out, then returned her attention to Lucus, wondering what she would do now. What was there left for her after this?

Outside, dawn was making its inchoate appearance. Honor sat on a rough wood bench next to a window, her hands folded primly on her lap, her body stiff with tension. She looked ravaged, her golden hair wild and unkempt. Dark blue shadows shaded the surface of translucent skin beneath her gray eyes that brimmed over with despair.

How did this happen? she wondered. Why? Was it really just a matter of hours earlier when Lucus had stood at the bedroom door watching her make love with Clay? Now, in her tired, confused state, it felt as if it had taken place a long, long time ago.

She watched Lucus pace feverishly before her. His

hands gesticulated wildly as he shouted, "I knew I shouldn't have brought you to New Mexico! I knew it! You've never been happy here . . . never . . . never!"

Honor couldn't bear to watch his anguish any longer. She turned away to look out the window. Dawn was indeed breaking, casting its golden glow across the great sweep of sky. Dark shadows were slowly, gently, being nudged away as the bright new day crept over the still land. She sighed deeply, wishing she were out there—away from the sharp edges of turmoil.

From the corner of her eye she stared at Lucus covertly, finding herself mesmerized by his moving figure. They had been at this far too many hours, his maunderings frightening her to the very roots of her being. All efforts to mollify him had failed. She no longer had the energy to keep on trying.

Sorely piqued, at one point during the long night Lucus had angrily stalked out, slamming the door behind him. He was gone for several hours, leaving Honor sitting silently, immobile, in darkness. When he'd returned, there was still no quieting him down.

Feeling the need to say something to him, she offered nervously, "It's not true that I've never been happy. There have been good times. I've never been sorry I left New York . . . not once." Her voice was tired, hoarse, sounding strange to her own ears. She wished she could crawl into bed and never get up.

"He said he wants to marry you."

"Yes," she murmured tonelessly, "I know that."

"Do you want to marry him?"

"How can I know what I want? I'm tired. I want to go to sleep."

"Damn it, Honor," he shouted, pounding his fist on a table, "you've broken one of God's commandments. You've sinned before God and before me."

She kept her eyes lowered and remained silent.

Lucus suddenly slumped down in defeat on a chair, rubbing his tired face. "What do we do now, Honor? What do we do now?"

Honor reflected torpidly, trying to sort out her

thoughts through the numbing haze of her fatigue. Her head ached, and her tongue felt thick when she spoke, her words almost slurring. "I'll leave, Lucus. It's best for both of us." Avoiding his eyes, she returned her gaze to the rising sun. At this moment the thought of being totally alone somewhere nourished her.

"Will you go alone?"

"Yes. I promised you that. I need very badly to sort out my feelings by myself."

"Where will you go?"

"I could reopen the house in Santa Fe." She thought seriously about that for a moment. "Yes. I will go there."

"I see."

She turned to look at him, then was sorry she had, for unchecked tears were streaming down his cheeks. Her heart lurched. She had never seen a man cry before. With a shudder that went through her whole body, she ran to him, falling on her knees, burying her head in his lap. "Please don't do that, Lucus. I can't bear it."

He moved his hand over her hair, stroking it. "You're the only woman I've ever loved."

She started to cry also. "Lucus . . . Lucus . . . Lucus."

His voice was shaky with emotion. "I know it's my fault. I've neglected you terribly. I haven't wanted to face it completely. But the caverns have gnawed away at my energies. I haven't had time for you . . . I couldn't make time."

"You did what you thought was best," she sobbed. "You're not to blame yourself for what happened yesterday. I'm to blame."

"But I've had to give the caverns, and God, *everything* of myself. For, to me, the caverns are God . . . in a concrete form you can touch. To have given you even a part of myself would have meant I loved God that much less."

Poor Lucus, Honor thought, poor, sad, confused Lucus.

"I've always believed the caverns were important, Honor. I'm linked to them by a . . . a higher order of intelligence. Bringin' the world to the caverns is my destiny. You were the first to see that. At least I thought you did."

In one terrible flash Honor saw Lucus as pitiful; immediately she cringed at the disloyal thought. A suffocating wave of guilt swept over her. Steeling herself against nausea, she murmured, "Oh, Lucus, I never meant for it to turn out this way."

He didn't seem to hear her. "It's my fault that you sent Elijah away. I know that. I wasn't much of a father to him. But I couldn't have loved him more if he were my own son. You know that, don't you?"

"Lucus, please stop torturing yourself. Stop it!"

He gently cupped his face with his hands and lifted it. "Tell me somethin', Honor. Are you in love with Clay Birdsong? I have to know."

Until now, this was the one question he hadn't asked. The one question she fervently hoped he would never ask. She stared into his eyes for a moment—helpless.

"Yes."

Clay stood firmly before Sophie, his mind clearly made up. "Go talk to Honor for me, Sophie. The train leaves for California at eight tomorrow morning. Tell her to meet me, Sophie. Tell her she must come with me."

Sophie's face reddened and her hands fluttered excitedly as she sputtered, "Oh, dear. Oh, dear. I was afraid something like this would happen. I just knew it."

"I love her, Sophie. She belongs with *me*."

"Oh, dear. Oh, dear."

Clay's voice grew impatient. "Will you go to her and give her the message? I must be sure you'll tell her."

"Yes, yes. I'll take the buggy out this afternoon. I'll do as you ask." She hesitated briefly, her brows creasing in concern. "Clay, do you really know what you're doing?"

The muscles in his jaw clenching, Clay's voice was hard and decisive. "I've never been *more* sure in my entire life." He reached for the doorknob, stopped by Sophie's words.

"Good luck, Clay."

He nodded and stalked out of the gallery, moving with long strides toward the hotel. There he would pack his meager belongings and wait out the long hours until it was time to go to the railroad station. He suddenly stopped in his tracks. Fear pitted his stomach with startling impact. What if she didn't come? He shook off the feeling, not admitting to the possibility it could really happen.

Once in his room, Clay stretched out on the narrow bed, his hands folded under his head, and lay deep in thought. His eyes moistened with emotion when he thought of his father's people, his father's blood flowing through his veins. The Indian knows there is no such thing as an accident, Clay reflected.

He pondered this, knowing without a doubt that his path had crossed Honor's for a reason. A reason neither he nor she could possibly interpret—yet. Something had drawn them together. This he was positive of. Something so awesome and powerful that it could not be denied.

Their love *was* right! It had to be. For what did his money and success mean if he couldn't share them with this woman and settle down? Am I to be a bird of passage all my life? he wondered. He shook his head. With her his life would have real meaning. He remembered with clarity the first time he'd laid eyes on Honor . . .

She was the most beautiful, most independent woman he'd ever come across. But it was more than her physical beauty, more than her self-determination, that had set Honor apart from others. She'd magnetized him. Somehow he could penetrate her surrounding aura, feeling the power of her soul.

Honor was his destiny. He knew it. He closed his eyes. She would come. She had to.

Honor sat in the dank surroundings of her kitchen listening to the rain falling in a steady rhythmic beat on the cabin roof. A hurricane lantern flickered, casting inadequate light on the dun-gray room. Her luminous eyes were riveted to the clock over the sink as the minutes ticked inevitably by.

It was seven-thirty in the morning. Pulling her attention away from the clock, she let her thoughts drift to Sophie's visit the evening before and the startling message Sophie had conveyed. After she had left, Honor had spent an unbearable night pacing the empty cabin. Her thoughts had been in a turmoil, sleep eluding her.

Clay's image continued to blaze through her mind. She looked back at the clock. He'd be leaving Carlsbad in thirty minutes.

She tried to organize the heady turn of events into some kind of structure—something that made sense. At this instant she couldn't consider going to California with him. Yet she still wanted him with a desperate longing. What was she to do? What did she want? *Really* want?

She'd never consciously thought about it before, but she suddenly realized that the underlying force of her life had been a long, intense search for the fulfillment of love. She'd been sure she'd found it with Julian, but he'd abandoned her. Opting for security instead, she'd turned to Lucus. But apparently even that she couldn't rely on.

Clay . . . Clay. He *was* different. Different from both Julian and Lucus. But how well did they really know each other? She closed her eyes for a moment, recapturing the feel of Clay's strong arms, her body trembling with excitement at the memory.

Seven-thirty-five.

Hugging her arms around her body, Honor rocked back and forth, anguish causing her temples to pound. Could she go away with Clay after what had happened? No . . . yes . . . she didn't know. She worried that such an alliance would only serve to compound her guilty feelings. For, despite the fact that she was leaving Lucus, she *was* married. The affair was wrong. Wrong from the start. She couldn't just pick up and leave with him. Not at all. Or could she?

Seven-thirty-eight.

Honor jumped to her feet with a start. Was she crazy to let him go out of her life? Happiness was a breath away. She would grab onto it. She'd waited too long for Clay—for someone like him. Somehow, in some way, they'd make it work. She must go to him. She had to be with him! Was there enough time?

The clock read seven-forty.

She didn't think about packing as she ran out into the rain to get the horse from the corral. After hastily fastening a saddle on the mare's back, she climbed on, racing against time, her body chilled from the cold shower that drenched her. She had to get to the train depot before it was too late. Focusing her thoughts intensely on Clay, she murmured, "Wait for me. Please wait for me."

The train whistle blew its ominous shrill, sending shivers up Clay's spine as he grabbed the iron handrail and lifted a leg onto the first step. He stopped and turned back, trying to ferret Honor out in the blinding storm, afraid to lose hope completely. At once his spirits collapsed. There was no sign of her.

"All aboard. All aboard."

She's not coming, he thought miserably. He took the steps two at a time, determined that their paths would cross again. Perhaps, he told himself, this wasn't the right moment for us. But somehow . . . someday . . . they *would* meet again. For how could he ever forget her?

Honor jerked the horse's reins to a stop and slid off the saddle. The rain pelted her mud-splattered body, but she was not aware of it. The only reality penetrating her senses was the sight of the train racing off in the distance, leaving a trail of puffy smoke. She ran into the ticket office to ask the agent if that had been the train bound for California. Aware that the agent looked at her oddly, she heard him dryly affirm what she already knew. She slumped down on a bench, suddenly very cold.

"Would you like to wrap yourself in a blanket, ma'am?" the agent inquired.

She nodded in acquiescence, feeling rough wool being draped over her shoulders. Suddenly conscious that she must look a sight, Honor felt a sad, diminutive twinge of self-pity. She jumped up, pushing the blanket from her shoulders, angry at herself for hoping . . . for what she had no right to hope for in the first place.

BOOK IV

Santa Fe, New Mexico

1902

Eighteen

DREW COURTENAY bounded from the theater entrance in a great rush, relieved to be finished with his managerial duties for the evening. Anxious to get home, he fleetingly savored the prospect of the cool bath that he knew would be waiting for him. The street was thick with New York theatergoers; he elbowed his way through the crowd with difficulty. Suddenly, over the vibrating hum of conversation around him, he heard his name being called.

"Drew! Drew Courtenay!"

Drew spun around, finding himself face to face with Julian Borg. He stared at him incredulously. "Julian," he gasped, "am I seeing things?"

Buoyantly, Julian threw his arm around Drew's shoulders. "I think I'm the one seeing things. It's been too long . . . too long." His words slurred and his breath reeked of alcohol.

Involuntarily, Drew stepped back. "How in the world are you, Julian? Have you been back in New York for very long? I tell you, you're a sight for sore eyes."

Julian laughed inanely. "Let's have a drink, shall we, and I'll answer all your questions."

"Of course . . . of course. Come home with me, why don't you? I'm finished here for the night."

"Good." Julian patted Drew's arm with affection. "I'll excuse myself from my friends. Give me a minute."

Drew watched Julian move through the mob to his circle of friends, his body weaving slightly. His ob-

vious inebriated state brought back memories to Drew
of all-night bouts of drinking he'd shared with
Julian in days gone by. He chuckled to himself. What
a time we used to have!

He grew serious, though, when thoughts of Honor
filtered through his mind. A letter had come from her
only yesterday, containing rather surprising news. In
light of this, he thought it an odd coincidence to have
run into Julian now—Julian, of all people. For an
instant Drew was suffused with a sense of foreboding.
He shook his head, pushing the feeling aside.

Drew opened the front door to his house, holding it
ajar so that Julian could pass through. "Go into the
library and make yourself comfortable. I'll get some
ice from the kitchen. I won't be a minute."

"Fine, old friend," Julian said. "Take your time. I
know my way around." He moved toward the library
and let himself in, leaving the heavily carved doors
open behind him.

Removing his black bowler hat, he tossed it hap-
hazardly onto a nearby mahogany table, along with
the jacket he'd been carrying on his arm. Wiping the
perspiration from his forehead with the back of his
hand, he then loosened his forest-green bow tie and
took off his detachable collar, tossing it aside. He
sank into a large, overstuffed chair and waited for
Drew.

After several minutes he began to sober up somewhat, his head clearing. Looking around the library,
Julian recalled all the times he'd been in this room
with Honor at his side. A sharp thrust of regret
stabbed at him.

Drew appeared in the doorway with a large bucket
of ice, which he deposited on the bar. "Here we are.
I've got a bottle of Napoleon brandy here, and
Scotch. Help yourself while I change into something
more comfortable. If there's anything else you want,
ring the bell for Flossie in the kitchen."

Julian looked up at him. "No need to bother the

maid for anything. I'll have some Napoleon, old friend. You go on."

"Fine. I'll just be a minute."

Drew ran up the long flight of stairs that led to his bedroom. He looked in on his filled tub with regret, then removed his damp clothing and put on a long maroon robe of a flimsy material that made crackling sounds when he walked.

His glance fell on his desk, where Honor's letter lay opened. How strange, Drew thought, that she had suddenly found herself alone at the moment, and now here was Julian. Did this coincidence mean anything?

He walked out of the bedroom, pausing to look in on Elijah in the darkened room next to his. He could hear the boy's even breathing, indicating Elijah was sound asleep. He drew in his breath and descended the staircase.

"Well, Julian," he said brightly as he entered the library. He moved to the bar and poured Scotch into a glass over chipped ice, then sat down to look at his friend.

Julian was as trim and fit-looking as ever, he thought, with the physique of a young boy. The only change evident in Julian's face was a puffiness beneath his inscrutable green eyes, giving him a rather dissolute look, but taking nothing away from his strikingly handsome features.

"Well, Julian," Drew repeated, "I can't tell you how good it is to see you. Tell me, what have you been up to all this time?"

Julian sipped his brandy carelessly before speaking. "I've been in England, as I'm sure you already know, just recently arriving in New York for an extended visit." He paused, his eyes suddenly full of mischief. "Do you remember that novel I was working on?"

Drew nodded.

"Well, I finished that some time ago. It was published in London . . . with a great deal of notoriety attached to it, I might add." He convulsed with laugh-

ter. "The British thought it too risqué. They're a bit
stiff over there, you know."

Drew joined his raucous laughter. "I would love to
read it, Julian."

"I'll see that you get a copy."

They were quiet for a time, each sipping his drink.
Drew watched a fly traversing a lampshade, suddenly
aware of the scent of decaying roses from the hallway
wafting into the room. He was rising to close the large
doors when Julian dramatically announced, "I've
come to get Honor back."

Drew turned to look at him, clearly startled.

"Where is she, Drew? What's become of her? I
must find her."

Drew couldn't quite believe Julian's audacity.
Damn the man! Honor isn't some little fluff of a person with no feelings. She's a proud and sensitive
woman who was heartbroken when the cad stood her
up. How like Julian to waltz back in after almost three
years and expect to resume where he had left off. The
more Drew thought about it, the angrier he got. He
could not resist the temptation of jabbing Julian with
the truth. "You're too late. About a year after you
left, Honor married a cousin of mine . . . a cowboy
from New Mexico . . . Lucus Kant."

Julian looked crushed at this news, his pride
wounded.

"She's still there," Drew continued, then pondered
for a moment. "Her son, Elijah, is staying with me
for the summer, as a matter of fact. He's upstairs now,
sleeping. You know, Julian," he added enthusiastically, "Elijah's an amazingly attractive child with a
bright, inquisitive mind—" He broke off as he noticed Julian begin to squirm in his chair.

"I gather you're in close touch with Honor, then."

"Yes . . . we've always corresponded."

"And—?"

"And what, Julian?"

"Is she happy, Drew? Happy with her life?"

Drew pushed back the gold pince-nez that had

slipped down his nose from perspiration. How much he wanted to lie. "I thought she was. I know she was happy for a time. But now . . . no . . . she's really not. I received a rather sad letter from her just yesterday."

Julian got up and paced restlessly about the richly decorated library. "What's wrong?"

"Apparently she's now estranged from my cousin. She didn't go into detail, but she's on the way to their home in Santa Fe, and Lucus is remaining in Carlsbad. Some distance away, I take it."

"I see."

"After all this time, Julian, can you really still be interested in Honor? And how can you be so sure she wants *you* back?" He worked hard to keep his voice nonchalant.

Julian sat down again, stretching his legs out in front of him and rubbing the cool brandy glass across his forehead. "I've never been able to get Honor Wentworth out of my mind. She's a woman not easily forgotten. She'll want me, all right. Married or not, Honor's tied to me in a hundred ways."

Julian's arrogance strongly irritated Drew, but he remained silent.

"I must see Honor. Seeing her again has become an obsession with me. It's the only reason I'm here in New York."

Drew abruptly set his drink down and removed a cigar from a long wooden box on the table next to him. "That's impossible," he said sharply.

"Nothing is impossible. What stops me from going to Santa Fe? You say she's separated from her husband. I'm not too late, am I?" His voice had a defiant edge to it.

Now Drew deeply regretted having told Julian this news. He groped for the right words, convinced that Julian was not thinking rationally. "Julian, you can't complicate her life any more than it already is. I don't know what happened exactly, but I'm sure she needs time to work it out. If you care about her, you'll let her be."

Drew bit off the end of his cigar and spit it into an ashtray, recalling the feeling of foreboding he'd experienced earlier in the evening. Fervently wishing he and Julian had never met again, he fiercely chomped on the unlit cigar, then pulled it from his mouth. He shook his head forbiddingly, saying, "Let the past rest, Julian. You can't go back. What's done is done. After all, she may be separated from her husband, but she's still a married woman."

This advice sounded lame even to Drew. Moral restraint had never been one of Julian's outstanding points, Drew reminded himself as he watched his friend down his brandy. His infamous escapades were a well-known fact in their circle.

Julian looked defiantly at Drew. "I think Honor is entitled to share in this decision." He was quiet then, avoiding his host's eyes.

Unexpectedly, the library door swung open, calling a halt to the conversation. Drew turned to see Elijah standing in the doorway in his nightshirt, rubbing his sleep-filled eyes.

"I woke up thirsty, Cousin Drew. I heard voices in here."

Drew moved to him. "Flossie is still in the kitchen. Go on out to her, child."

"Elijah, how good to see you again."

The young boy's eyes were suddenly alert as he focused them sharply on Julian. "What are you doing here?" he blurted accusingly.

"How big you've grown, my little man." Julian stood up and started for him but was stopped by the forbidding wave of Drew's hand.

"Go on, Elijah," Drew said softly. "We'll talk in the morning."

Elijah's gaze was riveted on Julian. "I asked what you were doing here."

"He's my guest, Elijah. Now please, go on."

"You keep away from my mother. Do you hear me? Keep away from my mother!"

Drew forcibly turned him away. "Elijah!"

Elijah sucked in his breath, staring first at Drew and then back at Julian. "All right, then." He slammed the door behind him.

Drew faced Julian, feeling slightly flustered. "He feels violently about you, doesn't he?"

Julian shrugged, returning to his seat and picking up his brandy. "He's just a child," was his only comment.

Drew was completely leery of Julian now. Any earlier feeling of camaraderie had disappeared without a trace. Elijah's unannounced appearance and reaction to Julian had thoroughly shaken him.

Drew was seriously worried for Honor, shockingly aware that Julian's strong will would carry him wherever he liked, even at her expense. Drew was utterly frustrated in the face of this. Didn't Julian Borg always get what he wanted?

After Julian left, Drew wearily ascended the staircase, hoping that Elijah had gone back to sleep. He was too tired for a confrontation now, hoping it could be put off until morning. Though he knew with certainty that Elijah would ask some uncomfortable questions. The boy had been badly upset on seeing Julian again, and he had every right to be, Drew supposed.

He'd so wanted Elijah's visit to be perfect, and until this evening it had been. Elijah seemed to like being with Drew as much as Drew enjoyed having him there. With Elijah's arrival, Drew's too-quiet bachelor home had quickly filled with noise and glee from this child who seemed to approach each moment of his life with a vibrant enthusiasm. How terrible it would be if this incident were to spoil Elijah's visit and their good feelings for each other.

He hesitantly passed Elijah's room, only to be stopped by his voice calling out. Drew sighed, then, entering, found Elijah sitting up in bed, his gas lamp still turned on.

"You should be asleep. Do you realize what time it is?"

"I couldn't sleep, Cousin Drew. I'm too mad."

Drew slowly sank down on the side of Elijah's bed, saying, "Nothing has happened for you to be mad about. I know you have good reason not to be especially fond of Julian, but he's gone now. You don't have to see him again. I promise you."

"I thought Julian went far away forever. Why is he back?"

"I expect he's returned to see his aunt. She's his only living relative. Surely you can understand that. I'm sure that after he's visited with her, he'll return to England." He silently hoped the tone of his voice was convincing enough. This boy was not like other children. He was too bright not to suspect a lie. Drew prayed that Elijah would let the matter drop.

"Are you sure, Cousin Drew, he's only here to see her and will be leaving again soon?"

"I'm positive," Drew said enthusiastically. "As I recall, that's exactly what he said to me, and I believe him. Now, please turn off your light and go to sleep. Or else you'll be too tired in the morning to do the things we planned."

"He won't bother my mother, will he?"

"How can he possibly bother your mother? She's many, many miles away from New York."

Elijah bit on his lower lip for a moment, his eyes downcast. Then he looked up at Drew forlornly. "I suppose you're right."

"You bet."

"All right, then." He lifted his arms to encircle Drew's neck, planting a moist kiss on his cheek. "Good night, Cousin Drew."

Touched, Drew kissed him in return and then laid him back down, tucking a linen sheet under his chin. Gently, Drew brushed aside a lock of Elijah's hair from his forehead, then turned off the light. He wondered if he should indeed warn Honor. Perhaps he'd best stay out of it. Sighing deeply, Drew wondered where the wings of desire would take her.

Nineteen

IT HAD rained most of the morning. When Consuelo came to call for Honor, the sun was just beginning to show through gray flocculent clouds, its brilliance falling on the wet earth in sharp streams of light.

Honor greeted Consuelo with enthusiasm as she sidled into the buggy seat beside her. They were off to Agua Fría, the Village of Cold Water, for the Saint Juan's Day fiesta. There, they would stay overnight at the home of Consuelo's uncle, Tío Rafael. The short trip offered Honor a sorely needed break from her solitary existence in Santa Fe, and she welcomed it.

Since her return, she'd deliberately kept out of the social stream she'd once been so involved with, forgoing the social amenities entirely and avoiding the people she'd known best, only seeing Consuelo infrequently.

Having no need to hire a cook, she shopped at Kaune's on San Francisco Street, stocking her cupboard with canned food imported from the States. She ate alone and spent her time sketching or sewing. It was the way she'd wanted it, yet today it *was* good to be out again. Perhaps, she thought, she was ready to relinquish her solitude and join the world again.

As they jostled along Honor smoothed her long blue skirt with one hand while with the other she hung on to her wide-brimmed hat, its clusters of purple grackles flying in the breeze.

"I am so glad you decided to come today, Honor," Consuelo offered, her words hurried. "My uncle so wants company. He lives alone now and is very lonely."

"Yes," Honor said, "I'm glad I—"

"It has been a long time since I have been to visit with him. Tío Rafael and I have been close since I was a small child. I have felt bad about neglecting him."

"I'm looking forward to meeting your uncle."

"You will like Agua Fría. It is a pleasant town. And my uncle's old house is most charming."

"Was it convenient for you to leave your children in order to make the trip?" Honor asked.

"The older children take care of the others," Consuelo answered nervously. "They will be fine." She lapsed into silence then, lost somewhere in her own thoughts.

It occurred to Honor that Consuelo was behaving oddly, first chattering nervously, then withdrawing abruptly. But Honor was too interested in the surroundings of Santa Fe to dwell on Consuelo's erratic behavior.

She never tired of studying the rutted streets that had once been faint paths made by barefoot Indians trudging across the red earth. Seldom providing a clear view for even a block ahead, the old Santa Fe Trail turned to the right, plunging down a hill and past a small stream, then twisted to the left to pass the San Miguel Church. Then still another bend. Adobe houses jutted out as though they marked the end of the road, but the road unexpectedly curved past them, following its own waywardness.

Honor drank it all in, fascinated by this city that had seemed magical to her from the first. Finally they reached San Francisco Street, and Consuelo pulled the horse to a stop at the plaza. They both looked across the river to their destination.

"You have never been to Agua Fría, Honor?"

"No, I never have."

"It is going to be a rough trip. Many stay away because of it."

Honor laughed. "I'm not afraid."

Consuelo shrugged. "Very well. We are off." She jerked the horse's reins.

The road to Agua Fría was narrow and difficult to cross, its muddy, rock-strewn banks constantly obstructing their path. The buggy jostled and careened across small streams and flooded ditches, nearly tipping over at one point. Honor gasped, anxiously turning to Consuelo. She was relieved to see her friend juggling the reins in an unconcerned manner. Her outward display of confidence comforted Honor somewhat.

Eventually, as they approached the village proper, the poor road conditions lessened. Honor slowly relaxed, her anxiety quickly becoming transmuted into wonder as she absorbed the sunny surroundings, catching fleeting glances of the people and the land as they rode on at an easy pace.

Everywhere, gardens and orchards burst forth in happy abundance. Great cottonwoods, piñons, and cedars raised their graceful limbs upward to the turquoise sky. Wagons traveled down the road, spilling over with laughing, brown-eyed children. The air was heavy with the sweet fragrance of hollyhocks climbing the courtyard walls.

Honor was suddenly aware that Consuelo was casting furtive glances her way. Inexplicably, she began to feel uneasy and confused in Consuelo's company. What could be wrong? She tried to put it out of her mind as they turned down a road leading to a white, decaying house with dark green portals. Tío Rafael, an old man dressed in a black suit, his broad-brimmed black hat resting atop an abundant shock of white hair, waited for them in the front yard, a pleased smile creasing his face.

Supper began by candlelight at a large table covered with white linen, set with delicate, pink-flowered china and ornate, highly polished silverware.

A thick soup called *albóndigas* was served as the first course; in it were small, round meatballs that had been rolled in blue cornmeal and boiled along with the soup. Then came enchiladas, blue cornmeal pancakes stuffed with chopped raw onion and melted cheese and smothered with hot chili sauce. Green peppers, fried a golden brown, were filled with chicken and cheese. Brown beans were heaped in large yellow earthenware bowls, and tender spring beans were served on long brown platters.

It all looked inviting, yet Honor poked at her food, unable to eat. A peculiar form of nausea pitted her stomach. Saliva collected profusely along the inside of her cheeks, and the room started to spin.

She was about to excuse herself from the table when the wave of sickness subsided as quickly as it had come, leaving her more than a little shaken. This had happened to her often over the past few weeks. Perhaps, she thought, she should see a doctor on her return to Santa Fe. She looked up to see Tío Rafael studying her, his white brows drawn together in an inquiring frown.

"The meal does not please you, *señora?*"

Honor's neck reddened with embarrassment. "Yes . . . yes. It pleases me. The meal is wonderful. It's just that I've never quite gotten used to the sharp spices used in Spanish cooking." She paused. "I'm sorry if I've offended you."

His frown disappeared and he smiled warmly at her. "You haven't offended me, *señora*. I only like my guests to be happy always."

She returned his smile and relaxed, unobtrusively pushing her plate away from her.

At the meal's end, sweet green melon and goat's milk cheese were offered for dessert. Honor ate both sparingly, with no apparent aftereffects. The three sat back while the Mexican cook cleared the dishes from the table.

Honor was keenly aware that Consuelo had hardly spoken a word since supper began. She wondered again what was causing her odd behavior.

Rafael brought his attention to Honor. "You are from the States, are you not, *señora?*"

"Yes, I am. From New York."

"And what are your impressions of the Southwest?"

"I have loved it from the first. It's always seemed to me that I belonged here somehow."

"*Sí.* I understand. Who could not feel this way? But you should have known New Mexico in my youth. Then we were proud caballeros." His brown eyes shone as he explained, "Caballeros were horsemen, *señora.* The first Spaniards were heroic men in a heroic time. That title merited respect then."

Honor looked at him with interest. "What did the caballeros do, *señor?*"

"What did they do? They came to this New Spain and planted it with the seeds of faith, art, and tradition. The conquerors cleared the land with fierceness and force, *señora,* but the caballeros brought with them and infused the whole country with the proud history of a people. In those days a horse was a luxury and the sign of a gentleman of means. The caballeros rode their horses with such pride. Such pride. But now . . . times have changed, have they not? Everything changes." He sighed.

Honor smiled at him gently. He reminded her more than a little of Miss Gilly and her reminiscences of a time gone by. How sad to live in the past, she thought, realizing that this was a plague of old age.

Rafael rose awkwardly from the table, his body lethargic and stiff. "You will excuse me. My old body needs rest. Please feel free to do what you wish." He looked directly at Honor. "*Esta casa está siempre a la disposición de usted.* My house is your house, *señora.*" With that he kissed Consuelo on the forehead and quietly left.

Honor turned to Consuelo. "Shall we go outside for a bit?"

Consuelo nodded agreement, following her out to the portico.

They sat in silence on hard chairs and Honor's thoughts drifted. She had seen Consuelo several times since her return to Santa Fe, but she still could not get over how she had changed. Consuelo's skin, once a satiny olive, had turned brown from the sun. Fine wrinkles were deeply etched around her eyes and mouth. Her black hair hung loosely down her back, and her oval face had become thin, slowly shriveling up from the dry air. Her dark eyes glistened and seemed to burn with an inner fever.

Honor recalled having once heard that Latin girls bloom early and fade early, after the long drain of childbearing. That, and siestas following all-night bouts of dancing and drinking wine, took their toll. She wondered what Consuelo's life was really like. How well did she know her? She was suddenly aware of Consuelo's voice repeating her name. She pulled her attention back to the sound of it. "What?"

"I said, there is a man in town asking about you, Honor." She was silent for a moment, waiting for a response. "Honor?"

"A man?"

"*Sí.*"

"What is his name?"

"His name? Let me think . . . He said his name was Julian Borg."

Honor stared at her, thunderstruck. It wasn't possible—she couldn't have heard right! *Julian!* She was speechless.

Consuelo prodded her again. "Do you know a man by this name?"

Honor nervously cleared her throat. "Why, yes. I did know someone by that name . . . years ago in New York." She forced a lightness into her voice. "Well, what a coincidence that he is in Santa Fe. Did you tell him where I lived?"

"*Sí*. Was that all right?"

"Why, of course. Of course." Honor felt strangely numb from shock.

Consuelo leaned forward. "Honor, do not think me bold, but there is something I must ask you."

Honor's heart stopped. Did she suspect something odd about Julian's arrival? She mustered up a weak smile. "Certainly, Consuelo. What is it?"

"Why have you left Lucus alone in Carlsbad? What happened between you?" She paused. "Is Lucus all right?"

Honor stiffened, resentful of this intrusion into her privacy. She was suddenly exasperated. All this was too much, she thought. Julian was in Santa Fe, and now Consuelo pressed her for details about her marriage. She took a deep breath before speaking. "Lucus is fine, Consuelo. I've already told you about the caverns he discovered, and that he works there as a foreman in the guano mines. I came to Santa Fe . . . because I needed a change of scene," she lied. "Carlsbad was lonely for me."

Consuelo looked sharply at her. "You can be lonely when you are with the man you love?"

Honor was instantly angry at her prying. Her voice was strained and deliberate. "Yes, one can be lonely even when they are with the man they love."

Consuelo looked contrite. "Forgive me, Honor. I did not mean to make you angry. I just worry about Lucus being alone—"

Sparks flashed in Honor's eyes. "You've always loved him, haven't you? I've suspected it for a long time." Consuelo started to cry, causing Honor to melt immediately. "Please don't cry, Consuelo. I don't hold it against you. People can't help who they love in this life." She hesitated, then asked, "Did you fall in love with Lucus before you married Estéban?"

"No. After."

"I see."

"No, Honor, you don't see." Consuelo pulled a handkerchief from her pocket and dried her eyes.

"Only a Latin would understand. My marriage to Estéban was arranged by our parents when I was thirteen. I was still playing with dolls. At fourteen, I had my first child. The years went by, but I never grew to love Estéban."

Honor was astounded. "You married when you were thirteen?"

"*Sí*. Then Lucus came into my life. I met him at a fiesta. So . . . it started. He made me very happy. I have never known anyone as kind and gentle as him. But what we had . . . it did not revolve only around sex. That was not important to me. It was the closeness we shared. I had never before felt so close to another person." She turned to face Honor squarely. "I . . . we had a child, Honor, my daughter, Lita."

Honor was incredulous. "Lucus has a child?"

"*Sí*."

"But how can you be sure it's his and not Estéban's?"

"I know, Honor. There is no doubt."

"Does Lucus know this?"

"*Sí*, he does."

"But he never told me."

"I suppose," Consuelo said, "that is not the sort of thing a man would tell his wife."

Honor's voice faltered. "Why do you tell me this now? For what purpose?"

"I thought . . . if you and Lucus were finished . . . I would take Lita and go to him in Carlsbad."

"Go to Carlsbad! But what about Estéban and your other children?"

"That doesn't matter now."

"But how do you know that Lucus would want you to come?"

"I have no pride left. It does not matter to me that you are the one he loves. I have waited many years to be with him, always believing that someday we would be together. I know he would let me stay."

Honor's head was swimming. She wished she could move back in time to yesterday and wrap herself once again in the tranquility of her solitude. Why did today have to happen? And now, on top of everything, Julian . . . and Consuelo! *Damn it all.*

She looked directly at the other woman, her voice sharp and angry. "Consuelo, Lucus and I are not finished. Not at all! He is still my husband and you must respect that. I am deeply sorry for all you've been through. But I cannot give you permission to go to my husband. It's impossible."

Consuelo's face was suddenly tired and drained, her voice wavering. "I am sorry to have upset you, Honor. I suppose it is unrealistic for me to go to him without being asked. But I have hope." She got up slowly and went inside, leaving Honor alone in the still darkness.

Damn you, anyway, Honor thought as she watched Consuelo close the door behind her. You gave Lucus the one thing I could never give him. A child. Damn you! She slumped back in the chair. Did that really matter now? She'd never loved Lucus, really. But her pride made it impossible to release him to another woman. Even if she did, it was too late for Consuelo. Honor could never reveal to her that Lucus was too troubled for any woman now. Hot tears slid down her cheeks. She wondered who, or what, she was really crying for.

Honor moved through the next day's festivities in icy silence. She had lost her taste for them. When Consuelo finally deposited her at home the next evening near dusk, it was with a great sense of relief that she shut the courtyard door and found herself alone again.

She had only just dropped her canvas suitcase on the *sala* floor when she heard a loud knock behind her. She opened the door to find a messenger bearing a note encased in a white linen envelope.

Honor stared at the envelope for some time, afraid to open it. What was she afraid of? she wondered. That it was Julian asking to see her, or that it was not from

Julian after all? The messenger waited patiently for an answer, kneading a large sombrero in his thin hands.

She turned away from him, helpless from her fears and lack of confidence. Julian still had powers over her, she thought. But after all, maybe he had changed. Perhaps if she saw him she wouldn't feel the same way. Time had changed her. Could Julian Borg be exempt from the ravages of years?

She was jolted back to reality by the sharp memory of all the pain he had caused her. Was she mad even to consider for an instant seeing him again? She hastily tore open the letter, her hands shaking.

Dear Honor,

I recently saw Drew in New York and he informed me that you were here in Santa Fe. What a coincidence! I had planned a trip to this part of the country for some time.

Would you think it bold of me to want to see you again? I am staying at the Exchange Hotel. Please, meet me here tomorrow night at eight for dinner. How I will look forward to it.

As ever,
Julian

Her voice subdued, she told the messenger to wait. Going inside, she sat at her writing desk and answered Julian's note.

Julian,

What a lovely surprise. Thank you for asking, but I really must decline. My appointment book is so filled, it makes my head spin.

I hope you enjoy your stay.

Regards,
Honor

It would only serve as a temporary respite. She could vividly recall his persistence.

Twenty

HONOR RETURNED from a late-afternoon visit with Dr. Morales in a state of shock. Her body shaking, she poured herself a glass of sherry with trembling hands, finishing it off in one gulp. She poured another and wandered aimlessly into the court-yard. It couldn't be true. Not now, after all this time.

Pregnant! Why now? she agonized. She didn't even know where Clay was exactly. And how would Lucus take this final insult to his manhood? *Pregnant!* It was Clay's child she was carrying, not Lucus's. *Lord!* How jealous she had been on hearing that Consuelo had given Lucus a child when she had been unable to. What an incredible turn of affairs.

Suddenly she panicked, thinking of Elijah. There was no reason to assume he would know anything about the circumstances, she consoled herself. He would naturally think the child was Lucus's. But if it looked Indian? How would she explain that to Elijah? He'd never suspected for a minute that he'd been born out of wedlock. There'd been no reason in the world for Honor to lose his respect by telling him. How awful if that should happen over this.

A gentle knock on the street door pulled her thankfully away from her thoughts. For the fifth day in a row, a messenger bearing a bouquet of yellow, long-stemmed roses stood before her. All were from Julian, with accompanying notes prodding her to change her mind about seeing him, pleading for a chance to speak with her.

Today her resolve never to see him again, as well

as her patience, was worn thin. He had finally caught her in a moment of weakness. She needed to be with someone, anyone, to get herself away from this house where she was forever locked in uneasy thoughts.

Besides, Julian was quite obviously not about to give up. Perhaps she'd better see him just once and have it over with. How would it look for Señora Kant to be out in the company of a strange man? she wondered.

To hell with propriety, she decided. An evening out would do her good. She returned a note with the messenger, agreeing that this evening they would meet for dinner.

At the threshold of the hotel bar, Honor tried to locate Julian in the darkness. She was again doubting the wisdom of their meeting. She'd hesitated before leaving her house, fussing with her hair far too long, changing her dress twice before at last being satisfied with her appearance. She had settled on a low-cut, green chiffon gown; velvet pressed to look like ribbing; decorated at the bodice with a profusion of white linen daisies and green velvet bows. Beneath it she wore a long-sleeved white eyelet blouse reaching to her neck. Her outfit was completed by a wide-brimmed evening hat with poufs of white lace.

Viewing herself in a mirror, she was still nervous and knew it, vowing that nothing would happen between them. She'd have dinner with him, but nothing more. Then perhaps he'd leave her be. She wouldn't worry about her problems tonight. She'd relax and enjoy herself.

Instantly Julian appeared before her. That smile . . . that warm, engaging smile entrapping her with its radiance. In spite of her resolutions, she felt a spark of attraction as she whispered, "Julian," extending her gloved hand in greeting. He lifted it, brushing his lips across her covered fingers, holding the hand just a fraction too long. Self-consciously she pulled away, having expected to receive a proper shake, not this European affectation.

"Honor, you look smashing," he said as he led her to a small round table set with a service for two.

"You look well, too, Julian."

"I've ordered dinner ahead of time. Was that all right?"

"Of course. That's fine."

"Will you have some sherry first?"

"I would love a glass." She watched him motion the waiter to them, knowing immediately that she had made a grave mistake by seeing Julian again. The attraction was still there—still strong. Her temples were beginning to throb.

Throughout dinner she mostly listened, often amused, as Julian regaled her with stories of England and the shining part of life there that was so grandly opulent. He related tales to her of fat-jowled men and fat-buttocked women caught in a lascivious maze of Victorian frivolity. She *was* enjoying herself. It seemed such a long time since she'd had a reason to laugh.

His life was quite a contrast to her pastoral existence of the past few years, she thought. She couldn't help but be impressed, titillated, sucked in as she'd always been by Julian's warmth and flair for drama. At the end of the meal, over rice pudding, came the inevitable exchange of questions.

Julian shifted in his chair. "What became of Gilly, Honor? I went to the house in Greenwich Village, only to find strangers living there."

"Gilly died just before I came to New Mexico. Her heart gave out. She was quite old." Uneasily changing the subject, she asked, "What about your book? Did you ever finish it?"

"I not only finished it, but it's been published in London. Just last year."

Her gray eyes sparkled. "How wonderful. I would love to read it."

"I'll give you an autographed copy." He paused,

leaning back in his chair and studying her before asking, "Tell me, what about you? What have you been up to besides getting married?"

"Well, I've taken up painting rather seriously. The gallery I own in Carlsbad has sold quite a few of my oils and watercolors."

"How exciting! You must paint one for me, Honor. Santa Fe is rich with atmosphere for an artist. I would love a scene of this city."

"Of course, Julian. I'd be happy to."

"Good. Good."

They lapsed into silence, which Honor broke by blurting, "What do you want of me, Julian?"

"Want of you? Why, nothing except to see you again." He reached across the table for her hand, whispering, "I've never been able to forget you, Honor."

She desperately wanted to ask him why he'd left her, but she couldn't frame the question. Perhaps, she realized, she really didn't want the answer. She wasn't ready to hear it. And it had happened, after all, a long time ago. She withdrew her hand from his touch.

Julian cut in on her thoughts. "Drew told me that you're separated from your husband. Is that true?"

"Yes."

"What went wrong?"

"I really don't care to go into it, Julian."

He laughed. "Still the same, aren't you?"

She looked at him quizzically. "Still the same?"

"You always found it difficult to talk of personal matters. You're an intensely private person, Honor Wentworth. I think that's why you're such an exciting woman. Everything about you is so veiled in mystery."

Honor was uneasy. The conversation was leading toward something she didn't want to get involved in. "I'm afraid I'm getting a headache, Julian. I really must go home now."

He grew quiet for a moment. "Let me accompany

you, Honor. You shouldn't be running about alone
at this time of night."

"There's really no need to. I'll be fine."

"No, I insist." He stood up and reached into his
pocket for some coins. Tossing them onto the table,
he came up behind her to pull out her chair.

She stood up reluctantly, letting him lead her out
into the cool night.

Julian pulled the buggy to a halt in front of her
house. "I'll walk you in, Honor."

She was about to enter the house, then turned to
say goodbye. "Take my buggy back to the hotel,
Julian. You can have it returned to me in the morning."

He blocked the doorway so that she couldn't get
past him. "Won't you invite me in for a bit, love? I
won't stay long, I promise."

"Really, Julian, I have a headache."

"Please. Just for a little while."

She hesitated, then acquiesced. "Very well," she
said, permitting him to follow her through the courtyard. Lighting a candle that stood on a table next to
the *sala,* she led him inside; then, after she brought
the fire to a blaze, they both sat on the Navajo rug in
front of it, warming themselves.

Quietly studying him, Honor thought Julian looked
tired, his green eyes faded. Her gaze fell on his full
blond mustache mottled with tobacco, then on his
tousled blond hair. Regarding his face carefully, she
suddenly saw him as the young boy he had once been,
vulnerable, sweetly innocent. Something tugged inside
her.

Honor let him fondle the thick honey-blonde
strands of her hair, allowing herself to be pulled to
him as he planted kisses on her moist lips. It felt good
to be close to a man again, she thought. In that moment she realized how lonely she'd really been.

She suddenly stiffened, realizing what she was doing, and drew away from him, suffused with guilt. At

that moment the memory of Clay flashed across her mind with startling force. But Clay was gone, she thought. *Gone.* Julian was here. Perhaps he *was* finally ready to give himself to her completely.

Honor was overcome with a longing to go back, wishing to recapture with Julian the shared memories and innocence of lost youth. Could she? Was it possible? Or was she merely deluding herself with this man who'd once hurt her so deeply? But at this moment the past was remote.

Yet nagging at the back of her mind was the problem of the unborn child growing within her. Clay's child. Clay, she thought, how I miss you.

She couldn't bear it any longer. Couldn't bear to be this physically close to a man without consummating her rekindled desires. Clay had brought her to the full peak of her womanhood, and she fervently needed to feel that way again. She threw her arms recklessly around Julian's neck, returning his caresses with a matching ardor. She was well past the point of reason.

Twenty-one

THE BED was cold and damp. Shivering, Honor jerked the twisted wool blanket up to her nose and hugged her arms around her shoulders. In her lethargy she wondered if the room was indeed all that icy, or was it the lack of warmth in her heart that was chilling her?

She turned over on her side and moved her hand over the pillow next to hers. With a start she fully awakened, staring at the empty portion of the bed. Again, *again,* Julian had not come home to her.

She sat up, calling out his name, then sank back, knowing she was alone. Why did he always do this to her? she fretted. How could this frightful situation with Julian Borg have happened in the first place? It was her fault. She should have known better and never have let him move in!

Dejectedly, Honor burrowed her head in the pillow, her profusion of honey-gold hair tangled around her. This liaison with Julian had cost her quite a bit, she thought bitterly; it had forced her to retreat from the predominantly Spanish community around her. The great, carved doors of Santa Fe were now closed to Honor, the remembered hospitality virtually nonexistent.

Nothing slipped by unnoticed by the people here, and certainly not her living arrangement with an Anglo outsider. Honor was now regarded as a tainted woman in their eyes. People kept their distance, studiously avoiding her. She often found herself walking up to once-friendly faces at the marketplace, only to be shunned. She held her head up higher, vowing to herself that she wouldn't let them see how much this hurt her. But she began to avoid the market, anyway.

All this, she numbly realized, and the fact that Julian demeaned her in the bargain. Where was he now? She turned over on her stomach, pounding her fist into the pillow. She didn't know how to cope any more.

Honor could no longer keep track of how often Julian had come home drunk and abusive during the past weeks. The days were running together, blurred and foggy. Periods of remorse would follow, combined with heady protestations of love. As if these displays could make up for his former bad behavior.

From one day to the next she never knew what to expect from him, finding herself living on a precipice of impending doom. Often, too often, he would not come home at all, which drove her into jealous temper fits. Like now, she thought!

Forcing herself out of her reverie, Honor climbed out of bed. Removing her nightdress before a long, oblong mirror, her attention was riveted to the reflected image. Refracted sunshine seeping in through sheer white curtains cast blotches of light on her still high and pointed breasts. Her gaze fell to her haunches, which seemed to grow wider by the day, then to her slightly protruding stomach.

She wondered how much longer she could conceal the truth from Julian about the coming baby. She picked up a hairbrush from the dressing table adjacent to the glass and gave her lackluster honey-colored hair a few strokes, only to drop her arm listlessly.

She moved closer to the mirror, tracing the outline of her reflection with a thin fingertip, wondering where that once-lovely girl had disappeared to. Hardly recognizing herself, she saw before her a woman with purple circles beneath large, almond-shaped gray eyes; her mouth was drawn and pinched. But she was still young; her twenty-fifth birthday was a few months away. How could she have changed so suddenly? Where had Honor Wentworth gone?

Suddenly he was there behind her, his image reflected above her bare shoulder. She jerked around to face him in an instantaneous fit of rage, screaming, "Where have you been all night? Where have you been?" Her voice was coarse and shrill.

Julian held out a hand to steady himself on a nearby table and laughed at her. "Out with a piece that's better than you, love." He laughed again.

The room became a blur to her. Forgetting her nakedness, she lunged for him, her fists pummeling his chest, shoulders, and arms. "I hate you, Julian Borg! I hate you!" she cried with savage vehemence.

Julian grabbed hold of her writhing hands, clasping her wrists so tightly that she winced and moaned from the pain. "You don't hate what I do for you in bed though, do you? You like that." He laughed triumphantly and held her wrists even tighter.

"You're drunk," she whispered in a thin, frightened voice, reeling against him. "You're always drunk."

"Do you know you look like hell?" Julian remarked sarcastically. "Small wonder I'm not always here."

"Why don't you leave, then?" she pleaded desperately. "For God's sake . . . just leave."

Julian released her, pushing her roughly away from him. He chewed his upper lip thoughtfully for a moment while staring at her. "One day I will." He pulled her back to him, holding her at the buttocks, kissing the hollow softness in her neck.

"I hate you, Julian Borg," she murmured. "I hate you." But despite herself, she was clinging to him with fervor, allowing herself to be eased backward onto the bed, allowing him to enter her. Why couldn't she do without him? When had he become an obsession?

It was the dead of night. Honor sat alone in the courtyard, a shawl pulled tightly over her dressing gown, her braided hair falling over her breasts. Bathed in moonlight, she sat frozen to the chair. She'd tried to sleep earlier, but, frustrated in her attempts, she'd finally gotten up and wandered outside.

Her chest felt tight, her whole being dull and weighted down by some silent, invisible force. She wondered if brandy might help her to sleep. Just as she was about to get up to go to the kitchen, she heard the sounds of a horse and buggy advancing toward the house. Was it Julian? Her heart lurched with anticipation.

After a few moments a loud knock on the courtyard door startled her. Why would Julian be knocking? she asked herself. She got up to answer it and was surprised to find Consuelo standing before her. Honor looked beyond her to see Lita bundled up in a large blanket in the buggy. "Consuelo, why are you out at this hour?"

"Could I come in for a moment, Honor?"

"Why, of course." She stepped aside to let her pass.

"I could not be sure I would find you up," Consuelo said.

"I couldn't sleep. I've been up for a long time."

Consuelo's eyes darted from Honor toward the direction of the house, then back again. "Are you alone?"

"Yes. Can I offer you something?"

"No. Nothing. I do not have much time."

"What is it, Consuelo? Why are you out at this hour with Lita? Is something wrong?"

"I have made my decision, Honor."

Honor stared at her blankly for a moment. "What decision?"

"I waited until the whole house was asleep," Consuelo continued, ignoring Honor's question. "Then I wrapped Lita up in a blanket and brought her to the buggy. I have our bags packed. In them is all we will need."

"What are you talking about, Consuelo? Why have you done this?" Honor suddenly grasped what Consuelo was going to say, and she didn't want to hear it.

"I am taking Lita and going to Lucus in Carlsbad. If he will have us, we will stay with him."

Honor sucked in her breath. "You can't do this. You're not thinking clearly. Please, Consuelo. Think!"

Consuelo's dark eyes flashed at her. "You cannot object to this. Lucus is nothing to you any more," she said defiantly.

"It's not for myself I'm begging you to reconsider. What about Estéban? What about your other children? My God, you can't just abandon them."

"Estéban and the other children will survive without me. My place is with Lucus. It has always been with Lucus. He has a right to see his child grow into womanhood."

"And what about Estéban's right?"

"I do not love Estéban," she declared firmly. "I cannot live the rest of my life without love."

Honor nervously wrung her hands together. Her

voice was now shaky and distraught, reflecting her inner turmoil. "Why did you come and tell me this? For what purpose?"

"I wanted to make sure you knew where I stand. If you were to change your mind and return to Lucus, I would put up a fight. That is what I wanted you to know."

"You're afraid of me." Honor's voice flattened.

"*Sí*. I am afraid of you. You are the one Lucus loves. But you do not deserve him. Only I love him. Only I can give him what he really needs."

Honor slumped down onto a chair. "You needn't fear me. I will not be returning to Lucus." She thought for a moment, then said, "There is something you must know, Consuelo."

Consuelo's eyes narrowed suspiciously. "*Sí?*"

"Lucus is not the man he used to be. The caverns have changed him. It's hard to explain what happened, but Lucus has gone inside himself. He's no longer connected to the reality of life around him. He's chosen another place to dwell in—a religious, spiritual plane of sorts. All this has finally brought him to a state of celibacy. He's a different man, Consuelo. He'd be no good for you any more."

Consuelo weighed Honor's words carefully. "Why should I believe you?" she finally asked.

"I expect you don't have to believe me. If you're determined to go, you'll soon find out for yourself. In all conscience, though, I can't let you leave without knowing this."

"If this is true, it does not matter to me. What I have in my heart for Lucus is bigger than just physical closeness. It is much more than that. Just to have him near to me . . . That would be enough."

"You are sure about that?"

"*Sí*," Consuelo said decisively. "*Sí*. I am sure."

"Then I wish you luck, Consuelo. I really do."

"You mean this, Honor?" She looked surprised.

"Yes, I do. You'll not have any trouble from me. Perhaps you *could* make Lucus happy. I certainly couldn't. Lucus is a good man. He deserves happiness."

Consuelo stared at Honor for a moment, then walked toward the gate. She paused to look back at her. "I wish you luck also."

Honor listened to the buggy speed off in the late-night stillness. At this moment her only thought was with Estéban. Poor man, she mused. What a mess this will make of his life. She paused for a moment, realizing that she had done the same with her own. As had all of them.

She finally got up and went to the kitchen for brandy, praying that sleep would come soon to obliterate the world from her troubled mind.

Honor reined in the horse abruptly and jumped from the buggy in haste. Running to the massive carved entrance of Consuelo's house, she banged on it with all her might. Estéban answered apprehensively; then, realizing it was Honor, he stared fixedly at her dress, which was torn in shreds from both shoulders.

"Please help me, Estéban," she cried. "Please . . ."

He reached out to grab hold of her arm. "Honor, calm down and tell me what has happened."

"It's Julian," she gasped. "He's gone mad. Completely mad. Oh, Estéban, I need help. Come home with me. Please come!" She pulled on his sleeve, leading him to the buggy. Heeding the urgency of her plea, Estéban moved quickly, taking control of the horse from her shaking hands.

As they raced off, Honor covered her fear-stricken eyes with her hands, trying to shut out the horror from her mind. "Oh, my God," she moaned over and over, "oh, my God. I thought he was going to kill me."

They found Julian writhing on the bedroom floor, his hands and protruding tongue trembling violently, a fractured lamp lying next to him. A trickle of blood oozed from a large gash on his forehead. Honor cringed in the doorway while Estéban bent down over him, cradling Julian's head.

"How long has he been like this?" Estéban asked.

"He woke up early this morning screaming . . . something about a tiger clawing him. He doesn't seem to know who he is or what's happening. What is it, Estéban? What's wrong with him?"

"Has he been drinking very much?"

"Almost nonstop."

"Go get Dr. Morales. Do you know where his house is?"

"Yes," she murmured, but she couldn't tear her eyes from Julian's tormented body.

"Go get the doctor, Honor," Estéban sharply directed. "We must have him. Go."

When Honor returned with the doctor, a hellish scene greeted them.

Julian was screaming at the top of his lungs, "Get it away from me. It's clawing me . . . ! Get it away!" Estéban was desperately trying to restrain him. A heated struggle was taking place on the floor as Julian resisted.

The doctor moved his large bulk toward them and told Estéban, "We must get him on the bed." To Honor he directed, "Go and bring some strong rope. *Pronto, señora.*"

Honor was unable to react, unable to think. Then she ran from the bedroom to the *sala* for the rope that encircled the saddle on the wall, Julian's tormented screams following her. When she came back, she saw him being forcibly dragged to the bed as he fought the two men with superhuman ferocity. Helplessly, she stood in the doorway.

As they pushed his frame across the bed Dr. Morales shouted to her, "Don't just stand there. We need your help. Bring the rope."

Honor did as she was ordered, watching with numb horror as Julian suddenly fell over in a slump. "What is it?" she cried. "Is he dead?"

"No," Dr. Morales answered, "just passed out." He looked at Estéban. "You tie his feet to the bottom bedpost while I tie his hands to the top." This task accomplished, he retrieved his bag. "Bring me a glass of water, *señora.*"

Unrolling a thin, neatly folded piece of parchment paper, he pulled open Julian's slackened mouth, poured a gray powdery substance down his throat, and washed it down with the clear liquid Honor proffered, causing Julian to gag violently.

Dr. Morales leaned back and relaxed, out of breath. "I will leave you a supply of this opium, *señora.* You may give it to him once every few hours to sedate him, if he needs it." He closed his bag and stood up.

"What's wrong with him, Doctor?" she gasped. "What happened?"

"This man drinks much, *señora?*"

"Yes."

"That is what I thought. It appears to me that he is suffering from delirium tremens. It is a common malady among heavy drinkers."

"Delirium tremens?"

"*Si, señora.* The D.T.'s."

Honor stared uncomfortably at Julian trussed to the bedposts. "Does he need to be kept tied, Doctor?"

Dr. Morales stared thoughtfully at Julian for a moment. "If I were you, I would keep him that way until you are sure he has calmed down. When he is better, tell him to come and see me. I will talk to him about his drinking problem and try to help him. But he must not be left alone for the present. You will be able to stay with him, *señora?*"

"Yes."

Dr. Morales asked Estéban, "You can take me home?"

"*Si,* of course." He looked at Honor. "I will come back, Honor. I will not be long."

Honor collapsed in an over-stuffed chair after they left, gazing at Julian's face now stilled in repose.

She couldn't move, remaining in one position until Estéban returned.

When he discovered her morose state of mind, Estéban pulled her stiff body to another room where they could speak freely. "What will you do now, Honor? You cannot continue to live with this man the way he is."

"I can't think ahead. Right now I will care for Julian until he's well again."

Estéban nodded and shrugged his shoulders. "I will stay with you for a while, Honor. I will not leave you alone."

"That is very kind of you, Estéban. Thank you."

Estéban studied her for a moment before saying in a low, hushed voice, "Consuelo has left me to join Lucus in Carlsbad. Do you have knowledge of this, Honor?"

She glanced at him quickly, then lowered her lashes to avoid his melancholy expression. "Yes, Estéban, I do. She came to see me the night she and Lita left."

Estéban's eyes clouded over with emotion. "This is sad for the other children. I do not know how to explain it to them. I woke up that morning to find, not her next to me, but a letter. What could I say to the children? It makes no sense to them." He paused for a moment, then continued in a broken voice. "Consuelo was always a good mother. Believe me, Honor, she always was."

"I believe you, Estéban," she said gently. "I know that she was."

"This action of hers did not surprise me, though. I have always known how she felt about Lucus. She would be shocked to learn that, but I always knew."

"If it's any consolation to you at all, Estéban, she's too late for Lucus."

"Too late? What do you mean?"

"I received a note yesterday from my friend, Sophie, in Carlsbad. She informed me that Lucus has entered a monastery."

"A monastery?"

"Yes. I told Consuelo before she left that Lucus had undergone a change. That he wasn't the man he used to be. She said she didn't care."

"But how does this affect your marital status, Honor? This is all so strange."

"I really don't know, Estéban. I expect I'll have to see a lawyer and try to figure it out. I don't know what I will do. In any case, my marriage to Lucus was ended long ago."

"I suppose, in many ways, mine ended long ago as well."

"Estéban," she whispered softly, "I am sorry." He cleared his throat. "But I do not think badly of her. These matters are best left to the *confesionario*. It now concerns only Consuelo and God."

"You won't try to get her back?"

"No," he said gruffly. "I will not. You cannot force a person to be where they don't want to be."

"Oh, Estéban, it's my fault. If I hadn't returned to Santa Fe, Consuelo might not have left. Perhaps none of this would have happened," she added, thinking of Julian.

"Do not foolishly blame yourself for the tragedy in others' lives, Honor. Only God determines destiny."

They both lapsed into silence. *Only God determines destiny*. Over and over, Honor repeated this statement to herself, seriously questioning its truthfulness. Don't we have any control over our lives at all? she asked herself. Is everything predestined? She thought back to the gypsy in Carlsbad and her ominous prediction: *"Her* end will be *your* end."

The gypsy believed that the unfolding drama of people's lives could be forecast ahead of time. Was that really true? In the end, are we all merely pawns in a universal, prearranged chess game? Honor wondered bleakly. She wouldn't let herself accept this idea. Free will, she thought, free will liberates us from a belief in destiny. Suddenly she felt small and helpless, caught in a microscopic web of uncertainty.

The sky was a clear, cloudless turquoise and the August air sweet with the fragrance of hollyhocks. Honor shuffled her feet impatiently at the threshold of the courtyard while she waited for Julian to exit from the house.

Today they would picnic. After suffering through Julian's long, nightmarish drying-out period, a picnic was just what they both needed. He *wouldn't* drink again. He'd promised and she'd believed him, determined to drive away bleak memories.

Over an early breakfast, they'd decided to spend the afternoon at an old abandoned fort Honor had once been to that rested on a high bluff one third of a mile northeast of the plaza. The buggy was loaded with a basket of fruit, cooked chicken, a book for Julian to read, and an easel and paint equipment for herself.

To anyone looking in, Honor thought dismally, it had the appearance of a normal family excursion. If only this were so . . . if only. As if out of nowhere Julian appeared, and they were off.

Santa Fe melted behind them as they quietly rode along an archaic wagon road that led to the large, mud-walled building of the fort, finally pulling up before the blockhouse. Once an observation tower, Honor knew from her past visit that the surrounding area was the highest and most favorable point from which to enjoy the extensive view of the vast horizon.

While they unloaded, no words were exchanged between them. They had not talked to each other very much at all lately, both hanging suspended in a unified state of numbing limbo. Away from him, she still enjoyed and derived pleasure from life. With him, she lived a joyless existence. But she couldn't bear the thought of being without him, of being alone. She sighed, smiling wanly when he suddenly looked her way.

His pale brows drew together in an inquiring frown, but he asked casually, "Are you hungry yet, love?"

"No," she answered. "But you go ahead if you want to. I think I'll sketch for a bit."

He nodded, laying a blanket down and spreading out their lunch. "Go on," he said roughly.

She pretended not to notice the edge in his voice as she turned from him and settled herself on the ground with drawing paper and a black crayon.

The sunshine and shadows were just right today, clearly marking one glorious mountain range after another, in almost interminable succession. Through a narrow gap in the horizon she could see the blue outline of a distant peak in the far southwest, fully seventy-five miles away. With all this panorama to choose from, she had trouble deciding what to draw first, finally settling on a snowcapped mountain peak to the east.

As always, she became enmeshed in her work, losing track of time and place. When the first sketch was finished, she set her crayon down and looked Julian's way. He was reading. She leaned back against a tree and stared at the uneven horizon before her.

For the first time she felt a sharp thrust of longing for Elijah's presence. Until this moment she had been grateful that he had been spared the torments of the summer. Her mind traced over the bits and pieces of memories that only she and Elijah had shared, remembering how they had joyfully joined together in the adventure of moving to a new life in New Mexico. Both had been full of optimism then, Honor especially happy over the prospect of Elijah's finally having a father. Where had that dream gone to? she wondered.

Now she desperately wanted to feel Elijah's small, warm body close to hers. Where had she been? Was she really so numb that the full impact of their separation had only just reached her?

Elijah will be home with me again soon, she consoled herself. But how will he fit into this arrangement with Julian? She felt helpless, torn between love for her son and a yearning to remain with Julian. Elijah, she thought, my son, my life. What am I to do?

She turned dejectedly toward Julian. Getting up, she joined him on the blanket, helping herself to a plump apricot.

"We have to talk, Honor," Julian said, putting down his book.

She shrank from him, her voice coming out faintly. "What about?"

"You know very well what about. We can't continue to live together in silence."

She looked away from him. "I know."

"Honor, I'm . . ." He hesitated, then went on. "I'm deeply sorry for all I've put you through. Deeply sor—"

"I know you are," she interrupted.

"Please . . . let me finish. I wish there were some way to make this up to you. I've put you through hell. But I really do love you. It's taken me a long time to face it, but I mean it with all my heart."

Honor felt nothing on hearing these words. She realized there had been a time when they would have meant heaven and earth, but it was too late. Then why did she still cling to this relationship? Would she ever find the courage to end it? She shrugged slightly as Julian resumed speaking.

"You're the only reason I came to Santa Fe. I came to find you, hoping we could still have some life together. But I'm in a muddle." He studied her expressionless face with rapidly diminishing self-composure. A curious hesitation entered his voice. "I don't know how my drinking could have become such a problem. I can't remember when I couldn't do without it. The past couple of years have somehow become a blur," he finished lamely.

Honor stared straight into his eyes. "Why do you drink, Julian? Do you know why?"

"No . . . not really. I only know I'm in emotional pain, and for a while, when I completely saturate myself with liquor, the ache goes away."

Her expression softened. "Julian," she murmured.

He suddenly looked grave. "That awful day when I said I would leave you . . . I didn't mean that. I need you, Honor. I could never leave you again."

Honor flinched at the memory of that day. She jumped up and moved away from him.

His voice was pleading. "Don't walk away from me. Talk to me, Honor. Please . . . talk to me."

She hesitated, then turned back, observing him almost regretfully. "Don't expect anything from me any more, Julian. I can't give you what you need. I probably never could. I didn't understand when you jilted me years ago. Now I do."

"Honor, that had nothing to do with you. It was something inside me that feared responsibility. Believe me."

"And now, Julian? How do you feel about responsibility now? Has anything really changed?"

She watched him mutely shake his head in bewilderment. Sighing deeply, she studied this tortured, handsome man who'd altered the course of her whole life—this man she couldn't seem to live without. Yet she knew they were strangers and would always remain so. She could never know him. What had brought them together again to share this strange journey through life? she asked herself.

At this moment Honor sensed he needed to hear something reassuring, but she had nothing left to offer him. Pitying him, she remembered that night when she'd pitied Lucus, too. Why, in the end, did she feel sorry for the men in her life? Would it have come to that with Clay, too? *Clay.* His name stabbed at her. She looked sharply at Julian, suddenly wanting to hurt him as much as he'd hurt her. "It's too late for us."

"No. That's not tr—"

"It's too late." Her voice bordered on a scream. "I'm pregnant, Julian. Pregnant!"

He stared at her incredulously. "We're going to have a child?"

"No, Julian. It's not yours."

"Does Lucus know?"

"No. But it doesn't matter, really. The baby is not Lucus's, either." She breathed a sigh of relief, the burden of her secret finally lifted from her. Now Julian knew. She stared at him defiantly, challenging him.

He looked at her steadily, in silence, then rose and walked away. Turning back to her for a moment, he flung out sarcastically, "History certainly repeats itself, doesn't it, Honor?" Then, with his back to her, he kept on walking.

She watched him go, tears stinging her eyes. All desire for Julian was absent from her life, as was indeed desire for any man. Where had it gone to? Her desire, like a wild, winged bird, had taken flight, leaving her encased in an empty, abandoned shell. She finally turned away from the sight of Julian, a profound loneliness enveloping her.

Twenty-two

A LOUD noise jarred Clay from the deep recesses of his sleep. He tried unsuccessfully to shake it away, but it returned with repeated constancy. Eventually groping his way back to consciousness, he opened his ebony eyes with a start, hearing a loud knocking on the door. He sat up, calling groggily, "Just a minute."

He turned to the young Indian girl huddled next to him under the covers. Patting her arm, he whispered, "It's all right. I'll get rid of whoever it is." He pulled the blankets away from his naked body and swung his muscular legs over the side, reaching for his faded blue pants lying on the floor. Pulling them on, he moved to the door and opened it a crack to see Cyrus Zabez greeting him with a jubilant smile.

"Whatcha doin' sleeping this time of day, you ol' hawk?"

Clay smiled. "Wait for me down in the bar, will you, Cyrus? I'll be there in a minute."

Cyrus stared at the slight opening in the doorway that prevented him from seeing further into the room. He winked broadly, saying, "Gotcha," and turned on his heel to descend the cracked wooden staircase.

Clay closed the door and moved to the girl, who was regarding him with wide, questioning eyes. "You can stay as long as you want. I've got to leave now." He sat down on the edge of the bed and pulled on rough wool socks and heavy boots, then reached for a shirt hanging over the side of a chair. Placing a beige hat on his head, he turned to look at her again before leaving quietly. What had brought Cyrus to California? he wondered.

Seated across from Cyrus, Clay lazily reached for the steaming cup of mud-brown coffee set before him. He sipped slowly, then leaned back in the hardwood chair, coming fully awake. "What brings you to Santa Rosa, Cyrus? Is something wrong at the mining operation in Carlsbad?"

"No. Well, yes. But nothing to concern yourself with."

"What is it?"

"Well, you see, Lucus has done gone, which sort of leaves us in a pickle."

"What do you mean, gone?"

"He's not foreman any more. He just up and left one day and said he's not coming back. He's an odd bird, that man."

Clay scrutinized Cyrus with interest. "Where did he go?"

"You're not going to believe this. Lucus has entered the confines of a monastery, telling all who care to listen that he's dedicating his life to God. Well, fine for him, but it left us without a foreman we can trust. I can't be there all the time with my other interests going, and here you are in California. Are you planning to stay here for good, Clay?"

"What about his wife?"

"I imagine I'll find someone else," Cyrus continued, seemingly oblivious to Clay's question. "Jake is filling in temporarily. Just wanted to know your plans, is all. It seems one of us should be around till we can put our finger on a good foreman. But listen, I don't want to worry you none. I didn't come all the way to California just to tell you this. I'm just having to journey to Oregon 'cause my wife wants to visit her people, and I decided to detour here first to let you know what's going on. I'll be back in Carlsbad next month sometime."

Clay waited until Cyrus had finished, then repeated, "What about Lucus's wife?"

"His wife? I'm told she moved to Santa Fe. Can't say what happened between them. As a matter of fact, she left not too long after you did."

"Did she?"

Cyrus studied him for a moment. "You have some interest in her, Clay?"

"You might say that."

"That's why she left Carlsbad!" He laughed, slapping his thigh. "I should have known, you ol' rake. Women sure like you. If I had a daughter, Clay Birdsong, I'd sure keep her locked up when you're around." He roared again.

Clay squirmed uncomfortably in his chair, frowning. "It was nothing like that, Cyrus. I was serious about her."

Cyrus's eyebrows knitted together quizzically. "Don't say? Well, I can't blame you none. That's one beautiful woman."

"You say she went to Santa Fe. Do you think she's still there?"

"Don't rightly know."

Clay nodded. "Tell you what, Cyrus. I'll go on to Carlsbad in a few days and see if I can find a new foreman. Put it out of your mind."

In a contained voice he maneuvered the conversation around to the finances of the mining operation, but beneath the surface Clay struggled valiantly to end the conversation so that he could escape and sort out his feelings.

Clay finally found himself alone in his room, staring thoughtfully out the dirty window. Nothing prevented him from stopping off in Santa Fe before going on to Carlsbad, he reasoned. She might still be there. There was always that chance.

Honor had hardly been out of his thoughts since he'd left Carlsbad. He couldn't count how many nights he'd lain in bed longing for her, recalling with startling clarity that morning when they'd made love, wishing she were always there next to him.

He'd driven himself crazy thinking about her, until he'd eventually sought solace with whores, following the same pattern here as he had in Carlsbad. But in the end that had never helped. The feel of another woman's flesh only heightened his need for Honor's. Hers was the only body he wanted. Damn it anyway, he thought miserably.

In frustration he reached for a cigar. He lit it, puffing profusely, angrily throwing the blown-out match across the room, wondering about the wisdom of chasing after Honor. She could have gone with him to California if she'd really wanted to. She could have! Perhaps his needs had been stronger than hers. Maybe he hadn't thought straight about this from the beginning. Maybe . . .

He quieted down, his anger making him feel ridiculous. An obviously overlooked truth might simply have been that she wanted to come but just couldn't get away on such short notice. Honor was the only one who knew the real truth. She *was* married. He'd given careful attention to that fact when he'd first realized his attraction toward her, yet had allowed himself to fall in love with her nonetheless, knowing at the time that Honor had considered him to be without any moral restraints on that issue.

But should he just walk back into her life again without notice? Yet if he didn't, he knew he was fated to live the remainder of his days in abject uncertainty. How would he ever know if their love had been real or imagined?

Clearly torn with conflict, Clay stayed in his room until the darkness of night enveloped him—pacing— worn out from the weight of his emotions.

It was ten A.M. when Honor found herself before the old, decaying adobe building that was the Exchange Hotel. She walked into the lobby and headed toward the entrance of the saloon. She waited there until her eyes adjusted to the dimness. She realized only too well that the saloon was a rendezvous for trappers, traders, merchants, and politicians: all male—a forbidden place for women. She shrugged her shoulders at this thought. Well past the point of propriety, she didn't care how it looked for her to be there.

She leaned against the frame for a moment, completely exhausted from staying up the entire night waiting for Julian to return home. No longer able to sit alone in the house for another minute, she had decided to take some action. She would find Julian and bring him back, knowing with certainty that he would be in the hotel bar. Glancing about the large room, she spied him playing cards.

She started toward him, acutely aware that her presence drew indignant stares in her direction, which she chose to ignore. Suddenly, she stopped, inexplicably sensing a familiar presence lurking in the shadows at the bar. Bewildered, she shrugged it off, straightened her shoulders proudly, and advanced to Julian's table.

Her heart sank on seeing his obvious inebriated state and the haggard, unshaven face that gave him, she thought, the terrifying look of a man gone mad. She hesitated, then reluctantly tugged at his shirt sleeve, the tone of her voice tinged with pleading. "Come home with me, Julian. Now. Please . . . come home."

He jerked his arm away from her, shouting, "Can't you see I'm busy? Get out of here."

"Julian, please," she prodded, ignoring the unabashed stares of the other men. "Please. You're drunk."

He thrust his chair away from the table and lunged for her, pushing her back by the shoulders. "Get out of here, you whore!" He pushed her again. "Let me be. I'll come home when I'm damned well ready to!" He spun away from her and returned to his seat, picking up his cards.

Her face hot with humiliation, she ran, somehow finding herself outside—falling—crying—not conscious of her body actually moving and getting her from one place to another.

Lying on the ground sobbing, she became aware of a masculine presence bending over her and gently touching her shoulder. Startled, she looked up and cried, "Clay! Oh, Clay!"

He lifted her from the ground and cradled her in his arms, crooning to her as to a small child. "It's all right now. It's all right. Everything's going to be fine . . . I'm here now . . . I'm here." He carried her back into the hotel and up to his room, all the while whispering endearments in her ear.

He placed her on the bed, removed her shoes, and covered her with a blanket. She fell into an immediate, exhausted sleep. He sat down in a chair next to the bed, never taking his eyes from her tear-stained face.

"I'm here," he murmured to her, "I'm here."

Clay let Honor rest on his hotel bed for three days.

He brought warm meals and stayed by her during the day, sleeping in an oversized chair at night. She still looked wretched, reminding him of a wounded soldier just returned from battle. He suspected she'd been through her own battle of sorts.

He wondered what she had really been through. She hadn't spoken much and he didn't press her. Instead, he'd filled in the hours with tales of his ancestors and his travels. He never hinted that he was curious about her entanglement with Julian. He'd wait until she was stronger.

On the fourth morning, seeing little recovery, Clay decided something had to be done. Honor was still unwell, still weak and without color in her face. He realized she couldn't very well remain in his hotel room indefinitely without causing further raised eyebrows, and he wouldn't consider bringing her back to her house. He'd asked around a bit and learned of her recent living arrangement with Julian. He supposed Julian was still in Honor's house. At any rate, Clay knew he was still in town.

So Clay began to search for a cabin to rent, finally locating one resting on the outskirts of Santa Fe. He knew the cabin would be difficult for most people to find, and he wanted Honor to recuperate in a remote area where she would not be subjected to gossip. At all costs, Julian must not be able to find her.

As the warm orange glow of sunset filtered through the panes, Clay told Honor of his plan. "It's a good location, Honor. A good place for you to be alone. I'll stay on here at the hotel and visit you every day. I'll bring you anything you need. You must have complete rest now, Honor. And this hotel room is not really the right place for it."

Honor was sitting stiffly before the window, a thick green blanket thrown over her legs. "I expect you're right, Clay," she said with a wan smile.

"Then I'll take you there tomorrow morning?"

"Yes, that will be fine." She regarded him seriously.

"You know, you're entitled to some kind of explanation for all this."

"I'm not entitled to anything. You don't have to tell me anything you don't want to."

"But I do want to tell you. I must."

Clay sat down on the edge of the feather-stuffed bed, facing her, relieved to have the mystery cleared up at last. "How did this happen, Honor?"

"You know I was living with Julian?"

"Yes, I do."

"It all seems so mixed up now. But you see, Julian and I were once engaged to be married. A long time ago . . . in New York. It was before I'd met Lucus. I dare say Julian was bad for me even then. This time around I should have known better. In any case, he'd heard from a mutual friend in New York that I was separated from Lucus, and he came looking for me. I resolved to be strong and not have anything to do with him, but in the end I weakened. I suspect loneliness played a large part in that, but I'm not making excuses for myself. He'd once meant a great deal to me, and seeing him again brought all those old feelings back."

Clay tried to be objective while he listened, but her words stung him. He experienced such a violent stab of jealousy that his voice came out sounding angry and gruff. "But how could you stay with a man who treated you so badly? If what I saw downstairs in the saloon was any indication of your life with him, it just doesn't make any sense to me at all."

Honor bit her lower lip, then said, "I know it's hard for you to understand, Clay, but I feel a great compassion for him. On the surface Julian appears to be the man who has everything. In reality he's lost . . . so lost."

"And you decided you were the one to save him."

"I expect it was something like that." She looked at him thoughtfully, her eyes misting over. "I can't imagine why you want anything more to do with me after this."

His anger gradually subsided as he stared at her in silence. Once he had regained control of his emotions, Clay said, "We'll leave for the cabin in the morning. All right?"

She nodded, no longer resisting, and watching the traffic in the street below. "All right."

Clay could not take his black eyes away from Honor's near-perfect profile, love swelling up inside him. Every fiber in his body yearned to hold her, to protect her from any more misfortune. Nothing could alter his feelings for her. What would happen to them from this point on he couldn't know, but he still cared despite everything. He always would. That he was sure of.

Tensely, Clay rode a sturdy palomino toward the cabin and the woman he loved, his dark hair rippling in the wind. He'd just left Julian, having met him for the first time. Inwardly shaken by their encounter and the shocking news Julian had thrust at him, he fervently hoped he'd never have to lay eyes on Julian Borg again.

Clay had not found Julian to be at all what he'd expected, and he wondered what Honor had ever seen in that weak and decidedly ineffectual man. He'd gone to see Julian with every intention of getting him out of Honor's house—out of her life.

When the amenities were over, they'd faced each other apprehensively. Clay had spoken first, lending the resonant words an emphasis and potent conviction as to make them unquestionable. "I'm ordering you to leave town. You've got three days to get your affairs in order. If you're not out by that time, I'm bringing the sheriff. This house is not your property, and you have no legal right to be in it."

Initially Julian had faltered, then looked back at him with amazement as he slowly absorbed the full impact of Clay's authoritarian directive. *"You're ordering me? Who the hell are you to dictate anything to me? What gives you the right?"*

"I want you out of Honor's life, Julian. Her welfare is now in my hands, and that gives me the right."

Julian's stare had changed his green eyes into frozen pools. "Not until I see Honor first."

Clay's own eyes had blazed with steel-like fury, though he kept the tone of his voice contained. "That's out of the question. I have Honor where you'll never find her. I've seen to that."

Julian had lapsed into an impotent rebellion. "Who do you think you are to keep her from me?" he'd shouted. "I demand to know where you have her!"

Clay, incredulous at Julian's gall, had lost his control, succumbing to the anger permeating him. "*You* demand? Who the hell are you to demand anything after the way you've treated her? You'll get near her again over my dead body. Is that clear?"

Julian, thoroughly defeated, had lowered his gaze to the floor, shuffling his feet restlessly. When he'd finally looked up, his mien suggested total indifference to the situation at hand. Nonchalantly he said, "You tell Honor I'm returning to New York and she can go to hell. Why should I waste my time on a whore, anyway?"

Clay's spine had stiffened at this last insult to Honor. "Why, you—"

"Well, I can see the truth hurts." With that, Julian had deliberately paused, eyeing Clay maliciously before slowly saying, "She's pregnant, did you know that? It's not my child. And it's not her husband's, either. Perhaps you should consider *that* before you take on the full responsibility of her!"

The chords of Clay's neck tensed with both shock and fury. In one stricken moment he'd become paralyzed; then, regaining his control, he'd lunged forward, his fist crashing into Julian's jaw, shouting, "You bastard! You'll go to any lengths to discredit her!"

Julian had toppled backward, falling, blood spurting from his mouth. He lay on the floor for a stunned moment, then fumbled in his pocket for a handkerchief. He looked up at Clay with venom. "You think I'm lying? Ask her yourself. Ask her."

Clay was momentarily dazed, then forced himself to turn on his heel and walk out, frustration and fury searing his guts . . .

Was she really pregnant? he wondered now as he drew closer to the cabin and Honor. And if she was, could the child be his? That was certainly within the realm of possibility. And if it was, why hadn't she told him?

Through a flux of disoriented, fragmented thoughts, Clay found himself experiencing extreme insecurity over his relationship with Honor, or rather, the seeming lack of it. He hadn't pressed her about their feelings for each other at all, neither touching her nor bringing anything serious into their conversations, not since that last day at the hotel. Perceiving that she needed to be alone, he had not infringed on her privacy, leaving her to recuperate and heal—only seeing her to provide her with groceries.

He'd never been insecure with any woman before, pondering how he could have gotten into something like this quite so deeply. He had to resolve this situation once and for all.

His thoughts wandered back to that day when he'd found Honor at the Exchange Hotel, reliving the shock of it all over again. He'd waited so long to find her, never in his wildest dreams expecting to discover her the way he did—ravaged and dissipated. It had been more than he could bear.

And now he had the knowledge of Honor's being pregnant to contend with. He really didn't think that Julian had lied about that. But what really plagued Clay the most was that Honor hadn't come away with *him,* but had chosen a man who obviously delighted in abusing and degrading her. Why? He would have given her anything—everything! Clay still would if he believed there was a chance for them.

As he moved closer to the clapboard cabin he was determined to bring it all out in the open. He had to know where he and Honor were headed, wherever that was, and if it was together. He had to know everything for the sake of his own sanity.

Clay found Honor sitting on the porch looking fresh and rested. It warmed him to see the shadows gone from beneath her eyes and the rosy color back in her cheeks. Studying her, he realized that her eyes had lost the haunted look that had characterized them when he'd found her. She was different now, emanating that quiet dignity he remembered so well. Now Honor seemed both at peace and happy to see him.

He sat down next to her, reaching into the pocket of his plaid shirt. "I picked up a letter for you at the post office."

She smiled as she looked at it. "Why, it's from Elijah. What a nice surprise."

"You look wonderful today. You're feeling better, aren't you?" His voice was strained in an effort to resist the urge to reach out and touch the golden glints in her hair.

She fingered the letter tentatively, then lay it unopened in the deep folds of her blue skirt. "Yes, I do." Her large eyes registering alarm, she asked, "What's wrong? You look uneasy."

"I just saw Julian." He watched her expression carefully. To his relief there was no noticeable reaction. "He's leaving town."

"I see."

"Are you sorry, Honor?"

"How could I be sorry? It had to end this way. We were going in circles."

Scrutinizing her intently, he said cautiously, "He told me that you're carrying a child. Is it true?"

She stiffened visibly. "I meant to tell you in my own way. I didn't mean for you to find out like that."

His throat constricted, and his voice was hoarse when he asked, "Is it mine?"

"Yes, Clay, the baby is yours."

He relaxed, then looked at her accusingly, unable to restrain what had been bothering him all along.

"Why did you choose Julian over me? I asked you to come away with me. There was no reason for you to carry this burden alone all this time. We could have been together. Why not me, Honor? I must know."

"Oh, Clay," she cried, reaching for his hand. "I *did* come that day. I *was* going away with you. But the train had already left. I missed you by only a few minutes. My God, I should have told you that from the first. I didn't realize—"

He pulled his strong hand away. "You should have waited for *me,* Honor. You had to know I would be back when the time was right. Did you really believe that I'd walked out of your life for good?"

"I was so confused after you'd left I didn't know what to believe, Clay. I had a terrible time with Lucus after that morning. With or without you in my life, I knew that Lucus and I would never resolve our problems. And I'd hurt him so deeply. At the time, it seemed the only thing left for me to do was to return to Santa Fe and be alone. To try to sort out my feelings. I didn't know what I wanted."

"And now, Honor? What do you want now?"

"I'm not sure."

Intensely studying her delicate face, he asked, "How do I fit in with that? How does our child fit in with that?"

Her large gray eyes downcast for several moments, she finally lifted her gaze to his. "I love you, Clay. I've loved you from the first moment I saw you."

"Then what's the problem? I'm here and I love you, too. You must know how much . . . We can put all that's happened behind us. We can have a future together, Honor."

"Perhaps you're capable of burying the past, Clay. I don't doubt that. But can I? I'm still so bruised . . . so confused."

"You must decide, Honor. If you let this chance for us slip through our fingers again, I won't be back," he declared urgently.

"Clay, I—" Her voice broke.

"Do you know what I think?" he said, his voice subdued and gentle. "I think you're afraid to accept my love. You can't live your life in fear, Honor. There comes that day of reckoning when you have to trust yourself enough to take a chance."

Her heart lurched as she recalled a similar conversation she'd once had with Lucus. Only then it hadn't concerned her. Or had it? What a mess she'd made of everything. "Could you give me a little more time, Clay?" she asked. "I really need it."

Clay looked away from her, gazing steadily at the surrounding meadow and the last flush of summer flowers that were paling in color. He thought deeply for a moment, then turned to her. "I have to go to Carlsbad. Why don't you come with me and stay with Sophie for a while? It'll give you more time to think everything through. If you choose to come with me, when I'm ready to return to California, we'll settle there. If not—"

"All right," she said softly. "That would be best, I think."

He got up, descended the porch steps in a single movement, and in long strides crossed the deserted meadow with no particular destination in mind. He would leave her alone for now. He needed to be alone as well to think this through.

Watching his powerful body disappear from view over a hill, Honor's heart ached with love for him. If only she had made that train and gone away with him. How different her life would be at present. Her recent experience with Julian blazed through her mind, shaming her. How could she have demeaned herself that way? It seemed as if another person had lived through that nightmare. Not her. Thankfully, it was fast receding from her consciousness.

Honor wondered about the duality of human nature, asking herself if in reality everyone wasn't more than one person at the same time—circumstances unearthing different people inside all of us. Staring off into the distance, she suddenly shuddered in the wake of the real truth about herself, forcing herself to confront it and deal with it.

She *was* afraid of love, incongruous though that seemed to her, for she'd always believed she'd been searching for it. But had she really? Or had she subconsciously sought out men like Julian and Lucus who would reject her in the end? Clay had perceptively tapped the hidden cause of her fear. He *was* different, and he frightened her because of it.

She couldn't bear to think about it any longer. Tears trickling down her cheeks, Honor diverted her attention to Elijah's letter. She opened it, warmed by the sight of her son's familiar scrawl.

Dearest Mama,
    Vacation is over shortly. Can't wait to see you and tell you about my summer.
    Where shall I meet you? Will you be in Santa Fe or Carlsbad?

                                        Your boy,
                                        Elijah

Walking inside to get a pencil and tablet, Honor sat down to answer him.

Elijah,
    I am returning to Carlsbad. How I look forward to seeing you again.

                                        Your loving mother

"I've committed myself on paper," Honor spoke to the empty room. Still, she wondered, where will the wings of desire take Clay and me. If only she knew.

Twenty-three

IT WAS a late, sunny Thursday afternoon when Clay halted the buggy in front of Sophie's small home in Carlsbad. He helped Honor down and lowered her small canvas suitcase to the ground.

She looked at him, her luminous eyes questioning. "Where will you be?"

"At the hotel till Sunday."

Her gray eyes widened with surprise. "Till Sunday? I thought you planned to stay for a while—till Cyrus returned."

"I don't think so. It won't take me long to find a permanent foreman, and the mining operation will keep till Cyrus gets back."

"I see." She stood still, reluctant to leave him.

"Do you want me to walk you in?"

"No," she said hesitantly. "I'll be all right." She paused before asking, "Will you be over before Sunday?"

Clay stared hard at her for a moment, and when he spoke his voice was harsh. "What do you want, Honor? For me to run over here every day looking for crumbs?"

She froze before him as his jaw muscles twitched. He was clearly stung by his own sense of guilt. "I'm sorry," he said gently, reaching for her hand. "I wish I could take that back. You're the last person in the world I want to hurt. I really didn't mean that to sound as cruel as it did."

"I know, Clay. Really, I understand. We're both under considerable strain."

"I'll be around." He released her hand. "You know where to find me, Honor."

She gazed at him searchingly. "I do so love you, Clay. Please believe that."

"I know. I know. Take care for now." He climbed into the buggy, jerked the reins, and steered away from her.

Honor watched Clay move down the dirt road until he was out of sight. She felt strangely bereft, heavy with a sense of great loss. A couple of days, she decided, turning back to Sophie's home. Just a couple of days to sort all this out. That was all.

"Well," Sophie said warmly, "let's enjoy some good gossip together. It's marvelous seeing you again."

"You really don't mind my staying here for a few days, Sophie?"

"Mind? I should say not. Why, it's a real treat having you. You stay on as long as you like." She lowered her large bulk onto a wicker chair across from Honor. "You're looking so well, Honor. Filled out a bit, haven't you? It's becoming."

Honor lowered her lustrous lashes for a second, then blurted, "I'm pregnant."

"Pregnant? My goodness. Is it whose I think it is?"

Honor nodded in affirmation. "It's Clay's."

"Well, what are you going to do?"

"I don't know."

"You don't know? Do you have a choice?" She paused. "He's not abandoning you, is he? He doesn't seem the type for that."

"No. Nothing like that. Elijah will be returning to Carlsbad sometime this week, and when he does, Clay wants the three of us to go with him and settle in California."

"Well, it's settled, then."

"No, Sophie, it's not at all."

"I don't see what the problem is."

"I'm as confused as you are, believe me. I'm so mixed up, Sophie. The problem is me. So much has happened that you don't know about. In Santa Fe I found myself reconciled with a man I'd once been engaged to in New York. It turned out horribly. A nightmare. When Clay showed up, I think I'd sunk as low as anyone ever could in this life. I can't understand how Clay still wants me after that."

"He loves you. When you love, you forgive. I hope you're not going to do anything foolish, Honor. You've got the new child to think of." She hesitated before asking, "Have you fallen out of love with Clay?"

"No. I still love him very much. But I've had nothing but unhappiness with men. How do I know it will turn out differently with Clay, Sophie?"

"I suppose you don't. After all, unhappiness is a woman's lot when she hasn't been lucky enough to find that one shining person. But you *have* found him. And what a wonderful man he is." She looked at Honor carefully, giving her words emphasis. "You don't want to end up a lonely old spinster like me, do you?"

Honor glanced away from her for a moment, then returned her gaze and said, "It just seems so much safer to remember what Clay and I had. Nothing can damage it then. It stays intact."

"I'm surprised at you, Honor. God put us on this earth to marry and multiply. Why do you complicate it so? Go to California with Clay and have done with it. The gallery is doing quite well now. I could continue to run it, or we could sell it. We could get a fair price for it, I'm sure."

"We'll discuss that later, Sophie." Changing the subject, she asked, "Have you seen Lucus at all?"

"Why, yes," Sophie answered breathlessly, "I run into Lucus in town every now and again. He always speaks of you."

"Could you arrange for a meeting between us? At the gallery, perhaps?"

"I suppose I could. What do you have in mind, Honor?"

"I mean to ask Lucus for a divorce. I don't know

what I'll do with my life exactly, but I do know I want to start fresh, with a clean slate, no matter what it is."

"Yes, yes, I can see that. Of course I'll arrange it. I'll get someone in town to deliver a message to the monastery. It's not too far out of town, you know."

"Do you think there's any reason why Lucus won't divorce me, Sophie?"

"Well, why on earth wouldn't he? My goodness, he'd better!"

"Sometimes I feel I've hurt him enough. My coming back this way and asking him for a divorce might be the last thing he needs. Tell me, Sophie, when you saw Lucus, did he seem happy?"

"Why, yes, as I think back on it, he did seem so. The times he spoke of you, there was certainly no bitterness attached. Not in any way."

"How I hope that's true."

Sophie reflected before saying, "How strange to think of Lucus living in a monastery now. Don't you agree?"

"Strange? No. Nothing is strange to me any more."

"It's good to see you, Honor." Lucus reached over to gently squeeze her hand that still bore a gold band. "You been well?"

Honor stood against a wall in the art gallery, observing him nervously, thinking that he'd lost weight. "Yes. And you?"

He was suddenly exuberant—pouring his heart out to her. "Great changes have come into my life," he said expansively. "More and more I'd felt myself bein' drawn into service . . . God's work. I had to find a direction for that feelin'. Then . . . I knew. At first the impact of my decision overwhelmed me. But I'm adjusted to it now. I know it's right."

"I heard that you entered a monastery, Lucus."

He smiled broadly at her. "I've really found myself, Honor."

Honor suddenly recalled with a shock that the

gypsy had prophesied this very thing. She'd completely forgotten about it. Now she looked at Lucus carefully, asking, "You're truly sure that's the life that will make you happy, Lucus?"

"It wasn't a hasty decision." His lean face became grave. "You know, after you left I felt as if my life was over . . . I lost interest in everythin'. Even the caverns. At first I thought you'd write, that a miracle would occur that would make things right between us again. But as more and more time went by and there was no word from you, I came to the realization that I had to adjust to bein' alone. I had to decide what to do with my life."

She winced slightly as he spoke, knowing she'd been so wrapped up in Julian that she'd never given Lucus a thought. Could she really have been so selfish not to have considered that he'd needed to hear from her? How could she have treated him like a stranger when they'd shared so much together? There would always be a bond between them. Their two years together had to count for something. She looked at him sadly, saying, "I'm very sorry that I never wrote."

He smiled gently. "It doesn't matter now. What does count is that my loneliness forced me to really think about my life. It was a happy day when I really knew what I wanted."

"What about the caverns? Have you completely abandoned them?"

"Why no, not at all. My work there isn't finished. Once I'd renewed my interest in life, I was drawn back to them again. I still cling to my dream of bringin' the world to them. To bring people closer to God by the very reason of the caverns' existence. I still believe that I've been chosen."

"And . . . Consuelo? What part does she play in your new life?"

This question visibly startled him. "You know she's here?"

"She told me herself. I know everything, Lucus.

How she'd always felt about you and . . . and that Lita is your child."

He nodded. "Consuelo and the child are stayin' at our old cabin. When she first came, I begged her to return to Santa Fe. I told her how wrong it was for her to abandon her other children. But she wouldn't have it any other way. I finally gave up tryin' to convince her. I'm sure one day she'll realize what she's done and go back. For now, she's content merely to remain close by. She knows there could never be anythin' between us physically again. She only asks that I visit occasionally."

"I see."

"And you, Honor? What are your plans?"

Her voice subdued, she announced, "I want a divorce, Lucus."

"To marry Clay?"

"I can't say for certain yet. Perhaps. But I want the divorce in any case. I think it's the only thing for us to do."

Matter-of-factly, Lucus said, "I feel sure that under the circumstances we could get an annulment. That would be the best way to go about it. You go ahead and do whatever has to be done. I'll sign any papers that're required of me." He paused for a moment. "I want what's best for you, Honor. I always have. I won't stand in your way."

"Oh, Lucus!" she cried, her face flushing with relief. "You don't know how much it means to me to hear you say that!"

The air around them was suddenly charged with emotion; they both lapsed into silence. Lucus finally broke it by asking, "How is Elijah? Do you hear from him?"

"Elijah is meeting me here in Carlsbad. I expect to receive word about his arrival at any time."

"Well, Honor, I know if you marry Clay it'd be good for Elijah. He used to hang around Clay at the caverns sometimes. He really liked Clay, I remember."

"Yes. Clay likes Elijah also. He's mentioned that to me."

Suddenly Lucus grew serious. "I hope you don't feel torn about anythin', Honor. I've had a lot of time to think about us. Look, I married you knowin' full well that you weren't in love with me. I'd believed you would learn to love me. I took the gamble . . . and lost. But I carry with me the memory of the good side of our marriage. I could never forget how it was for us at first in Santa Fe. Or that you were right at my side when we discovered the existence of the cave. You changed my life in a way you could never really understand. That'll always be enough to sustain me."

To her relief his eyes didn't register any pain as he spoke. He *was* at peace—happy. It emanated from his kind dark eyes. She was so glad for him. Her voice broke as she said, "I'll always care about you, Lucus. You brought into my life the first real emotional security I'd ever known with a man."

His eyes moistened, and he dabbed at them with the back of his hand. "I may have brought you emotional security, but in the end I know only too well how I failed you. I'm deeply sorry that I couldn't have been more of a man for you. But perhaps it was meant to turn out this way. Perhaps it was God's will . . . to free me from earthly temptation to carry on His work." He hugged her tightly.

"You've always had fire, Honor Wentworth. Promise me . . . promise me you'll never change." He released her, saying, "Give Elijah my love."

"I will, Lucus." She turned and walked out into the blinding Saturday morning sunlight, knowing that whatever they had been to each other—good and bad —had not been in vain. Their lives had been touched by each other and changed because of it. They had both grown immeasurably, swept inexorably toward their own separate destinies. They couldn't have prevented this final separation, couldn't have held back the forward flow of movement. Their marriage had to end.

She'd never regret that she'd been Lucus's wife. After all, she thought, if Lucus hadn't brought her here when he had, there would never have been a Clay Birdsong in her life, nor his child growing within her. This was terribly important, she realized.

She stroked her hand rhythmically over her stomach. A new life grows within me, she thought. A new shining life! Through her it would enter this world, where it would hopefully live without fear.

A brilliant smile spread over her face. In that fraction of a moment something lit up inside her, bringing everything into focus again. She knew she would continue to grow with Clay, too. To deny herself, to deny Clay's child the opportunity to grow with him, would be unspeakably selfish. The nagging fear was gone. All that remained was the urgency to be close to the man she loved. Now she knew what she must do, what she had always known she would do.

She quickened her steps, approaching the hotel where Clay was staying. She rushed to the desk clerk and asked for him, only to be told he was not in. She left a message and headed for Sophie's brimming over with happiness.

Sophie greeted Honor at the front door, impatiently curious, her words rushing out excitedly. "Well, what did Lucus say? Is everything all right? What happened?"

Honor laughed at her friend's bubbling personality, glad that Sophie was Sophie and would never change. "It's all right. Everything's settled. Lucus has agreed to an annulment."

"And Clay?"

"I stopped at his hotel, but he was out. I left a message that I'd been there."

"You've made up your mind to marry him?" Sophie asked hopefully.

"Yes!"

Sophie clapped her hands together gleefully. "I'm

so happy for you! Well, come on in. The telegraph office delivered a message for you." She rushed in ahead of Honor to hand her an envelope lying on a table.

Honor ripped open the envelope anxiously and read the message. She looked up at Sophie, smiling. "Elijah will be here tomorrow. How I've missed him! Won't it be wonderful having him back at last?"

"I should say. What will you do now?"

"All the way home I've been thinking about the caverns. I'd like to see them one last time before I leave. Can I use your buggy?"

"You mean you're going to the caverns now? All by yourself? In your condition?"

Honor laughed. "Sophie, don't be such a worrywart. I'll be fine. Do you need the buggy or horse this afternoon?"

"Why, no. I don't. You can use them."

Honor ran into her bedroom to change her clothing, calling out to Sophie, "If Clay comes by, tell him I'll be back sometime this afternoon. Will you?"

"Yes," Sophie answered in a worried tone, "I'll tell him."

Sophie had just settled down in a porch rocker with a book when she spied Clay approaching on horseback.

He dismounted from the palomino and climbed the front steps. "Honor here, Sophie?"

She jumped up from the rocker. "I'm so glad you're here, Clay. I'm really worried about her."

"Has something happened?" he asked anxiously.

"She's taken the buggy to the caverns. All alone. She wanted to go down, she said, one last time before leaving Carlsbad. I don't think she should be there by herself. I didn't like it one bit. But there simply was no talking to her."

Clay froze for a moment, inexplicably frightened. He didn't think it was Sophie's anxiety that made him feel this way, but rather his own premonition that something was not right. He had to agree with Sophie. He didn't like it, either. Something . . . something was really wrong. "When did she leave?"

"A couple of hours ago."

"I'll go to her." Fairly leaping down the porch steps, he swung into the saddle, his heart pounding out of his chest, dug his spurs into the horse's flanks, and took off at breakneck speed.

Sophie stood watching him until he disappeared around a bend in the road. She wondered why she had let Honor go so easily. She could have stopped her if she'd really set her mind to it.

Honor moved toward the orange-cast cave entrance that was suffused with an eerie stillness. She slowly turned full circle, watching for swallows that had always swooped down and up the sides of the opening, delighting her with their exuberance. There was no sign of them. Strange . . . Her gaze traveled to the surrounding canyons, searching for the ever-present turkey vultures. There were none in sight anywhere.

She looked up for a moment to see billows of puffy white clouds resting against the azure sky, then down at the ground and the reseda brimming over with vibrant verdancy and a riotous mass of flowers.

She couldn't remember when color had ever seemed so vivid to her. Looking up again, staring at the firmament, she suddenly wished she could reach up and touch it. Smiling at the thought, she turned her attention back to the cave.

There was a certain mystery about this place that might never be unraveled, but it didn't matter now. She only knew that she had to see the caverns and move through their majestic splendor once more. Whatever good or bad they might have brought into her life, she would always be indebted to them for their very existence, and for the profound experience of beauty they had given her. One last look, she thought. One last touch.

It struck Honor that Lucus had missed something

important here. To him the caverns represented the sole symbol of God. What Lucus has missed, she told herself, is that we are also living symbols of His perfection, and the love we have for each other is the greatest affirmation of God's existence. How sad that Lucus didn't see that.

Honor glanced at the mine shaft, vacated for the day, and moved to the edge of the pit. A rope ladder still hung down where Lucus had made his first descent. The steep slope downward, the sheer drop to the floor of the bat cave, did not fail to give her that familiar queasy feeling, but it soon passed.

Adjusting her knapsack, she slid her body over the side and found a footing. She grabbed the rope and slowly began the descent, the ladder undulating beneath her. Halfway down she suddenly heard—felt—the rope ripping under her grip!

She strangled a scream, quickly grabbing onto a sharp, protruding rock. Realizing that the rope had rotted, she rapidly mulled over the possibilities for an alternative course of action. If only she had the strength to climb back to the top. But she knew she was too far down to make the ascent, and too far up to jump to the bottom without seriously hurting herself.

In her terror the whole scene felt like a nightmarish replay of something very familiar. The dream that had always plagued her—that was it. She was living her dream. Dear God, she thought. Dear God!

She moaned as her fingers cut into the jagged edges of the rock and started to bleed. Her head was spinning from shock. She saw the blood, felt the pain, but none of it seemed real. Was this a dream, too?

Unexpectedly, through the web of her terror and confusion, she heard her name being called and looked up to see Clay's face. Half relieved, she had a flash of desperate fear that he was too late. How long could she hold on this way? "Clay!"

He disappeared and then was back again, casting a

rope into the pit alongside her. "Grab it, Honor," he ordered. "Grab the rope and hang on."

"I can't let go," she screamed. "I can't!"

"Grab the rope! One hand at a time."

She forced herself to calm down, doing as she was told, reaching for the rope with both desperation and hope. Inch by inch, she felt herself being pulled to the top, until at last she was close enough to reach out to him and fell to the ground, her body racking with sobs.

Clay held her tightly for a time, then lifted her up and carried her to a clearing. He set her down and turned her hands palms upward. Reaching into his pocket for a handkerchief, he dabbed gently at the raw wounds. His voice shaking, he murmured, "I love you. I love you."

"Oh, Clay!" She clung to him with all her energy.

His bronzed hands moved to her hair, tenderly pulling out the combs until the shining, honey-gold abundance cascaded in swirls down her back, burying his face in it. He covered her face with kisses, moving his hands down to cup her breasts, finally lowering his cheek to rest on her stomach.

Reaching down to cradle his head gently in her hands, Honor was secure in the knowledge that his love had given her life new dimension and courage. She was home at last.

EPILOGUE

HONOR STOOD on a hill and watched the sun coming up over a mountain, pushing away the dark shadows that enveloped her. She felt as if she were looking at the world for the first time all over again, for never had it seemed so new and bright.

Today was the beginning of everything, and she was filled with peace. Yesterday was becoming remote, she thought as she patiently waited for Clay to return from the train depot with Elijah. Their future hung expectantly in the air around her.

She suddenly squealed as she felt a kicking motion inside her, and she touched her stomach with a sense of awe. For the first time the child had moved within her. A signal that he was here, too, and not to be forgotten.

Hearing her name being called, she turned to see Elijah, now so tall and straight, standing at the foot of the hill with Clay by his side. She rushed down the hill—running through space to reach them—the wind whipping her long skirt around her.

With outspread arms she moved joyously into the inner sphere of their love, without a backward glance.

About the Author

PAULA DION, born on May 20, 1939, in the Bronx, New York, is a new arrival to fiction, *Wings of Desire* representing her first entry into the world of publishing.

A graduate of The American Academy of Dramatic Arts, she spent six years in the New York theater, the basis of which sharpened her perception of characterization and sense of drama, both, she feels, helpful tools to writing novels.

After her marriage and the birth of her children, she spent a number of years at home devoted to family life. Finally reseeking an outlet for her creative drive, she began her new career just four years ago as a nonfiction magazine writer, specializing in personality profiles. Before long the irresistible attraction of fiction had ensnared her.

She and her French-Canadian husband, Charles Dion, their daughter, Dominique, and son, Jourdain, currently reside in Las Vegas, Nevada. For relaxation away from her typewriter, Ms. Dion bike-rides with her family, is a compulsive reader, and also finds time for another interest, embroidery.